ISSUE #6

GEAR*SHARK*

MAGAZINE

WHAT'S MEANT TO BE
WILL ALWAYS FIND A WAY.

CAMBRIA *HEBERT*

ISSUE #6

GEAR*SHARK*

MAGAZINE

#FATE

CAMBRIA *HEBERT*

*"Fate decides who comes into your life.
Your heart decides who stays."*
—unknown

Will they put a
ring on it?
@speed_demon
@TMask when's the
wedding?
Married in
secret?
GearShark
Interview Request...
Missed Call:
Ron Gamble
...
We want a wedding!

In 2001, The Netherlands became the first country to legalize same-sex marriage.

ONE

Drew

The constant vibrations and incessant dinging of my phone was disturbing my sleep. Why the fuck was it going off like this so early in the morning anyway? Didn't people have any respect?

Flinging an arm out, I reached for my person.

All I found was the dent in the mattress where he should have been.

Cracking open one eye and feeling mighty grumpy about it, I glared at the empty spot. "T!" I bellowed, my own voice just as bad as the chiming phone.

The noise of an elephant rumbling down the hallway barely registered before the bedroom door smacked against the wall and something big and smelly launched itself onto the bed.

"Oomph!" The sound burst out of me as my whole body jolted under the impact. "Holy hell!" I wheezed. "Bad dog!"

My legs were jackhammered by the dog's frantic tail as it slapped me over and over. I looked up just in time to see a giant, slobbery tongue coming at me.

"N—" I started to protest, but it was too late.

The sandpapery, dog-breathy, drool-covered tongue smacked against my face and licked all the way across my nose.

"Jesus! Are you trying to find my brain?" I asked but then started to laugh.

The beating from the tail increased tenfold.

Palming the side of the uber hairy monster's head, I pushed it aside to rescue my face from his dog breath. "This is not the morning kiss I had in mind, Fry," I grumped but rubbed his ear affectionately.

"I still can't believe I let you name that dog French Fry," Trent commented, his large body filling the doorway of our bedroom.

"Let me?" I wondered, fending off more dog tongue. "It's too early for this!" I complained, pushing him off me.

The dog rolled onto his back, paws up in the air, and gazed at me longingly. This mutt was smelly, clumsy, and filled with drool… but he was still my boy. So of course, I scratched his belly.

Trent stopped beside the bed, shirtless and with a big white mug in his hand, effectively stealing away any attention I was giving Fry.

His college football career was several years gone, but he still had that body. Wide shoulders that I knew sometimes carried the weight of the world. Rounded, defined biceps, which dominantly caged me in when he took me in bed. Cut abdominals my fingers knew intimately and a V-shaped muscle that disappeared into the band of his designer boxer briefs.

He noticed my perusal. Beneath those boxers, his cock jerked because he liked it.

We'd seen each other without clothes a million times. I would argue I knew his body better than my own.

It didn't matter.

The same excited electricity buzzed throughout my body whenever he was close.

"You left me in this bed alone." I criticized, still fondling his mostly naked body with my stare.

"*Your* dog had to piss."

Smiling, I asked, "That coffee for me, frat boy?"

He smirked. "Maybe."

I reached for it, but he drew back just enough to be out of reach. A grumble broke out of me as my eyes narrowed. "You know I need my a.m. fuel."

Eyes glittering, he said, "So do I."

Sliding my tongue across my teeth, I pushed up onto my knees, the tangled blankets falling away.

I was sporting some major morning wood, despite the attack from our giant dog-child. Nothing else seemed to matter when my guy was standing there looking like a snack.

Because the dog was still on the bed between us and Trent was still standing too far away, I crooked a finger at him.

Pursing his lips together, he pretended to think about the request. Just when I was about to lose all my patience, he chuckled, a sound that made my scalp tingle. His knee hit the mattress, his upper body leaning close.

I had bedhead, morning breath, and my scruff was out of control.

I kissed him anyway, the kind of kiss that wasn't shy, and even though it rang with familiarity, he sank into me like we were brand new.

A low moan vibrated the back of his throat while his palm rubbed over my unshaven jaw. He still loved the feel of stubble, and by the way his tongue delved deep to attack mine, I would say he also had a fondness for morning breath.

Sliding a hand up his chest to cup my palm around the side of his neck, I settled the pad of my thumb against his rapidly beating pulse. I lifted my other hand to delve into his mussed hair, raking my fingers through the blondish strands before palming the back of his head to bring him even closer.

The hint of coffee on his tongue delighted me, and I sucked his upper lip between mine before pulling back to lick over his mouth.

Blinking his eyes open, he smiled, somehow making it seem as if he could see all of me even though his eyes never left mine.

I loved that look. The one that made me feel like I was all he saw, the center of his universe, and the blood keeping his heart pumping.

Once, long ago, when these feelings between us were new and scary, I wondered. I wondered what would happen if the chemistry between us fizzled out, if whatever pulled us together suddenly let go.

The thought scared me so much I banished it from my mind, refusing to ever let it resurface. I wasn't scared of it now, though, because I knew the answer.

I saw it in Trent's eyes.

Nothing.

Nothing like that would ever happen because the love between us would never go away.

"Here," he said gently, offering me the coffee I knew he'd made just the way I liked it.

Fry jumped off the bed to probably chew something he wasn't supposed to, and we ignored him, thankful to be alone.

Instead of settling against the pillows, the headboard, or holding my own weight, I leaned into his warm, secure side as one of his arms wound around my waist.

I was right about the coffee. It was exactly how I liked it.

Cupping the warm mug against my chest, I sighed, leaning into him a little more. One benefit of being with another guy was he had the size to take my weight. He had the bulk to surround mine.

My eyes slipped closed as his fingers teased my hair and I knew not one care in the world.

Bzzz. Bzzz.

My eyes popped open. "I've just about had it with that fucking thing."

An inaudible chuckle vibrated Trent's body. "Ah, that explains why you're awake already."

I made a rude sound and went in for more coffee.

"I should have taken yours downstairs with mine," Trent murmured, rubbing his palm over my shoulder.

Tilting my head, I glanced out of the corner of my eye. "Yours going off like that too?"

He made a sound, which I knew was an agreement.

"What's going—" I started to sit up, but he pulled me back, anchoring both arms around me.

"It's nothing,"

"It could be Ivy or the kids." I tried to sit up again.

He tightened his hold.

Remember just seconds ago when I was saying how awesome it was to date someone whose strength and size matched my own (okay, fine, he was a little bigger)?

I changed my mind.

"Trent," I growled.

"I already checked, Forrester. It's not the family. They're okay. I called up and talked to Romeo just to be sure."

Pacified for the moment, I relented. "Then what is it?"

"Same shit… different day."

Oh. I knew that tone, that restrained annoyance.

This time when I sat up, he let me. Leaning over his body, I placed the mug on the side table and drew back so I was facing him.

"What did they print this time?"

His upper lip curled a little. Then he sighed. "Those vultures took some photos when we were in town a few days ago."

My mind sifted through what we'd done that day, and I couldn't think of anything that could possibly make the news.

Of course, from experience, the press was really good at making shit up. "I didn't even notice anyone taking pics."

"Me either," he muttered, rubbing a hand over his jaw. "Can't even let your guard down to walk down the street."

"We were holding hands?" I asked, trying to recall if we had been that day. Truth was I had a hard time paying attention to that anymore. It used to be something I was conscious of… but not lately. Trent was mine. I could hold his hand if I wanted to. I was fucking tired of having to think about every time I touched him in public and if it would rile up the media.

We were two men, not a fucking circus attraction.

"Mmm." He agreed. "And we were walking past a jewelry store."

Realization struck. "Ah, the marriage thing again."

"If I had a fucking penny for every time someone asked me when we were getting married, I could buy a small country."

I leaned in. "Would you name it after me?"

He laughed, pushing my face back. "No."

"Maybe I should get a ring, put it on one of my fingers. Really get everyone in a tizzy."

Trent smirked. "Our phones would probably explode."

"Might shut everyone up," I said, watching his reaction.

"They'd just find something else to gossip about."

"T—"

The expression on his face darkened as though a sudden storm churned up within him. "We're not getting married because the press wants us to, Forrester."

"You think it would be because the press wants it?"

The muscle in his jaw ticked, and he let out a breath. When his stare came to rest on mine, it softened considerably. There it was again, that all-encompassing stare that made me feel swallowed whole.

"I don't need a piece of paper to prove how much I love you. I already have everything I could ever want. Hell, Forrester, I have more than I ever thought I'd have. You don't mess with perfection when you have it. You don't rock a sailing boat in the center of the sea."

"Perfection, huh?" I echoed, my heart slowing to a heavy thud. I didn't know how, but this guy always had a way of making me feel like I was back in middle school and experiencing my very first crush.

His hand slipped around the back of my neck, tugging me forward until our lips met. Craving more, I climbed into his lap, and the sounds of our deepening kiss filled the bedroom.

Trent kissed roughly this morning, ownership in every slash of his lip. His tongue sliced over mine, making me relent and surrender.

All at once, he wrapped both arms around my back and went forward, pinning me against the mattress with his broad, naked torso.

"I want you," he growled, pushing up my chin so he could drag his lips across my unshaven jaw.

I parted my lips to answer, but his finger penetrated my mouth as he moved down my body, lips latching onto my nipple.

I forgot about talking. I no longer heard the notifications going off on my phone. All that existed was Trent and the perfection we'd found between us.

In 1998, Alaska and Hawaii were the first states to ban same-sex marriage.

TWO

Trent

NRR *Season Opener*

Perfection isn't an illusion.
I met it, held it in my hands.

There was no warning. In life, there never is. One moment, life was a picture-perfect puzzle with all the pieces finally in place.

Bam!

The bright-yellow race car went airborne, all four tires abandoning the pavement and taking along all sense of reality.

Standing on the top of a giant rig, I gazed over the track with my frozen heart lodged tight in my throat.

I blinked. I blinked again.

The car was sailing, tilting at an angle it didn't belong. Time stopped. Everything was reduced to astonishingly noiseless moments.

Moments in which I couldn't think. I couldn't feel. I could do absolutely nothing but stand there stunned.

No…

Metal being torn apart by asphalt boomed into that wretched silence, so loud and so overwhelming I fell onto one knee. Shattering glass and the echoes of moaning, screeching, and rupturing thundered over any thoughts I struggled to have.

Time now snapped back to life, and everything was on fast-forward.

My heart jolted back to life, beating so hysterically inside me it felt as if it would burst out of my throat at any second.

Thrusting up to both feet, my entire body trembled so much everything around me vibrated too.

The intense, overbearing sounds of the crash were only made louder by the absolute hush that followed. For a track this size, packed to the brim with people, you could have heard a pin drop.

It is the sound of death.

"Drew!" I yelled, but it came out in a shaky whisper. I grabbed the headset and yanked the mic so close it smacked against my teeth. *"Drew."*

Silence.

I gazed out across the pileup. Drivers were climbing out of their cars, emerging from the smoke and wreckage.

Pacing toward the end of the rig, I peered about, looking for one person.

My person.

His car was upside down… what was left of it anyway. It teetered on the shell of what it had been just moments before. One tire was completely gone and so was the passenger side.

"Forrester," I pleaded, starting my decent down the ladder. *"Baby, answer me."*

Whoosh.

That was not the sound of his voice. It was the sound of flames igniting. Flames so close his headset picked up the noise.

I don't know if I let go or if I jumped. Hell, maybe my limbs just stopped working. I hit the ground with a hard smack, but I didn't linger. Rolling with the impact, I got up and started running.

People were screaming. Sirens pierced the air. The announcer was saying something, but it wasn't the voice I was listening for.

As I weaved through the people, the vehicles, and whatever else stood in my way, I stared at the wreckage. I waited to see his body walk out of the huge clouds of smoke. I looked for his outline lit by the growing flames.

He didn't appear.

He didn't speak.

I couldn't remember the last thing we said to each other before he got in that car.

Vomit ripped up my esophagus. My eyes watered from the velocity of it. I forced it back down and kept running.

I felt hands trying to shove me back.

I felt my skin break and stinging pain across my knuckles.

Flames. Destruction. Desperation.

Why can't I see him? Hear him?

Why can't I feel him?

More singeing pain scorched me, and close by, someone screamed. They didn't stop screaming.

Restraints were shackled around me, but there was no restraining a rabid tiger.

I fought and clawed until the only cage surrounding me was the one my lover was also in.

He was there, limp and unresponsive, body cradled by the perilous claws of death. I was being taunted. Challenged.

The first wave of agony penetrated my shield of determination. It was unlike anything I'd ever felt before. I collapsed, momentarily crippled.

Death was indeed the most wicked opponent.

Still, even in that moment, my eyes found Drew just before the savage lick of flames built a wall between us.

Death would have to do better than that if it wanted my entire life.

Perfection isn't an illusion.
I met it, held it in my hands.
But then it slipped right through.

In many countries, such as Sudan, Saudi Arabia, and Iran, gay people can be sentenced to the death penalty.

THREE

Drew

Some drivers would tell you that racing is an addiction. The rush you get from flying over the pavement, the high from this kind of speed equals the same chemical reaction in the brain a man gets from gambling or drugs.

You know what else addiction can bring?

Life's end.

In my ear, T croaked my name. I heard him plead for the sound of my voice.

I tried so hard to answer, so fucking hard to let him know I was still here.

My body and mind didn't obey. It was almost like they weren't mine to command any longer.

I never realized how heavy a price addiction could have... until it cost me Trent.

FOUR

Trent

I was numb.

But I hurt so goddamn bad.

How could I feel both?

I guess some agony couldn't be masked even by insurmountable trauma. I sat here, alive, staring at two wide swinging doors that were achingly still, but everything inside me had been brutally scraped out and tossed away like rotten trash.

The only reason I was still breathing was because my heart hadn't been inside my chest when I was hollowed out. My heart didn't reside inside me at all. Right now, it lay on a gurney, fighting for his life.

If his heart failed him, mine would be there to keep him safe.

I would offer up my own life to make sure Drew had his. I would give up every last drop of blood, every breath in my body, and serve my soul to Satan himself.

Not Drew.

Anyone. Anything. But *not him*.

One door swung open, and a nurse dressed in scrubs stepped out. The chair skittered across the floor with the force I used getting up. Her footsteps stuttered, and when I advanced toward her, she cowered back, a look of alarm crossing her features.

"How is he?" I asked, my voice strangely hoarse.

"Excuse me, sir?"

"How is he?" I demanded.

"I-I don't know who you're asking about."

"Drew Forrester. He was brought in from a car accident," I said, impatient.

A little of the alarm slipped from her eyes, and interest replaced it. "The race car driver?"

"He's mine!" I roared. "Tell me how he is!"

She started inching to the side. "I wasn't in there with him."

My whole body slumped, and sorrow so vacant and scary began to take over.

"Jesus," someone swore close by, and suddenly, my sagging weight was supported. "Trent!"

He had a familiar voice.

"Security!" someone else bellowed.

"Seriously? He's half out of his mind with grief. Just look at him! Why hasn't anyone called *him* a doctor?"

Even though the nurse's voice was the most unfamiliar one, it was the only one I really paid attention to. "He was very angry. I told him I didn't know the patient status." She quickly tried to explain. The entire conversation was a waste of time.

A helpless noise scraped my already raw throat. *"Please,"* I pleaded, swaying on my feet. "Just tell me if he's still alive."

"*Christ.*" The voice closest to me swore again. "Could you just see? Consider it a personal favor."

"Right away, Mr. Anderson." The nurse agreed and rushed back through the doors.

I tried to follow, but my brother's arms wrapped around me from behind. "Just wait. She's coming right back."

"Rome," I whispered.

"I know."

He couldn't possibly know just how bad I hurt right now. Just how fragile the entire world seemed. But I knew he cared.

Braeden stood right beside Romeo, both of them slightly behind me. Romeo didn't let go of me, and I didn't try to move away.

I stared at those doors.

I waited.

My chest ached so bad. It was a pain I'd never felt before. What if that pain meant my heart was failing Drew? What if it meant when she came back, it would be to tell me something that would absolutely kill me?

The door swung open, and my brothers drew in a collective breath. I didn't breathe, though. I would never take another breath if Drew didn't either.

"He's still in surgery," she reported. "He's alive."

A deep sob ripped out of my throat, and I would have collapsed had it not been for Rome. He lifted me, and Braeden stepped in front of me, holding his palms out as if he thought I would fall again.

I did.

I fell against his chest and started to cry.

Without hesitation, his arms wrapped around me in a tight hug.

He didn't hug as tight as Drew. No one hugged better than Drew.

He's still alive.

Another wrenching sob ripped out of me, and I crushed the shirt against B's back in my fist.

"He's alive." Braeden assured me, letting me practically rip his clothes. "He's going to stay that way."

My entire body shook as I cried, but I wasn't embarrassed. I didn't have that emotion inside me. I might not ever again. In fact, I felt immeasurable shame that I might have ever been embarrassed about any of the feelings Drew brought out in me.

Something large and warm wrapped around me from behind. As I sniffled into B's shirt, I realized it was Romeo and that they both were hugging me. In those moments as I crumbled while Drew fought for his life, it was my brothers who held what was left of me together.

As of 2017, there were 150,000 registered same-sex marriages in the United States.

FIVE

Trent

"Trent?" A small, tentative voice called me.

Even in the panicked, out-of-body, and ragged state I was in, it was a voice that couldn't be ignored. Lifting my head, I looked over Braeden's shoulder to where Rimmel stood. She was drowning in Romeo's hoodie, her hair was a wreck, and her eyes were puffy and red.

I didn't have the voice to ask her what she wanted. My sister understood.

"I've brought a nurse. You need to get looked at—"

Despite her gentle, caring tone, I bristled. "I'm not leaving."

"You can just go down the hall—"

"I said no!" I barked, shoving back from my brothers.

Romeo laid a hand on my shoulder, and I shoved it off. "Don't start with me, Rome."

"You're bleeding all over yourself. And your wrist…" Rimmel pleaded, taking a step toward me.

The second she came closer, Braeden and Romeo both held out an arm in front of me. I didn't blame them. I was wild right now, and she was as gentle as a lamb.

The nurse beside Rimmel glanced between us all as though she wasn't sure what to do.

"Wouldn't it be better to get that taken care of while Drew is still in surgery? When he gets out, you're going to want to be at his side… He's going to be upset when he wakes up and sees you bleeding everywhere."

A pang of hurt pierced me.

"If you get an infection, you won't be able to see the patient," the nurse added. "It will put him at risk for one too."

"Just get me a Band-aid." I compromised.

"You need more than a Band-aid!" Rimmel exclaimed. All fight seemed to drain out of her then, making her sway on her feet.

Romeo was at her side instantly, supporting all her weight.

"Just go," he told me firmly. "The rest of us won't move from this spot. If anything happens, we'll come get you."

"Please Trent." Ivy begged. I hadn't even realized she was here.

Turning, I saw her sitting close by, her face stained with tears, and the front of her top wet from where they fell. Her blond hair was, for once, a wreck, and all her makeup was smeared.

Drew's sister. The person closest to him, right after me.

Making a sound, I went to her. Braeden rushed after me, but I shoved him back. When I dropped onto my knees in front of her chair, she fell into my open arms and started openly weeping.

My throat was blocked with pain and emotion. I couldn't swallow, barely able to draw a breath.

"He's going to be fine," Ivy said against the side of my neck. "My brother is way too stubborn."

Flashbacks of the way he'd looked lying limp on the pavement assaulted me. Covered in blood. White as a ghost. No life. No expression…

"Trent?" Rimmel said from behind.

Abruptly, I stood up, looking at the nurse through blurred eyes. "Just down the hall, right?"

"Yes, I've got it set up for you already."

I followed her direction, turning back to look at the OR doors more than once.

"Sit here, please," the woman instructed, and I moved on autopilot, doing as requested. "You have glass in your hands and arms. I'll need to remove it."

"Go ahead," I answered, staring at the door.

"And you have second-degree burns on your wrist. How did this happen?"

"What?"

Ripping my eyes from the door, I glanced down, noticing the state of my wrist and hand for the first time. The flesh was bubbled up, raw and oozing. Nicks and cuts were all over my forearms, and I definitely saw some glass.

I guess I was bleeding everywhere.

Not that it mattered.

"What caused the burns?" she repeated patiently.

#

Thick smoke stole the oxygen from the air while roaring flames tried to create a wall between me and Drew. I didn't need air, but I would die without him.

Forcing back the crippling anxiety, I dragged myself forward, reaching for my guy. The smell of singed flesh filled the enclosed space, but I ignored it.

Shaking fingers closed around the sleeve of his drive suit, and I gripped on for dear life. His outfit was flame-retardant. At least it was against these flames that had yet to grow.

My body burned and shook with effort as I pulled Drew toward me with one hand. He was caught. The harness meant for safety was now holding him hostage.

Suddenly, the door on his side was ripped away, and emergency workers reached inside.

"It's too mutilated over here. He's trapped!"

"The harness," I yelled, praying my hoarse words could be heard over the fire extinguishers and sirens. "Cut it the fuck off!"

Drew's body was like a ragdoll being tossed around as they roughly and swiftly cut through the binds. The second he was free, his body slumped toward me, and I caught his head before it could fall into the flames.

Shaking and dizzy, I held his head away from the fire as I briefly wondered where the fuck his helmet had gone. There was blood. So much blood.

A blast of white filled the interior, and the flames trying to devour us were snuffed out.

"Hold on. We'll come to your side," someone yelled.

I wasn't waiting. I'd had to squeeze through wreckage and crawl through glass to get to him. The fire might be out now, but the intense smell of gasoline permeating the air created a sense of urgency.

Still cradling his head, I reached forward with my other hand, feeling the skin on my arm rip.

"I'm getting you out of here, Forrester," I vowed and started towing him closer.

He was dead weight, and the car was crushed around us. Tears streamed down my face, and vomit rose up the back of my throat again as I towed him out of the wreckage, trying to be quick but careful.

When his head and shoulders cleared the car, I collapsed back into random pieces of wreckage littering the ground, Drew's head cradled in my lap.

I might have blacked out after. Or maybe my brain refused to recall anything else.

It didn't matter, because Drew made it out.

# # #

"Ah, there was a fire in the wreckage," I finally answered, hollow.

"You were in the car too?" she asked, surprised.

I shook my head. "I crawled inside to get him."

"Isn't that what the emergency responders were there for?"

My eyes snapped up to her, intensity radiating off me with a menacing vibe. "If your entire life was lying inside a bashed-in car that was literally on fire, would you leave it up to a stranger to save them?"

She cleared her throat, lowering her gaze. "He's very lucky to have someone who cares so much."

"I'm the lucky one," I echoed, turning all my attention back to the door.

What if my luck is finally running out?

"Are you sure you don't want some pain medication? Perhaps a numbing injection so I can clean and wrap all these wounds…"

"Just do it," I said. "I won't feel it anyway."

She didn't argue, and I ignored her while she worked. Every shadow, every body that walked by the room we were in, made my body tense.

I don't know how long it took her to do whatever she was doing, but a little later, I felt her patting my arm.

My gaze cut to where she was touching me, then lifted.

Slowly, she withdrew her hand as if she knew she'd just been poking a sleeping tiger.

"I apologize, but you weren't answering."

I made a sound. "What?"

"You need stitches," she explained, gesturing to one of my palms, which had a deep cut on the meaty part below my thumb. "The glass went very deep."

"No," I declared. "I don't have time."

"You will just continue to bleed."

"Wrap it." My voice was impatient. "I need to go."

"I wouldn't recommend—"

I silenced the unwanted advice with a single glance.

"I'll just wrap it." She relented.

Ivy and Braeden stepped around the doorframe, and I shoved up to my feet, knocking over the small tray of bloody scraps. "How is he?"

"Blood…" Ivy began.

Everything around me swam. The absolute worst thoughts started attacking me. "What?" I asked, reaching out to steady myself on the chair.

"The hospital doesn't have any more of what he needs." She finished, and everything around me came back into focus.

"Take mine," I declared, swinging around to look at the nurse.

"We would need to see if you're a match—"

"We are." I interrupted. "I have the same blood type as him."

"Are you certain?"

I made a rude sound. "Of course! Stop wasting time and tell me what to do."

"I'm probably a match too," Ivy said.

I held up my hand. "I've got this."

"Are you sure you should be donating blood to Drew when you've already lost some?" Ivy worried, pointing at my hand.

I noted the freshly dripping blood.

"Stitch this up," I told the nurse, planting back in my seat.

"You said you didn't want stitches."

"Well, now I do." Before, it didn't matter if I bled or not. But now… now that Drew needed my blood, I wouldn't waste another drop.

"I'll numb—"

"No," I declared. "Do it now. The faster the better."

"It's going to hurt."

I laughed. Nothing—and I mean nothing—would ever hurt worse than Drew's life hanging in limbo.

"Can I donate the blood here?"

She shook her head once. "You'll have to go down to the lab."

I glanced around at Braeden. "Can you go tell them to get ready? Give them my name and birthday. All my info is in their system already. Drew's too." I cleared my throat. "We got tested together last year. They'll see we're a match." My gut twisted, stabbing hot pain cutting through my middle. I'd always made sure he was protected. That he was safe.

Just look at us now.

"I'm going now." Placing his palms on Ivy's shoulders, he leaned down to look into her eyes. "You stay here with your brother, okay, blondie? I'll be right back."

She nodded, tears welling in her eyes.

Braeden disappeared, and I tapped my foot impatiently, waiting for the stitches to be finished.

"He must have lost a lot of blood," I announced a few minutes later to no one in particular.

"Yes," Ivy echoed.

"It's a good thing he has people ready and able to give him what he needs." The nurse remarked, focused on my hand.

I'd give Drew every last drop of blood in my veins if that was what he needed. There was nothing—literally nothing—that I wouldn't do for him.

The divorce rate of same-sex couples is fifty percent lower than heterosexual couples.

SIX

Drew

There is a place between living and not living. I woke up there. The sounds were loud and disruptive. None of them made any sort of sense. And the beeping. The constant beeping, as if every moment I had left was being counted.

At first, I didn't understand. I looked for Trent, only to see people dressed head to foot in scrubs, masks over their faces, and only their eyes on display.

I didn't know any of these people.

I didn't know any of these sounds.

Where is Trent?

Where am I?

Suddenly, the view of the room changed. I was no longer staring up at the faces concentrating down at me. Instead, I was above them, looking down.

Fear unlike anything I'd ever felt before squeezed my chest. Not only was I looking down at strangers, but also at myself.

There was a tube going into my nose and something else sticking out of my mouth. My skin was nearly translucent, and the veins beneath looked blue. All my clothing was cut away. So much skin was exposed… all of it cut open. All of it bloody.

Forcing my eyes away, I swallowed back the lump clogging my throat.

The doctor said something, and a tool appeared for him to take. Someone was up by my head using giant tweezer-like things to pull out pieces of something that made a small *pinging* sound every time they tossed one into the waiting bowl.

Something stuck grotesquely from my chest. I could see right inside my own body.

"Get someone in here to set that leg!" a man yelled. "And get me some blood! His pressure is dropping!"

I was in trouble. Even though I felt nothing, I knew what I could see.

A woman in scrubs pushed into the room, timid and slightly wary. "The family is outside. They're demanding an update."

"He's alive!" the doctor snapped without even looking up.

She scurried away, and I rushed to follow. *Trent.* He was probably going out of his mind. I hit the door and bounced back. I ran for it again.

Blocked. Trapped. Unable to leave.

Whirling back around, I looked at my limp form. Was I tethered to my body? Did that mean this wasn't as bad as it looked?

The rhythmic beeping signaled my life meter slowing.

"We're losing him!" someone yelled.

I raced back toward myself, standing next to the monitor that was suddenly displaying a flat line.

"Get me a crash cart!" someone yelled.

Chaos and bodies rushed around. A sudden uncomfortable feeling clutched my chest.

"Don't you die on us!" the doctor grunted, leaning over.

The sound of the flatlining beep made me woozy, and I felt like I was fading away.

"Here's the blood!" A woman rushed in.

More chaos. A surge of electricity jolted my body. The door to the room swung as people rushed in and out. Bright light, the purest, most incandescent I'd ever seen, shone just outside the room.

It beckoned…

I started forward, turning my back on the ragged, nearly dead form I'd lived in for almost thirty years.

Warmth suffused me, pushing back the woozy feeling, wrapping me up in a warm hug. I thought it was the light. The closer I got, the more at ease I felt.

"Don't give up, Mr. Forrester. There's a man down in the lab who gave this blood just for you. He would have given us every drop he had if we'd allowed it."

Turning my back on the light, I stared at the woman leaning over me. After another few adjustments, she stepped back, and my eyes fixated on the tube of red liquid flowing from a nearby bag right into my arm.

The beeping started again, slow at first, but it was there.

Multiple sighs echoed around the room, but I fixated on what flowed inside me.

The strength. The warmth. The life… It wasn't coming from that beautiful glow outside.

It was Trent.

Just as my life was fading away, he offered up some of his.

Existing there between my battered body and a halo of light, the choice was clear. That light, which seemed so splendid just seconds ago, no longer held any appeal.

The only direction I wanted to go was wherever Trent was. Taking a step toward the operating table, I doubled over in pain.

So. Much. Pain.

I reached out, trying to steady myself, but when you are in between life and death, there is nothing tangible to hold you up.

Despite the immeasurable agony I knew was waiting the second I climbed back into my body, I staggered toward it anyway.

Fixing my gaze on that line of blood, I imagined Trent beside me, both his hands wrapped around one of mine.

I wouldn't leave him. Not for peace. Not for comfort. I would endure my heart stopping over and over again because that man would burst in here and restart it himself if he had to.

That kind of loyalty… That kind of love…

It could never be beaten. Death wasn't my fate today.

Trent was.

Searing pain took over everything the second I was back on the table. The doctors and nurses were somber and worried. Hurt cloaked me, driving out everything, dragging me under. Even though I was terrified of being alone, the blood flowing into my veins whispered…

I'm here.

SEVEN

Trent

They told me to sit down a while since I'd been in a traumatic event and then donated blood.

Blood I had to practically force them to take. Apparently, taking it from someone already injured, blah-blah-blah, wasn't good protocol.

Fuck protocol.

Drew needed it. And because of that desperate need, they took what I was offering. I gave two pints, though they tried to cut me off at one. I started yelling about death and suing…

Then Romeo walked into the blood bank.

Drew—and hell, even I—was a celebrity of some sort. But Romeo? Around here, Romeo Anderson was like a god who walked on water.

They took the second pint, and Romeo stood over them all, smiling while I snarled and glared.

I wasn't a guy who liked to make a scene. I was quiet, enjoyed lying low in the background… but that didn't mean I wouldn't step up if I needed to.

The second the IV was out of my arm, I pushed up out of the seat.

"Sir, please, sit down. Have some juice." The nurse appeared, carrying some OJ and a cookie.

A freaking cookie.

I oughta shove that cookie—

"Thank you so much, Leigh." Romeo cut off my thoughts as if he knew exactly what I was about to do. "I'll just take this," he said, grabbing the juice and cookie from her and smiling. "I'll make sure he sits down upstairs by the OR. That's where our family is."

She smiled and giggled.

Romeo put a hand on my shoulder just as I stepped forward.

"Let's go."

Out in the hall, I looked at him. He tossed the cookie in a nearby trashcan. "I know," he said, all charm gone and weariness instantly in place.

His blond hair was mussed, dark circles were under his eyes, and his shoulders seemed heavy. I felt bad for my behavior back there, bad that Rome had to basically make sure I didn't snap. We were all dealing with this, not just me.

But I couldn't bring myself to offer up any support. I didn't have any in me. Everything I had was being channeled toward Drew.

"No word?" I asked gruffly.

"None," he said quietly. "They took your blood back but haven't said anything."

"It's bad, Rome," I whispered, the words wrenching out of me and cutting me up on their way out. The edges of my vision were blurry and slightly dark. Every once in a while, dark spots would float in front of my eyes, but I ignored it.

My brother stopped abruptly, grabbing my shoulder and pulling me around, wobbly on my feet. His fingers tightened, and his eyes narrowed. "Trent?"

"I'm fine."

"We don't know how bad it is yet."

Swallowing, I let my eyes find his. I let him see everything that went down to my core. "I pulled him out of the car. I saw him."

"I know." He swore. The hand on my shoulder wrapped around the back of my neck. "We've got this, okay? All of us… we're going to be here. Drew wouldn't dare try and quit this family, 'cause he knows—"

The words ripped out from the deepest, most frightened part of me. "What if he doesn't have a choice?"

Romeo fell silent. The hand holding the back of my neck pulled, and I swayed forward. He hugged me in the middle of the hallway. Florescent lights buzzed overhead, the scent of antiseptic drowned the air, and desperation clung to every single piece of me.

I couldn't live without him. Everything before Drew was so long ago, so far away it was literally obsolete. If the earth couldn't exist without a moon, then I couldn't exist without my other half.

"C'mon," I said, clearing my throat and starting forward again. "I need to be up there."

The second we stepped off the elevator, I rushed forward.

"Trent." Romeo beckoned, making me glance back around.

"There's so many of us that they moved us into a waiting room."

Frowning, I started to shake my head.

"C'mon," he clapped me on the back. "It's just off the hallway where you were sitting before."

The second we stepped in, everyone in the room jumped to their feet. When they saw it was us and not a doctor, they deflated.

It was immediately obvious why the staff here moved us into a waiting room. Everyone was here. Almost the entire family. And everyone's eyes turned to me.

Words failed me. If these people were looking to me for some sort of encouragement, for some sort of positive words that would help cut the grimness of the atmosphere, they would be disappointed.

A blur of movement caught my attention, and then a body nearly plowed into me. Thin arms wound around my midsection, and a bleached-blond head pressed against my shoulder.

"We got here as soon as we could," Arrow said, his voice muffled against my shirt. I glanced down at the kid (Arrow would forever be a kid to me, despite the fact that he was a married, grown-ass adult), slightly taken off guard by his sudden show of affection.

Glancing up, I found Hopper standing off to the side. He was focused on Arrow, but when he felt me looking, our eyes met. A sense of understanding washed over me, for in the depths of his gaze was a haunting sort of pain.

He'd once lost someone to an accident like this.

If anyone in this room could understand the depth of pain I felt, the rawness of excruciating fear, it was him.

I wondered briefly what it cost him to be here, and I hoped I remembered later to tell him how much it meant that he showed up regardless.

Arrow's arms tightened around my waist, and I remembered he was there and that my arms were still limp at my sides as if I had nothing left inside of me, not even a hug for a kid I knew considered Drew his best friend.

Feeling completely drained, my eyes automatically sought out the source that kept me full. I went around the room, searching for that one face… but he wasn't here.

I knew Drew wasn't in this room, yet my heart still looked.

Another body came forward and added to the hug I was already receiving. Curly black hair tickled my chin when Joey wrapped her arms around me and her brother-in-law.

"We're all here for you both," she whispered.

Against me, Arrow nodded.

Over their heads, my eyes locked on Lorhaven, the guy in the room I liked the least. Maybe because of that, looking at him was easier. Because I knew he wouldn't have any expectations of how I should be. It didn't matter. He'd think I was an asshole regardless.

Oddly, that brought me comfort.

He was still wearing the suit he'd been racing in, which made me remember he'd been in that race too.

"Did you get caught up in the pileup?" I asked, my voice sounding like sandpaper.

He wasn't offended I didn't even know. Hell, I hadn't thought of any of the other drivers at all. The second Drew's car went airborne, he was literally the only person to exist.

"I managed to get out," he replied. "I tried to come help you, but the bastards wouldn't let me through."

Someone came into the room behind us, and I spun, the force of my movement shaking off both Joey and Arrow. Once again, disappointment stabbed me, and impatience coiled my nerves.

"It's better you stayed out of it," Gamble said, tucking a phone into the inside of his suit jacket. His tie was askew, and the top few buttons of his dress shirt were undone. He gestured at me the second his phone was put away. "Getting this one out of hot water is enough."

"Me?" I echoed.

He nodded. "My lawyers have it handled. No need to concern yourself."

Seeing the blank look on my face, Braeden stepped forward. "Do you remember anything from the accident?"

Blood. Glass. Drew being nearly mangled in the mess that had been his car.

I shook my head.

"You took out a few guys on the asphalt," B explained. "They tried to hold you back from the wreckage."

A low rumble vibrated my chest.

The corner of B's lip turned up. "You Hulked out, bro. It was pretty impressive."

"Braeden." Ivy warned, her voice way less challenging than usual.

He shrugged. "Figured he should know. It's trending on social right now."

I didn't care. If people got in my way while I was getting to Drew, they deserved what they got.

"You own half this hospital, don't you?" I said to Gamble. "Can't you get someone in here to tell us something?"

"I've been assured that we will get an update immediately. I've also made sure the best doctors in this hospital are taking care of Drew. He will get the best care possible."

Romeo's phone went off, and he lifted the screen. "It's Liam," he announced before stepping into the hall to answer.

"Liam?" Joey asked.

"Liam Mattison," Braeden explained. "The Olympic snowboarder. We spent some time at his ski resort over the winter. He probably saw the news…"

Everyone quieted, and I started to pace.

"Trent," Rimmel said, wrapping her cold hands around my wrist. "You look too pale." Holding out the juice Romeo had brought, she pushed it into my chest. "Please drink this."

I took it but didn't agree to drink it.

"Romeo's parents are on their way," she whispered. "Braeden's mom too."

"They should just stay home with the kids," I said, staring at the door. "Driving across the state isn't necessary."

"We're family," she said plainly. "It is."

"I'll send my plane," Gamble interjected. "They'll get here faster."

Rimmel didn't even argue. It reminded me just how bad the situation was. She went off with Gamble to make arrangements for the plane, and I was left standing there… raw.

Two doctors appeared, wearing wrinkled blue scrubs, caps on their heads, and masks hanging around their necks. They both looked weary, and seeing them that way made dread rise in my throat.

Even as I rushed forward, I had to flatten a hand against my chest because the pressure was so intense.

"How is he?"

"Next of kin?" the doc asked, glancing around at the sea of faces.

I grabbed the front of his shirt. "*Me*. You can talk to me."

Reaching between us, Romeo pulled my fist off his clothes and cleared his throat.

"We're all a little on edge, Bruce," Gamble said, stepping forward. "Tell us some good news."

The doctor glanced back at me and stepped forward eagerly.

"We had a few close calls, but he's come through surgery."

My stomach hit my feet. "Close calls?" I rasped.

"To be blunt, he flatlined."

I swayed, but Romeo and B stepped up behind me, offering the support of their football player frames.

"We brought him back, and now that his blood volume is stable, so is he."

"I want to see him." I started past.

"His injuries are extensive."

I stopped breathing.

Ivy and Rimmel started crying.

"How bad?" Romeo asked, tucking his wife under his arm.

"His ribs broke, which punctured his lung, causing it to collapse. The medical term would be tension pneumothorax, which means the puncture was serious enough it required us to insert a chest tube that will need to stay in place for several days. We also plated a few ribs… to put them back in place."

"I need to see him," I demanded, ragged.

"I'm afraid there's more."

There was no bracing myself. There was no brace that would make any of this okay to hear. To know. To feel.

"Say it already!" I bit out.

The doctor pinned me with level eyes. "His left tibia is broken. The tibia is the larger bone in the lower part of the leg that supports your body's weight. He will have to be in a cast for several weeks."

I nodded. That was okay. A broken bone was to be expected.

The other doctor cleared his throat. "The patient also has a traumatic brain injury."

My hand went to my face, covering my mouth. Silently, Hopper stepped up beside me, so close I felt the heat coming off his body.

"If he hadn't been wearing a helmet, he probably wouldn't have made it."

I stumbled backward. Hopper caught me around the waist and held.

"He required twelve stitches in his head after we pulled out some fragments of the shattered helmet. Along with a concussion, there is some swelling of the brain and a few broken blood vessels."

"Because of his injuries, we have placed him in a medically induced coma."

I made a sound. Ivy turned into Braeden.

"This will ensure the protection of the brain while the swelling and pressure subsides."

"How long?" I asked.

"It really depends on him. Most medically induced comas last less than two weeks."

All sound in the room seemed to fade away. I saw the doctor's mouth moving. I saw Ivy asking questions and a few others say things.

I heard nothing.

Not even the sound of my own heart beating. The sound of my lungs breathing.

My vision started to narrow and blur. Like a curtain was closing on everything, the world started to go dim.

Someone's face swam in front of mine. Their lips moved, features concerned. I was too far gone to answer… and then there was nothing.

Approximately two-thirds of married same-sex couples are lesbians. One-third are gay men.

EIGHT

Trent

The world came back in a burst of light and sound. My lungs seized violently, making me cough. The vivid scent of ammonia clung to the insides of my nostrils, and my fingertips curled against the cold floor…

Wait.

The floor?

Blinking, I looked around from my position sprawled on the waiting room floor.

"Trent?" Romeo asked, leaning over me, concerned.

"Fuck," I muttered, rubbing a hand over my face. "I don't have time for this."

"It's going to keep happening until you take care of yourself." Someone scolded.

"I want to see Drew."

"He's still in recovery. You can see him once he's moved to a private room," announced the doctor who was holding some smelling salts.

Shaking my head, I heaved up off the floor. Romeo pulled me up with him, but I rebuffed his support.

Facing the doctor, I said again, "I want to see Drew."

"He's in recovery."

"Maybe we could make an exception this one time," Gamble interjected smoothly.

"You're next of kin?"

"We live together," I said.

His eyes widened a bit. "Oh, so you're married?"

I deflated. "No."

"Is there a blood relative here?"

Ivy stepped forward. "I'm his sister."

She looked like hell, and if Braden wasn't holding her up, she probably wouldn't be standing. Still, she lifted her chin, her gaze unwavering.

"My brother would want Trent," she said. "Trent is his guardian."

Trent is his guardian.

I don't know how or even why, but those words gave me something nothing else had. As I stood here practically crumbling, they reminded me of my purpose. Drew was weak right now. I would be strong.

Slowly, the doctor shook his head. "This is something we don't normally allow, but since our benefactor, Mr. Gamble, has asked..."

I started for the door.

"You need to change first," the man called.

"Okay," I said, still going.

"And wear a mask. And disinfect your hands."

Stopping in the hall, I poked my head back around the doorframe. "I'll do whatever you tell me to do. Let's go."

The doctors followed me out into the hall and instructed a nurse, who led me to a room, handing me a stack of hospital scrubs, a cap, facemask, and something to cover my feet. I took it all, dumping it on the bed, and started taking off my bloodstained clothes before she was even out of the room.

"Take your time." She began.

"Just wait right outside the door. I'll be there in a minute."

When she was gone, I cleaned up as best I could considering one of my wrists and hands was almost completely wrapped up.

I discovered some glass in my knee as I was changing. I pulled it out, tossing it in a nearby trashcan. A nearby cabinet had some bandages, so I doused the cuts in antiseptic and strapped on a couple Band-aids.

My entire body trembled and my legs felt wobbly as I followed the nurse down the silent, somber hallway.

At a white curtain, she paused and turned back. "Don't be alarmed with the way he looks. He's stable."

Swallowing thickly, I nodded.

"There's a chair beside the bed."

"I'm going," I said, cutting off whatever else she might say. I didn't care. All I cared about was the man on the other side of that curtain.

Dragging in a shuddering breath, I pulled the curtain back and stepped around.

#

How could a man who took up so much space inside my heart and world look so small?

How could fragile and lifeless explain someone who smiled so big, hugged so hard, and kissed until he consumed my soul?

Tubes and wires were everywhere, making him look like the victim of a science experiment and not the recipient of life-saving technology. White walls, white blankets, and the steady beeping of monitors made me wish this was some sort of bad dream.

It wasn't a bad dream. This was a nightmare. And it was real.

The thick fabric of the curtain separating us from the rest of the world strained beneath my grip as I stood there frozen and staring.

I'd wanted nothing more than to see this man. But seeing him like this? This was the worst torment I would ever experience in my entire existence.

Still, I would not look away.

Shuffling toward the bed, I fixed my gaze on his face, noting the colorless pallor nearly matching the white bandages circling his head. His blond-ish hair stuck out around them, giving me a tiny glimpse of the Drew I knew and loved.

A sob ripped from my throat, and I nearly choked trying to hold it back. I wouldn't do this here. I wouldn't do it in front of him. Drew needed strength right now, and strength was what I would deliver.

Moving closer to his side, I couldn't help but stare at the ventilator covering the lower part of his face, and the sound of it breathing for him made goose bumps rise along my arms.

"I would trade places with you in an instant if I could," I told him.

He didn't respond. He couldn't. I wasn't sure when he would again. Without looking away, I pulled the chair as close to the bed as I could. His entire body was buried under blankets, but I wanted his hand.

Gently, I lifted the blankets to gaze beneath them. He wasn't wearing a shirt, and my eyes went instantly to the chest tube inserted into his torso. My stomach heaved, and I squeezed my eyes shut before reopening to study the massive bruising all over his chest, the swelling around his ribs, and the bandaged incisions.

Lowering into the chair, I reached for his hand. His fingers were limp but warm. I wrapped my hand around them and carefully replaced the covers over his torso. His leg was in a sling that elevated it off the bed. The cast was thick and white, covering everything from his knee down, except for his toes.

Slipping my other hand under the covers, I wrapped it around his hand too. Despite seeing him this way, touching him gave me comfort. Being here, having eyes on him, was something I was so grateful for.

"We're going to have to talk about this profession of yours," I told him, trying to sound firm.

The only sounds that answered were the beeping of the monitor and the whirring of the ventilator.

"They said you almost died in there," I whispered, my hands gripping his tighter. My lower lip wobbled, and intense pressure squeezed my chest. "Thank you, baby," I said, the wobble moving from my lips into my words.

Bowing my head, I rested it on the edge of the mattress while skimming my thumb along the back of his hand. "Thank you for fighting in there. For coming back to me." Lifting my face, I let the tears fall, pretending they weren't even there. "Don't worry about anything, okay? I'll take care of everything. I'm your guardian. Ivy said so."

The mention of his sister reminded me.

"Everyone's here. Romeo, Rim, B, and Ivy. Lorhaven, Joey, Arrow, Hopper... even Gamble himself. Romeo's parents and B's mom are on their way. The doctors here wouldn't dream of not doing right by you. Gamble pays most of their salaries." I tried to joke, but none of this was funny.

"All you have to do is heal. All you have to do is come back to us. To me."

Lifting out of the chair, I leaned over the bed, lowering toward his forehead. "You're so banged up," I said, almost scared to touch him. "It's okay," I said, not wanting him to think I was upset with him. I whispered, "I'll be gentle."

As I brushed my lips over his forehead, a heartbeat of peace moved through me. I hoped he felt it too, because even though it was brief, the relief was incredibly real.

Not ready to pull away, I kissed him again.

Lowering back into the chair, I kept my hold on his hand. "Take as long as you need to heal, Forrester. I'm going to be right here. I won't leave your side."

We sat in silence for a while, but I began to worry he might think I'd left him alone.

"I love you," I whispered. Then I whispered it again.

And again.

And again.

Children raised by same-sex couples face the same adjustment/difficulties as children raised by heterosexual couples.

NINE

Drew

The dull static sound filling the room drowned out everything else with its eerie tone. It was so dark here I couldn't see where it came from, and I didn't know where I was.

This place was cold… empty somehow.

I didn't like it. I wanted to go home.

I tried to sit up, but my limbs didn't obey. I tried again, but I was paralyzed, as if my body were no longer my own to command.

Panic cut through the haziness, assailing me, making my already tight chest squeeze.

I fought against the binds holding me down, but I was weak. I called out for help, but my voice wasn't mine either. I opened my eyes and saw nothing but shadows.

Fear rushed over me like a thousand tiny spiders, a thousand footsteps scurrying over my skin and making me want to scream.

I couldn't.

Where was I? What was this place? How did I get here?

How did I get free?

Loneliness taunted, and I wasn't sure which was worse: being afraid or being alone and afraid.

The crackling static seemed to fade away, and sudden foreign sounds burst into the shadows. Someone moaning. Something beeping. A voice I didn't recognize.

My heart felt like it would gallop right out of my chest. I wanted to fight or flee so urgently, but my body wouldn't move.

A heavy scraping sound from close by jolted my system with adrenaline.

What is happening? Let me go!

The overwhelming sense of loneliness gnawing at my mind began to ebb away. The chaos and confusion inside me began to fade with it. Something warm and reassuring wrapped around me. I felt the strength in the touch… and something else.

There was something else.

Haziness dragged me down. The clarity I was beginning to find was being cancelled out again, replaced with that awful static. Why didn't someone turn off that broken TV?

"I'm going to be right here. I won't leave your side."

I knew that voice. It was familiar. It was comforting.

I fought the fog trying to pull me under, searching through the dark for more of his voice. I waited and waited, anxiety enveloping me once more.

"I love you."

There he was.

"I love you."

I wasn't alone.

"I love you."

Fear abated. Calmness washed over me like the sea. And the darkness? The darkness might have my body, but it was that voice that commanded my heart.

I stopped fighting, letting myself be pulled under, but I was no longer afraid because there *was* something else.

Some*one*.

Trent.

GS
ISSUE #6
GEARSHARK

A study from 2011 states 1.7% of adults identify as gay or bisexual and 0.3% identify as transgender.

TEN

Trent

Drew was moved out of recovery and into the ICU. The intensive care unit had a lot of rules, one of them being only two visitors at a time.

I remained planted beside his bed, holding his hand and making sure there weren't long periods of time when no one spoke. The doctors said even though he was in a coma, there might still be bursts of moments when his brain was lucid and aware of his surroundings. He might be confused. He might be afraid and trying to understand what was happening.

I didn't know how much Drew could comprehend right now. It didn't matter. Even if there was only the slimmest chance he heard me, I would continue to talk. I would continue to reassure him.

The family rotated in and out, one by one, not even asking me to let someone else take my spot. When they'd gone through the rotation, Ivy appeared back in the doorway, and I held out my arm, inviting her close.

Dashing the tears off her cheeks, she rushed forward, climbing into my lap and putting her hand over mine and Drew's.

"I always knew racing was dangerous and risky, but I never thought this would happen," she said, watching over her brother.

"Me either." I agreed, once again internalizing everything that happened in the past few days. As Drew's lover, this accident was traumatizing.

As his manager? I felt responsible.

Over and over, I went through everything I'd done with the team to prep him for the NRR season opener. We left early to drive across Maryland to New Revolution Racing's headquarters and its home track.

This place was pretty much our home away from home. It wasn't new territory. Drew had his own garage there. His own handpicked pit crew. The track had been built by Gamble and all the NRR owners. It wasn't an old or shoddily built course.

His car was in tip-top shape. Nothing about it had been compromised yet this season because this had been the opening race.

What did I miss? What did the crew miss? I wanted to call the crew boss, but I didn't trust myself to not lose my shit on the phone so I remained silent.

I'd been his eyes and ears during the race. His spotter. He trusted me to watch over him… and I let him down.

If only I'd seen it coming sooner. If only I'd been able to warn him.

Maybe he wouldn't be lying here right now. Maybe he wouldn't have almost died.

He flatlined.

The horror of knowing that Drew's heart literally stopped beating altered me in a way I had yet to even understand. I felt the change deep. I just didn't know the consequences of it yet.

"You're doing good, ba—" I started to tell him, then glanced at Ivy still situated in my lap. "Forrester. You're doing real good. We're here, okay? We love you."

"You must be exhausted," Ivy said, leaning against me, not even mentioning the way I almost called her brother baby in front of her.

"I'm fine," I answered.

"Do you think he's in pain?"

"I hope not," I said, sweeping a glance over his relaxed face. "Isn't that the whole purpose of the coma?"

She whispered, "He looks really fragile."

"That's why we'll be strong for him."

Ivy's hand slipped away from ours when she curled a little closer into my lap. Using my free hand, I smoothed her blond hair away from my face and rested my chin atop her head. "Romeo's and B's parents just checked into the hotel we're staying at."

"You can go see the kids. I'll stay with Drew."

"I want to stay a little longer."

"Try and get some sleep, okay? It's been a long day, and Jax and Nova will be all over you when you go because they haven't seen you in a few days."

"We drove down here to watch my brother in his season opener… not for this." Her breathing hitched, and I ran my hand up and down her arm. "I'm glad the kids stayed back at the compound. I'm glad they weren't there to see this."

"Me too," I replied, hoarse.

We lapsed into silence, and I went back to the ever-repeating checklist in my mind. What happened out there? Why did this happen?

One minute, life was perfect. The next, everything was falling apart.

No warning. No way to stop it.

All that was left was to endure.

Unsure how much time passed, I stroked my thumb over Drew's hand. "I love you," I told him.

"He knows you're here," Ivy said, her voice a near whisper.

"I thought you were sleeping."

"When I close my eyes, I see the accident. His car flipping… smashing into the cement wall."

"Shh." I murmured, "Try not to think about it."

"Is that what you're doing?"

"No."

When she sat up, Ivy's eyes met mine. The blue was muted, the whites bloodshot. The tip of her nose was pink, and her lips were dry. "We're all here for you too, okay? I know you want to be strong for Drew, but don't suffer alone."

A nurse in all white came into the room, sparing us a brief smile. "Visiting hours are about over."

"I'm not leaving," I said.

"The ICU doesn't allow overnight guests."

"You don't have to consider me a guest."

"Sir, hospital policy—"

I sat forward, making sure Ivy didn't fall out of my lap while still keeping one hand on Drew's. Despite the temper boiling inside me and burning my throat, I kept my voice calm. "I don't care what hospital policy states. If you want me out of this room, you'll have to call security. And make sure there's an entire team of them, because a few guys won't do any good."

She opened her mouth, closed it, then started backing out of the room.

"Wait," Ivy said, straightening.

The nurse glanced back, wary.

"Is there a reason you came in here other than to tell us about visiting hours?"

"I need to check his vitals, and the doctor will be making his rounds…"

I stood from the chair, carefully placing Ivy on her feet. "Come look at him."

The woman shuffled from foot to foot.

Ivy went to her side. "I know he looks all big and grumpy, but he's just worried. He definitely won't stop you from making sure Drew is okay."

Ivy gave me a look that said I needed to get it together.

I sighed.

"I apologize for being gruff. Please come check him out, make sure he's okay. I'll stand over here." I assured her, moving across the room. My feet and legs felt heavy, as if they were weighed down with sand.

Nodding, the nurse went to Drew's side, and Ivy walked to the door. "I'm going to go check in with Gamble," she said. "You'll be okay?"

Checking in with Gamble = making sure no one hauled me out of here in handcuffs for refusing to leave.

I nodded. "I'm good, sis. Go."

When Ivy was gone, the nurse glanced back at me, cautious. I smiled, but it didn't seem to help much. Couldn't say I blamed her. I probably looked like a dead man walking, and my smile was probably scary.

"Looks like he's in good hands. Mind if I step into the bathroom a moment?"

She nodded, relieved.

Before stepping away, I came forward, making her pause in her task. Gently, I smoothed a few strands of wild hair back and then leaned in to press my lips against his forehead.

"You watch over him for me, okay?" I told the woman.

Her entire demeanor changed in that moment, every feature on her face softening and the set of her shoulders relaxing. "Of course." She agreed, her lips curving into a warm smile.

Retreating into the bathroom felt like resisting the pull of a super strong magnet, but I made myself go. The last thing I wanted to do was scare the staff and make it harder for them to take care of Drew.

At the sink, I turned on the faucet and glanced up. My reflection caused me to do a double take.

Fuck.

No wonder all the nurses were scared.

My short hair was wild and tangled. It stuck out in places it shouldn't even be long enough to stick out. My eyes looked like Ivy's, but I didn't have the excuse of mascara smudging. They were bloodshot and heavy-lidded, blood smearing over one cheek. A few nicks and cuts dotted my skin, and my cheeks sank in as though I'd been stranded without food for weeks.

Leaning over the counter, I splashed cold water across my skin, ignoring the sting from the scrapes. When the water slipped between my lips, I realized my mouth was dry so I swallowed a few palmfuls before grabbing a paper towel and haphazardly mopping up my face.

The scrubs I was dressed in were kind of scratching and annoying. The cuts in my knee burned and probably needed a new bandage, but I didn't care.

Glancing down at my wrapped wrist and covered stitches, I noted the dull throbbing of pain and then ignored that too.

The doctor was standing over Drew's bedside when I came out of the bathroom.

"How is he?" I asked.

Glancing up from the laptop in his hands, he replied, "Stable. I don't want to be too optimistic, but he seems to be improving."

Going to Drew's side, I fished under the blanket for his hand. "You hear that, Drew? You'll be out of here in no time."

"The nurse made you aware of our overnight policy?"

I bristled.

"I would recommend that you go home. Shower and get some rest. You can't be any help to him if you don't take care of yourself."

"I'm not leaving."

The man held up his hand. "I've informed the overnight staff that you are permitted to stay. Please be discreet."

"Thank you," I said, the fight draining out of me.

"We can't offer you anything but the chair you've already been sitting in. And I warn you. Staff will be in and out frequently through the night."

"Don't worry about me. Just do what you need to do for Drew."

When the doctor was gone, I noticed the nurse still loitering on the other side of the room.

"I'm sorry if I scared you before."

She shrugged. "You love him."

"Yes," I deadpanned. "I do." Then because I knew exactly the kind of world we lived in, I added, "I hope you won't hold that against him."

She smiled. "Definitely not. In fact, I think I might be kind of jealous."

"I think you might be our favorite nurse." Giving Drew's hand a squeeze, I said, "Right, Forrester?"

On her way out, the nurse nearly collided with Braeden. "Oh, I'm sorry. Visiting hours are over."

"I just wanted to let him know we're leaving," B said, smiling down at her. My brothers had a way of making most women look like shorties.

"Make it fast."

Braeden winked. "Of course."

I returned to the seat as B came into the room, the lighthearted look in his dark eyes gone, in its place an apprising, somber expression.

"We're all heading out. The 'rents are all here with the kids. I'm sure they will be over first thing in the morning."

"Weren't you supposed to check out tomorrow?" I remembered. "If you all need to, you can crash at our apartment." Drew and I kept a small apartment on this side of the state because we spent so much time here for training and races. It was a small one bedroom, but it would do in a pinch.

Braeden held up his hand. "Everyone is moving over to Gamble's estate."

My eyes widened. "What?"

"Joey and Gamble insisted. No one is leaving until Drew's out of this coma and we know for sure there's no brain damage."

I made a choked sound. The idea that Drew had brain damage was unbearable.

B stopped abruptly and gave my shoulder a squeeze. Clearing his throat, he went on. "Apparently, the place is big enough,"

"It definitely is," I echoed vaguely, thinking of the giant white mansion that I used to think was too big for just Joey and Gamble. Since she got married, she and Lorhaven had bought their own place and now it was just Gamble living there.

"One of us will bring you some clothes and shit when we come tomorrow. You want anything else?"

I shook my head. "Ivy—"

"Don't worry about Ivy. I'll take care of her."

I nodded.

"Don't hulk out while we're gone, okay? We're the only ones big enough to stop you."

I nodded. "I won't do anything that will compromise Drew."

"He's going to be okay."

I glanced back at Drew lying there with stitches in his body, a ventilator breathing for his lungs, and more machines than I cared to count monitoring his every moment, and I hoped like hell Braeden was right.

Some states don't allow same-sex divorce because there are no divorce laws to permit it.

ELEVEN

Trent

I was afraid if I closed my eyes too long, Drew would disappear. At some point, I did doze off, and when I woke, my head was lying on the mattress beside him, both of my hands wrapped around his.

And there was a blanket.

It was horribly itchy and scratching, and it was also ugly. But it was draped around me in a caring way that oddly bruised something deep inside me.

After all the protests to even let me sleep here. After all the warnings that they could do nothing to make me comfortable. Even after all the fear I'd put into the nurses, they'd still brought me a blanket when I'd finally succumbed to exhaustion.

My eyes were barely focused when I lifted them to Drew. The lighting in here was dim, the curtains closed, and the harsh fluorescents overhead turned off for the night. He was still in the same position as before, his body unmoving and pale.

The sound of the ventilator still made my skin crawl, and as I sat back, I peeled the blanket up gently, making sure the tube sticking out of his chest was still in place and not doing anything it wasn't supposed to.

I whispered a few phrases, reminding him that I was there, and then gently brushed his hair back even though it wasn't in his face.

I worried about him lying so prone, about the muscle loss and the stress immobility might cause his limbs.

Carefully, I perched on the edge of the mattress and gently rubbed his arms and massaged lightly between his fingers. "I know you aren't a morning person, Forrester, but anytime you want to open up those baby blues, I'd be grateful."

I knew he couldn't, not yet. The meds he was on would make it impossible. Still, it seemed like any kind of encouragement, any kind of conversation would be better than none.

Afraid that my weight was too much for the bed, I stood, glancing down at his leg supported in the sling.

His toes looked slightly blue. Frowning, I moved down, carefully wrapping my hand around the exposed toes. They were icy cold.

Anger and worry slapped into me. "Fuck," I muttered.

I'd been dozing off while his toes were getting frostbite. What the hell kind of hospital was this? Snatching the blanket off the chair, I draped it over his foot. The sling sort of tilted from the weight of the itchy wool, and I panicked, thinking it would cause undue stress on the broken bone.

Taking it off, I paced a little, wondering what to do.

I could get a towel from the bathroom. *No. They're itchy too.*

Where'd this place get their linens? Shitquality.com?

The blankets covering his body were too big and heavy for his sling. Annoyed that as I stood here and debated, his toes continued to freeze, I ripped my shirt over my head.

It was just a scrub top, but it was warm from my body heat. And it was light. Gently, I put it around his exposed toes, tying the ends around the cast to hold it in place. Once that was done, I wrapped my hands back around them, letting some of my body heat sink into the fabric and hopefully into his skin.

The door opened, and the nurse from last night came in, smiling. "Good morning, Trent."

"You're still here?"

"I'm getting off shift now. I wanted to come check in with him one more time and say bye."

"Thank you for watching over him last night. And for the blanket."

She smiled slightly. "He looks better this morning."

"Yeah?" I asked, hope lighting up my insides. I'd forgotten how good hope felt… even just a glimmer of it. "You think so?"

I moved up the bed to stare down at his face.

She checked a few monitors and nodded. "Definitely. His pulse is stronger, oxygen level is better."

I sank into the chair, so grateful for any good news that I could barely stand.

"You hear that, Forrester? You're a model patient."

"Your presence must be good for him."

I glanced up. "Really?"

She nodded. "The patients who have someone by their side always do better than the ones who don't. Keep doing what you're doing. I think it's helping."

"Will you be here tonight?"

She nodded.

"What's your name again?" I asked, sorry I hadn't thought to ask sooner.

The embarrassment must have shown on my face because she giggled. "You had more on your mind than my name."

I grimaced.

"It's Katie."

I repeated it to help me remember, then turned back to Drew.

At the door, she called my name. "What happened to your shirt?"

"His foot was cold."

She giggled again. "You should check out the gift shop."

I nodded, even though I had no intention of leaving this room.

The doctor came in, also noting that Drew's vitals seemed better. He would be going for another CT scan to check the swelling on his brain. When he was gone, I reached for my pocket to realize two things:

1) I was wearing scrubs, not pants.
And…
2) I had no clue where my phone was.

"I don't want to talk to anyone anyway, unless they're you," I told Drew. Then I told him I loved him.

For probably the millionth time since yesterday.

I hoped it annoyed him. Then he would be forced to wake up and tell me to shut it.

The door to the room opened, and Ivy and Braeden walked in. Ivy looked exhausted but, for the most part, better than the night before. Her hair was pulled back from her makeup-free face, and a pair of large black sunglasses were perched on her head.

"How is he?" was the first thing out of her mouth.

"I wanted to call… but I lost my phone."

Her eyes widened, and she rushed forward. "Is something wrong?"

"No. He's doing better."

Tears welled up and spilled down her cheeks. "Oh, thank God!"

Reluctantly, I released his hand and stepped back, giving her room to move in beside him. She began fussing over him and sniffling.

Braeden stepped up and held out a large white cup. The scent of coffee wafted toward me, and I took it gratefully. "Thank you."

"Where's your shirt?" B wondered.

I pointed to Drew's foot.

"This is a university hospital. The best in the state. And that's the best they can do?" B grumped.

"The blankets here might as well be made of sandpaper."

"I brought you some clothes." He held out a hot-pink bag. When he saw me notice, he rolled his eyes. "The bag is Ivy's."

Any other time, I would have smiled, maybe asked him if he was the one who was gay, but I didn't have the energy for that. I didn't have the energy for anything that didn't involve Drew.

After another sip of the coffee, I delved into the bag, my hand closing around soft fabric.

"We didn't have the key to your place, so I just brought you some of my shit."

"Thanks," I told him, going across the room to exchange the scrub shirt around Drew's foot for Braeden's shirt.

When I had it tied in place, I put the now-wrinkled doctor shirt back on.

When I turned back, B was watching me. I shrugged. "It's softer than this."

"He does look better," Ivy said, holding her hand out to Braeden. "Come see him, B."

B went to the side of the bed.

I ignored the rest of the clothes he'd brought and drank the coffee instead. Then I took advantage of the familiar people around Drew and went into the bathroom.

Coming out with a warm cloth in my hand, I went around to the opposite side of the bed to gently wipe his arm and hand.

"Romeo and Rimmel will be here later. They're staying with the kids, and his parents are on their way."

I wiped what I could off his face, then went back to rinse the cloth. While I was in the bathroom, B and Ivy moved to the other side of the bed so I could wash his opposite side.

"Do you want to go eat?" Ivy asked as I worked.

"No."

"Take a shower or get any of your stuff?"

"No."

"How are your burns and stitches?"

"They're fine."

I felt rather than saw her look at Braeden. He cleared his throat.

Before he could start in, I looked up. "I'm fine. As long as I can be here in this room and be with Drew, I'm fine. You don't have to worry about me."

"Drew would want me to take care of you." Ivy reasoned.

"If Drew wants someone to take care of me, he can wake up and do it himself." I said it without heat. Without anger. I was too weary for anger, and I knew my family came from a good place. Then, because I didn't want to sound like an asshole to my sister, I said, "Let's just all focus on taking care of Drew right now."

"Exactly my thoughts."

Everyone whirled around at the intrusive voice coming from the doorway.

All the air whooshed out of me as if I'd been violently punched in the gut when I saw the familiar face. The familiar, *unwelcome* face.

"Dad!" Ivy gasped. He stepped into the hospital room, and Drew's mother stepped in behind him. "Mom?" she echoed. "You're here."

"Of course we're here. We got on the first flight we could after you called," his father said.

Adrienne, Drew's mother, rushed toward the bed to stare down at her son and sob. "Oh, my baby," she crooned, reaching for his hand.

My back teeth slammed together. I didn't want her to touch him.

B cleared his throat, and I looked up, locking my eyes on his. He held my stare, offering silent comradery.

"Oh, Burke, just look at him." Adrienne sobbed.

I had to bite my lip to keep myself from telling her not to be so noisy. She was going to upset him with all that blubbering.

"Drew," I said, leaning down to speak quietly. "Your parents are here to see you. Your mom and your dad."

"How is he?" Adrienne said, desperately looking to me for answers.

"Don't ask him!" Burke clapped out, making my spine straighten. "Why would you ask him anything about our son?"

My tongue slid over my teeth.

"Trent's been taking very good care of Drew since he got out of surgery," Ivy told them.

Adrienne clearly wanted an update about her son, and she divided her gaze between me and her husband.

"Why haven't you been sitting with him?" Burke asked Ivy. "He's your brother! You should be here!"

Braeden stepped around Ivy, leveling a stare at his father-in-law. "Watch the way you talk to her. And she has been here. We all have."

"You shouldn't be here," Burke said, pushing past B to stare at me.

"I think it's you who shouldn't be here," I said quietly.

He had the gall to look surprised. And offended. "Are you kidding me? That's my son!" he said, pointing a finger to where Drew lay.

"Funny. I thought you disowned him."

The man's face turned beet red, and Adrienne sucked in a breath. The cloth in my hand had gone cold, so I set it aside and adjusted the blankets so they covered more of his chest.

"Oh, let me help you," Adrienne said, grabbing the other side to help me gently pull them up.

"Thank you," I said. "The doctor was just here," I started to tell her.

"Don't talk to us about our son!" Burke yelled.

"Dad!" Ivy whisper-yelled. "Lower your voice."

"I don't want an update from you. I'll hear it from his doctors. Or from his sister."

"I was the one that sat beside him all night," I said patiently.

Burke's face reddened once more. Disgust whipped through his eyes, and the harshness of it pierced my already bleeding heart. "Get out."

I blinked.

"I said get out," he growled again, flinging a finger at the door.

"No."

A vein in his forehead actually appeared. It looked like it was in danger of exploding. Stalking forward, he grabbed me by the front of my shirt. "What did you just say to me?"

"I said no."

Across the room, Ivy made a sound of distress, and Braeden stepped forward, a grim look locked in his eyes. "Don't do this here, Mr. Forrester. Not in front of your son. He's been through enough."

"You have the nerve to stand over my son as he lies there half dead? You're the reason he's lying there at all, but you want to act like the hero? You want to act like you actually care?"

At my sides, both my hands balled into fists.

I used the beeping of his monitors to anchor me. To hold me in check. I wouldn't do this here. Now. In front of Drew.

Braeden's muscled arm went around Burke from behind and easily pulled the man away from me. "I think we should step outside."

"Oh, I'm not going anywhere. He is!"

The door opened, and a nurse appeared. Shock registered on her face, and then she frowned. "Why are there so many people in here? Only two allowed at a time."

"I'm sorry, we were just leaving, and then my parents came..." Ivy hurried to say.

Burke jerked away from Braeden and straightened his shirt. "I'm the patient's father. And his mother," he said, pointing to Adrienne.

"We still only allow two visitors at a time."

"And I was just telling everyone to leave," Burke declared.

"We'll all go. One of you stay behind with Trent, and then you can switch off." Ivy reasoned. She turned to the nurse. "Trent is Drew's guardian. His next of kin."

The nurse nodded in understanding.

"No!" Burke practically roared, rushing across the room to shove his hand down into the bag Adrienne had around her wrist.

"Burke." She gasped, nearly stumbling with the force of his tug.

He pulled out a stack of stapled papers and stalked back to the nurse. "I have no idea why any of you think that… man over there is next of kin for my son, but he isn't."

"We live together. We're in a relationship," I said, impatient. "You know this. The entire country knows this." After I was done speaking, I glanced at the monitors to check Drew's vitals, worried that this kind of environment would upset him.

"Two men cannot be in a relationship. You aren't married. You have no legal rights over my son."

I blinked, feeling stunned. "What?"

He waved the papers at the nurse. "As Drew's parents, we are the next of kin. I have the legal documents proving this."

The bottom fell out of my stomach, and a twisty, jittery feeling took over my middle.

Not married. Legal documents. Next of kin.

"This is a copy of Andrew's will. We are clearly named as next of kin. No one else should be allowed in this room unless I allow it."

He turned glittering, hard eyes on me.

"And I don't allow that man to be here."

My hand gripped the edge of the mattress, and a low whirring sound filled my head.

"Drew has a will?" Ivy asked, stepping forward to take the papers from the nurse.

I stared at her as she shuffled through them, pinning all my hopes, pinning all my fear on her… praying to God that she would look up and say that man was lying.

"This is from years and years ago…" She glanced up at Braeden. "From long before he ever moved to Maryland."

"It doesn't make it any less legal," Burke intoned. He turned to me. "Get out. You are hereby banned from this room. From seeing my son."

"Dad!" Ivy begged, grabbing his arm to pull him around to look at her. "Dad, this is insane. Drew would not want this. Drew would want Trent."

"Your brother has been brainwashed by that… *fag*."

Ivy gasped and let go of him as if he'd burned her.

"Whoa," Braeden intoned, stepping up.

I couldn't even react. I was too stunned. Too overwhelmed by the implications of this entire conversation. This man… This man who literally disowned his own son had legal rights to keep me away from him? To keep me away from the person I loved most on this planet?

The chair made a thudding sound when I dropped into it. My knees felt weak, and I just needed a moment.

I glanced at Drew, at his face, which was still so beautiful despite the bruises, the ventilator, and bandages.

This man was everything to me. The sun. The moon. The air I breathed. My blood literally flowed through his veins now.

Without him, I was just half.

A chunk of matter without its heart. Without any life.

I knew his father hated me. Hated *us*. But this?

Tearing me away from the bedside of a man I sincerely loved with every fiber of my being?

It was unimaginable. It was cruel.

At some point during my mental breakdown, I'd reached for Drew's hand. I'd entwined his fingers with mine.

"Get up," a cold, unfeeling voice said over me.

I glanced from our linked bodies and up into the unsympathetic face of a man that dared call himself a father.

He slapped the packet of papers into my chest and dropped them, letting them collapse into my lap.

Lifting the papers, I glanced down at the words, but they were nothing but a jumbled, blurred mess. As I slowly lowered them back into my lap, a bead of moisture dropped onto the paper.

At first, I thought it was rain.

Then I realized it was my tear.

"I'm going to have to ask everyone to settle this elsewhere. This is not good for the patient," the nurse said.

I didn't even know she was still here.

"Perhaps I should call the police." Burke threatened. "Let them remove the problem."

I heard Ivy talking, maybe begging her mother. I didn't hear. I just stared at Drew, wondering how the fuck things had gotten like this.

Burke reached down, his hand squeezing my wrist above my fingers where I held Drew. "If you truly love my son, you wouldn't make such a scene and put his health in jeopardy."

Is that what I was doing?

Suddenly, the man was gone, and a loud thud hit against the wall behind me. I glanced around at Burke, who was staring, shocked, at Braeden.

"I know you're my father-in-law," B growled, "but you aren't even acting human."

"I'm calling security," the nurse announced.

"Wait," I said, drawing everyone's attention. On wobbly legs, I stood. "Don't do that. I'll go."

It felt as if all the oxygen had been sucked from the room, and for a moment, I didn't hate that ventilator, because it was providing air to Drew that wasn't tainted by… *this.*

I turned around to Drew, focusing solely on him, clutching his hand, trying to make mine stop trembling. Swallowing thickly, fighting the knot of emotion in my throat, chest, and gut, I leaned over his still form.

"I have to step out for a few," I told him, swallowing again. "Ivy will be here with you. And I won't be far. Keep doing what you're doing."

"Let's go." I felt Burke step toward me, but I also felt Braeden step in his way.

"I love you," I told him, not caring who heard. Suddenly wondering why love was so fragile… why love wasn't created equal.

I kissed his forehead, and Burke pretty much went nuts.

I heard Braeden hauling him out of the room as I stood and slowly untangled my fingers from my love's.

"Even if I'm not in this room, I'm here with you," I told him.

Then I did the hardest thing I'd done in my life to date.

I left him lying there alone.

TWELVE

Drew

A glimpse of awareness pushed back the hazy, shadowy world I was trapped in. Gentle ministrations, a warm rag sliding over my skin… Everything was okay.

He was here.

I sank back into oblivion… until I woke up to a nightmare.

There was chaos, and the terror, so ready to pounce on me, reached out its boney claws. Why couldn't I move? Why couldn't I see anything? And the sounds… so many foreign sounds.

I searched through them all for the one I always recognized. All I heard was yelling. Someone was angry…

Perhaps the man who trapped me here.

Panic gripped me, and I knew torment. What if the man who was holding me hostage had also gotten hold of Trent? I couldn't even help him.

The yelling stopped. Warmth surrounded me and so did a feeling of safety.

"Ivy will be here with you. And I won't be far. Keep doing what you're doing."

What did that mean?

"I love you."

I love you too. I might not know anything else, but that much I knew.

The warmth I'd grown used to feeling, the comfort that kept the worst of my panic at bay, started to slip away.

"Even if I'm not in this room, I'm here with you."

Wait! I tried to yell. *Where are you going?*

No one could hear me. No one could answer.

A sense of hollowness enveloped me, and this cold, ruthless place became scarier than before.

Don't go! I begged.

But it was no use.

He was already gone.

In 2012, Portland, Maine, was voted the eighth "gayest city in America".

THIRTEEN

Trent

As I sagged against the wall outside Drew's room, the door made a definitive click when the nurse closed it behind me.

So close… but somehow so far away.

I was tired. *So* fucking tired. So tired my own body seemed like too much to hold up. Giving all my weight to the wall, I bounced the back of my head against the concrete as I stared unseeing up at the ceiling.

I could barely digest what was happening.

And even with the confusion, part of me was roaring. *How could you let this happen? How could you just give up like that and walk away?*

Not away. Never away.

I did what I did because, above everything else, I had to protect Drew. He couldn't protect himself right now. I had to do it. And right now, that meant stepping out of the room I so badly wanted to be in.

Listening to his dad spew hate was not good for him. Listening to us fight and go at each other would only set back his healing.

He had a traumatic brain injury, for Christ's sake! I didn't know what the fuck his father was thinking barging in there like this, but it wasn't of his son. That was for sure.

Not married. Legal documents. Next of kin.

I made a mistake. I'd made so many.

"Excuse me."

Pulling my head away from the wall, I glanced down. A man who was several inches shorter than me stood there. I almost snarled until I saw the kind eyes and set of scrubs he was wearing.

"Are you a doctor?" I asked.

"A nurse." He corrected. His voice was a little on the high side. Or maybe he was just cheerful. I didn't remember what it was like to feel cheerful.

When I said nothing else, he cleared his throat.

"We don't allow visitors to stand in the hallways," he said gently. "We need to keep the halls clear."

"Yeah. Right." I agreed, pushing off the wall completely.

He stepped back a little. "You have some height on you."

I made a sound and turned. Out of the corner of my eye, I saw him reach for the handle of Drew's door.

"Wait," I said,

He looked back.

"Are you Drew's nurse?"

"One of them."

I held out my hand for him to shake. He complied, and as he did, I made a request. "Please take good care of him. If he needs anything—and I mean anything— please tell me. I'll make sure he gets it."

"Wow, that's a good friend."

"He's not my friend. He's my everything."

Surprise flickered in the nurse's eyes, and then it cleared. A wide smile filled out the lower portion of his face. "I understand."

I scowled. "Is that some kind of dig?" I said. "Because if you're some kind of… homophobe, I don't want you stepping into that room at all."

Pulling back, I started searching out the head nurse. No, fuck that. I was going to find Gamble. I would not have any more toxic people around Drew. His father was bad enough.

"I'm gay!" the man blurted out.

I stopped, turning. Through narrowed eyes, I apprised him. "I'm not in the mood for bullshit."

His nose wrinkled. "Why would I lie about that?"

"You be surprised the shit people do."

His shoulders slumped, and a flash of understanding shone through his green eyes. "I have an idea of what you're talking about."

I glanced over him from head to toe. My "gaydar," as some people might like to say, was nonexistent. Probably because I didn't give a rat's ass what people preferred. It wasn't my damn business. So he didn't "look" gay to me.

"I'm wearing pink scrubs." The man pointed to himself.

Yeah, I guess he was. I shrugged. "So?"

"So I'm saying I'll take good care of your boyfriend."

"Yeah, okay." I agreed. "My name's Trent. If he needs anything at all, I'll be around. Please tell me… not the man who calls himself his father."

"Patrick." He pointed to himself.

"Trent," Braeden called from the other end of the hallway. I turned to see him standing there with Romeo's dad, who was a lawyer. Exactly who I needed right now.

"Thanks again," I called and jogged away. It physically hurt the farther away from Drew's door I got.

In the nearby waiting room, I heard Ivy's pleading voice and Burke's much louder, angrier one. Somewhere in the middle was the sound of Drew's mother.

"Get her away from them," I told Braeden. "She doesn't need that."

"She thinks she can get through to them," he said miserably.

"There's a bit of a situation?" Romeo's father, Anthony, asked, concern in his tone. Behind him, Romeo's mother stood.

I held out the papers Burke had tossed at me. "Can you please tell me if this is legit?"

He took them, frowning down.

Turning to Rome's mom, I said, "Do you think you could go sit with Drew for a few? He's alone right now…"

"Of course!" she replied, already stepping around her husband.

I told her the room, and she started away. It took everything inside me not to run along behind her and slip into his room too.

Braeden had gone back to Ivy's side, and I stood anxiously waiting for Anthony to thumb through the legal shitstorm.

He sighed and looked up. The expression on his face was like a sucker punch right in my kidney.

I deflated right there like a balloon with a giant hole. "It's legit."

"It appears so."

"But it's so old," Ivy insisted, coming up behind us.

"The age of the document doesn't matter. It's the legality of it."

She made a small sound. "But Trent and Drew live together."

Mr. Anderson looked at me warily.

"Just speak plainly," I told him.

"Legally, your relationship with Drew means nothing."

The words ripped a hole in me.

"The fact that they let you in that room at all is, frankly, a miracle." He went on. "You aren't a blood relative, you aren't a spouse, and you aren't next of kin."

"But he is next of kin!" Ivy argued, clearly upset.

"In the eyes of everyone who knows them, yes. But not in the eyes of the law. And unfortunately, in these types of situations, it's the law that matters."

"But my parents disowned him!" Ivy fussed. "And now my father is trying to ban Trent from even seeing my brother!"

"He's within his legal rights."

Bracing a hand on a nearby wall, I stared at my feet. "So you're saying if we were married, he wouldn't be able to keep me out?"

"Maryland does recognize same-sex marriage. So yes. If you were married, he wouldn't be able to do this."

The regret I'd been buried under since yesterday was getting heavier and heavier to bear.

"Did someone say marriage?" Burke interrupted, stepping out of the waiting room, followed by Adrienne.

I really didn't want to think badly of Drew's mother, but damn, the way she scurried around behind that hateful man like she was happy with any crumbs he left behind made me physically sick.

"This conversation doesn't involve you," Braeden snapped.

"Any conversation about *my* son most definitely does."

"Suddenly, he's your son again?" I snapped, spinning to stare at him.

"He will always be my son. And this is the perfect opportunity to get him the hell away from the likes of you. You can get any lawyer you want to look over those papers, but they'll hold. And marriage? You can forget about that right now because I will never allow my son to marry someone like you."

Remember how I said I was too tired for anger?

I lied.

It rushed up from the soles of my feet so fast it consumed me without pause. One moment, I was standing there stunned and defeated by his hateful words, and the next, I was plowing my fist into his yammering mouth with nothing but desire to shut him the hell up.

Adrienne screeched as her husband flew backward into the waiting room, where he fell flat on his back.

He lay there stunned from the hit for long moments, and I stalked forward, shaking out my fist. Straddling his body, I leaned down and grabbed a handful of his shirt, yanking his upper body off the floor.

His nose was bleeding all over the lower half of his face, but seeing him bleed didn't give me any satisfaction.

"If you so much as breathe even an ounce of this hate near Drew and fuck up his recovery," I growled, pulling him up a little farther off the floor, "I. Will. Kill. You."

"Did you hear that?" Burke wailed like the chickenshit he was. "That was a threat! Call the police!"

I shoved him down, his body hitting the floor like a ragdoll. "I make promises. Not threats."

Scrambling to his feet, he looked at his wife and then Ivy. "You see? This is what I'm trying to keep away from my son!"

I laughed. "If you were that worried about your son, you wouldn't let him lie in the hospital room alone while you stand out here and toss insults at me."

Adrienne gasped and went rushing down the hall.

"What kind of mother needs reminding of that?" I muttered.

"Why don't we take a walk, son? Cool off." Anthony cajoled, putting his arm around me to lead me away from Burke.

"I can't go anywhere." I protested.

"Just to the end of the hall," he said.

"Just leave and don't come back," Burke said, his voice nasally.

I turned, pinning him with a hard glare. He faltered and took a step back, then hurried away, and I didn't ask where he was going. Maybe to clean the up the blood dripping all over his face.

"I'll stay with Drew," Ivy offered, giving me a tentative look.

I softened, looking at her. She was afraid I would blame her for her father's bigotry. "Thanks, sis," I said, deliberately calling her that. "I won't worry as much if I know you are beside him."

Her eyes filled with tears.

I shook my head. "Don't do that, okay? I know."

Her arms went around my middle, her face buried into my chest. I hugged her back, trying to offer her comfort but unable to take any.

When she pulled back, she went down the hall toward Drew's room, and I stared after her longingly.

"What can we do?" Braeden asked, bringing me back to the moment.

Anthony stepped into the empty waiting room, and we followed. He sat, and I dropped into a seat beside him. A wave of dizziness swept over me, but I pushed it back.

"You could file a suit petitioning for guardianship," he told me but then shook his head. "But honestly, you won't win. You have no legal claim to Drew."

I dropped my head into my hands.

"As a lawyer, my first recommendation would be to try and work out a compromise with the other party… but considering what just happened."

"He deserved a lot more than one punch," I growled.

"So if Trent can't take away his next of kin status, is there anyone else who could?" Braeden asked.

"A blood relative," he answered. "Maybe Ivy."

"No," Braeden and I said at the same time.

Shaking my head firmly, I continued. "I'm not putting Drew's sister in the middle of this. It's already bad enough. I'm not doing that to her."

Braeden slapped me on the back. "I appreciate that, man."

"The easiest thing you can realistically do is wait for Drew to wake up." Mr. Anderson surmised. "When he does, he will ask for Trent. It won't matter what his father says or wants, because Drew will be able to decide for himself."

A heinous, sickening thought haunted me. I started to speak, but I couldn't choke out the words. Both men looked at me, concerned.

Clearing my throat, balling my fists in my lap, I pushed the words out. "What if… what if he has a…?" I couldn't do it. I couldn't bring myself to put it out there.

"What if he has some brain damage." Braeden finished for me.

"Ah." Romeo's dad considered. "Well, if Drew is, ah, incapacitated…"

I made a sound.

"Then his father would be in charge of his care."

I burst up out of the chair, wobbling from the force of the movement. "I—I c-can't." My voice cracked, and all I could think about was getting out. I had to get away.

"Trent." B grabbed me, but I pushed him off.

"Let me go." I begged, heading for the door.

Before stepping away, I turned back. "Please don't leave him here alone."

"I swear." B vowed.

I made it into the elevator where I was blissfully alone. The second the doors cut me off from everyone else, I slid down the wall and cried.

FOURTEEN

Trent

Despite the strong desire to get away, I didn't go far.

I couldn't.

I was invisibly tethered to the man who lay upstairs.

Tethered by friendship.

Tethered by love.

And now tethered by blood.

He was such a part of me that sometimes it felt we were the same person.

But it didn't matter. *How could it not matter?*

How could black and white words typed on paper mean more than feelings, more than physical bonds? How was it that a man consumed with so much hate could have the advantage over those who loved to the fullest?

This was why. Why I thought I'd been doing the right thing. Why I'd built the life we had.

I thought I was protecting Drew.

Was everything I believed wrong?

Maybe not wrong, but narrow-minded?

I laughed out loud at the thought. The hollow sound echoed through the empty hallway I'd escaped to.

Narrow-minded. It was comical and borderline ridiculous that I would consider myself this way, especially after everything that just went on upstairs.

Ever since our first kiss—hell, ever since I realized that I loved Drew as more than a friend—I had one goal.

Protect him.

I was zealously protective of Drew. Not only because I loved him, but because he loved me. Drew loving me was literally the most significant, precious gift that I would ever get, and it almost hurt to accept that love because I knew what a heavy price he would pay for giving it.

Once upon a time, I'd even tried to end the relationship before it barely even got started. Drew fought for us that night, and in the end, I couldn't deny him anything. I couldn't push him away.

So shielding us became my number one goal.

And now, as I sat here on this cold tile floor in an empty hallway of a hospital wing that quite possibly was abandoned, I considered something.

Perhaps I'd protected us too well.

Perhaps in my compulsive need to keep us safe, I'd actually made us vulnerable. And in that, I'd been too narrow-minded.

Instead of considering the world at large, I'd created one of my own.

How else could I explain the stunned shock still trembling my organs, still making it hard to draw in a breath? If I hadn't been so narrow-minded, so trusting in the small world I'd created, I might have seen this coming.

I might have been able to block the attack.

I didn't.

And now here I was. Here *we* were.

Drew and I weren't so naive that we thought everyone accepted same-sex relationships. Hell, we knew entirely too well they didn't. We both had been disowned by our parents. I'd been attacked and beaten, and there was a time when Drew thought he might lose his job.

In addition to that, the hate comments online overflowed. The disgusted looks and the muttered slurs never went away.

I think I'd become too good at blocking it all out. At keeping it away from us. Drew and I lived in a little bubble, a safe bubble of acceptance, and within it, we flourished.

Our blood might have shunned us, but our family enveloped us. Gamble opened his home and took on an "underdog" in love with another man as the face of the NRR. *GearShark Magazine*, who had major influence and brand recognition, gave us a platform to tell our story and to gain support.

It wasn't that we didn't know how cruel the world was. It was that we created our own world where love was all that mattered.

I'd shielded us too well behind the walls of our family compound, behind the gates at the NRR, and by ignoring the majority of the hate flung at us online. We remained private but not secretive. Open but not in-your-face.

I'd thought it was the best thing.

I was a fool.

I didn't want to rock the boat, mess with the perfection we'd found. I was afraid if we got married, it might shift something irrevocably.

Something shifted all right. But it wasn't because we were married. It was because we weren't.

Not fully committing to him, being openly together but not obtrusively married, was the most dangerous thing I could have done to Drew.

And now he was lying upstairs, victim to not only a horrible accident, but to his parents who only wanted to control him instead of love him.

If I had asked him to marry me, I would still be at his side. If I had taken a chance that a change in our relationship would have made it better instead of ripping it apart, then things might be different right now.

There was so much regret inside me. Could I have prevented that accident? Could I have protected him from his parents? Was he lying upstairs scared and feeling abandoned?

Letting my head fall into my hands, I felt the world tilt around me.

I messed up, Drew. How am I going to fix this?

In 2004, Massachusetts became the first state to legalize gay marriage.

FIFTEEN

Trent

It had only been an hour, but I needed to see him. The tug in the center of my body made me ache. My soul wanted him and rebelled against me for not being there. I had no doubt if it could escape its own body and go to Drew, it would.

Hell, the ache was so severe I considered cutting a hole in me to set it free.

The hallway was empty when I came around the corner, and I didn't hesitate. I went briskly down the hall as if I weren't doing something that would cause a ruckus. It wasn't even necessary for me to go in the room. It would be enough just to see him, to gaze at him through the window or through a crack in the door.

Anything to reassure myself that he was okay would be better than not knowing.

Someone walked by, making me immediately duck my head. Nerves gripped the back of my neck and my shoulders tensed, but I kept going. The door to his room was ajar. My eyes briefly closed in thanks.

Glancing around once more, I crept close, peeking around the corner toward Drew's bed.

It was empty.

Forgetting all about the rules and the care I took to be inconspicuous, I let the door hit the wall when I shoved it wide and barged into the room.

"Where is he?" I demanded, my eyes frantically searching every corner of the room. Rushing into the bathroom, I looked in there too.

Rationally, I knew he wouldn't be there. He was in a coma, for fuck sake. He wasn't taking a piss, but rationale didn't factor into the intensity of my internal freak-out.

As I hurried toward the empty bed, all oxygen stuck in my throat.

A rough, hard grip wrapped around my forearm and pulled. "I thought I told you that you aren't welcome in this room."

"Where's Drew?" I asked, my chest heaving from lack of breath.

"That's not any of your concern." Burke sniffed.

His nose was swollen, and there was dried blood on his nostrils. One of his eyes was blackening, but I didn't give a damn.

"Everything about Drew is my concern." He was still holding my arm, and I wrenched it away.

"I could take my son out of this hospital and put him somewhere else, and you would have absolutely no say."

"You can't do that," I said, reaching out to steady myself on the side of the bed.

The empty bed.

Dear God, did this man somehow arrange to have Drew transferred this fast? Would he really put his own son at risk by moving him while he was in a coma?

He wouldn't...

"I most definitely can."

My stomach was hollow and empty, yet I felt it heaving up whatever was inside into my throat. "Please just tell me where he is. Is he okay?"

I thought I saw a flicker of something in Burke's eyes. Humanity maybe? But it was there and gone so fast I couldn't decide.

Folding his arms over his chest, he glared. "You know this is your fault, right?"

"What?" I asked, trying to keep up. Why wasn't he answering?

"Drew is in a coma right now. He almost died because of you."

"I checked the car," I said weakly. "I had the entire team go over his car."

"He wouldn't even have been in that car if you hadn't convinced him to defy his family and become a driver."

"That's what he wanted. Drew has always wanted to drive. You know that."

"All I know is that cars were just a hobby to him until he met you and turned his back on everything he was raised to be."

I looked around the room again. "Did the doctor come get him? The nurse?"

"This is your fault." He persisted, taking a step closer.

I felt like something terrible was closing in, like I was being cornered and trapped. My instinct wasn't to fight back, though. Oddly, it was to fold in on myself. To retreat.

Where is Drew?

"I take responsibility for the accident," I admitted. "It was my fault. I didn't want this to happen…"

"If you had left him alone, if you hadn't dragged him down with you, he wouldn't be being punished right now."

"Punished?" I questioned.

"Punished for this lifestyle. For…" His face twisted in disgust. "For living with another man."

I made a choked sound, incredulous. "You think this happened to Drew because he's gay?"

"My son isn't gay. But you are. And my son got caught up in your punishment."

The room tilted. I couldn't comprehend what he was saying *and* not know about Drew at the same time.

"If you had just stayed away from him, he wouldn't be like this. He wouldn't be gone."

All the noise in the room stopped. The silence was deafening. All my organs dropped toward my feet, and the soul still trying to tug out of my chest seemed to wither. "G-*gone?*"

"Whoever will you latch onto now that my son is not here?" the man taunted.

But I didn't notice the provoking tone. All I heard were the words. All I felt was my entire life collapsing around me.

I sank onto the floor, the side of the bed the only thing keeping me upright. I felt as though I'd been dropped underwater. Like I was sinking deep below the surface of the sea. It weighed me down, made me sluggish, and muted the entire world around me.

Someone dropped down in front of me, shaking my shoulder and calling out my name.

Ivy.

Her face was pale, her blue eyes wide. I saw her lips moving. I saw her shaking me, but I heard nothing. I felt nothing.

Suddenly, she was gone. A much larger form dropped down in front of me. Blond hair. Blue eyes.

"Drew," I said, reaching out, grabbing a fistful of his T-shirt.

"He's fine," a voice that was *not* Drew's replied.

I blinked.

Grabbing me, giving me a rough shake, Romeo spoke again. "Trent, Drew is fine. He's getting a CT scan."

I yanked his shirt, aggressively pulling him close. "He's okay?"

"I swear. He's getting tests done. He'll be back up in a few."

Relief poured into me, restarting my life and filling my lungs with air. "Thank God," I whispered, then grabbed Rome's shirt again. "You swear?"

"I don't lie to family." Romeo confirmed, holding my stare directly. "C'mon, let's walk downstairs and see how it's going."

I pushed up off the floor, Romeo giving me a hand.

Ivy bounced from foot to foot near Braeden, and out of the corner of my eye, I saw Adrienne standing on the other side of the room.

"What the hell did you say to him?" Romeo snarled, turning toward Drew's dad.

"The truth."

"He said Drew was gone," I echoed, still feeling the boney, ice-cold fingers of death piercing my heart.

Ivy made a sound. "How could you? I told you how much they love each other. I begged you not to do this. Why won't you listen?"

"How could I?" Burke said, staring at his daughter. "How could you?"

"*Me?*"

"Burke." Adrienne intercepted meekly on behalf of her daughter.

Clearly, B thought it was just as meek as I did, because he stepped forward and spoke to his father-in-law in a calm, deadly manner. "There is a limit to my patience. My wife is off-limits to your sewage."

Burke glanced between Ivy and Braeden for a few moments, then relented.

Ivy turned her back on him and came to my side. "Let's go check on Drew," she said, reaching for my hand. As she did, she realized it wasn't empty. "What's this?" she asked, gesturing to the bag I'd forgotten about in my hands.

"I got it for Drew."

"Let's go give it to him." Ivy took my hand, and we started for the door.

"You're sure he's downstairs?"

"Positive," she said.

"I meant what I said." Burke's voice stopped me at the door. When I glanced over my shoulder, I couldn't see him because Romeo and Braeden had formed a formidable wall between me and Ivy and her parents.

Romeo hitched his chin at me to keep walking, to just ignore whatever he was about to say.

"If you won't stay away from Drew, I'll have him moved. I'll put him somewhere none of you will be able to find him."

All the blood drained from my face.

"This is one of the best hospitals in the country," Romeo snapped, spinning around. "Moving him would only set him back."

"Well, a downgrade in treatment would just be one more thing that man can add to the list of things he's done to my son."

A sob broke out of Ivy, and she started forward.

I caught her hand. "Don't," I said low. "You should stay out of it."

"I will not!" she snapped, sounding mad as hell.

Braeden moved out of her way when she charged forward, obviously seeing fire in her eyes.

"I've tried to give you the benefit of the doubt. I always believed you would come around because underneath all your hate, you actually love Drew. But this…" Her voice shook. "What you've done today… I can't be neutral anymore."

"Ivy," Braeden called.

"I've made up my mind," she tossed over her shoulder. He relented. "You're out," Ivy announced. "Out of my life. Out of my children's lives."

Adrienne gasped and rushed forward to stand at her husband's side. Burke's eyes narrowed. "You would cut me out of my grandchildren's lives?"

"I just did. You are no longer welcome at my house. You are no longer welcome in Nova's and Jaxson's life. I don't want any part of your... disgusting behavior around my babies."

Burke cut a glance at me. "You would really side with him?"

"Ivy," I called, not wanting this.

"You're damn right! He's my family! He's Drew's family. *Drew's choice.* I always thought maybe you and Drew would find a way to mend your relationship..." Her voice fell away, and she shook her head. Putting her hands on her hips as if she needed to fortify herself, she lifted her chin. "But *nothing* will ever repair this. Drew will never forgive you. And I won't either."

Ivy spun, tears glittering in her eyes but her head held high.

"Ivy," Adrienne pleaded.

Her face crumpled, but then she rebuilt it and turned around with grace. "I'm sorry, Mom, but my decision includes you too. I know you haven't exactly said the things Dad has, but you stand idly by and follow him with a closed mouth. For that... you are just as horrible as he is."

"But Nova and Jax." She begged.

"They're no longer your concern." Ivy's voice rang with finality, and the silence that followed her exit was deafening.

"Braeden." Adrienne tried after she was gone.

He made a motion with his hand. "Don't even try. I'm with my wife one hundred percent. Don't come around my kids... 'cause it will only upset them when I toss you out."

Braeden left the room. Then Romeo was at my side, motioning for me to go. We all went down the hall as a unit, and if I wasn't still so unsettled, I'd say we probably looked like badasses.

"Ivy," I said when we were all waiting for the elevator.

"This isn't your fault, Trent. None of this. And what I just did back there… it was the right thing. I won't have my kids around his toxic beliefs."

Braeden put an arm around her shoulders. "You're hot as hell when you put assholes in their place."

"What if they try and keep you away from Drew too?" I worried.

"They wouldn't dare." Ivy seethed. "Besides, I'm a blood relative. Dad already told them to keep me updated."

The sound of the elevator sliding into place behind the doors made me look up anxiously. Now more than ever, I had to see him. I had to assure myself he was okay.

A bell dinged, the doors slid open, and two orderlies pushed a bed out of the car. Lying in it was Drew.

SIXTEEN

Trent

My body swayed toward his. I wasn't dizzy. I didn't trip. I just knew exactly where I belonged.

The metal railing on the bed was cold against my palms when my hands wrapped around it to help the orderlies bring the bed the rest of the way out of the elevator.

The center of my chest ached when I stared down, taking in every little detail I could. He looked exactly the same as this morning, except the bandage around his head was gone. I reached out to touch him, wanting to check the stitches on his head.

"Who are you?" one of the orderlies asked, his voice brusque.

"Family," I said.

Ivy rushed forward. "I'm Drew's sister. These are his brothers,"

The orderly nodded. "We need to get the patient back to his room to hook up all his equipment properly."

"Could we maybe have just one minute?" Ivy asked sweetly.

"That's not—"

"I'll take him from here," Patrick said, appearing from around the corner. He was still wearing the same pink scrubs, and this time, I noticed he had a diamond stud in one ear.

"You sure?" one of the orderlies asked.

"Of course," he replied, waving his hand at them.

"Look at these strapping football players. They can help push him back to the room."

The orderlies seemed doubtful.

Romeo stepped forward and smiled. "Nice to meet you guys. I'm Romeo."

They forgot about Drew and focused on the football stars before them. Part of me was pissed off they would forget Drew that fast, but the other part of me was grateful.

I wondered if Romeo ever got tired of being a charmer.

"I can give you like two minutes," Patrick whispered, leaning in.

"I won't forget this," I told him sincerely.

Ivy stood close by but angled her body, trying to give me some privacy with my guy. I didn't care. These past few days changed me. Being guarded didn't seem so important anymore. Suddenly, all those times we were discreet when we wanted to touch or when I'd held back precious words until we were alone seemed like such a waste. I should have said everything I felt the second it bloomed in my heart. I should have touched him instead of denying us in case someone else might be uncomfortable.

I did a lot of shit for other people. People who didn't know me. People who might judge. People that didn't even matter.

All that mattered was Drew.

If he died, I would live with those regrets. Those lost moments. And they would haunt me like unsettled ghosts.

As Romeo, B, and those men chattered away about football, Patrick and Ivy basically stood guard.

I forgot about them all.

Leaning over the bed, over the body of the man I loved more than myself, gently, I brushed my fingers over the side of his head.

"You're just using this as an excuse to not comb your hair," I told him softly, trying to give him a smile.

He wouldn't see it. But I was hoping maybe he would feel it.

I managed the smile, but it caused tears to well up in my eyes. God, I felt like a giant wuss. I wasn't a crier. But since this happened, I'd never cried so much in my entire life.

That didn't matter either.

Perhaps I'd been too guarded with my emotions in the past too.

The ventilator was still breathing for him, and I missed the view of his lips. Of his smile. Of his ocean-blue eyes.

Blinking back the tears, I caressed the side of his cheek.

"I brought you something," I told him, glancing down at his casted leg. Reaching into the bag I was carrying, I pulled out my recent purchase.

"It was black or this," I said, holding up the tie-dyed fabric. "You probably would have picked the black, but I wanted to give you a rainbow. Where'd your shirt go?" I asked, moving down the bed toward his foot. "Guess they thought it didn't belong there." I shrugged. "It was B's shirt anyway. He can buy a new one."

"I heard that." B chimed in.

His toes were cold again. The ache in my chest intensified. If I had been with him, his toes wouldn't be cold like this. They would have been covered and warm.

Taking the tag off the cast cover I purchased, I tossed the bag on the floor and slowly, cautiously worked it over his leg. A cast cover was basically a large sock made to go over a cast. I didn't really know what people used them for. Hell, I hadn't even known they made these things until today.

All I knew was that it would keep his toes warm.

When I was finished, I stared down at the bright multicolored fabric and smoothed my hand over it.

Patrick cleared his throat, and mine constricted. Holding up a finger, I went back up beside Drew, leaning over his body again.

"Keep fighting, Drew. I'm here. I'm not going anywhere." I had no idea if he heard me.

He looked so still and quiet. Not at all the man I was used to seeing.

After pressing my lips against his forehead and then on the bridge of his nose, I pulled away just slightly. "Love you," I whispered.

"Would you mind giving me a hand, boys?" Patrick asked my brothers.

"Wait." I stopped them, pulling the blankets up around him and making sure his hands were covered. Then I walked alongside the bed until we reached the waiting room at the end of his hallway.

The rest of them kept going, and I stopped and watched until the bed disappeared into his room. Inside the waiting room, I dropped into a chair, staring off into space.

Someone cleared their throat. I looked up.

Four sets of eyes stared back at me.

"I didn't know you guys were here," I said, taking in Joey, Lorhaven, Hopper, and Arrow.

"Who's the douchebag standing in Drew's room like a Nazi?"

"Hitler's descendent," I muttered.

"You give him that busted nose?" Lorhaven asked.

"Yep."

"It's his father, isn't it?" Arrow asked, a knowing tone darkening his voice. Everyone, including me, looked at him. His cheeks turned pink, and he squirmed in his chair uncomfortably.

Hopper rested his hand on the top of Arrow's thigh, and almost instantly, he calmed.

The power of a touch. The *right* touch. My stomach twisted. *Does Drew need my touch right now?*

"Yeah," I said. "It's his parents."

"He's one of those dads." Arrow went on, his voice haunted and perceptive.

"A—" Lorhaven began.

"It's okay," he replied to his brother. "We aren't the only ones with a fucked-up father."

"I thought Drew's dad disowned him," Joey practically whispered.

"He did. But he sees Drew's weak state as the perfect opportunity to separate us and control Drew."

"What do you mean?" Hopper asked.

"He has some old will. He's next of kin. He's forbidden me to see Drew."

Lorhaven shot up out of the chair he was in so forcefully it banged into the wall. Everyone sitting alongside him barely reacted. They just looked up, mildly surprised.

That's what happens when you're a guy prone to attitude. No one is surprised when you get pissed off.

"Are you fucking serious?" He fumed.

"Do you think I'd be sitting all the way out here if I wasn't?"

"I'll break something else…" he muttered and charged forward.

Joey bolted up, but I was faster, sliding into the doorway and pushing him back.

"Stay away from him, Lorhaven."

He turned, incredulous. "Guys like that—"

"He threatened to take Drew somewhere else and not tell us where."

Lorhaven's eyes rounded, and all the fight left him.

Joey pressed a hand to her mouth, muffling the sound she made.

"You can't do anything that will piss him off any further. If he takes Drew…" My voice fell away.

A strong hand slapped onto my shoulder and squeezed. "That's not going to happen." Romeo vowed.

Glancing over my shoulder, I saw him, Braeden, and Ivy.

"How is he?" I asked, turning.

"He's fine. The doctor will be up to tell us the test results soon."

"No one stayed with him?" I worried.

"Two people in the room at a time." Ivy reminded me. "My parents are both in there."

"My father wanted to let you know that he will be here tonight. He had meetings today," Joey told me.

I nodded and sank back into the seat.

Everyone sat down. No one talked, but the solidarity we all exuded spoke volumes. One person stepped in, glanced around, and backed out.

I don't know how much time passed before a cup of coffee appeared under my nose. It smelled good, but my stomach revolted just looking at it. "No thanks," I muttered, not even glancing up.

The cup followed me when I turned away from it.

"I said no—" I began, irritation clear in my voice, but then I saw who it was. "Rimmel." I amended. "I didn't know you were here."

"I was at the hotel with the kids and B's mom. But Romeo's parents came back and London fell asleep, so here I am."

"Kids okay?" I asked.

She nodded. "I brought you this." She tried giving me the coffee again.

I made a face.

"Trent," she scolded. "Take it."

I did, and then she climbed in my lap. I blinked a few times, stunned, then gazed around for Romeo. He was sitting nearby, watching us. When he saw me looking, he smiled lightly.

Dude knew I was grumpier than an old man with a bad case of hemorrhoids and wanted to sit here alone and brood.

He also knew I wouldn't rebuff his wife. Rimmel was pretty much the entire family's soft spot. No one could deny her, and if we tried, Romeo would kick our ass.

I was pretty good at keeping people at arm's length. Except for Drew.

And then Rim snuck in, just a little bit closer than the rest of the fam.

She was so small. Even after having three kids, she fit in my lap with room to spare. Swinging up, her legs dangled slightly over the armrest, and she tucked her cheek against my shoulder.

I knew she meant well. Hell, I loved her for what she was trying to do.

But honestly?

Just between you and me…

This made me feel worse.

This reminded me that the only comfort I truly wanted was from Drew. The only person I wanted in my arms was him. My stomach flipped and dipped with emotion, and my throat struggled to swallow.

I put an arm around her and said nothing, because even if I didn't feel any comfort, I hoped maybe she did. And if she did, then that was enough for me.

"Drink that," she insisted, pushing the cup up toward my face.

Like the good brother I was, I drank some of it and then made a face as it went down. "How much sugar did you put in this, sis?"

"It's caramel," she replied. "You need the sugar."

"Well, there's enough sugar in this cup to give me diabetes."

"It's not that bad," she said, slipping her arms around my waist and hugging me. "You gave all that blood yesterday, and I know you haven't eaten since before the accident."

"I'm not hungry."

"I know."

We fell into silence, and I drank more of my diabetes in a cup. The warmth of the liquid felt good against my throat, making me realize how raw it was.

"I heard what he did," she said after a few minutes.

The arm I held around her stilled. I made a sound, acknowledging her words.

"He's wrong," she said plainly, lifting her chin a little so her head, still resting against my shoulder, was angled up toward mine. "I know it feels like all of us are sitting still, just allowing that man to do and say these awful things, and I honestly can't imagine how hard it is for you to even sit here."

"You're on top of me. Makes it hard to get up," I joked, trying to lighten things up. Trying to stop myself from shattering completely.

She poked me in the midsection, making a small sound. "None of us agree with him. None of us are actually sitting still." Her small hand pressed against my chest.

When Drew put his hand over my heart, his palm covered it. It felt like he was actually holding my heart.

"Not in here," she whispered, drawing my gaze. "We're all outraged. We're all screaming inside. We all hate the unfairness of this situation. Just like you, we know it's best for Drew if we just tow the line… try and keep the peace."

I cupped the back of her head. "I don't want anyone fighting this battle but me. It's just me he hates… Drew needs the rest of you."

She nodded. Behind the glasses, her wide brown eyes were empathetic. "We're all here for him."

"Thank you, Rim."

She grabbed my hand, giving it a squeeze. "But we're here for you too. Don't forget that, okay? You're our family too. Not just Drew."

I nodded.

"Trent?"

"Hmm?"

"It isn't you that man hates. Not really. He just hates seeing proof that everything he believes is a lie. Love doesn't have limits, and if there has ever been proof of it, it's you and Drew."

Emotion clogged my throat. I lifted the coffee to my lips but then decided not to take a sip because I was afraid it wouldn't go down.

"You know you're my favorite, right?" I whispered, leaning in to kiss the side of her head.

She giggled. "Drink your coffee," she instructed.

I made a face but obliged. "Do you think if I go into sugar shock, they'd let me share a room with Drew?" It was meant to be a joke, but the way I said it conveyed way too much longing.

"He's going to wake up soon. And when he does, it's you he's going to ask for first."

Hope and fear grabbed me, creating a violent game of tug-of-war inside me. Hope that, yes, Drew would soon open his eyes. And fear that when he did, he might not know me.

In 2017, Seattle elected its first lesbian mayor: former US Attorney Jenny Durkan.

SEVENTEEN

Trent

I spent the night in a waiting room chair, occasionally so restless I would wander down the hallway and steal glances through the window into Drew's room.

The staff would cast glimpses and whisper every time they walked past. A couple times, they spied me creeping down the hallway, but they never said a word. Maybe they were scared of me. Maybe they thought I was pitiful.

I couldn't help but wonder whose side they were on. If they also agreed with Drew's father that someone like me was too corrupt to be around him. If they thought the love I felt for Drew was somehow invalid because we were both men.

Invalid. Other people didn't have the power to void out something a man felt. Did they? Emotions, in a sense, were sort of like opinions. Though they often differed, were any of them wrong?

Emotions and opinions were expressly owned by whoever held them, and just their presence made them real. But just because I might not agree with someone else's opinion or how they felt, it didn't mean whatever it was somehow cancelled out.

Yet here we were, being punished regardless.

No one had the right to tell me how to feel, but in turn, I couldn't make others understand.

A light nudge on my shoulder brought me out of the half sleep I'd been floating in. Katie, one of Drew's night nurses, stood there with nervousness written all over her.

I jumped out of the chair like it was on fire, adrenaline lighting my veins and making my heart pound fitfully.

"What is it?" I demanded. "What happened?"

Braeden jerked awake in a nearby chair. "What's wrong?"

Ignoring him, I grabbed the nurse by the shoulder, giving her a light shake. "Drew?"

Pressing a finger against her lips, she shushed me. "He's okay."

Expelling a forceful breath, I bent at the waist, pressing my hand against my chest. "Jesus Christ," I swore. "You scared the shit out of me."

"Shh." She reminded me.

As I straightened, my eyes narrowed. "If nothing's wrong, what are you doing here?"

"We're going to be changing shifts soon." She began, dividing her stare around the room as though she was making sure we were alone. Leaning in, she whispered, "Do you want to see him?"

Instant intense longing was a lightning strike of pain right into my chest. "Seriously?"

She nodded. "You can't tell anyone. I could lose my job."

I held up my hands in surrender. "I swear to God."

She smiled and motioned for me to follow.

I glanced back at Braeden. "Cover me."

"Will do."

The hallway was still dim and quiet. I wasn't really quite sure what time it was, but I didn't care. The palms of my hands grew clammy, and nerves coiled in my lower belly. It was like finally getting to see someone after a long time apart. Like meeting up for a first date, eaten alive by worry.

Katie walked into the room first as if she was just doing her normal rounds, leaving the door slightly ajar.

Quickening my footsteps, I rushed soundlessly, slipping inside the room without pause. The second my eyes fell on the bed, my stomach flopped. I don't remember walking across the room, but then I was there, close enough to reach down and take his hand.

"Drew." His name fell from my lips like a prayer, and gratitude rolled into one.

The chair I'd kept so close to the bed wasn't there, so I dropped onto my knees, my whole body in contact with the side of the bed. Lifting his hand, I pressed my cheek against it.

While I was sitting out there in that uncomfortable seat, I'd thought of so many things I should have said. A thousand words I'd wanted to string into sentences to hopefully explain just how much he meant to me.

A thousand words instantly forgotten.

I couldn't speak. It was overwhelming just to feel. Just to hold him in my gaze.

Close by, Katie cleared her throat. I'd forgotten she was there.

Not pulling my eyes off Drew, I said, "I owe you. Ten times over."

"The look on your face is payment enough."

"How long do I have?" I asked, pressing a kiss to the back of his hand.

"Not too long. The day staff will be here soon, and then visiting hours will start after that…"

I heard what she didn't say. Drew's parents would be back. They didn't even try to spend the night. He didn't even ask if they would bend the ICU rules and let someone stay with his son.

Instead, Drew lay there alone for hours while I sat down the hall in hell.

I'd thought so many times about sneaking in here. But I was afraid.

Afraid there were more people on Burke's side than mine.

Afraid if I got caught, Drew would be shipped away to some secret location.

Thinking of that, my heart squeezed. "You're sure this is okay?" My neck pricked with the desire to glance around to make sure no one was watching. But that would require looking away from Drew.

I'd spent too many hours desperately wanting to see him.

She made a sound. "The supervisor just left. It's just me and a few others right now. No one will say a word."

"Thank you," I whispered, standing up so I could caress his cheek.

I stayed as close as humanly possible until she came back and told me it was time to go.

# # #

"How is he?" Braeden asked when I stepped back into the waiting room.

"About the same," I replied, dropping into a chair. The relief I felt from being able to see and touch Drew for even a short while was extreme. Though relief was a good feeling and often made one feel lighter, this time it was heavy.

"You look like shit," Braeden remarked, standing over me with his arms crossed over his chest.

"So do you."

"Yeah, well, sleeping in a waiting room sucks."

"You should have gone back to Gamble's."

"We're fam. I'm not letting you sit here all night alone. And someone has to be here in case you hulk out again."

I gave him the finger. I was too tired for anything else.

B slid into the chair beside me. "Why don't you come back with me? Take a shower. Get some food."

"I'm not leaving."

"I get it. I really do. If that was Ivy…" His voice trailed away. Clearing his throat, he went on. "But if you keep going like this, you're going to collapse. Then you won't be any help to Drew."

"I'm not leaving him here alone."

"He won't be alone."

Angry, I spun toward him. "His dad is just waiting for a chance to whisk him out of here undetected. The second I turn my back, he'll have Drew out of here, and I swear to God, B."

"I won't let that happen." A new voice joined the conversation.

Surprise took some of the intensity out of my voice. "Romeo."

As he came into the room, he reached out, giving my shoulder a squeeze. Rimmel appeared from behind him, glasses perched on her nose and an oversized hoodie taking over her frame.

"What are you guys doing here so early?"

Rimmel handed me a coffee. I grimaced. "It's how you usually drink it. No extra sugar." She confirmed.

Oh. Well. I would take it. "Thanks."

"We're here to relieve you two." Romeo informed us.

"How's Ivy?" Braeden asked.

"She was still sleeping when we left. But she's okay."

Braeden nodded. "I'll bring her and my mom over when visiting hours start."

"Valerie and Tony will be over later this afternoon," Rimmel said of Romeo's parents.

Even though not everyone could go back and see Drew while he was in the ICU, it still meant something that they all came here day in and day out. They seemed to take unspoken shifts, making sure Drew was always surrounded by people who loved him.

Braeden stretched out his back. "C'mon, T. You can ride with me."

"I told you I'm not leaving."

"You've been here for three days," Romeo said as if I didn't know exactly how long I'd been here. How long Drew's life had been hanging in the balance. "You look like a zombie."

I ignored him.

"You smell," Rimmel inserted.

All three of us looked up at her. Romeo made a low amused sound.

Her cheeks turned pink, but she made a face and put her hands on her hips. "You do. You're stinky! And you haven't changed any of your bandages or put anything on those burns."

"I don't care about me," I murmured.

B leaned over and not so discreetly took a whiff of me. "Bro," he exclaimed, wrinkling his nose. "She's right. You're ripe."

"You might not care about yourself right now, but Drew does. He's going to wake up soon. Do you really want to"—Rimmel paused, considering her words—"be in this condition when he does?"

"You have my word that I will not let anyone take Drew out of here while you're gone. I won't let anyone mess with him." Romeo vowed. "It's not even visiting hours yet."

"That doesn't matter," I argued.

"I'll stand outside his door like a guard if it will make you feel better. I'll stand there until you come back."

I glanced up, sort of touched by the tenacity in his voice. "You'd do that?"

"Damn right I would." Romeo agreed.

"Me too." Rimmel agreed. "No one would get by me!"

Romeo patted her on the head. "You're the toughest of us all, baby."

I shook my head. Just the thought of leaving this hospital made my stomach twist.

Romeo went on. "Even if it's only an hour. Shower. Change. Eat. Maybe grab some clothes for Drew for when he wakes up."

"Get your ass out of that chair, Trent," Braeden grumped when I didn't move.

Reluctantly, I stood. Dropping an arm around my shoulders, B started walking toward the door, but my feet remained planted.

"Go." Romeo insisted. "I've got things handled here."

The entire way down in the elevator, I fought the intense urge to rush back upstairs. Clammy sweat broke out across my forehead, and the palms of my hands were hot. The not-so-soft material of the scrubs I was wearing suddenly felt very restrictive, and I wanted to rip them off.

Braeden cleared his throat as the elevator slid to a stop on the main floor. "So, um, you should know the press is camped out down here."

I cursed.

The doors slid open.

New York City has the
highest number of
same-sex marriages in
the United States.

EIGHTEEN

Trent

"Oh my God! There he is!" someone yelled.

Gasps, scurrying feet, and the blur of people rushing toward us caught me off guard.

"Trent! Trent Mask!"

"How is Drew?"

"Is Drew still in the ICU?"

"Can we get a statement?"

Dipping my head, B and I marched through, making it so they had to clear a path for us to walk.

"He looks awful."

"The rumors must be true!"

I stiffened, and my feet stalled. Rumors? What rumors?

Braeden put a hand on my shoulder, nudging me along.

Flashes went off, burning my irises and making me even surlier than I already was. More camera clicks and cellphones floating around, all of them trained on us.

The wide glass doors opened, and cool morning air rushed around us. The sun was barely up.

"Please, Trent! Give us an update! How's Drew?"

"Are those injuries from when you climbed into the wreckage?"

The hum of a strong engine and the squeal of tires at the edge of the sidewalk turned heads. I recognized the vintage black Camaro instantly. The passenger door opened, and Arrow's blond head popped out from the back seat. "Get in!"

The press turned rabid once again as we practically dove into the car. When we were barely in, Hopper revved the engine and peeled away from the curb, plastering me into the back seat.

"Looked like you guys needed a hand," he called from the driver's seat.

Arrow's eyes focused totally on me. "Is Drew okay?"

I nodded, and the worry in his stare calmed. "What are you guys doing here so early?"

"Came for an update before *he* got here," Hopper answered, meeting my eyes in the rearview.

A bitter taste filled my mouth. "Is he giving you a hard time too?"

I thought maybe he just hated me because of Drew, but apparently, his hate extended to all gay men.

"Nothing we can't handle. Just trying to avoid the drama."

Leaning back, I sighed. "The press has been like that for three days?"

"They were worse on the first day," Braeden answered from the passenger seat in front of me.

"How much worse can they be?"

"You don't want to know," Arrow quipped.

I sat up. "What?"

Braeden reached around and smacked Arrow on the head. "Not cool, Biebs."

Keeping one hand on the wheel, Hopper snatched Braeden's wrist before he could pull it back. "Touch him again and you can walk."

"Hopp," Arrow admonished.

"It's cool," Braeden swore, not taking the threat too seriously.

"What aren't you telling me?" I demanded, leaning around the seat to stare at my brother.

"It's just the same old shit. You know how the press is. We just didn't want to burden you with it. You have enough to deal with right now."

"Nothing having to do with Drew is a burden," I said, glancing out the back window, thinking of asking Hopper to turn around.

"Keep driving," B told Hopper, knowing exactly what I was thinking.

I glared at him.

He sighed. He looked wrung out, bloodshot eyes and rumpled clothes. He'd slept in the waiting room with me all night last night. I knew it wasn't just for me but for Ivy too, but still. He was there.

I couldn't be mad at him for long.

"I need to know what I'm dealing with." I reasoned.

"The clip of you going postal on the track and fighting your way into the wreckage is burning up the internet... and the national news."

"I thought Gamble took care of that."

"Yeah, he paid everyone off so they didn't sue your ass. That just gave the press more headlines."

"Fucking great," I muttered.

"No one in the fam has released a statement or talked to the press. They're hungry for an update on Drew. The only thing they know is that he's in the ICU."

"What else?" I asked, sensing there was more. B wouldn't have been that irritated at Arrow if there wasn't something else.

"Don't worry about it." He tried.

"Arrow?" I called.

Hopper made a noise. "Don't fucking drag him into it."

"Then you tell me." I challenged.

He took a turn a little too fast, but none of us even winced. This was how it was when you were friends with racers. "Someone at the hospital leaked some shit."

I leaned around the seat to glare once more at Braeden, silently telling him I wanted the information. And I wanted it from him.

Rolling his eyes, he pulled his cell from his pocket, tapped the screen a few times, and then handed over the phone.

Kept Apart...
GS

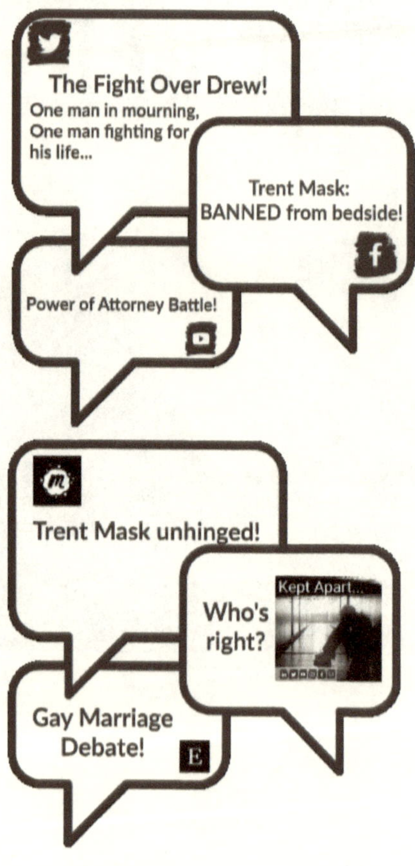

Sighing, I handed the phone back to Braeden. "How'd they get that photo?" I asked, thinking of the private, lonely moment I thought was mine and mine alone.

Turns out nothing was off-limits to the world. I couldn't even grieve without someone snapping a photo.

I could beat myself up for not seeing them lurking, but what good would it do? I had no room left inside me for that. All my internal space was currently being used up.

I reached down for my phone, realizing I didn't have pockets… nor did I know where my phone was.

"Let me see it again." I motioned to Braeden.

He handed his cell back over.

"Unlock it, asshole," I snapped, holding it out.

After scanning his fingerprint, he handed it back.

Romeo answered on the first ring. "He's fine, Trent."

"Are you sure?" I asked, not even asking how he knew it was me.

The phone beeped in my ear.

"Look at it," Romeo said.

Pulling it away, I glanced down at the new text. Tension seeped out of me the second I saw the pic of Drew through the door window.

I stared at it for long minutes, and Romeo waited me out.

When I finally pulled my eyes away, I said, "That's a shitty photo."

"My bad. Next time, I'll try to get his good side."

I half smiled. "Thanks."

He grunted.

"The press hasn't come up there, have they?"

"Fucking vultures," Romeo spat. "No. They aren't allowed in the ICU."

Right. That was good.

"This is why we didn't tell you about the press," Braeden said, directing his words toward the back seat. More specifically the man sitting beside me. "More to worry about."

"He was going to find out sooner or later," Arrow bitched back.

"Call if anything happens," I told Romeo.

"Will do."

"But Braeden's phone. I don't know where mine is."

"I know." His voice remained patient.

"Send me another picture."

"I'm hanging up now."

The call cut off, but seconds later, another pic came through. It looked a lot like the first one, but I didn't care.

Muffled pain broke through my intent staring, and I realized I was gripping the phone so tight the stitches in my hand were pulling.

"I'll just hold this for another minute," I said to Braeden.

As I was staring at the shitty photo of Drew, another notification came up on screen. Curling my lip at it, I surrendered the phone to my brother.

"There must be someone in the hospital leaking info," Hopper said as he drove. "How else would they know about the next-of-kin fight… and that photo?"

Arrow glanced around. "There's already videos of you and B coming out of the hospital."

"Have his parents talked to the press?" I asked.

Calling Drew's parents by their names was very difficult these days. It was hard to call a person by their name when they acted anything but human.

"No," Braeden replied.

The next thing I knew, Hopper pulled up to the Gamble estate front door. Braeden opened his door and got out, popping the seat up to make room for me to climb out.

"You coming?" he asked.

"I shook my head. I'll go to the apartment."

Braeden hesitated, coming back into the Camaro. "I'll go with you."

"No." I insisted. "Go check on Ivy. See your kids."

Again, he hesitated.

"We'll stay with him," Hopper told him quietly.

"I don't need a babysitter," I bitched.

Braeden ignored me to fist-bump Hopper and then reached back to ruffle Arrow's hair.

Hopper's eyes met mine in the rearview. "He's an asshole."

"He's family."

The ride to the apartment was silent. I hadn't cared about my missing phone until now… until I felt completely cut off from Drew.

There were press vans parked outside our building. The vans were obvious, even if they tried not to be. Some photographers just stood openly on the sidewalks, waiting for a glimpse of something photo-worthy.

The second the Camaro was noticed, they started aiming their cameras. Hopper drove into the parking garage, making sure none of them followed the car before the gate closed. I hadn't even considered the press until now. It never even entered my mind what the rest of the world was saying about Drew's accident.

They ceased to exist for me.

All that had mattered the last three days was making sure Drew woke up… and worrying that he might not know me when he did.

I didn't think about the fact that the press would be playing out every ounce of family drama they got a whiff of.

Now that I knew?

It still didn't matter. As long as they stayed away from Drew, I didn't care.

"The net is pretty divided," Arrow said quietly. "It's an outright debate over who's right: you or Drew's parents."

"Let them talk," I said wearily as we climbed out of the car. The parking garage was dim and quiet, the smell of gasoline and oil tinting the air.

It reminded me of Drew, and my throat squeezed.

Halfway to the building entrance, the distinct sound of a camera shutter filled the air. Immediately after, sneakers pounded on pavement and then a bright light flicked on, nearly blinding us.

I stopped walking, tossing a hand up to shield my eyes.

"Trent! Is it true Drew's family doesn't want you around him? Were you kicked out of the hospital?"

"You aren't supposed to be here," Arrow said. "Get out!"

"Is this why you never got married? Because his parents forbid it?"

A low grumble built in my throat. "No comment," I bit out and started for the door.

The jerk-offs rushed me, the camera thrust back in my face. The lights making me recoil, and someone else latched onto my arm.

I reacted.

Wrenching my arm free, I spun, putting all my weight behind the fist I punched forward. The asshole who put his hands on me went flying back, landing on his ass. Next, I lunged at the camera with the offensive light, smashing it onto the concrete.

Hopper put a hand on my heaving chest. "Enough," he advised quietly. "Let's go."

"My camera!" the man yelled. "You busted my camera!"

We headed toward the door.

"I'm going to sue you! You fucking fag!"

I stopped.

Spots swam before my eyes.

Hopper grabbed one arm. Arrow grabbed the other.

"Keep walking, Trent," Arrow whispered. "He wants a reaction. They have more than one camera."

It was hard. So hard to deny the sudden, violent anger boiling in my veins.

"Let's go call and check on Drew." Arrow cajoled.

I blinked.

"You can use my phone." Hopper promised.

We started walking again, the reporters still yelling even after we made it inside.

NINETEEN

Trent

The hollowness that assaulted me the second I stepped inside rocked me back on my heels.

His scent permeated the air.

His laugh echoed off the walls.

His presence was everywhere: in the sweats tossed over the back of the couch, the packets of ketchup littering the counter, his Xbox controller laid on the coffee table.

Moments caught in time. Life in this apartment frozen until he walked in and it all started up again.

I couldn't do this. I couldn't live in a world without him. I couldn't even comprehend it.

If Drew didn't wake up, who would put toothpaste on my toothbrush every morning? Who would buy the shampoo I liked?

I stopped in the doorway of the bedroom, bracing my weight on the frame. If I walked in that room, it would be gone too, our life that had been left on pause. Inside the room, we were still untouched.

The last time we were in there, we were together. We were both whole and healthy. The air practically shimmered with remnants of who we were. Of what I desperately wanted back.

I'd given Drew everything. He'd broken down walls I'd built over the course of my entire life. My father never wanted me. My mother only did her duty. I learned young to be a friend but never let anyone get too close. I learned it was better to be a loner than to feel alone among people who were supposed to care.

Then Drew walked into Screamerz.

His Mustang literally crashed through every wall I'd ever erected.

I'd been afraid. So fucking afraid.

But then suddenly, the fear wasn't as paralyzing because we could be afraid together.

I was alone again.

Standing here haunting this happy place like a ghost, tarnishing everything we'd left behind with everything we'd come to be.

All I saw when I gazed around was Drew. I felt him. I tasted him. I could even hear him.

"Frat boy! Get your ass in here. This shower is too big without you!"

"Take off your clothes and come over here."

"I love you, T. I love you more than anyone."

I bowed my head, my fingers aching as they gripped the wooden frame. A hand covered mine, and I glanced over my shoulder.

Hopper stood there, solemn understanding in his eyes.

I turned toward him, and one of his arms wrapped around my back. I probably—no—I *would* have been embarrassed at any other time. I wouldn't even have hugged him, let along clung to him like I did now.

Clinging to Hopper was better than being eaten alive by the love Drew and I left behind in this house.

Wait. *No.*

I wrenched backward, stumbling over the threshold of the bedroom and bursting the untouched bubble of happiness that remained.

It hurt. It fucking hurt like being burned by the blazing sun… but this was better. I'd rather cling to what Drew and I had and be eaten alive by it than try to hide.

Hopper stayed where he was. He didn't approach, but he didn't back away either. Arrow's blond head flashed behind him. He turned whispered something, and then his husband disappeared into the other room.

I swallowed. My skin was vibrating.

"The first time I came back to the place I lived with Matt," he said quietly, "it felt like he died all over again."

"Drew's not dead." I swore.

"No. He's not. Hold on to that."

I nodded, the simple words somehow giving me strength.

"Instead of mourning all the love you feel in this house, let it fill you up."

My eyes whipped up to his.

He half smiled. "I really do get it."

"I'm sorry," I said sincerely. Pain like this had a way of making a man forget other people could suffer too.

"Don't be sorry," he answered. "I made my peace with things a long time ago. But I still remember, and I know how you feel."

I went around to a nearby dresser, pulling open the door. Drew's scent wafted up around me like a cloud, and I shut my eyes. On the top of his stack of T-shirts was one I'd gotten him several years ago. It had the label of his favorite ketchup brand on the front. It was worn from being washed so many times. And it was his favorite.

A vision of him standing in front of me, smiling, wearing that shirt, his blond head messy and jaw unshaven, flashed before my eyes.

It made me smile.

Blinking back the tears, I grabbed the shirt and a few others, along with a bunch of other shit, and jammed it all into a duffle bag. Next, I grabbed some clothes for myself and a pair of Drew's boxers and shut myself in the bathroom.

I wasn't supposed to get my stitches wet. I ignored that rule. The water stung every cut and scrape on my body, and when water hit the burns around my wrist, sounds of pain hissed from between my lips.

When I was done in the shower, I pulled off the bandage covering the stitches and then dabbed off the water droplets. My knee was bleeding, so I had no choice but to apply a few bandages. All the other open cuts, I ignored.

The burns on my wrist looked kinda gross, but I didn't have the stuff I needed to cover those so I didn't bother.

Remembering the way Rimmel looked when she told me I smelled, I brushed my teeth and then ran a comb through my wet hair.

Once dressed in a pair of jeans and a T-shirt, I shoved some more stuff into the duffle and headed out. Before leaving the bedroom, though, I stopped, feeling a tug on my heart.

Pivoting, I glanced around again, taking in some of the love. A love so strong it stayed behind even when we physically weren't here.

I breathed deep. My tank was empty, startling so. Slowly, I began to fill up, recharging. The bed was still rumpled from the last time we were in it.

The alarm clock Drew hated so much lit up my bedside table. A copy of *GearShark* and a random sock littered his.

A photo of us on the day he'd become the first NRR champion was framed on the dresser.

My tank didn't fill completely. It wouldn't until Drew opened his eyes. But it was fuller than when I first stepped in here. I was calmer too.

And less stinky.

Arrow and Hopper were standing in the center of the living room when I came out.

"Why didn't you sit down?"

"It's not our place," Hopper said, knowledge in his pale-blue eyes.

He didn't want to disturb any memories I might have with Drew. He didn't want to somehow erase them or taint them.

I nodded, overwhelmed by the consideration. Also, sad that he knew how this felt.

Hell, he had it worse.

I couldn't imagine. I didn't even want to.

"We can go," I said, gesturing to the door. "Romeo didn't call, did he?"

"No." Hopper confirmed.

I hoped that meant everything was fine.

"I'm hungry." Arrow complained when we stepped into the elevator.

"You're always hungry," Hopper refuted, affection clear in his tone.

"We rushed out early this a.m.," he grumped, rubbing his stomach.

A low laugh filled the small car, and Hopper put his arm around Arrow, drawing him into his side. "All right, babe. What do you want to eat?"

Arrow glanced at me. "What do you want, Trent?"

"I'm not hungry."

He made a sound. "Well, I'm not eating unless you do."

"Take pity on me," Hopper said. "If I don't feed him, he'll be impossible to deal with."

Arrow made a face.

"I know what you're doing," I commented.

"Is it working?" Arrow beamed.

I sighed. "Fine. You can hit up a drive-thru. Then it's right back to the hospital."

I really didn't want to eat, but maybe if I did, I wouldn't feel so dizzy.

Same-sex marriage wasn't legal until the 2000s but same-sex couples were getting married on TV in the 90s. *Friends* and *Roseanne* showed same-sex marriage in 1995 and 1996.

TWENTY

Trent

When I stepped off the elevator, Romeo was standing there waiting.

"What's wrong?" I asked, anxious.

"The doctor wants to take out the chest tube and take him off the ventilator."

My heart rate skyrocketed. "When?"

"Pretty much now. We were trying to stall until you got here."

"Why didn't you call?" I demanded, racing down the hallway.

He kept up easily, saying, "Because the doctor just came in and announced it."

"The parents here?"

Romeo made a sound of agreement.

Rounding the corner, I jerked to a stop, surprised to see the doctor standing in the waiting room with the rest of the family.

"Doctor?" I said, completely focused on the man in the white coat as I rushed forward. "You're taking out the chest tube?"

"Mr. Mask," he said, turning when I spoke.

A loud throat cleared. I didn't have to look to know who it was. His angry vibes were stinking up the room.

I wanted to punch him again. I ignored him instead.

"Is it safe to do that already?" I asked, forgoing the pleasantries.

The doctor glanced back at Drew's father, clearly unsure if he should answer.

"We're all family here, Doc. Tell him whatever he asks." The familiar yet unfamiliar voice drew my attention.

I glanced over, then did a double take. Turning completely toward the newcomer, I felt my eyes widen. "Camden?"

Ivy tucked her arm in his and smiled widely. "He just got here this morning."

I'd only met Drew's brother once before, and that was before we started dating.

"Trent." He greeted me, stepping forward and offering his hand. "You look a lot worse than the last time I saw you."

"It's been a rough few days."

His face sobered. "I know. That's why I'm here."

I slid a glance at Ivy, and we exchanged a look.

"I called in reinforcements." She spoke quietly.

Camden always told Drew he supported our relationship, so maybe Ivy thought having him here would help with their dad.

But I couldn't help but worry. Saying you supported a relationship from afar was a lot different than doing it when it was right in your face. And doing it in such stressful circumstances would only make it harder.

So while Ivy seemed to think Camden would be an ally, I reserved the right to be cautious.

Cam nodded slightly to me, as if he could almost hear my thoughts. He resembled Drew. Blond hair, blue eyes, near the same height.

Cam didn't have the same sex appeal Drew had, though. At least not to me. He didn't have overgrown messy hair or an unshaven jaw, and he was dressed more neatly than Drew. Instead, he was dressed in a pair of dark jeans and a short-sleeve polo.

"As you were saying, Doctor?" he asked.

"Drew is down getting X-rays right now. I want to make sure his lung is functioning properly, not filled with fluid, and that the lung is capable of filling with oxygen. If the X-ray looks good, then, yes, I think now would be a great time to remove it. Chest tubes can be quite painful for patients, so it's better we get it taken care of before he's out of the coma."

"Is he coming out of that too?" I asked, hopeful but also scared.

"Not quite. We need to remove the tube and the ventilator. Once that is done and he's breathing on his own, we can begin thinking about reducing the anesthesia keeping him in the coma."

"W-will he be able to wake up on his own?" I worried. "You're sure the coma is medically induced?"

"The swelling in his brain has gone down considerably. There is still some there, but it should all subside soon. Based on the tests we've run, there is no reason to believe he won't wake up."

"But what about his brain? Is there… damage?"

"Who do you think you are, asking all these questions?" *he* inserted, coming closer.

"Dad." Camden spoke. His voice was quiet and flat. His father glanced over. "We all have these questions. Let the doctor talk."

The doctor went on like he wasn't in the middle of some bitter family war. "We won't know the full effect his head trauma had on his brain until he wakes up."

The sound of movement in the hallway had everyone turning around. Drew's bed came into view, and I shot out the room faster than anyone else.

"Drew," I said, slipping my hand into his. "Doc says you're getting better."

"If you'll excuse me, I'll go check the radiology results and be with you shortly." The doctor excused himself.

The entire family filled the hallway, surrounding Drew's bed.

Patrick appeared, relieving one of the orderlies. "Let's clear the hall," he announced. Today he was wearing forest-green scrubs. "Would you mind giving me a hand?" he asked nonchalantly.

I nodded, gripping the bed rail.

"Just one minute—" Drew's father began.

Camden cut him off. "Dad, I want to talk to you."

"I'm busy right now, son."

"I just got here. You don't have time for me?" He countered.

Romeo cleared his throat, moving to the other side of the bed. "I'll give you a hand."

I expected Burke to pitch a fit behind me. He didn't. Maybe Camden would be an asset to this situation after all.

Once Drew was back in his room, all the machines were hooked up properly and the orderlies were gone. Patrick rechecked everything, then caught my eye and winked. "I've got to make rounds. Let's pretend I forgot you were in here."

I nodded enthusiastically.

When he was gone, Rome stood beside the bed, staring down at Drew. "We're all pulling for you, man."

"There's a chair over there," I said, gesturing across the room. "Pull it up."

Romeo shook his head. "I'll leave him to you. I'll be outside if you need anything."

"Thanks," I said, still focused entirely on Drew.

When he was gone, I picked up the duffle I'd dropped near the door and pulled out a blanket I'd shoved inside.

It smelled like our house and was ten times softer and warmer than anything this hospital had. It was blue had French fries all over it. Carefully, I spread it out over him and then checked to make sure the cast cover was still in place.

"I missed the shit out of you," I told him, leaning in to kiss his forehead.

We sat for a while with me talking randomly, holding his hand, and stealing glances at the door, waiting to get kicked out.

When the door finally opened, I resolved myself to a scowling father but instead got the doctor.

"Good news," he said, glancing up from his laptop. "Oh, I didn't realize…" He faltered. "I thought you weren't allowed to be in here."

"I just really wanted to make sure he was okay," I said, playing it off. "What's the good news you mentioned?"

"Oh, uh, I'll just go get the next of kin."

I deflated when he turned away.

"I'm here," Drew's mom said, coming around the corner. "You have news about Drew?"

The doctor glanced at me once more.

Resigned, I stood, reluctantly slipping my hand from Drew's. "I'll go," I told them. "Thank you for allowing me a few minutes," I said sincerely.

Even if I was aching considerably, I was still grateful. Any minute with Drew was a minute to be thankful for.

"You can stay," Adrienne said, surprising me and the doctor. Her face flushed, and she avoided my open stare. "Do you have the results?" she asked.

"Yes." He confirmed. "The lung looks great. No fluid, and I see nothing that suggests it won't be able to hold oxygen."

I sank against the wall and breathed a giant sigh of relief.

Patrick stepped into the room, wheeling a tray of covered supplies.

"I'm going to go ahead and remove the chest tube." The doctor went on. "Then we will remove the ventilator."

Adrienne nodded. I stayed by the wall, hoping she would forget I was there and not change her mind about my presence.

"If you want to step out…" He gestured to the door.

She agreed readily, walking out. It offended me.

"I'm staying," I announced. Forget trying to be invisible.

"It's not necessary."

"You said it's painful for patients. Coma or not, Drew has some kind of awareness. Someone should be here with him," I insisted. Shifting my stare to his mother, I said, "He shouldn't have to endure any of this alone, even if it is hard to watch."

Her cheeks paled.

I didn't feel bad.

"Fine, but you'll need to remain quiet." The doctor allowed.

I said nothing.

Adrienne hesitated.

Still holding her stare, I spoke quietly. "Please. Let me stay."

Her lips rolled inward. She looked into the hallway, probably wondering about her husband. To my surprise, she nodded.

The relief was seriously real.

Patrick hurried to shut the door behind her as if he also thought she might change her mind. Then he readied all the supplies while the doctor put on some sterile gloves.

I kept my word and stayed quiet and out of the way. Well, until they flipped the blankets back and started the process of removing the tube inserted between his ribs. Unable to stand back any longer, I moved slowly toward the bed.

Once there, I took Drew's hand in both of mine.

The doctor glanced up at me but then went back to his work.

I didn't watch what they were doing, but my stomach clenched just the same. I focused on Drew's face, on any flicker of pain or awareness. He remained unchanged, but I held his hand anyway, gently stroking over it with my thumb.

Thankfully, it was a quick procedure, and soon the tube was gone and a large bandage put in place.

I leaned down and whispered, "It's over, Forrester. You did amazing."

The doc pulled out his stethoscope and listened to Drew's chest for a few minutes, then looked up. "Doing good."

"Yeah?" I echoed, hopeful.

"Let's go ahead and remove the ventilator."

"It's not too soon?" I stressed, gazing back down at him.

"I don't think so. Lungs heal fairly quickly, and ideally, we would like Drew to be breathing on his own. Once he's doing that, we can transfer him out of the ICU and bring him out of the coma."

I so badly wanted Drew to wake up. I wanted to see recognition in his eyes, a smile on his lips. Still, I hesitated because it didn't matter what I wanted. What mattered was what was best for him.

After a moment of debate, I nodded. "Go ahead."

The doctor didn't bother to point out that it wasn't even my decision. It was Drew's parents'. I appreciated that.

I had to stand back when they pulled the tube out of his throat. My stomach churned watching him lie there helplessly while the doctor and nurse leaned over him, doing things I knew would probably hurt if he was awake.

It was the first time I thought maybe his coma was a blessing in disguise. At least this way he felt less pain.

"Now what?" I said when the vent was removed.

"We see if he breathes on his own."

Forgetting I was asked to stand back, I came forward and took Drew's hand. "Take a breath, Forrester."

Doc, Patrick, and I stood there watching and waiting.

Drew's chest expanded.

Then again.

The relief was so incredible that chills broke out across my skin and scalp. My body tingled as I gripped his hand and willed him to keep breathing.

The doc listened to his lungs again. A few minutes passed, and then he looked up. My eyes asked him what my mouth could not.

"He's breathing on his own. Lung function is good."

I blew out the breath I'd been holding, making my chest cave. "Thank God," I prayed under my breath. "Thank God."

"We'll keep an eye on him. Check his oxygen saturation in a short while." The doctor directed his words to Patrick, who nodded.

"Will do."

Then he turned back to me. "He's doing well."

Tears welled up in my eyes, and I tried to blink them back. The relief was so great I couldn't contain it.

The doctor put his hand on my shoulder. "I'll go tell the family."

Nodding, I swiped at my damp eyes.

The second they were gone, I laid my palm over his chest and nearly cried all over again when it rose and fell with his gentle breath.

"It's so good to see your face again," I whispered, roaming every inch of him. Unable to resist, I stroked my fingertips across his chin and jawline. "Your scruff is turning into a beard."

The cuts on his cheeks stood out against the paleness of his skin, and there were marks on the lower portion of his face from the ventilator.

He was still the most beautiful person I'd ever seen.

In fact, he was even more beautiful to me now. Even in this condition. Actually, *because* of this condition. He was alive and breathing on his own, which was honestly the most beautiful thing I'd ever seen.

Moving slowly, still feeling the rise and fall of his breath against my palm, I leaned in. The anticipation of him didn't make me hurry. Instead, I reveled in it. I'd never taken Drew for granted. I'd always known just how incredible it was that he loved me. Now I cherished it even more.

The moment my lips brushed against his, my heart stuttered and the fingers lying against his chest spasmed lightly. Emotion welled up, making my throat feel tight and my head dizzy. Even so, I kept the kiss brief and gentle so as not to interfere with any breathing he was trying to do.

"Your lips are dry," I told him, rubbing the pad of my thumb across them. "Your mouth probably is too."

I poured a glass of water and pushed the chair as close to the bed as possible, sitting down with everything I needed. Unwrapping a large Q-Tip-looking thing, I dipped it into the glass, lifting it to dampen his dry, cracked lips.

On the second pass, too much water dripped off the tip and trailed across his jaw. Gently, I swiped at the excess water, feeling a kind of peace I hadn't known in days.

I almost felt guilty for the moment of ease I felt.

I wasn't sure I deserved it.

The door opened, but I didn't look up right away.

"What are you doing?" his father demanded, breaking any sort of calm we had.

"His lips are dry," I replied, keeping my voice low and even.

I'd never been one to hate anyone. Usually, I just remained indifferent and wasn't too quick to anger—unless it involved a threat to Drew.

But this man? He taught me pure hate.

How ironic that it was his son who taught me pure love.

"You've taken advantage enough for one day. Get out."

"Aren't you going to ask?"

"Excuse me?"

"The first thing you did was yell at me. Aren't you going to ask how he is?"

He paused, then replied with an indignant tone. "The doctor just told us he was fine."

"I would think you would want to ask the person sitting beside him. Or come forward and ask him yourself."

"He can't answer me right now."

"Yes," I said softly. "He can. You just have to listen."

He went silent, but his presence was still suffocating.

Ivy came into the room. I felt her stare between us. "Trent, is he okay?"

I glanced just briefly at her father, as if to say, *See? Your first thought should have been him.*

"Breathing on his own," I said proudly. "He needs some lip balm."

"Let me get my bag," she announced, then rushed out of the room.

She returned seconds later with her bag and a small jar of something in her hand. "Here," she offered, taking off the lid.

I sat back, giving her space, but she held it out to me. "You do it."

Automatically, my eyes slid toward her dad, who still stood watching. Ivy shifted, blocking him from my sight.

"His lips are chapped."

I applied the balm to Drew's lips, then set it beside the bed for later.

"You brought a blanket," Ivy said.

"The ones in this place aren't good enough."

I felt Ivy's hand in my hair. "You doing okay?"

I nodded. "Better now that he's breathing on his own."

Ivy wrapped her arms around my shoulders and hugged me tight.

"Thank you," I whispered against her.

"Cam's a good distraction," she whispered back.

Patrick bustled into the room. "I need to check some things, and the patient needs some rest. Two visitors at a time."

"I'll go," Ivy offered, pulling back.

"He's going," her father snapped, reminding us he was still there.

Ivy started to argue, but I put a hand on hers. "You stay. I'll be in the waiting room."

Her blue eyes were conflicted.

"It's fine." I promised, giving Drew one last lingering look before silently taking my leave.

It wasn't that I wanted to go, but I also knew how lucky I was to be at his side today. I didn't want to push his father too far because I was still afraid of what he might do.

Over half of the
same-sex couples in
the US are in
California.

TWENTY-ONE

Drew

Sometimes there was silence. Sometimes there was the crackle of static and distant sounds I didn't understand.

Sometimes a strange sensation of anger and tension permeated the room.

Fear.

Loneliness.

But sometimes there was warmth. There was a voice that reached through everything else, a voice with a powerful ability to become the center of the dark universe I floated in.

Awareness burst over me, along with the brush of cool air. I tried to recoil, but my body still felt like it belonged to someone else. People stood over me. Foreign sounds and hazy voices filled the air.

Vivid fear that they were here to do me harm gripped my heart and incited panic throughout my limbs. An odd tugging sensation somewhere in my middle made me want to scream.

What is happening?

Safety enveloped me, sort of like a blanket in the cold or an umbrella buffering the rain. Skin against skin wiped away the worry, and the tug in my chest seemed a little less scary. Then it was gone. But the feeling of safety remained, and soon, the voice I always recognized accompanied it.

There he is. Where've you been?

It was quieter now, and the pressure in my chest was gone. Some of the binds that seemed to be tying me down were gone.

The urge to suddenly gag and cough nearly choked me, but I couldn't. Instead, I lay here feeling the burn of needs I couldn't meet.

Lips brushed over mine, quieting the worst of the unrest disturbing me. Cool moisture soaked my lips that felt entirely too dry, and then the hum of quiet voices floated somewhere nearby.

"He's going." The harsh words broke into my peace.

The warm touch, the gentle presence started to pull away.

Wait! I yelled. *Stay!*

He vanished again, and haziness closed around me, only to be interrupted by the sound of the voice I'd been seeking.

He wasn't calm and gentle this time, though. He was yelling.

According to a 2017 study, there are more than 10.7 million LGBTQ adults in the United States.

TWENTY-TWO

Trent

The unauthorized photo circling the web was whipping everyone into a frenzy. Rumors flew, harsh debates waged online, and apparently, the family's silence about Drew and his condition only made matters worse.

I didn't want to deal with this.

But not wanting to deal with something didn't make it go away. In fact, it made it worse.

A painful lesson I'd been learning lately.

"The media is camped outside the Gamble estate," Braeden announced, coming into the waiting room, his mother following closely behind.

I got up when I saw her. "Caroline," I said. "Thank you for being here."

"Of course I would come," she said.

"Where's Ivy?" B asked, looking around.

"With Drew."

"Everyone else?"

I shrugged. "I'm not sure about Romeo and Rim. I would think that Drew's mom is with Camden."

"I'll go see if you can go in and see him," B told Caroline, heading for the door.

"Wait," I called. "What were you saying about the press?"

B made a face. "They're stalking the Gamble estate, and the number of people downstairs has doubled since you and I first left this morning."

"I just chased a few out of the cafeteria," Romeo informed us, coming up behind Braeden. He had a coffee in his hand, and Rim was carrying a juice. "There was one in the stairwell too."

I cursed.

Braeden pulled the backward hat off his head to run his fingers through his hair before putting it back in place. "That pic of you has gone viral." He made a face. "And now there are a bunch of shots floating around of us leaving the hospital."

"I should have just stayed here," I muttered.

"This isn't your doing," Caroline said sternly. "Those people have no limits."

"Your zombie-like appearance got the rumor mill all whipped up in a frenzy again. The woman at the information desk downstairs said she gets nonstop calls from people trying to get updates about Drew."

"Maybe we should release a statement." Romeo considered.

"I can't think about that now," I said. An anxious feeling washed over me, and the urge to go down the hall and put eyes on Drew made me pace.

"You don't have to. We'll deal with it."

"I don't know." I hedged. "What if it makes things worse?"

A flash of black slid down the hallway, something I might not have noticed if I hadn't been looking at Romeo in the doorway.

The hairs on the back of my neck rose.

"Move." I gasped, pushing between my brothers and out into the hall.

Someone dressed in a black hoodie and jeans walked along the wall, slowing when he approached Drew's room. The thick red strap I knew belonged to a camera draped around the back of his neck.

"Hey," I called out.

The person halted but didn't turn. Suddenly, in a fit of movement, he rushed forward, bolting directly inside Drew's room.

I was already halfway down the hall when I heard Ivy gasp.

"Who are you?" Drew's father called.

The bright flash of a camera flickered inside the room, and the obnoxious sound of photo after photo being taken filled my head.

My hand slammed down on the back of his shoulder, making his body sag under the hit. Squeezing, I pulled him around, ripping the hood off his head.

"What the fuck do you think you're doing?" I growled low.

"Let me go!" he yelled, his legs running but his body stationary.

Holding tight, I looked over to where Drew lay. "He okay?" I asked, surveying every inch of him.

"He got pictures," Ivy said, pointing at the intruder.

The man's body slammed against the wall, and his face wrinkled in pain. He tried to run, but I shoved him back, using my body to block his exit. Roughly, I ripped the camera over his head and whipped it onto the ground.

The sound of it shattering and breaking apart was satisfying.

"Didn't you hear?" I said, deadly quiet. "No press. No pictures."

The little shit's face flushed with anger, and his chin lifted. "Yeah? Well, I still got a story. He's still in the ICU. He's in a coma. And you weren't even at his bedside." He smirked. "Headlines for days."

Rage flashed before me like a thunderstorm that came out of nowhere.

The second I moved, all the color drained from his face. The camera skidded somewhere across the room as I grabbed him by the back of the neck and dragged him up. His feet dangled over the floor when I lifted him so our eyes could meet.

"You think that's a threat?" I asked, quiet. "You think you coming in here with your fancy camera and bad attitude will shake me up?"

I felt my nostrils flare, and when they did, his eyes widened.

He started to speak, but I squeezed the back of his neck harder and turned so he could see the bed. "Take a long look," I intoned. "The man I love is lying in that bed. And yeah, he's in a coma. But you think threatening me with more headlines is going to get you somewhere? Wake the fuck up, man. I'm already living my nightmare."

I threw him on the floor, and he scrambled back, looking up at me in fear.

"If you don't want to know what it's like to live in your own personal nightmare…" I walked over and bent at the waist to stare him down. "I suggest you get the fuck out of here and don't ever try and take pictures of my family again."

He lunged for the broken camera.

I growled.

He dropped it and raced for the door.

"Hey, asshole," I called just as Romeo and Braeden blocked the entrance into the hall.

He stopped, his shoulders so tense they nearly reached his ears.

"I see any of this in the news or hear even a whisper anywhere on the streets, there is nowhere you will be able to hide."

Romeo and B parted, and the guy ran off.

Braeden went right to Ivy, taking her by the shoulders. "You okay, blondie? He hurt you?"

"I'm okay." She assured him.

Trying to get my anger under control, I went to Drew's side, double-checking he was unharmed.

"If it wasn't for you, the press wouldn't be breaking into the ICU for photos and a story."

My back teeth gnashed together.

"Man, you just don't know when to quit, do you?" Braeden snapped, turning to block Ivy from any view of her father.

"Are you saying I'm wrong?"

"Yes." Romeo and Braeden spoke unanimously.

"I think that violent outburst I just witnessed was enough to get a restraining order against you. Who knows when you could snap, my injured son the victim?"

I backed away from Drew as my eyes narrowed. "The fuck you just say to me?" I spoke deadly quiet, causing both Romeo and Braeden to straighten.

"With a restraining order, you wouldn't even be able to set foot on the same floor as my son."

I lunged. Romeo was ready and used his body like a barricade, trying to keep me back.

"Let me go!" I yelled, trying to fight past him.

Romeo wrapped his arms around my midsection and dug his feet in. "This is what he wants, Trent. Don't give it to him."

"I've had just about enough of these petty threats, nasty sneers, and disgusting words!" I burst out, still fighting Romeo. "Do whatever you want, you hateful son of a bitch! It won't matter, because the only way I'll stay away from Drew is if I'm dead."

"What on earth is going on in here?" Adrienne worried, rushing into the room with Camden on her heels.

"Call the police, Adrienne," he instructed. "Apparently, a legal document isn't enough to keep him away. So we'll have to put him in a cell."

Bam!

Drew's father fell back against the wall and slid down, a shocked look on his face.

Braeden stood over him, chest heaving, shaking out his fist. "If you weren't my wife's father, you'd be in the ER right now."

Romeo let me go, and I stood. I wasn't the one who hit him, but it was still satisfying to see him go down.

A few nurses rushed into the room, along with an orderly in all white. "What is going on?" Patrick exclaimed. "Why are there so many people in here?"

"I want everyone out," Burke said, using the wall to help him lever back up to his feet. The corner of his mouth was bleeding and already starting to swell. It would match well with his black eye and busted nose. "Everyone!" he yelled. "I am next of kin, and no one is allowed in this room anymore. No one!"

The staff threw everyone out.

In the hall, my head buzzed and my hands shook. Whether it was from anger or regret that I'd lost it in front of Drew, I wasn't sure.

Hell. Maybe it was both.

"If you don't keep to the waiting room, you will all be banned." The supervising nurse warned everyone. "This is intensive care. There are patients here who are seriously ill. This is disruptive and dangerous."

"I apologize," I said, staring at the floor. "Reporters are starting to come into this wing, even though it's prohibited—"

"That's no excuse!" she snapped.

Everyone turned to go toward the waiting room, me being the last.

He came out of the room just after and spoke to the nurse. "Whom do I speak to about having a patient transferred to another facility?"

My hands balled into fists, and about a thousand emotions pummeled me at once.

Just as I was about to turn back, Romeo put his arm around my shoulders, nudging me to walk. "He knows you can hear him. He wants another reaction. Don't give it to him."

"He can't take Drew," I whispered, hurt breaking through everything I had going on inside.

"We won't let him." Romeo vowed.

But Romeo didn't have a say either. The only person that could truly put a stop to him was Drew, and he was in no condition to do it.

TWENTY-THREE

Trent

Three weeks a man could survive without food.

Three days a man could survive without water.

Two days. I'd been kept away from Drew for two days. How long could a man survive without his heart?

Not much more.

Desperation clung to me like a bad odor. The joints of my fingers and hands ached in exhaustion from being clenched for so long.

Every single second of the last two days, I had fought. Every single second, the cells in my body, the blood in my veins, pulled me to Drew.

Yet I resisted. I had no choice.

It was a battle inside me that continuously waged. So many times I'd started to storm in there, only to be dragged back by the small shred of reasonable thought I had left.

If I went in there, I would lose it again. I would do way worse to Drew's father than punch him in the nose.

I'd definitely land my ass in jail. Then I would be even farther away from Drew.

Just hang on.

The mantra became a heartbeat inside me.

Just hang on a little longer.

The doctors were slowly decreasing the medication that kept him in a coma. Soon, he would wake up. Soon, he could end this excruciating separation.

Please, God, don't let his brain be damaged.

The very last thing I needed to do was give that asshole anything else he could use against me.

But holy hell, the urge was intense. I nearly shook with the desire to feel his flesh split beneath my knuckles. The satisfaction of seeing even just a fraction of the fear and pain he'd caused me flicker in his eyes had the same kind of pull as a drug.

I kept my ass in the chair. I kept my eyes off that man. Because as much as I wanted to retaliate against him, I wanted to be with Drew more.

The love in my heart outweighed the hate. Wouldn't it be nice if everyone operated the same?

Right after Drew was breathing on his own and right after I was threatened by the staff to chill the fuck out, he was transferred.

I'd nearly pissed myself when I saw his bed being moved. I thought old man asshole had made good on his threat to take Drew away.

Just as I was about to go to war, Ivy rushed in, throwing her arms around me. "He's being moved out of the ICU! They said he's stable and out of the worst danger!"

It took a moment for her words to sink in. When they did, the relief I experienced was indescribable. Some feelings just couldn't be put into words. Some feelings were far greater than any word a person could speak.

For the first time since the accident, I found some comfort, and I hugged Ivy back until new worry assaulted me.

"Where are they taking him?" I asked, muscles tensing anew.

"The third floor," she replied, pulling back.

"No." I shook my head. "No, no, no. Romeo!" I bellowed, not knowing where he was, but knowing he would hear. "Braeden!"

B appeared first, coming around the corner instantly. Romeo rushed in shortly after. Both of them were clearly ready for anything.

"They can't put him on the third floor. The place is crawling with press," I demanded, pacing. "It's just asking for trouble."

Romeo nodded. "I'll see if there is a higher floor available. Maybe a VIP room."

"This is exactly why that man shouldn't be in charge. He has no fucking clue," I muttered. Turning to Ivy, I asked, "Think your father will listen to Romeo?"

She frowned. "I don't know." Her lower lip wobbled. "He's so difficult. I don't even recognize him. I keep trying to recall if he was like this when I was little, but—" Her words stopped and she sniffled.

"It's okay, blondie." B consoled her, putting an arm around her, pushing her face into his chest.

Her arms wound around his waist. "I'm glad you decked him."

Braeden half smiled, patting her head. "Anything for you, baby."

Romeo came back with the doctor in tow. "The VIP room is full."

I cursed under my breath. "There has to be somewhere you can move him that will be less obvious," I implored the doctor.

"I should probably talk to his next of kin…"

I swear I felt a piece of my back tooth chip off when my jaw grinded. "That's not important right now!" I bellowed. "His safety is!"

"I know!" Ivy perked up, snapping her fingers.

Everyone glanced at her. "Can he have a room in the labor and delivery wing?"

"Where babies are born?" Braeden asked, dubious.

She nodded vigorously. "That would be the last place the press would look. It would definitely take them longer to find him there."

I nodded slowly. "You're right. I'll call and get some guards for the door too. That way when he is found, they won't be able to get in the room."

Ivy turned toward the doctor. "Is this possible?"

The doctor frowned.

Romeo stepped up with the charm he wielded like a sword. "I'm sure Ron Gamble will be really grateful that you would go above and beyond for one of his drivers. A driver that just happens to be the New Revolution Racing champion."

"I think we could make that work." He nodded once.

What a douche canoe. If I didn't have the country's highest-ranking quarterback standing there and a friendship with the richest man in the state, this doctor wouldn't even give us the time of day. Everyone deserved to be treated equally.

Few people ever were.

"Let's go talk to my parents," Ivy insisted, grabbing the doctor by the wrist and dragging him away.

Braeden made a sound as he watched them go. "That dude don't stand a chance against her."

"I'm calling in some bodyguards," I said, reaching for my phone.

A phone I still didn't have.

"Fuck!" I swore.

"You can't be cussing like that when we get to the baby wing." B scolded.

I leveled him with a hard stare. "Give me your phone."

He handed it over.

And so here I was, camping out in the waiting room of the labor and delivery wing, waiting for Drew to open his eyes. Waiting to see if his brain was unharmed in the crash.

I couldn't even fathom him looking at me with blank eyes and no recognition. It might kill me.

No. It wouldn't. I'd rather have him here looking at me as a stranger than not here at all.

I shot to my feet for the thousandth time and started to pace.

"You're going to wear a hole in the floor," Lorhaven informed. Joey smacked him in the back of the head. "Ow, woman!"

"Don't you woman me," she growled. "Leave him alone. He can pace if he wants to."

"You don't baby me like that," he muttered, wrapping his arms across his chest.

"That's because there isn't one thing about you that's soft."

I couldn't help it. I rolled my eyes.

Lorhaven chuckled under his breath. "Don't you know it."

Joey giggled, and I wanted to puke. "Why isn't he awake yet?" I wondered, running my hands through my hair. "It's been days. How much medicine did they give him?"

"I'm sure he's doing everything he can to wake up." Rimmel assured me.

I stopped pacing in front of her chair. "He looked okay last time you saw him?"

I'd asked her this hundreds of times. I'd asked everyone who had been allowed in the room—which actually was very few. But even that bastard Burke wouldn't deny the sweet face of my sister asking to see Drew.

I could ask her a hundred more times, though, and she would act like it was the first time. Scooting forward in the seat, feet dangling over the floor, Rimmel caught my hand, giving it a squeeze. "He looked good. Honest. I put some of that balm on his lips for you."

I nodded. "You talked to him, right? Let him know I was still out here?"

"Of course I did. I also told him you smell, refuse to eat, and your injuries look like dog meat."

I made a face. "You've been hanging out with Rome too long."

I went back to pacing. Rimmel giggled behind me. Seconds later, I felt her arms wrap around me from behind. Even though I'd literally been punching anyone who pissed me off, scaring the staff, and yeah, okay, I kinda smelled… this one still didn't hesitate to hug me.

"He's going to wake up soon."

I let her hug me for a few, then patted her arms. She went back to her seat, and I resumed pacing.

Out in the hall, Patrick went by.

I raced out after him, calling his name.

He turned and smiled. "We meet again."

"You'll be seeing a lot of me in the next few weeks."

He made a gesture with his hand. "No complaints here."

"Any news?"

"Not yet. He's still stable. Not awake."

I nodded, eyes falling to my feet.

A light touch on my arm made me look up. Patrick was much closer now, his eyes cast upward to meet mine. "I promise I will tell you the second anything changes."

I nodded.

"Honestly," Patrick said, stepping closer and dropping his voice, "I know things are… tense with this situation, but I think you know whose side I'm on."

I did, and it was exactly why I'd asked Romeo to use his persuasive powers yet again to suggest a few of the nurses who'd been taking care of Drew in the ICU continue to do so. Turned out that wasn't usual protocol.

Neither was Drew almost dying. So I did what any man would do. I threw money at them. Patrick, Katie, and one other nurse were now assigned to Drew exclusively.

Yeah, yeah. I was bitching about people being treated equally and fairly earlier. Didn't you also hear me say that wasn't how this world went 'round?

If you can't beat 'em, join 'em. Besides, this was one of the only things I was able to do for Drew right now. If I couldn't be beside him, then I could at least make sure the people around him were quality.

Well, except for that soul-chewing, foul-mouthed man whose name I would not say. The only power I had over that man was the ability to inspire hatred.

He didn't even know I was paying extra for these nurses. If he did, he probably would have had them fired.

"I really appreciate it," I told Patrick sincerely.

He patted my arm and then went back to work.

A wave of dizziness swept over me, and the raw skin on my wrist burned. Blowing out a breath, I gazed down the hall to the bodyguards standing post outside Drew's room. One saw me looking and nodded slightly.

They also were aware of the situation. They also were told I wasn't allowed in that room.

But they also knew who was signing their paycheck.

Wearily, I rubbed my temples. The dull thudding in my skull was annoying, and the sandpaper feel of my eyelids was equally so.

And who the fuck is crying?

My God, the sound had been background noise to this hellish day for far too long. Pulling my hands from my head, I gazed around.

Now that I focused on the crying, it seemed even worse than before. That kid sounded worse than I felt.

The thought was strangely unsettling. I mean yes, this was the baby wing of this hospital, and newborn babies cried. But they didn't cry this much.

Did they?

I shook my head. I had five nieces and nephews. Not one of those kids cried as much and as fitfully as that baby.

Where the hell were its parents? The nurses?

Didn't anybody give a shit it was obviously miserable?

They say misery loves company. I didn't agree. Because the misery I heard in that baby's wail was not anything I took joy in.

Without realizing it, I started to walk, following the sound.

TWENTY-FOUR

Trent

The wailing seemed to grow more insistent the closer I came. Or maybe it was just because it was louder.

Whatever the reason, I didn't like it.

I'd grown used to having kids around. On our compound, there wasn't a day that went by when I didn't see them. And when Drew and I were traveling for races, I missed the rug rats.

Hearing a baby cry so diligently made me uncomfortable.

Around the corner, the nursery came into view. You know, that place where families could go and stare through a large glass window to look at all the babies who'd just been born. Following the sound, I went there, gazing through for the source of the noise.

There were only two babies lying behind the glass. Both of them swaddled and asleep in their bassinets. One had a pink hat; one had a blue. Confused, I glanced around, knowing the crying was nearby, but not knowing where.

When I gazed into the nursery again, a small bout of movement caught my attention. There. Near the corner of the room, away from the other babies, was a bassinet. Inside it, I could see a baby flailing about.

Concerned, I glanced around for a nurse. Why wasn't anyone doing anything? Should babies just be left alone like this? Was that one sick? Why wasn't it swaddled and sleeping like the rest?

And who the hell put that baby in the corner?

Quickly, I went around as close as I could get to the baby, but it was still too far to see. He was still screaming his head off, and it was giving me anxiety. I didn't need any more anxiety.

I thought about how painful it was to walk away and leave Drew alone in that room before. How empty and achy I'd felt. How I still felt that way, knowing I couldn't be beside him.

That baby in there was the same. Alone. Obviously upset. And someone left him there alone.

What the fuck kind of hospital was this?

I was going to have to get Gamble on the phone. Dude needed to whip this place into shape.

The baby threw out a fist, and the tiny appearance of it felt like a punch in my gut.

Enough.

Walking with clear purpose, I went back around, found the door to the nursery, and walked right in. The lights in here were bright, and everything was sterile. I went right to the side of the bassinet and stared down.

Something heavy shackled around my heart. Something that didn't hurt at all.

The baby was tiny. Smaller than any of Rimmel's or Ivy's. Hell, he was even smaller than Joey's daughter.

He was completely uncovered. The blanket I assumed had been swaddled around him was kicked away, his arms and legs exposed to the air.

He was trembling. Trembling quite terribly for such a small body.

"Hey, now," I said quietly. "What's with all this noise? Are you freezing cold?"

The baby kept squalling, not even sparing me a glance.

"I get it," I told him. "I'm pissed off with just about everyone in this place too."

After another quick glance around for a nurse, seeing no one, I hesitated no more. Smoothing out the blanket (which was just as shitty as Drew's), I lifted the little guy into the center and turned him into a burrito.

The trembling of his arms and legs concerned me, making me worry something was wrong, more than low body temperature.

"Why you so tiny?" I asked him gently, lifting him out of the bassinet and into my arms. "You're smaller than a little peanut."

The baby paused in crying long enough to stare up at me with very dark eyes.

"You hungry?" I asked, swiping a tear off his cheek.

He started fussing again, and my body started swaying. That's what we always did with Rim's and Ivy's kids. The wailing went down a notch but didn't stop.

"Progress," I told him, spotting a rocking chair on the other side of the room. Settling into a smooth rocking rhythm, the baby quieted but still squirmed and trembled quite a bit. As I rocked, he fussed his mouth, searching around.

Nearby was a bin filled with supplies, among them a wrapped pacifier. Snatching it up, I ripped it open and held it out for him.

It was the kind that you could put your finger inside to help hold it. The baby tried to latch on, and after a few unsuccessful attempts, he started crying again.

"Whoa," I told him. "Let's keep it calm. Try, try again."

This time I put my finger inside it, holding it in his mouth. He latched on and didn't let go. As he sucked, he made unhappy noises around it but stared up at me with intensely dark eyes.

"You and me, we have something in common," I told him. "Stuck in this hospital and not happy about it. Who left you alone in here anyway? Where's your mom? Your dad?"

His limbs started kicking around again, so I tucked him a little closer against my chest for security.

"You're not supposed to be in here," said a woman wearing scrubs with teddy bears all over them.

"Aren't you supposed to be?" I said, keeping my voice low and unchallenging.

"We're short staffed today. I had to run down the hall."

"I got tired of hearing him cry," I said simply, gazing back down.

"He's a she."

I glanced up, surprised.

The nurse smiled. "She's a girl."

"Well, her hat wasn't color coded like the others." I defended myself, glancing at the pink and blue striped garment.

"The parents usually do that. The striped ones are hospital given."

"Well, why didn't her parents give her a hat?" I demanded, quietly. "And a better blanket. The blankets here suck."

The nurse smiled and stepped farther into the room.

"Where are her parents anyway? Who lets their kid cry like that?"

"This is the first time I've seen her quiet since she came." The nurse came closer, peering down at the baby's face.

"She was cold. And pissed off someone shoved her in the corner." As I spoke, I pulled her against me just a little closer.

"The heat lamp is over there. We had her under it earlier for warmth."

"She's been crying all day."

"Babies in her condition usually do."

"That's no excuse—" I stopped midsentence. "In her condition?"

The nurse nodded.

"She's sick?" I worried, glancing down at her again. She fussed and kicked me in the chest. "What's wrong with her?"

"NAS."

"NAS?" I echoed. Then feeling like I was getting some top-secret info, I glanced around. The last thing I needed was some pissed-off parents demanding I get tossed off the floor because I touched their precious daughter.

Then I'd have to get pissed they left her in here alone to cry.

Then it would get ugly, and *he* would use it as more ammo to keep me away from Drew.

Fuck, I was exhausted.

"Maybe you should get her parents," I said, starting to stand. "I'm sorry I came in here. I just…" I glanced down. "I didn't like hearing her scream like that."

"Stay," the nurse said, putting a hand on my shoulder to stop me from rising.

"What?" My voice was incredulous.

She pulled her hand away and offered a tired smile. "It's been a really long day, and it's really nice to not hear her scream."

"But what about—"

"She's an orphan."

My back hit the wooden rails of the rocker when I sat back. "An orphan?"

"A ward of the state. She's here because of her condition."

I glanced down again. Her eyes were still focused on me, tear-filled. Her cheeks were red and blotchy, and her body was still tremoring. Around the paci, she would fuss and latch on, only to repeat it all over again.

She was tiny. Probably barely five pounds. And she was alone.

Just when I thought the world was cruel, it showed me how much crueler it could be.

"What's wrong with her?"

"Neonatal abstinence syndrome," the nurse replied. At my blank look, she smiled and said, "She was born to a drug addict. Basically, she's going through withdrawal."

My heart turned over. "Who would do that?" I muttered, tucking the blanket around her a little closer.

"I think you'd be surprised how often it happens."

People were so fucked up. It seemed incredibly unfair a little peanut like this would pay the price.

"Is that why she's shaking so bad?" I asked.

The nurse nodded. "It's a symptom she is experiencing."

"That why she's so small?"

She nodded. "She's probably hungry. Do you want to feed her?"

"I'm allowed?"

The nurse went across the room to pull out some kind of premixed bottle. "Honestly, no. But like I said, she's never this quiet when I hold her."

"I'm just bigger than you. More arm to hold her close."

"You're pretty good with kids," she said, doing whatever she was doing with the bottle.

"I have three nephews and two nieces."

"I know."

At that, my eyes shot up. She smiled. "Your entire family is famous in Maryland, and well, this entire floor is talking about our unconventional guest."

Is that why she was more willing to let me hold this baby? Because she already knew who I was?

"If you know why I'm here, then you must also know I've been banned from Drew's room."

She nodded. "That means you have time to feed her, right?"

After a moment of looking between her and the bottle, I shrugged. "Sure, why not?"

"It's a special high-calorie formula that she needs."

The second I pulled the pacifier out of the baby's mouth, she started to scream and kick.

"You pack an awful big punch, peanut," I told her.

It took her a while to latch onto the bottle, but once she did, she stopped crying. The nurse offered some pointers and positioned her head better, then stepped back.

"She likes you." She observed.

"I like people who feed me too," I quipped. But underneath, something warm spread in my chest. It was a nice reprieve from the insane stress I'd been feeling.

"Drew," I said, glancing toward the door.

"How about I go peek in on him while you feed her? I'll come back and give you an update."

"You'd do that?" I asked, desperate for any kind of information.

"For a guy who managed to give me a few minutes of peace? Absolutely."

She went off to check on Drew, and I leaned back in the rocker a little farther, glancing down at the baby.

Her eyes were on me again, and I smiled.

"A girl, huh?" I said. "I guess I deserved all those kicks for assuming your gender."

The bottle popped out of her mouth, and she let out a yell.

"Women," I muttered, gently guiding it back.

She went back to eating, I went back to rocking, and both of us found a little bit of peace in this place.

"You're kinda cute," I told her a few minutes later.

She kicked me again.

I smiled.

A survery conducted in 2019 reports that six out of ten Americans support same-sex marriage.

TWENTY-FIVE

Drew

Slowly, I began to float to the surface. My limbs, which had been weighed down before, seemed more buoyant, and responsiveness tingled throughout me. Haze draped over me like heavy fog on a cold, damp morning, clinging to every thought I tried to form. The static in my head was still there, but it didn't drown out everything now. It was a background sound to everything else happening around me.

Sometimes I would pick out a voice or recognize a sound. Other times, that stupid fog disguised everything, confusing me.

Impatience burned my veins because a sense of urgency prickled the awareness I did obtain.

I didn't know what was wrong, but something was.

Trent. Where is Trent?

Is he being subjected to the same thing I am? Does whoever have me trapped here also have him?

I tried to open my eyes. Darkness clung.

I tried to use my voice. Silence adhered.

Despite it all, I fought for consciousness. I fought until exhaustion dragged me down, only to wake up and fight again. The cycle seemed endless, and the fear of being trapped inside my own skin without anyone knowing I was here was scarier than the fear of actually dying.

I was lost and wandering, trying to find the right way to escape. I searched for the direction, silently asking for the voice I knew could lead me home.

Home. I want Trent.

Sharp pain struck me, radiating throughout my midsection and thumping like an extra heartbeat at the base of my skull. Instinct pushed me to retreat, but I wouldn't go back.

I'd rather feel the vicious bite of pain than go back to that strange underwater existence. I'd rather hurt with family than suffer alone.

My eyelashes fluttered, fingertips flexing. Light burst over my consciousness, making my eyes blink and tear.

"Drew?" Someone called me.

I blinked again. Everything was so bright and hazy.

"I think he's waking up." A person leaned over me, and I stared, trying to bring them into focus. "Someone get the doctor!"

"Drew?" A hand wrapped around mine, and I squeezed it back.

A low sob filled the room.

The outline focused. Features became visible. Long, blond hair, fair skin. Worried blue eyes.

I tried to smile, but the uncomfortable stretch in my lips made me stop. I made a sound, worried something was wrong.

Why is there so much pain? Why is the room so bright? Where was I?

Ivy leaned over me, her body blocking some of the overwhelming light. Someone else stood behind her, but my eyes stayed on her. My sister.

"Sis," I spoke, not even recognizing my own voice.

She nodded, tears flowing down her cheeks with alarming speed.

"Wha—" I started to ask, then gagged.

"Braeden!" she called frantically.

My sister was replaced by the large frame of my brother, his size making me realize… "It's okay, man. Easy. Take it easy."

Braeden slid his arm under my shoulders, slightly lifting my upper body as I gagged.

"You're in the hospital. You had an accident."

An accident?

A sudden flash of my car going airborne, the earsplitting sound of grinding metal.

"Answer me, baby!"

My eyes widened, and I looked up at my brother, the shock of realization halting my heaving stomach. Any of the weight I'd been supporting on my own surrendered to Braeden, and he easily lowered me onto the pillow.

Frantic, I glanced around. The first person my eyes landed on was the last person I expected.

My father.

Beside him, my mother.

I looked back at Braeden and Ivy, realizing they both looked like hell.

I tried to speak, but it came out like a pitiful croak.

"Easy," Ivy hurried to say.

On the other side of the bed, my mom leaned over me. "The doctor is on his way."

The pain radiating throughout my body made it hard to breathe. My throat felt like it had been ripped out and then shoved back in. The weight on my chest was so severe I actually looked down to see if I was being restrained.

I glanced back at my father.

I tried to sit up, but my arms were like wet noodles and moving them hurt.

"Ivy," I rasped.

"I'm here, Drew. I'm here."

Not caring every syllable felt like the stab of a thousand knives, I spoke anyway.

All I said was one word.

"Trent."

South Africa was the first country in Africa to allow same-sex marriage.

TWENTY-SIX

Trent

Commotion in the hallway had me leaping out of my seat. Everyone sitting around also jumped up.

"What's going on?" Joey worried as I rushed into the hall.

Down near Drew's room, Camden was speaking frantically to a nurse he'd flagged down. My heart nearly exploded out of my chest when she nodded and rushed toward the nurses' station to pick up the phone.

I started to run down the hall but caught myself. Putting both hands on the back of my neck, I fought a battle inside me as I paced.

I knew I couldn't run back there. If I did, it would get ugly. Again. It would probably push *him* over the edge.

Drew was getting better. The doctors were saying he could wake up anytime. Maybe whatever was happening was a good thing.

What if it isn't?

The bottom literally dropped out of my stomach, and I pressed a hand to my guts.

What if there was some kind of complication? What if his lung collapsed again and he couldn't breathe?

Or worse.

What if he finally woke up but didn't know anyone?

The doctor came rushing past, hurrying toward Drew's room.

"Doctor," I called, desperate.

The man glanced around but didn't stop. "I have to see a patient."

That patient was my entire universe.

He was the sun, the moon, and every star in my sky. And I had no idea what was going on.

Fuck this. I would just go to jail. As long as I knew he was okay, jail would be tolerable. I rushed forward, only to be dragged back.

"You can't do that," Lorhaven advised, restraining me.

"Fuck you, Lor!" I spat. "Let me go."

"Think," Hopper cautioned. "Think before you go running down there."

"I can't!" The words burst out forcefully. "I can't think of anything when I don't know what's going on!"

"I'll go see," Romeo said, stepping around us all.

"Fuck you and your charm, Rome! I should be the one allowed in there, not you!"

He gave no reaction, just started down the hall at the same time Ivy burst out of the room, skidding into the center of the hallway.

When she saw me, her eyes widened.

I shoved away from Lorhaven, stumbling forward, then stopping dead in my tracks.

I didn't breathe. My heart didn't beat.

We stared at each other for a fraction of a second. Everything stopped.

"He's awake." She all but gasped the words.

Joy, anxiety, and fierce longing restarted my world and nearly buckled my knees.

"He's asking for you."

A piercing squeaking sound cracked through the quiet hall when my sneakers pushed off the polished floor. I ran down the hallway like there was a vast fortune waiting at the end.

Because there was.

I ran so fast I nearly passed the door, but my hand shot out and caught the frame. My body jolted back, and I crashed into the wood.

Everyone in the room looked at me, but Drew was all I saw.

His eyes were open. The second mine collided with them, I felt like I'd been hollowed out all over again. I'd hoped for this moment a million times. I'd hurt for it. I'd planned to be at his side, reassuring him that everything was okay.

Look at me now.

I was the one who needed reassured.

I hated myself for it, but even that deep loathing couldn't make me shake the sudden anxiety squeezing my heart.

What if he didn't know me? What if his father got to him and he, too, sent me away? What if the blue eyes I'd discovered myself in suddenly saw me as a stranger?

"T," he called to me.

My legs were shaking, but I pretended they weren't and stepped farther into the room. Staring at him, putting one foot in front of the other until I made it to the end of the bed.

"You need to let the doctor do his job," *he* said, trying to ruin this moment. Trying to steal something else from me.

"Do you know me?" I whispered, praying and begging all at the same time.

Drew gestured with his hand, beckoning me closer.

I rushed forward, nearly tripping over my own feet to fulfill his request. The sound of a scuffle broke out behind me, but it was short lived and something I completely ignored.

"You look like shit."

I nodded. "You look beautiful."

His body was still completely relaxed against the bed, but his fingers lifted, reaching toward me. "Why you still over there, frat boy?"

A sob broke free from my throat. Lips quivering, I closed the distance between us, reaching out to take his face but hesitating just before contact. "You know me, right? I can touch you?"

"Since when do you have to ask?"

The dam inside me splintered, and emotion I didn't even know I'd been holding back rushed free.

"Drew." I wept, gently cupping the sides of his face and leaning in. "I've been so fucking crazed," I confessed, gently resting my forehead against his. The ache in my chest turned into full-blown pain, and if it wasn't for the emotion leaking out of my eyes, I probably would have exploded.

One of my tears dripped off my face and onto his. His movements were sluggish when he lifted his hand and wiped my cheek. "It's okay, now, T. Everything's okay."

I dropped my head into the side of his neck, letting his words sink in as I weathered the storm of relief.

The infamous Roman Emperor Nero is said to have married two men (at different times).

TWENTY-SEVEN

Drew

I didn't know much right now. My brain was sluggish. Pain and discomfort radiated throughout my entire body, and even though I was finally awake, haziness clung to the back of my mind.

Even through all that, I sensed the underlying currents vibrating in the room. Tension, anger, and fear tinged the air with unwanted odor.

Trent was openly weeping against my neck. The cool slipperiness of the tears leaking from his eyes slid over my collarbone, and the trembling of his large, usually steady frame unnerved me.

I glanced over him toward my family who was literally crowding the room. Everyone was here, staring at us with mixed expressions of relief and worry.

It must be bad. I must be really hurt.

The doctor cleared his throat. "I need to check the patient."

Trent sucked in a deep breath and pulled back. "Please go ahead."

The man cleared his throat and came forward, then turned to face everyone crowding around. "I know it's a happy moment, but if I could get the room. Once I'm certain there's nothing needing immediate attention, visitors are welcome back in."

Toward the back of the room, Hopper, Arrow, Joey, and Lorhaven filed out. I glanced at Romeo and B, who remained rooted in place. Interesting.

My father cleared his throat. "Out! Everyone out."

Romeo gave me the briefest glance.

It was enough.

Trent turned as if he were going to also vacate the room. I reached for him, though he was a little too far away to touch.

"Where you going, frat boy?"

He stopped and turned back, something shimmering in his eyes.

The doctor, who obviously was aware of whatever the fuck was going on, stepped in. "Drew, would you like Mr. Mask to stay in the room with you?"

What the fuck kind of question was that?

"Yes," I said, reaching for his hand again. This time, T saw and came forward instantly.

Romeo and Braeden relaxed.

"We'll be down the hall," Romeo said, and they left.

I glanced at my parents, noting the dark look on my father's face. My hackles rose almost immediately. "You can wait outside too."

"You would have him in here over your own parents?" He accused. "You have no idea how he's behaved!"

Trent stiffened, and I gave his hand the strongest squeeze I could muster, which honestly was pathetically weak.

"Just go," I said, growing wearier by the minute.

"We'll be right outside, honey," Mom said, offering me a weak smile, then ushering my father out.

The minute they were gone, I looked up at Trent.

He smiled, but it couldn't hide the look deep in his eyes. A look that pained me more than any physical wound I had.

I wanted to ask, but the doctor took over, shining lights in my eyes and asking so many questions I became frustrated. I wanted answers, not questions.

"What's wrong with my leg?" I demanded partway through the freaking inquisition. It was propped up by some kind of sling and I was pretty sure it was in a cast, but all I saw was a bunch of obnoxious color.

"The largest bone in your lower leg is broken. We had to perform surgery on it, and now you are in a cast. Because it is the bone that supports your body's weight, you will likely need to do some physical therapy in a few weeks to help regain your balance and strength."

I made a sound. "Why the hell does it look like a unicorn threw up all over it?"

The doctor cleared his throat.

"Your toes were cold." Trent defended.

"You put that there?" I asked, incredulous.

"I wanted to give you a rainbow," he replied, his voice echoing with pain.

Every ounce of frustration I felt drained away. "In that case, I like it," I declared.

The lines and creases furrowing Trent's face softened. Fuck, he looked bad. I'd never seen him look so wrecked.

"Yeah?" he asked, still unsure. "I can go get you the black one."

"Unicorn throw-up is my new favorite color." I confirmed.

I'll be damned if that didn't make him happy. It was cute as fuck… but it also scared me. Trent wasn't normally this soft. At least not on the surface.

What have you been through, T?

"How long have I been here?"

"Five days," the doctor replied.

"Five," I echoed, trying to comprehend the fact I'd lost five days.

"You spent almost the first four in the intensive care unit and then were moved here."

"Where's here?" I asked, glancing around.

"This is actually the labor and delivery wing. We thought it would be a quieter place for you to recuperate."

My gaze shifted to Trent.

"We were trying to hide you from the press," he explained.

I yawned, the simple action making me wince.

Trent was there immediately. "What hurts?"

Everything. "My throat. My mouth," I said, tentatively reaching up to finger the corners of my lips. They felt raw and cracked.

Trent snatched something off the bedside table and uncapped it, dipped his finger in, and brought it to my lips. Slick relief smoothed over the dry areas, making me sigh.

"You will have quite a bit of discomfort for the first few days," the doctor explained while Trent smoothed the balm over my mouth. "You were on a ventilator, and your throat is probably swollen. I suggest some liquids, but go easy because you may gag at first."

Trent put aside the stuff and poured a cup of water, holding a straw to my lips. Tentatively, I took a sip. The burst of cool liquid over my tongue and dry mouth was overwhelmingly satisfying, and instinctively, I took another long swig.

My throat seized up, and the water came spraying back out as I heaved and gagged. Trent pulled his shirt off in a flurry, gently patting all the water off me and dabbing at my chin.

Every cough and heave that shuddered through me made sharp pains stab my chest. Freaking out, I looked at T.

"I got you." He assured me, sliding his arm under my shoulders and lifting. Automatically, my body gave in to his, allowing him to support my weight as he mopped up the rest of the water. My eyes were tearing from the burning in my throat, and my stomach churned from the force of the gag.

"You're okay," Trent whispered. "We'll take it slow."

Eventually, the spasms subsided, and I collapsed against him all over again.

"Your skin is warm," I murmured cuddling into his chest. How long had it been since we'd touched? Suddenly, I felt starved. Utterly denied of the physical contact I relied on just as much as air. If I had the strength, I would have pushed him down on the bed and climbed on top of him.

"Are you cold?" He fretted. "I'll get another blanket."

"No." I stopped him, tugging him close again. "I want you."

The doc cleared his throat. I'd forgotten he was there. "It appears that you are doing fine. Brain function seems to be as it should, and there doesn't seem to be any permanent damage."

"You thought I had brain damage?" I asked, alarmed.

Because T was so close, I heard his thick swallow. "There was some concern." He hedged.

"I'll want to run a few more tests, probably do another brain scan, but I'll give you a while to orient yourself."

I turned back to T. "How long's it been since you've shaved?" I asked. His entire jaw was covered in stubble.

"Me?" He scoffed. "You have a full-on beard." Reaching up, he scratched lightly at the thick hair that had grown in.

"The nurse will be in soon, and I'll get an order in for that scan," the doctor told us. "Get as much rest as possible. You will probably sleep often, which is completely normal."

"But he's out of the coma, right?" Trent worried.

"Yes." Doc assured us. "If the pain you experience becomes overwhelming, call a nurse and we can up your pain medication. But you should expect discomfort for a while."

"How's your chest?" Trent asked, taking his free hand and gently touching the center. He had to be uncomfortable, half leaning over the bed, my body pinning one of his arms against the pillow.

He didn't complain. Not at all.

"Oh, and one last thing." The doctor came closer to the bed.

When was this guy going to leave?

The air around T altered as though he was suddenly afraid of whatever the doc would say. Dividing my stare between him and the man in the white coat, I asked, "What?"

"I need to stress the importance of keeping a calm, relaxed atmosphere. I realize that Drew is awake, but stress takes a heavy toll on the body and his injuries are still very new and severe."

"I understand," Trent said, serious. So serious that he eased away from me to stand straight and face the doctor. "Drew comes first."

The doctor nodded, but doubt clouded his features.

I didn't like it. I didn't like the way he was sort of indirectly scolding my guy. "What's this about?"

Trent shook his head once. "Nothing to worry about."

My eyes narrowed, and it caused shooting pain in my skull.

The doctor and Trent still stood there, almost having a silent conversation. Suddenly, Trent's shoulders slumped.

"Drew?" he asked, his voice low and laced with regret.

"Yeah?"

"The doc needs to have a word with you. I'll be just outside the door."

"What?" I echoed, confused.

He looked like he wanted to say more, but he glanced back at the doctor and pressed his lips together.

"Wait." I called him back.

Two sets of eyes looked at me. "Whatever you have to say, you can say it in front of Trent."

"I think it's—"

"Just say it." I cut off the doctor.

"As a patient, you have certain rights." He began.

My face scrunched up, sending more shooting pain through my head. Reaching up, I cupped my forehead.

Forgetting he was supposed to be leaving, Trent was at my side immediately, gently cupping the back of my head.

"What's wrong with me?" I worried.

"You have stitches," Trent answered gently. "Your helmet busted and cut your head open."

I leaned into his hand and closed my eyes.

"Drew?"

I reopened them.

"Could you tell the doctor if it's okay for me to be in the room with you?"

I wanted to laugh, but the look in T's eyes was far too serious for a joke. The doctor stared, waiting for my decision as if this were some kind of court of law.

"Of course I want Trent in here with me."

"So you give permission for him, Trent Mask, to be allowed in the room? You don't feel pressured in any way to agree?"

"What the fuck are you asking me?" I half groaned. *Why would anyone think I wouldn't want him in here?*

A shady memory of me wondering where he was and worrying came over me. Was that not a dream? Had that actually happened?

The look on Romeo's face flashed into my mind. The fact that T wasn't beside me when I opened my eyes. The fact that he looked like he'd been beaten, robbed, and hung up wet. My parents standing beside the bed…

Oh fucking Christ.

I looked back at Trent, suddenly extremely alarmed, and rasped, "What'd they do to you?"

A look passed behind his eyes, a look he worked very hard to hide.

I hadn't seen a look like that for many years. Not since we'd struggled to admit our feelings and he was scared of everything he thought his love would take from me. The look he would get when retreating into himself, into a hidden place behind his heart.

"Nothing," he answered, his voice steady. "Everything's fine now that you're awake."

Anger I didn't understand gave me strength. I focused back on the doctor. "I want Trent in this room. Trent is my number one."

"Understood." The doctor nodded and then left the room.

Finally, we were alone.

But I couldn't entirely enjoy it because I was freaking the fuck out.

"Trent."

"Thank you," he said, stroking the side of my face.

"What the fuck is going on?"

"Lay down." He instructed. "You need to take it easy."

"I don't want to lay down. I want answers," I demanded. The cost of me trying to use my regular voice and not the scratchy, raspy one I was sporting threw me into another fit of gagging.

T did the same as before, tucking his arm and shoulder under me, offering me a place to lean, somehow absorbing the worst of the pain and calming me.

Collapsing against him, I sighed. "I feel like I was hit by a truck."

"More like a few race cars and a cement wall," he replied, haunted.

"Lay with me."

His face drew back so he could stare down. "What?"

"I want you in this bed with me."

"The IV and your ribs…"

"You're going to deny the patient?" I pouted.

He melted. "I'll give you anything you want."

"Get over here."

Instead of coming around to the opposite side of the bed, he went across the room to a duffle bag I hadn't even noticed and pulled out a shirt.

I shook my head. "Leave it."

He carried it closer but didn't put it on.

"You lost weight," I said, taking in his bare torso.

"So have you."

I patted the bed.

Kicking off his shoes, he gingerly got into the narrow bed, lifting the French fry blanket and covering us both. I settled against him, breathing in the familiar scent of his skin, soaking up the warmth he radiated.

Newfound peace washed over me, soothing some of the most intense pain I felt.

"Did you bring this from home?" I asked, glancing at the blanket as he tucked it closer around me.

"I never want to go back there without you again."

"I'm sorry," I whispered, settling just a little more against him. "I've put you through a lot."

"Watch yourself." He cautioned, his hands hovering around me as I moved. The second I settled, he continued. "Don't apologize for something that isn't your fault."

I started to say something, but his lips at my hairline made me forget I was speaking.

"It doesn't matter," he said between kisses, then pressed one more. "The only thing I want you worrying about is healing."

I tried stretching out my arm across his waist, but it hurt and I had to draw back. The huff of irritation turned into a cough.

"Stubborn," Trent muttered. "Lay still."

I turned my face into his chest. "I missed you," I grumped. "And now I can't get close enough."

"What's that?" he asked, leaning his ear closer. "You said you need a human Band-aid?"

I'm pretty sure that's not what I said, but T shifted so that he basically spooned against my side, gingerly putting an arm across my waist, clearly knowing where all my injuries were because he avoided them. His jean-clad leg rested over mine, and his face was so close his nose bumped my cheek.

"Is this close enough?" he whispered against my ear.

Tingles broke out across my scalp. Grasping his arm, I smiled. "For now."

TWENTY-EIGHT

Trent

Out in the hall, the peanut I'd met was quiet.

Inside this room, Drew was awake and in my arms.

I wanted to revel in the moment as long as humanly possible. I never wanted to let this feeling go.

No, nothing was perfect. Far from it.

But everything was okay.

It was enough.

More than enough.

The smile I wore, pressed against Drew's neck, didn't fade. Even after I'd lost the struggle to keep this moment from turning into a memory and drifted off to sleep.

TWENTY-NINE

Drew

There was a low knock on the door before it opened. Romeo poked his head inside the room, glancing toward the bed.

He saw us there and slowly started to back away.

"I'm awake," I told him, not having to whisper because my voice was just that raspy.

The door pushed wider, and he stepped inside, followed closely by Braeden, who gingerly shut the door behind them.

"We can come back later." Romeo spoke quietly, stopping beside the bed. Following his stare, I glanced down at the way my hand automatically cupped around T's face and over his ear, protecting him from any sound.

The desire to protect him was incredibly strong right now. So strong I didn't even think about it. My body and mind, even though injured, acted on instinct. I wasn't even sure why, but it was a feeling I couldn't ignore.

"No, stay," I replied, gesturing to a couple nearby chairs.

Beside Romeo, Braeden folded his arms across his chest. "Dude finally passed out."

"Guess he can finally breathe," Romeo murmured.

Trent had barely moved since climbing into this bed. He was still wrapped around my body like a self-proclaimed human Band-aid. His face was pressed into my neck, and every breath he took tickled my skin.

But seeing the way our brothers were staring at him, I was beginning to think perhaps it was me who was the Band-aid right now.

"He hasn't slept?" I questioned.

Romeo shook his head. "Barely. He only left the hospital once, and that was to shower and pick up some clothes."

"He hasn't eaten either," Braeden added.

My stomach dropped. "He hasn't eaten or slept in *five* days?"

"I think Arrow and Hop got him to eat a burrito the other day," B replied.

"Rim's been force-feeding him coffee with sugar," Romeo added.

The mention of Rimmel made me glance to the door. "Where is everyone else?"

"Ivy and Rimmel had to go check on the kids. The doctor said you had to go for tests, and they wanted to give you time with Trent. They'll be back in a bit," Braeden said.

"Joey and Lorhaven went to tell Gamble you're awake. Hopper and Arrow will be back later… They, uh…" His voice stalled.

"They what?"

"Your dad makes them uncomfortable," Braeden put in. "Actually, I don't think Hopper gives a shit, but he doesn't want the kid around all that."

The kid = Arrow.

He was a grown adult. A married, grown adult, but he would always be a kid to us.

"How long have my parents been here?"

"They got here the day after your accident," Romeo replied, his tone clipped.

Glancing down at T, I confirmed he was still deeply asleep. The smudges under his eyes looked like bruises.

"It's been bad, right?" I asked. "That's why you two are still here and not with Rim and Ivy. You stayed for Trent."

Both of them remained silent. They looked tired too. Tired but determined.

"What happened while I was out?" I pressed.

"Trent didn't say anything?" Braeden asked.

I shook my head. "He told me everything was fine and passed out almost the second he lay down."

"Sleeping in the waiting room ain't comfortable," B quipped, rubbing his back.

My eyes flashed up. "The waiting room? Why wasn't he in here?"

My brothers exchanged a look.

I made a sound. "Start talking."

"T ain't gonna like this," Braeden muttered as he went to get a chair from the other side of the room.

I shifted my attention to Romeo, knowing I would get the answers from him.

"You remember drafting up some kind of will when you were like eighteen and left for college?" he asked, sitting down in the chair nearby.

Braeden put his chair beside him, and the two sat side by side like two big bodyguards, filling up the entire side of the room.

I frowned. "That was years ago."

"In it, you named your parents next of kin." Romeo looked at me with knowing eyes.

At first, I didn't know what this had to do with anything, and then realization reared its ugly head. "You can't be serious…" My voice was incredulous.

B nodded. "Pops showed up, waving that document around, and kicked Trent out."

I jolted up, the sudden movement jarring my midsection, and breath hissed between my teeth.

Trent made a sound, and I winced, pushing back the discomfort and putting my hand on the side of his face, attempting to settle him.

This was a conversation best had while he was asleep.

Sure, I would be able to drag answers out of Trent, but he'd probably downplay it. By the way everyone was acting, this was not a situation that needed downplaying.

The look I saw in T's eyes earlier worried me. Most people didn't realize it, but Trent was fragile. Maybe not physically or even mentally. But emotionally, he was vulnerable. He hid it well, but this man internalized everything. If Romeo and Braeden were worried enough to stay here and watch over him and to basically go behind his back and tell me what's been happening, then this was serious because Trent was probably worse than even they knew.

"Maybe you should get some sleep first," Braeden suggested, watching me gingerly settle back.

"I've been sleeping for almost a week." I rebuffed, sliding a quick glance at T. He was still sleeping soundly, his deep, even breathing a comforting sensation. Before looking up to speak, I put my hand over his ear again to muffle our voices.

"You're telling me that my parents showed up with some dust-covered will and declared they were in charge of me while I was out, and their first order of business was to get rid of Trent?"

"It was your dad breathing all the fire, but your mom went along with it."

"That explains the doc wanting confirmation about letting him in here," I murmured.

"He hasn't seen you in almost two days," Braeden said quietly.

I looked up sharply, my stomach tying into an uncomfortable knot.

"He sat in the waiting room the entire time," Romeo added. "He stayed with you in recovery after surgery, then slept beside your bed the first night. He didn't leave your side at all until *he* showed up and threatened him."

"Why didn't you punch him in the face?" I demanded, rage filling me.

"Trent did."

Braeden sat up, a little mischief in his brown eyes. "Dude, Trent has been punching everybody."

"*What?*"

"Gamble paid off three people to keep him out of the slammer."

The blood drained out of my head, and the headache I'd woken up with intensified.

Romeo slapped B in the midsection, giving him a warning glare.

B wasn't intimidated and just shrugged. "It's true."

I looked down at the injuries marring Trent's wrist and hand. It looked like painful, open burns and stitches in his palm that were slightly swollen. "That what all this is from?" I gestured toward him.

Romeo nodded. "He's the one that pulled you out of your car."

"He did what?" A theme was emerging from this conversation: me freaking the fuck out about everything I was told.

Silently, Romeo pulled out his phone, hit the screen a few times, leaned forward, and held it out for me to watch the muted footage.

It was from a news station, coverage from the wreck at the track. It was chaos. Flames were everywhere, overturned cars, cars with bashed-in ends… metal everywhere. Emergency vehicles with flashing lights covered the scene, and water was sprayed, trying to put out the fires.

As if there wasn't enough chaos, more seemed to erupt in the corner of the screen. Leaning in, I watched a man I recognized very well yelling, trying to push through the blockades and emergency crew.

They wouldn't let him pass.

He wouldn't take no for an answer.

Astonished, I watched Trent use his size and sheer panic to literally fight past anyone who got in his way. He punched and kicked and used his body as a literal battering ram. It was like he was running down the football field, making mincemeat out of anyone who rushed him.

Except this wasn't a game.

Leaving a trail of bodies behind him, he vaulted over a partition and ran through the wreckage. The camera stayed focused on him all the way to the back of the wreck where my car was lying upside down against the cement wall.

I recoiled a bit, seeing my car like that. Knowing I was inside.

Those thoughts didn't linger, though. Trent punched out someone else who tried to stop him from going closer, and then he climbed over the car before dropping off the top and disappearing between the wreckage and the wall.

"What the fuck was he doing?" I muttered, still watching, though I couldn't see him.

"You were trapped inside. Your door was so damaged they couldn't get to you."

More people rushed around. I noticed flames glowing from inside the shattered windows. "It was on fire," I whispered, glancing down at the burns on his wrist. "*Jesus*," I swore.

"He pulled you out, and the crew finally made it around to get you."

"Why isn't this shit covered?" I demanded, seeing his injuries in a whole new light. "And why do his stitches look infected?"

"He wouldn't let anyone touch him. He only got the stitches because he didn't want to waste any of his blood in case you needed more."

In case you needed more.

I was stupefied, shock rendering me speechless. No thoughts could form in my head. I was absolutely dumbfounded by everything I'd heard. No. By the emotions hearing this brought forth.

"That dude ate, slept, and breathed nothing but you," Braeden said quietly. "Even after your father tossed him out and threatened him. I've never seen anything like it."

I marveled, gazing down at the big guy so gingerly wrapped around me. I was the one in the accident, but T was the one who suffered the most. So loyal. So selfless, dangerously so.

I love him. I loved him so goddamn much I knew without a shadow of a doubt that the reason I was still alive right now was because of this man.

Grazing my fingertips over the shell of his ear, I stroked the side of his head. As I did, the rest of B's words penetrated my emotion-swollen brain.

"Wait." I glanced up from T. "My father threatened him?"

"More than once," Romeo said, his voice deadly quiet. "Threatened to transfer you to some unknown location where no one could find you. Threatened to get a restraining order against him to keep him out of the hospital. Even threatened to put him in jail."

My hand fisted in the blanket. The blanket Trent had brought here and covered me with. I couldn't even imagine if someone tried to take him away from me when he needed me most. Hell, I'd damn near gone out of my mind when he was jumped and beaten up a few years back… and he was conscious the entire time.

"Why would they do this?" My voice was strained. I felt as though I were a dormant volcano that had just gone active. Hot lava boiled and churned under my skin, just waiting to explode.

"You know, I could give you some bullshit about grief making people crazy." Romeo began, shaking his head. "But that man doesn't even deserve the benefit of the doubt. He's cruel."

"Why would they even come here?" I muttered, my mind still reeling. "They disowned me."

"Pops saw it as a chance to get you back. I think he was hoping your head would be fucked up and he could take advantage and turn you against Trent," Braeden informed.

"That would never happen," I swore vehemently.

"It's just good to see you awake." Romeo agreed. "You shortened all our lives by about ten years with this shit. The family just wouldn't be the same without you."

A hard ball of emotion settled in my already inflamed throat. Emotion welled up behind the back of my eyes, threatening to spill out. "I almost died," I whispered.

They didn't have to tell me. I knew. Whether it was dreams, knowledge, or just intuition, I completely understood how close I came to almost never coming back.

Trent made a soft sound, cuddling against me a little tighter. Almost like he sensed my inner thoughts. As if he, too, understood just how close we came to being ripped apart. My body groaned a little with the shift of his weight, but I ignored it.

"You better apologize to your sister for that shit," B demanded. "She's been a mess."

I nodded. It seemed I had a lot to apologize for. Pondering that, I stroked my fingers through T's hair. It was kinda sticky. Pulling my hand up, I made a face. "When's the last time he showered?"

Romeo grinned.

"There's more you aren't saying," I said to them both.

"Look. Your dad is a jackass. That's all you really needed to know," B replied. He cleared his throat. "And yeah, Ivy banned them from her life and from our kids' lives."

I sighed heavily, regret making my head drop against the pillow. "Fuck." I'd never wanted my sister caught in the middle of any of this.

"She's had enough, bro. And I'm glad. I don't want that asshat around my kids either."

I nodded, understanding. It was for the best, but that didn't mean it wasn't hard to accept. My sister lost her parents, and what made it even worse is that she was forced to make that choice.

"I'm sorry—"

"Don't do that." Romeo cut me off. "Don't apologize for shit that isn't your fault. That's not why we told you all this."

"Why did you?" I asked, curious. I knew full well that Trent probably told them not to say anything.

Romeo and B exchanged a look, and the bottom fell out of my stomach once more. When Rome got out his phone, I braced myself.

After a moment, my brother glanced between me and the phone, debating. Not saying anything, I hitched my chin at him, silently telling him to hand it over.

Rising out of his seat, Romeo came next to the bed and turned the phone around.

A picture speaks a thousand words.

This one also dragged me down to that place where it felt like I was being buried by water. Where everything was muted and far away.

Even though I sat in a room with other people, with lights and sound, all of it instantly muffled.

The ache… Dear God, the fierce ache blooming inside me could quite possibly consume me alive. If I hadn't understood just how harrowing things had been while I was under, it was now excruciatingly clear.

Hand trembling, I reached for the phone, pulling the photo closer, eyes glued to the screen as if I were hypnotized.

Yes. That. Maybe I was. The despair and loneliness captured in this photo was so strong it spilled out of the image, chaining itself around my heart.

A man sat alone in a darkened hallway, hunched in on himself, cut off from the world. His body appeared heavy, the cold, apathetic wall the only thing there to offer support. His shoes were missing. My eyes kept going back to that detail again and again. Where were his shoes? Why did his clothes look so thin and ill-fitting?

The way this man curled in on himself, ducking his head, hiding his face… it was like he hurt so much he wanted away from even himself.

Without thought, I stroked my fingers over the image, trying to offer comfort to a man frozen in time. To a memory of pain so severe I felt it even though I hadn't even been there.

"What is this?" I rasped.

"That's a photo circling around the internet. An unauthorized photo of the man clinging to you right now like you might disappear," Romeo answered quietly. "This is what he looked like when your father basically stole the validity of your relationship out from under him. It's also the reason we told you all this." Pausing, Romeo rubbed a hand over his unshaven jaw and sighed. "Yeah, it's unfair to put this on you. Fuck, you almost died. But so did he." Romeo tapped the screen as if to remind me of the photo.

As if it was something I would ever forget.

"He needs you right now. We've done as much as we can. But the only one who can really protect him against your family is you."

Crushing the phone against my chest, I glanced up. There was wetness on my cheeks. I was crying.

The sound of the door opening behind us was like a gunshot ringing through the room. The emotional bubble my family stood in burst, and the rest of the world came crashing in.

"Time for those tests," some dude in scrubs announced, walking right in like he was invited.

The currents in the room hit him, and he stopped. "Oh, ah…" he said, swinging a piece of paper in his hand at his side. "I interrupted something."

We all stared at him.

"I can come back," he offered, his eyes gliding to Trent. "I wondered when he would crash."

I felt my dry, cracked upper lip curl. "Don't look at him."

Braeden made a choked sound.

Romeo leaned over, prying away the phone still clutched to my chest. "This is Patrick. He's been one of your nurses since you got here. He, ah, gave T a few chances to see you when other people wouldn't."

I stared back at the nurse, seeing him in a new light. "You helped Trent out?"

"We all need someone on our side now and then."

I nodded, slow. "I appreciate that."

He nodded, and the light caught on the diamond stud in his ear. "Of course. It's nice to see you with your eyes open."

Against me, Trent stirred, lifting his head to glance at me. His eyes widened when he saw me looking back.

"Wha—" He nearly gasped, instantly pulling his body back and holding his arm up off my waist. "Drew?" He worried, pulling farther back. "What's wrong? Did I hurt you?"

"I'm fine." I reached out for his hand, trying to pull him back.

"Is it your ribs?" he asked anxiously, pushing up to tug the blankets off me to look at my bare chest.

"What's with you dudes having no shirts on?" Braeden drawled.

Trent spun, realizing we weren't alone. "You guys are here?"

"We're keeping Drew company while you drool all over the place," Braeden teased.

Trent's hand flew up to his lips, checking to see if he was indeed drooling. It made me smile. He looked all rumpled, sleepy, and totally confused.

The ache in my chest returned. *How could anyone hurt him? How could anyone say such ugly things to this man?*

Forgetting about B's joking, his attention turned back to me. "Do you want me to get the nurse?"

"I'm already here," Patrick announced, waving.

Trent's eyes turned back to me. "How long was I out? What's going on?"

I smiled softly. "You were tired, huh?"

His eyes softened, returning to a sleepy expression. "I guess you were just comfortable."

Braeden made a sound. "All right. I'm out before I puke. Rome, let's go get the girls. Ivy's probably jumping out of her skin to see Drew."

Romeo glanced at me. "You guys will be good if we head out for a bit?"

I felt Trent assessing us as I nodded. "Yeah. Go."

They were at the door when I called out to Romeo. When he glanced back, I made a request. "Your dad in town?"

He nodded.

"I want to see him. Gamble too."

"What's going on?" Trent asked, immediately alarmed.

Romeo nodded, and. he and B left.

"Drew?"

"Everything's fine." I assured him, taking in every inch and angle of his face. I'd seen him a million times, but suddenly, it seemed I was looking through new eyes, eyes that had seen him at his lowest moment. Eyes that had stared in the face of death and come back.

Unable to help myself, I reached out with wobbly, weak arms to cup his stubble-covered jaw. "I really fucking love you."

The edge of his mouth lifted, and a spark of joy lit his hazel eyes. At the same time he started to answer, that dude nurse cleared his throat.

I'd thought he left.

Trent turned. "You need something, Patrick?"

It irritated me the way Trent said his name. Like they knew each other. Like that dude was familiar to him.

"Drew needs to go for those tests."

"Right," he replied, standing up from the bed. "The orderlies out there? You need help with the bed?"

Patrick rotated a little more toward him. His eyes lowered.

He was totally checking out Trent!

Oh, hells no!

I made a sound, then coughed. He was there instantly, sliding his arm around my shoulders, staring down with stark concern. "Tell me where it hurts."

I kissed him.

There was the briefest jolt of surprise, but he recovered with lightning speed, lips softening against mine and kissing me back without hesitation. The familiar hum of sexual tension hummed between us, and my lips clung to his, maybe because they were so dry or maybe because they knew where they belonged.

"It's better now," I told him, easing back.

The skin around his eyes crinkled, and I wanted to kiss him all over again.

"Uhh," Patrick said, "I was going to ask if Mr. Forrester thought he could go in a wheelchair now that he is awake, but—"

"I can do that," I said, leaning around T. "You wanna go grab one for me?"

"Sure thing."

The second he was gone, Trent gave me a look.

"Put your shirt on."

He laughed. "Are you being jealous right now?"

I made a face. "He was checking you out."

"He knows he's got no chance."

"He's gay?" I practically accused.

Trent nodded.

"I want a new nurse," I demanded.

"Don't be ridiculous."

I made a sound that caught in my throat and made me heave. The motion hurt my ribs and made me double into myself.

Trent cursed softly. His skin was smooth, his temperature warm when his arms came around me.

"Easy," he whispered, gently rubbing my back. "You need to stay calm."

I didn't speak because it burned too much when I did and my chest squeezed with pain. Exhaustion swept over me like a heavy blanket, trying to push me into the bed.

"I'll get you a new nurse, okay?" Trent vowed softly. "I swear to God, I've never looked at him as anything other than someone to help you."

I remembered what Romeo said about Patrick making it possible for Trent to see me.

"No." My voice was low. "He can stay." Lifting my eyes to his, I said, "I'm just being an asshole."

Trent smiled. "I'll take you any way I can get you."

The image of him crouching in that dark hallway flashed behind my eyes. "I'm sorry." My voice cracked on the words.

How would I make this up to him? How could I undo the damage my own parents wrought?

"Hey," he practically crooned, scooting closer on the bed. He shifted so he could wrap both arms around me, bringing his chest in to hug me carefully.

Not caring if it hurt, I wrapped my arms around his waist, pressing my nose against his chest.

He felt good. So damn good. All the lingering loneliness and fear clinging to me from when I floated in that dark place shied away from the light he shined on me. My fingertips curled in, clutching his bare back.

"Don't apologize again. For anything. Whatever you want. Whatever you need. I'll do it. I'll be it. I'll get it."

Turning my face, I laid my cheek against him. "What about you?"

"What about me?" he echoed.

"You've been through enough. Possibly more than me."

He stilled, careful, and pulled back. "What did Romeo say to you?"

"Stuff I needed to know."

He squeezed his eyes shut, and the muscle in his jaw worked. "He had no business—"

"He's family. It's his business."

Gold flashed in his eyes when they reopened, reminding me of lightning.

"Frat boy." I began. The door to the room opened, and I wanted to scream.

"Found you a ride," Patrick declared, pushing in the empty wheelchair.

"Put your shirt on," I grumped.

Suppressing a smile, Trent stood and dutifully pulled on the shirt. It was one of mine.

"We'll get you up slowly, and if it ever feels like too much, just say the word."

I was ready to get out of this bed. I wanted to move. I wanted to see how rusty my body was, how much strength I'd lost while lying here.

Patrick came forward to help me, but Trent intercepted him. "I'll do it."

Once the sling propping up my leg was down and the IV pole was beside the chair, Trent helped me sit up.

A wave of dizziness swept over me, and I could feel my heartbeat in my skull. Feeling winded just from sitting up, I closed my eyes and hid my face against his shoulder.

"Maybe this is too much," Trent said over my head to the nurse.

"No. I'm good." I lifted my head. "Let's do this."

Reluctantly and at the pace of a pregnant turtle, Trent helped me stand. Well, I was upright. Can't really say I stood, because he supported almost all of my weight.

My muscles stretched and pulled with the new position, and some of me trembled with effort.

Once I was sitting in the wheelchair, I was breathing slightly heavy.

Trent crouched near my feet, putting the cast up onto the footrest. I caught his hand before he could stand. "We're going to talk later."

"I'm not going anywhere." He promised.

"Shall we?" Patrick asked cheerfully.

"I'll push," Trent offered, moving to the back of the chair. "You grab the IV pole."

The trip down to wherever the hell we were going was quiet, and when the time came for T and me to separate, he knelt in front of me again. "I love you."

"More than French fries." I finished.

He kissed the top of my head and stepped back.

"You two are cute AF," Patrick crooned.

I would have rolled my eyes, but it would just make my head hurt worse.

"Hey, frat boy," I called when Patrick wheeled me away.

"Just say it," he said, holding out his arms like he was offering up the universe.

"Don't go punch Romeo."

He pursed his lips, suspicious that I knew exactly what he was thinking.

"He only did what he thought was best."

After a minute, Trent lowered his arms and nodded. "All right, Forrester. If that's what you want."

"First time I've ever seen him give in to anyone," Patrick murmured as we went.

I shrugged. "He's mine."

"You're lucky."

I made a sound, acknowledging his words. I thought about making sure he knew not to bother making a play for my guy. But I didn't bother. Some things I didn't even need to say. Besides, I was too fucking tired. I needed to save my strength for the people who really were a threat to me and Trent.

THIRTY

Trent

It was probably a good thing Romeo and Braeden left the hospital. It made it easier to keep the promise I'd just made to Drew.

I really did want to punch Romeo. He shouldn't have said anything to Drew. At least not right now. He was in a precarious state. He was fragile. I didn't want anything getting in the way of his recovery.

With the fam not here, Drew's parents in the waiting room, and his nurses changing the sheets on his bed, I wasn't quite sure what to do with myself while I waited. For the first time in what felt like forever, I wasn't buried under crushing grief and anxiety. Still, the aftereffects weren't easy to shake. And just because Drew was finally awake didn't mean everything was back to "normal."

Whatever the fuck normal was.

But right now, it seemed okay to give myself a couple minutes of chill.

Familiar crying echoed down the hall. My little peanut was pissed off again.

No. Not pissed off. Withdrawing from a drug addiction she didn't choose.

That pissed *me* off.

I wasn't the kind to judge. I'd been judged too much in my own life to be inclined to do it to others. But this was a kid, man. A baby.

A helpless, innocent life. I knew addiction was a disease. It wasn't simple to overcome. But why? Why in God's name would anyone do that to a child?

Without hesitation, I went down the hall to the wailing peanut. I wasn't sure if the same nurse was still on shift, but the least I could do was peek in and see if she was okay.

The bassinet she lay in was still in the corner of the nursery. What I assumed was the heat lamp was switched on above her, but she didn't seem too happy about it.

The other two babies I'd seen before weren't there, and she was completely alone. I didn't like that. At all.

My hand closed around the handle of the nursery entrance, but before I could open the door, someone spoke behind me.

"Who are you?"

I turned.

A nurse in purple scrubs stood there. Her long hair was pulled back into some kind of braid. When our eyes met, hers lit up with recognition. "Trent, right?"

I nodded. "How'd you know?"

"Sam told me about you."

"Sam?" I questioned, drawing a blank.

"The nurse who was here before."

I nodded, realizing who she meant. "Right." Glancing through the door, I gestured toward the baby. "I heard her crying again."

"Go ahead," she offered.

Surprise made my eyes widen. "Really?"

She nodded. "Sam says Jane likes you a lot."

"Jane," I echoed. "That's her name?"

"Not really. It's just what we put on her bracelet. Jane Doe."

No parents. No name. She was completely alone.

Going directly to the bassinet, I didn't hesitate to reach down and scoop her up. "You have something against blankets?" I asked, pulling her against my chest. "You probably wouldn't be so cold if you stopped kicking them off."

Peanut cried angrily, her body trembling mightily.

"All right now." I cajoled gently. "I get it. That blanket is stupid anyway."

She felt tiny and fragile in my arms. I worried she would break if I held her too hard, yet at the same time, the urge to hug her tightly was fierce. The hat on her head was gone. She probably managed to get rid of it too. The downy hair on her head was nearly black and perfectly straight.

Sitting down in the same rocker as before, I cupped the back of her head and pulled her away from my chest so I could get a good look at her.

She fussed and cried; her face flushed with anger. I frowned, seeing a scrape across her cheek. That hadn't been there before.

"What happened to her face?"

The nurse came around to look down. "Ah, looks like she scratched herself. Babies do that sometimes. She's very active with the tremors and shakes, so that probably happened."

Making a sound, I tucked the baby back into my chest, holding her tiny head against me with my palm. My hand was bigger than her skull.

"Can I have a blanket?" I requested.

The nurse handed over another scratchy, lame blanket with the same generic pink and blue stripes that her lost hat had.

"Isn't there any other way to calm her down?"

"She's not due for her next dose of medication for another hour," the nurse said, checking her chart.

"What medication?"

"Methadone."

"What the hell are you giving her that for?" I demanded. My harsh tone made Peanut cry more. "All right now. I'm sorry," I apologized, rocking her a little more.

"It's so she doesn't have to go cold turkey into withdrawal. It actually helps lessen her symptoms."

"Where's her mother now?" I grumped, knowing the woman probably had a body full of demons but angry with her just the same.

She shifted uncomfortably. "She died of an overdose shortly after giving birth."

"And she just left her here?" I pressed, wanting answers.

The nurse didn't answer right away. Instead, she watched me with the baby for a minute. "You know, skin-to-skin contact might calm her."

"What?"

"If you take off your shirt and let her lie against your bare chest, she might calm down."

With Peanut in the nurse's arms, I pulled the T-shirt over my head, tossing it on the arm of the chair. Taking the baby back, I laid her against my chest, patting her back.

She squirmed and fussed but then surprisingly calmed.

The nurse smiled. "Sam was right. She likes you."

My heart squeezed a little, making me glance down. Her arm was still swinging wildly, and I worried she might scratch her face again. Gently, I pinned it down at her side while rubbing her tiny back.

The door to the nursery burst in, and a blur of movement low to the ground whirled by.

"That's my sister!" a small, yet strangely fierce voice bellowed. A small fist pummeled against my thigh. "Let her go!"

"Whoa," I mused. "Who's this?"

A boy with dark hair and equally dark eyes looked up, his face pinched in anger. "That's my sister! Put her down!"

"This is Travis," the nurse said before turning her attention to the boy. "We know she's your sister," she said, mildly amused, and leaned down. "She was crying, so he picked her up."

"She's not crying now!" the boy insisted, glaring at me.

I half smiled. "'Cause she likes me."

"She likes me more!"

Taking a seat in the chair, I invited him closer. "Come say hi to her."

Travis came closer, coming around so he could stare intently into the baby's face. She was calm now, but upon glancing down, I saw her eyes were focused on the little boy who so fiercely barged in to protect her.

"She likes you too," I told him.

Travis reached out and touched the baby's cheek with his finger. Then he looked up. "She's mine," he told me.

His hair was overly long and cut unevenly. One side shagged over his ear, and the other looked as though it was cut just above it. He was tall and thin. The clothes he wore were too short and appeared worn.

"This is your sister?" I asked, keeping my voice low and soothing.

He nodded.

A woman poked her head into the nursery. She looked harried and tired. "Travis! I told you not to run off."

"I want my sister," he announced.

"I'm sorry, Mary," the woman said, not coming farther into the room. "He wouldn't stop asking to come here. He's quite the little troublemaker." The woman gave the boy a hard look.

He turned away from her and looked at his sister again.

"He can see her for a while." Mary agreed.

"I'll just go sit in the waiting room. I'm exhausted," the woman said, barely sparing a glance at me before retreating.

She didn't wonder who I was? Who she was leaving around this kid?

"That your mom?" I asked.

"No!" he yelled. "She's mean!"

Peanut fussed at his outburst, and he reached out to pat her back. "Don't worry. I won't let her be mean to you too."

My heart summersaulted. Such fierce loyalty for such a young age.

"How old are you?" I asked him.

"I'm five," he told me proudly. His dark eyes were slanted, and I wondered if he was part Asian. Glancing back down at Peanut, I noticed she, too, had the same look as her brother.

"And your name is Travis?"

He nodded.

"My name starts with a T too. I'm Trent."

"Are you going to take my sister away?" he asked, lower lip wobbling.

Maybe it was because my emotions were already frayed and raw. Maybe it was because of the tiny baby who was soothed by my presence. Or maybe it was knowing that this kid had obviously had it rough and was trying to figure out what was coming next, but tenderness consumed me.

I shook my head, trying to collect my emotions. "No way. I'm just rocking her until she falls asleep."

I wasn't sure he believed me, and honestly, I didn't blame him.

Gesturing to his fist, I asked, "What do you have there?"

Holding out his arm, he showed me the toy clutched in his hand.

It was a Matchbox car. A mustang. Smiling, I asked, "You like cars?"

He nodded.

"Me too. I have a mustang too."

"They go fast."

Tightness squeezed my throat. Fast cars weren't really that cool to me right now. "What other kinds of cars do you have?"

He glanced down at it, not answering. I wondered if maybe it was his only car.

"Show me how it drives," I said, pointing at the floor.

He glanced at his sister first, then dropped down to "drive" the car across the floor.

When he crawled off after it across the room, Mary came closer. "That's his foster mother out there. She brings him every day. Sometimes she leaves him here for hours at a time."

"Can she do that?"

"Travis is a handful, and he's fiercely protective of his sister. The only time he really behaves is when he's here with her."

"They're Asian?" I asked, sliding a glance back to the boy who was reaching under an empty bassinet for his car.

She nodded. "Their mother was Korean. From what we know, his father is American." Leaning closer, she whispered, "They don't have the same father."

I digested that.

Peanut started moving restlessly against me, her mouth searching around for food. "Do you have a bottle?"

Mary smiled and went to get it.

Travis came running back, car clutched in his hand. "My sister is sick."

I nodded. "I know. She'll be better soon." I wondered how long it took babies who were born to addicts to recover. I wondered if there would be any permanent side effects this baby would have to live with.

Mary handed me a premade bottle. Noting Travis still watching, I said, "Is it okay if I feed your sister?"

He thought about it, then nodded.

"Do you want to help?"

He hesitated, not knowing what to say. He was clearly very apprehensive around people, which made me kind of sad. He wasn't anything like the boys we had running around our compound, with open, trusting smiles.

"C'mon," I urged once Peanut was in my arms and had the bottle in her mouth. "You hold it."

He reached out, but his thin arms weren't long enough. Lifting him by the waist, I sat him on my knee and motioned for him to take the bottle. He held the bottom of it while his sister sucked the nipple.

"You're better at this than I am," I told him.

He didn't say anything, but the smallest of smiles curled his lips.

THIRTY-ONE

Drew

The longer I was awake, the more awareness set in. Yes, there had been pain from the minute I opened my eyes, but I was almost instantly focused on everything around me instead of within me.

After lying still for a CT scan, getting some bloodwork, and enduring another X-ray I'd had some "quiet" time to process everything.

The stitches in my head itched, but when I went to scratch them, my head screamed with pain.

What? I was gentle. It's not like I was trying to rip them out.

My entire midsection was sore and stiff, breathing wasn't as effortless as before, and the bandages wrapped around my midsection made me curious as to what was beneath them.

The cast on my leg was heavy. All of my limbs felt weak.

It hurt to talk. It hurt to swallow. Fuck, it even hurt to think.

I want Trent.

When he wasn't standing in the hall we'd left him in, a surly, irrational grumpiness came over me. I wanted eyes on him. I wanted eyes on him every minute.

How hard had it been for him to be forced to keep his eyes off me?

"When can this come out?" I complained, motioning toward the IV taped to the back of my hand. That hurt too.

"Might be a day or two yet," Patrick said, pushing past the place where Trent had knelt in front of the wheelchair.

Inside the elevator, Patrick pushed some buttons, then settled against the nearby wall. "Don't worry. He'll be upstairs."

My eyes lifted to his.

He smiled. "He's always here. Even when they tell him to leave."

Frowning, I asked. "They told him that a lot?"

The nurse nodded.

"But you let him see me."

"A couple times. I did what I could, but it wasn't much."

"Because you're gay?" I asked, not mincing words. I almost died. Almost dying cut out a lot of bullshit in life. "Or because you got a thing for my boyfriend?"

Guess I wasn't exhausted enough not to claim my guy after all.

"Both?" Patrick shrugged.

I grunted. The action hurt my throat and made me cough. "Least you admit it."

"He's hot, a fact I'm sure you are well aware of."

I choked again.

"Calm down." Patrick patted me mildly on the shoulder. "I'm not the type to steal someone else's man."

"Like you could." I threatened. I might be in a wheelchair, but I would kick this guy's ass. I was starting to regret telling T to keep him around.

"I definitely couldn't," he said as the elevator slid to a stop and the doors readied to open. He positioned himself at the back of the chair, and I grabbed onto the IV pole to help him out. Even my finger joints were sore.

"He's one hundred percent devoted to you." The nurse continued as we went into the hall. "Most men, including myself, would turn tail and run off if they had to listen to some of the things I heard said to him."

Lowering my head into my hand, I sighed.

"Drew!" My mother's voice rang out a little farther down the hall.

Groaning, I looked up.

"Oh, honey," she crooned, rushing forward. I hadn't seen her since Nova's last birthday party. Ivy never invited my parents to my niece and nephew's birthdays, but they came anyway. I just stayed away from them and tried to avoid a fight.

Lesson learned. Avoiding a fight had been the wrong way to handle this thing.

"Mom," I said, not bothering to smile. My lips hurt too.

"We've been so worried." She reached down and patted my arm. "Here, let me help," she said, reaching for the IV pole.

"No." My voice stopped her.

"Andrew," my father said, coming out of the waiting room to stand beside my mother.

Looking at him turned my stomach and made my hands tremble.

"We—"

"Not now," I said, trying to sound firm. "Just go."

"Go? We've been waiting almost a week for you to wake up!" Mom exclaimed. "We've been worried sick."

Anger burst through my exhaustion. "Worried? If you were that worried about my health, then you wouldn't have kept the best medicine away from me."

Mom's eyes widened.

Dad's lips thinned into a line. "If you are talking about that man—"

"He's not *that man*," I snapped. "He's..." My voice faltered, my brain stuttering out. Calling him my boyfriend sounded insignificant. It sounded like an insult. It wasn't a good enough word to describe everything Trent was to me. To describe everything my parents tried to take.

"Don't even know what to call him, do you?" Dad said, low.

I turned away. "I don't want to see you right now."

Patrick started walking again, pushing my chair down the hall. The security guards who were stationed at the door (not sure why that was necessary) came the rest of the way down, flanking the chair.

"Keep them out."

Mom gasped behind me.

Doesn't feel too good, does it?

"Wait," I told Patrick, and he stopped the chair.

I tried to glance over my shoulder, but my body didn't rotate and my neck hurt like hell. So instead, I just lifted my voice. "I don't want to see you right now. But I will. Just wait."

Without saying anything, Patrick pushed me the rest of the way into my room.

It was empty.

The bathroom was dark.

Unease curled low in my belly, and the toes on my unbroken leg curled under. Had he gotten into it with my parents again? Had they said something that sent him over the edge? *Is he sitting alone in a darkened hallway again?*

I need him.

"Hey!" I rasped out.

One of the guards peeked around the doorframe. "Me?"

"Where's Trent?"

"He was here awhile ago."

"Let's get you into bed," Patrick offered.

"No." I refused. "I want to know where Trent is."

"I'll find him for you once we get you settled."

"I'm not getting in that damn bed until I know where he is!" I bellowed.

Then I gagged.

Real tough, Forrester. Real tough.

It didn't matter how much I hurt, how much I wanted to lie down. I wouldn't be able to rest until I had eyes on him.

"Well, there is somewhere he might be."

"Take me there," I ordered.

"It's not far, so I guess it would be okay." He agreed.

Halfway down the hallway, I had a thought. "Why is it you know where he is?"

"Nurses talk, honey," he drawled.

I didn't even bother asking. I didn't care.

The nursery came into view. You know, that place where all the babies stay behind the glass wall so people could stare at them like they were zoo animals.

"Why are we here?"

"Because that's where your man is."

Furrowing a brow, I glanced up. "What?"

Patrick didn't answer right away, but the second we were in front of the glass, he made an affirmative sound. "Found him."

"Where?" I said, unable to see through the window because of this damn chair. I started to push up, but my arms trembled under the effort and one of my feet was not available for standing.

"Hang on," Patrick cautioned, going around the corner and opening a door.

When he came back, I scowled at him.

"You'll want to see this for yourself," he explained, pushing me forward into the doorway of the nursery.

"Why—" I started to ask why he thought Trent would be in the nursery, but then I saw.

Words perished. My heart stumbled, then paused. Every ache and pain throbbing in my system muted, and he was literally the only thing in focus.

The only thing I felt.

Raising my hand for Patrick to stop the chair, I paused in the doorway and stared.

What happened inside me was an oxymoron. A war of opposite emotions, fighting so hard they fused to form something I'd never experienced before.

It eclipsed all.

And in the center of it was him.

Trent had fallen asleep again, but this time, it wasn't wrapped around me. This time, it was with two tiny people wrapped around him.

His wide frame filled a wooden rocking chair, head tipped to the side. His hair was rumpled and messy, his normally clean-shaven face stubbled with shadow. One arm rested across the armrest. The other was wrapped around a baby who looked frighteningly small against his chest.

His shirtless chest.

I was out for five days. How had he picked up the habit of not wearing a shirt?

I couldn't even be salty or jealous, though, because his shirt—which was actually *my* shirt—was draped over the baby curled against him.

In his lap was another child, not a baby, who was also fast asleep, leaning his head against T's other side. The boy had a car clutched in one hand and a baby bottle in the other.

Fierceness and tenderness melded in my chest. My heart, which had stuttered, was working again, thumping unevenly while the strange sensation of butterflies filled my stomach.

They say when you die, your life flashes before your eyes. They were right.

But that was nothing.

Nothing compared to seeing your future spelled out for you as plain as day.

The desire to possess was so strong it hurt, but I embraced that pain. It was the kind of pain I liked. It was the kind of pain that made everything else fade away.

No. I couldn't call T my boyfriend. I couldn't even call him my person anymore.

If it seemed like an insult before, it was downright cruel now.

The sight of Trent sitting in that chair, cuddling kids I'd never even seen before, realigned everything. Including the beat of my heart.

Patrick started to move around me, but I caught the hem of his shirt and tugged him back. "Let him be," I whispered. *Let me look at this sight just a little longer.*

My voice woke up the boy sleeping in Trent's lap, making him turn toward us and rub his eyes. The second he noticed they weren't alone, he jerked up. All the innocence I'd seen cloaking him in sleep completely evaporated.

The boy's movement made the baby startle and start to fuss.

Trent jolted awake, tucking the baby closer against him.

My heart clutched. *I always thought...*

Trent looked first at the baby, then at the boy, who pointed in our direction. Following his aim, Trent saw me sitting there. In the briefest of seconds before realization settled in, our eyes connected, and with that connection, a much deeper one formed. As if he, too, had just been introduced to our future.

He smiled.

I smiled.

The baby started to cry.

"Drew?" Trent said, bursting whatever weird moment we just had, eyes widening. "What are you doing here?"

"Tests are done. Couldn't find you."

He started to swear, then grimaced, glancing at the kids. "I fell asleep. I'm sorry."

"Who's that?" the boy asked, staring at me.

"That's my other half," Trent explained as if the kid would understand. "His name is Drew."

"What happened to your leg?"

"Drove my car too fast, and I broke it."

"You must not be a very good driver," the boy said.

I started to laugh but ended up clutching my middle.

Trent's jean-clad legs appeared in my line of sight, and he leaned down to my level. "You should be in bed."

"That's what I said," Patrick quipped. "He refused to do anything until we found you."

Trent's thumb and finger curled around my chin, lifting my face so our eyes could meet, and he whispered, "I'm not going anywhere. I'm sorry I wasn't waiting in the room."

"Who's that?" I asked, glancing down at the baby.

Pulling back just a little, Trent adjusted the baby so she was cradled in his arms and I could see her face.

"It's a girl," he cautioned.

"Of course she is."

He glanced up, surprised. "How'd you know?"

"Like a face that beautiful would belong to a boy."

"That's my sister," the little man said, inserting himself in my view of the baby.

"Your sister?" I asked, feeling my brows rise. "I have a little sister too."

"Travis!" a woman called, coming into the room.

We all turned to see a nurse and a harried-looking lady step in.

"Hey, Mary." Patrick waved at the nurse.

"It's time to go, Travis."

"I don't want to!" he yelled.

The baby started to cry, her body shaking in a way that made me frown. Trent stood, bringing her with him, tucking our shirt around her body, then tucking a hospital blanket around that. He held her tightly, and I almost wanted to tell him to be gentler.

"I said it's time."

"No!" Travis fussed, stomping his foot. His little face was drawn into a fierce scowl.

"You'll bring him back later, right?" Trent asked the woman.

She blinked up at him as though she just noticed he was there. "Uh, sure. I'll bring you back tomorrow, Travis."

Travis's lower lip quivered, and Trent lowered in front of him. "I have to spend the night here tonight," he said. "Drew is sick like your sister. So how about I keep an eye on her for you until you get back?"

Travis nodded once.

Trent held his fist out to the boy, who looked at it, confused.

Chuckling, Trent stretched it out to me instead. I pounded mine against it under Travis's watchful gaze.

Once we finished, Trent held a fist out to him.

This time, he smacked his against it. The difference in size between that little boy and my man made my heart quiver.

When the boy and woman were gone, Trent carried the baby into the corner of the room, putting her down in the bassinet. I watched him pull his shirt away, and I heard her instantly start to fuss.

He lowered the shirt again, and she quieted.

His eyes found mine.

"Better leave it," I told him.

"She really likes him," Mary, the nurse, said to me.

It seemed a little weird that Trent had this new world he was part of that I knew nothing about.

"You've been in here before?"

"A couple times," Trent answered, turning from the baby.

I glanced past him and frowned. "Who put that baby in the corner?"

Trent tossed up his hands. "That's what I said."

"That's where the heat lamp is," Mary explained.

"Thanks for letting me hang," Trent said.

"Thank you for giving the entire floor a break from the crying." And her eyes dropped to his naked torso.

What was it with the people around here? Women *and* men checking out what was mine.

"How'd it go?" Trent asked, leaning over the chair into my space. I thought about kissing him like I did when I caught Patrick checking him out, but he frowned. "You're in pain."

"I was," I echoed, running my eyes over his face.

"C'mon," he said, grabbing the handles of the chair and the IV pole. "You're going back to bed."

"Frat boy!" I pretended to be scandalized. "There are people present."

"Har-har." He pretend laughed. "The only thing you're going to be doing in bed is sleeping."

As long as it was with T, it was all right with me.

THIRTY-TWO

Trent

"I don't like it, frat boy." Drew's hoarse complaint made me pause while tugging the blankets around him.

"Like what?" I asked, ready to fix whatever it was.

Gently, his hand reached for mine, tugging it away from the blanket and into his lap. The pad of his thumb stroked over the inside of my palm, making tingles race over my scalp and down my spine.

"This," he answered, showing me the unattractive state of my wrist, then turning my palm to show me the uncovered stitches. "You haven't been taking care of yourself at all."

"I'm fine." I rebuked gently, unsuccessfully attempting to tug my hand away. His grip was weak, but refusing any kind of touch from him was beyond me. Especially since there were so many days when I wondered if I would ever be blessed with it again.

"You aren't fine," he argued. "That looks like dog meat. And these"—he pointed accusingly at the stitches—"look infected."

I frowned, looking at the wounds once more. I guess it did look a little gnarly. "Don't touch it," I fussed, this time using more strength to pull away. "The last thing you need is any kind of infection."

"But who cares if you have one?" He accused.

"Drew," I said patiently.

"I get it." His voice was gruff, but his eyes still latched onto the wounds. "But it's enough now, T. I want that shit cleaned up. I don't like seeing it. I don't like knowing you're hurt because of me."

Making a light sound, I went to him, cupping the back of his neck and staring until his eyes met mine. "Nothing about any of this is your fault."

"You reached through a fire for me, didn't you?"

I sucked in a breath. "How'd you—" I realized. "Romeo," I swore. *What the fuck did he tell Drew?*

"You crawled through wreckage not even the rescuers were willing to go through."

"They were working on clearing a path," I bitched. "You didn't have time for that."

"You assaulted people."

"They should have stayed out of my way."

"You reached through a fire for me, Trent," he repeated.

Furrowing my brow a bit and tilting my head, I asked, "Did you think I wouldn't?"

He made a strangled sound that made him wince with pain. Caressing the back of his neck, I leaned in to briefly kiss the corner of his mouth. "I would do a lot more than that for you."

His hands were cool when they cupped my face, and the intensity of his sky-blue eyes gave me that butterfly sensation in my stomach. "They were horrible to you."

My heart squeezed, I had to work to swallow. "It doesn't matter."

"Don't." His fingers tightened against my cheeks. "Don't act like the hurt you feel is somehow unimportant."

But nothing would change it. And keeping all of that shit away from Drew made me feel better, so why bring it up? Why let it make an already grim situation darker?

"I know what you're doing," Drew intoned, sighing. "You're pulling—" His eyes strayed to something behind me. "Patrick," he called, lifting his voice so it would carry out into the hall, but it cracked partway through the call.

Alarmed, I jumped up off the bed, wondering why Drew was suddenly calling for his nurse.

Patrick, who was walking by, paused. "Did you call me?"

"Come here," I called so Drew wouldn't have to. Then I faced him again. "What's wrong? You need some more pain meds? You need the bathroom? You—"

"I need Patrick to clean up your wrist and hand."

It took a minute to assure myself it wasn't him who needed something. Relieved, I let out a breath. "Seriously."

"Patrick, can you do that?" Drew ignored me to look at his nurse.

He nodded. "Sure. I'll just go get some supplies and be right back."

He bustled out of the room, and I lifted a brow at Drew. "You're going to let him touch me?"

"Don't try and get out of it, Trent." He warned.

Damn. How'd he know what I was doing?

"But put on a shirt, huh? I'm sick of everyone in this place gawking."

Ahh, there it was. Pressing my lips together to stop the grin trying to split my face, I went for the duffle bag. "People keep needing them," I told him, still rather pleased he was jealous. After a few minutes of digging around in the bag, my hand was still empty. I turned toward Drew, sheepish. "There aren't any left."

Annoyance and exasperation flashed over his features. It was pretty fucking cute.

"I'll have Patrick get you some scrubs," he muttered. "After you get cleaned up, you can run home for more."

All amusement vanished when anxiety consumed my insides.

"*No.*" The word ripped out almost savagely. Drew glanced up immediately. "I'm not leaving. Don't ask me to do that. I won't," I said, rushing to where I'd tossed the shirt I used earlier to dry up the water. Scooping it up off the floor, I held it out. "I'll just put this on."

Drew leaned forward, wincing a bit but not relenting, and snatched the fabric out of my grip. "Come here."

I went.

He patted the side of the mattress, so I lowered onto it gingerly.

"Closer."

I started to protest.

"*Closer,*" he demanded.

Making sure the IV line was nowhere in the way, I scooted farther on the bed. A bed that was definitely not made for two men of our size.

His arms wrapped around my midsection; his body pressed against my side. Worry assailed me first because of his condition, but it was eclipsed almost instantly by something far more overwhelming.

Relief. Quiet.

Love.

Sometimes I wondered if he knew just how incredibly powerful he was. There was no one else on this planet, no one else in existence, who had the ability to crumble my walls while at the very same time give me strength.

It was incredible and so overwhelming tears bunched behind my eyes, blurring my vision.

I kept my face turned away because although I was no longer fighting a panic attack, I was equally overcome. Trying to control my emotions had been a real issue for me as of late.

It was embarrassing. I was stronger than this.

The stronger they are, the harder they fall.

I could feel the thickness of his beard against my skin. The solid width of his chest against my side. His cheek seemed cool against my shoulder, and even though he'd been here for countless days, he still smelled like home to me.

Swallowing thickly, I held still, not wanting him to let me go, but also not wanting to cause him discomfort.

"Take it," he whispered. "Let yourself accept the comfort I'm trying to give you, T."

"*Drew.*" I warned him not to do this. Not to pierce my heart this way.

"I don't know what to say," he whispered, holding on to me. "There are no words to take away what they did to you. But I can give you something."

I didn't look at him, but my head tilted in his direction. Looking down, I glanced at where his arms wrapped around me, and under them, I felt the way my heart thudded heavily.

"I can give you me."

I stilled.

"I know you've had me a long time now, frat boy. Over five years. And not once did I ever doubt us. They tried to take me. They tried to make you doubt me. Us. They made you feel abandoned and unworthy."

"Drew." I cautioned again, emotion so thick rising in me that it was physically painful.

"I almost died," he whispered. "It feels like a dream now, but I know it's not."

Unable to speak, I wrapped my hand around his arm, gripping him close.

"I heard the steady flatline of the machines attached to me. I saw myself lying on the table, and a bright light opened up on the other side of the room."

I tried to lurch up. I tried to run away. I couldn't hear this. I couldn't see the vivid pictures he painted in my mind. How many times had I almost lost him over the last week? How many times would I have to relive it? This had been my worst nightmare, and it changed me.

It changed everything.

"Listen," he said, holding me with strength that honestly surprised me. "Please, listen."

I collapsed back onto the mattress because I wouldn't deny him any request. And even though I wanted to run, the only place I could go was to him.

My head bowed, chin almost to my chest, as his arms encircled me once more.

"That light was beautiful, and it beckoned me."

A choked sob broke from my throat.

"You gave blood to me, right?" he asked.

"How'd you—" I began, then realized. "Romeo."

"Not Romeo." He denied.

My eyes found his. He smiled, gently wiping a tear clinging to my cheek. "I feel you inside me. You're practically my DNA now."

The bottom fell out of my stomach. "How—"

"I saw the nurse bring in the blood you sent. I watched it flow into my lifeless arm... into my emptying veins. My life, which had been fading fast, was restarted by you. I turned away from that beautiful light and climbed back into my ravaged body. Do you know why?" he asked, suddenly, pushing up my chin so he could look into my eyes.

I shook my head.

"Because I'm not going anywhere without you. Not ever."

Another sob ripped from my throat, and my body slowly wilted until my forehead was on his shoulder and his palm rubbed over my shuddering back.

"What they did was cruel and ugly. It hurt you, and that is something I will never ever forgive or forget. But it doesn't matter. My parents could ship me to Alaska and put you in a cell, but we'd still be together. No one will ever be able to take the bond we share."

My hand climbed up his back, my fingers clutching against the hospital gown with every inch I went.

No longer able to hold it in, a sound ripped from my mouth, making me turn my face into the crook of his neck. All the pieces I'd managed to hold into place despite the cracks and fractures literally making me look like a roadmap crumbled. I couldn't hold it in any longer, couldn't hold it back.

"I was so scared you were going to open your eyes and look at me like a stranger. That you would believe the things *he* said." I confessed, pushing even closer into his neck.

"Ah, baby," he murmured, cupping the back of my head. "There's too much of you inside me for that to ever happen."

Salty wetness slid between his skin and mine, taunting my lips. The tip of my tongue slipped out, licking against his neck, soaking up the liquid emotion. Need spiked my veins like vodka in a glass of OJ. Before I even knew what I was doing, my lips latched onto his skin and sucked gently. The motion calmed the storm raging in me. It tempered down the most intense emotion and allowed me room to breathe.

The hand on the back of my head tightened, the pads of Drew's fingers digging into my hair.

A small, needy sound filled the space around us, which must have been me because Drew responded by tilting his head a little to grant me further access.

With a growl, I sucked deeper, satisfaction blooming across my midsection like an earthquake.

"All right," Drew murmured, using barely any pressure to pull me back. "As much as I don't want to stop you…"

There was a popping sound when I pulled back from his neck, realization crashing over me like a fucking tidal wave. Horrified, I stared down.

Drew made a sound, cutting off the thought. "Up here." He beckoned, forcing my stare up to meet his.

Searching his eyes, I looked for any sign that I somehow hurt him. *Jesus criminy! He literally just told me about his near-death experience, and what did I do?*

I turn into Dracula and suck on his neck!

His laughter made me blink.

Oh my God.

His smile was gorgeous. It broke my heart into pieces and put it back together so perfectly it was like it was never broken at all. I'd missed that smile, the flash of his teeth, the dimple I knew was hiding beneath his beard. I missed the warm sound of delight that vibrated his throat and the way his eyes lit up with joy.

"Trent?" His smile vanished, and he grabbed the hand I'd pressed unknowingly against my chest. "What's wrong? Are you sick?"

I shook my head. "No. Sometimes it just hurts to love you this much."

His eyes softened. Everything about him softened. His hair, which needed a cut before and was now making him a contender for Sasquatch, fell into his eye.

I pushed all the hair up away from his beautiful face. "You were laughing." I tried to scowl but failed.

"If anyone is Dracula, I think it would be me. I'm the only with your blood swimming in my veins."

I blinked, whispering, "You can hear my thoughts?"

He smiled again, this one just as devastating as the last. "I can." He confided. "Some of your thoughts are dirty as fuck, frat boy."

He was messing with me. I was gullible as hell. I did have a dirty mind, though.

He laughed. "You said it out loud, frat boy."

Grasping his jaw, I pushed his head back, glancing at his neck. "There's a mark," I said darkly, but deep down, I was fucking proud of that mark.

"Good." I guess he was proud of it too.

"Did I hurt you?" I asked, brushing a thumb over it.

"The only thing that hurt was making you stop."

"I got, ah, caught up… What you said…"

Pressing his forehead against mine, I saw his smile in his eyes. "We have an audience in the hall," he whispered.

I went on red alert, shoulders stiffening.

Drew curled a hand around my neck, keeping me close. "That's the only reason I stopped you."

I made a mental note to be more in control of myself. If he couldn't be trusted to stop me from basically attacking him, then I had to be on alert. Dude was in no condition for any kind of foreplay.

"Do you think they heard what you said?" I whispered. His words still echoed around inside me, feeling like a summer night's breeze, soothing the worst of the day. Soothing almost a week's worth of hell.

"I only care if you heard."

Swallowing, I bobbed my head. "I heard."

"I meant every word, Trent. I'm still alive because of you. And not just because of your blood… Because I love you. Because even in death, you were my only thought."

I was getting choked up again. If I didn't get this shit under control, I was going to have to surrender my man card. It would have to go wherever Romeo's and B's went. "I love you too. So much."

"If you don't want to leave this hospital, don't. I won't ever send you away." In an act I felt intensely endearing, Drew dragged the pad of his thumb over my eyebrow like he was smoothing it down.

Pressing my lips together, I gathered up his hands, kissing the backs of them.

"That hurts." He pouted, staring at the IV taped across one.

I kissed it again.

"Knock-knock!" Patrick said rather loudly, rapping on the doorframe.

Maybe I should have been embarrassed. Wait. No. I *would have* been embarrassed if anyone had overheard the kind of exchange Drew and I just shared just a week ago.

Now?

Now I didn't give a flying fig (that's right, I said fig) if he recorded it and posted it online. Maybe the "perfection" I'd been trying so hard to maintain could take some notes.

Still holding Drew's hands, I glanced around at the man as he waltzed right into the room. "Got the supplies," he said, holding up some type of basket.

I made a face. Drew tugged my hand. "I don't like seeing it, Trent."

I relented.

"We're here!" Ivy chimed, walking in the room, followed by Rimmel, B, and Romeo.

Both girls came rushing over to Drew's bedside, both of their lower lips wobbling.

"Drew! Do you have any idea how worried we've been?" Ivy wailed, sniffling.

Chuckling, I got up from the bed to give her and Rim some room.

"Ives," Drew said, "sorry to make you worry."

She handed me some bag, then gingerly wrapped her arms around his neck.

"Watch his head," I cautioned.

Yeah, it was ironic. Me telling her to be careful after I was sucking on his throat.

"Come over here," Patrick called. "There is more room to work."

Everyone looked between me and the nurse. I held up my wrist, then started across the room.

"Shirt." Drew reminded me.

"Bro, this hospital is not clothing optional," Braeden quipped.

"I'm fine with it," Patrick bantered.

Drew made a sound, then started gagging. Ivy and Rimmel descended upon him like mother hens, and there was no way I was getting through.

I wasn't anxious, though, not like before. I guess his words really did help calm something inside me. Instead, I poured him a glass of water and set it close for when he needed it.

"Dude." I levelled Patrick with a look. "It's not happening."

Just because I was calmer didn't mean I'd put up with people upsetting my person.

"I know, but I can still enjoy the view."

"Braeden!" Drew gasped.

"I got this," B said, grabbing the nurse, who frankly was half his size, by the neck. "You got to go."

"It was a joke!" he squeaked. "What about his wrist?"

"I'll wait 'til Katie gets here tonight," Trent called.

"I was seriously just joking."

"Get new jokes," B said, pushing him into the hallway, then closing the door in his face.

Gingerly, Drew settled back against the pillows, exhaustion clinging to his every fiber. I went around to adjust the pillows at his back, going as far as propping up the hand with the IV in it on a pile of blankets.

When I was done, I took in both sisters with a thoughtful stare. Patting my jeans, not feeling what I was searching for, I glanced up, panicked.

"Your wallet is with us," Romeo told me.

My shoulders slumped in relief. Perking up, I asked, "You find my phone?"

"No. Drew's either."

"We need new phones," I informed Drew.

He shrugged.

"What do you need your wallet for?" Ivy asked.

"I want to give you some cash to go buy some decent blankets for this bed."

Ivy waved away my words like the offer of money was silly. "We'll go."

Rimmel nodded enthusiastically.

I picked up the wrinkled, slightly damp shirt. Ivy made a sound of distress and ripped it from my hands. "*What* is this?"

"My shirt."

"Where did it come from, the trashcan?"

I shrugged. "It was on the floor."

Rimmel and Ivy both made a face. "That's worse!"

Romeo and B laughed.

"You can't wear this," Ivy insisted.

"It's the only one I have left," I argued. "You see what happens when I walk around without one." I smiled slyly. "People can't control themselves."

Drew grumbled, and Rimmel wrinkled her nose. "You smell again. And your hair is starting to look worse than mine."

"But, sis, you're so pretty," I rebuffed.

"Because I shower," she deadpanned.

Ivy picked up the bag I'd set on the chair and held it out. "Here, we brought some clothes. And shower stuff."

Rimmel pointed to the adjoining bathroom without saying anything.

Romeo chuckled.

I looked at B for help.

"You're ripe." Then he held up a hand. "So frankly, it's impressive that fruity nurse still hit on you."

"Fruity?" I echoed.

"Braeden James." Ivy scolded.

"If you don't take a shower, we're all going to be in trouble." Braeden accused.

"We'll keep Drew company." Rimmel bobbed her head, the messy bun bouncing.

Glancing at Drew, he smiled. "Go."

Despite the audience, I leaned down, brushed the hair away from his forehead, and kissed it. "I'll be right back."

"Wait," Rimmel said when I was almost in the bathroom. When I came back out, she grabbed a coffee cup I hadn't even noticed Romeo holding and brought it over to me. "Drink this."

I stared at it dubiously.

"It's the way you normally drink it," she said.

I brightened and took it. Before closing myself in the bathroom I turned back to glance at Drew. It was like he was waiting for me to look, because he was already staring in my direction.

Both of us smiled.

THIRTY-THREE

Drew

I was back there. In the dark where my eyes didn't see, my mind struggled to understand, and I was prisoner to something I didn't understand.

I fought against it, but the darkness clung, making me afraid.

Screeching metal, crunching gravel, and the unmistakable whoosh of flames consumed me. Unable to see, all I could do was hear the cringe-worthy sounds and feel the intensity of the heat from the fire.

My lungs seized and pain shot through my chest so forcefully that it lingered along my arms and legs.

"Drew." The familiar voice beckoned, shattering the firmest grip panic had on me. "Drew, wake up."

My eyes shot open, and I gasped for breath as if I'd been somehow robbed of oxygen. I folded in on myself, clutching my chest. Breath was necessary, but it hurt so much.

"You're having a nightmare." Trent soothed, somehow gathering me in his arms without causing any additional pain. "It was just a dream."

Collapsing into him, I let him support all of my weight. I worked on gentling my breathing, trying to assure myself there was plenty of air and I didn't have to gulp.

My throat hurt, and the faint smell of smoke lingered in my nostrils. A cough racked my body, and Trent tightened his hold.

When I grasped his forearm, the IV sticking out of the back of my hand tugged, the sharp pain bringing me fully into reality.

Tilting my head back, I greedily sought T's face.

"You're okay." He assured me.

I believed him.

Clutching his arm a little tighter, I leaned up, and he met me halfway. Our lips fit together like two halves of the same whole. Neither of us moved. Trent just pushed a little closer, sealing any gap between us and offering up exactly what I needed in the moment.

When at last I was calm, I pulled away, laying my head against his chest.

"Do you remember the accident?" T whispered.

The room was dim. I wasn't sure of the hour, but it was likely the middle of the night.

I made a small sound. "Not really. Just…" I paused, trying to put into words the way it made me feel. "Just the fear and confusion."

Trent moved, my body going with his, and then a cup with a straw appeared in front of my lips. "Drink this."

I obeyed the command, sipping slow and cautious at first, then going back for more.

"Do you want some pain meds?" he asked once the cup was set aside.

I shook my head. "I just want you." Pushing his shoulder so he would lie against the bed, I followed, wanting to wrap myself around him.

"Forrester." He stopped me. "Your ribs."

"Please, hold me."

Even in the dim lighting, I saw his face go soft. His entire big body melted into the bed like salt into a hot fry.

Mmm, French fries.

I didn't ask him to hold me often. If I wanted held, I'd just wrap my arms around him. Asking denoted a certain type of vulnerability… a vulnerability I didn't realize I shied away from until now.

Now it seemed important. Or maybe now I was just so vulnerable it was impossible to hide.

This accident shifted things, made me desire to wield to him. It made me want to cling in ways I would have suppressed before.

"C'mon, baby." Trent beckoned, his voice like velvet.

He held still while I fit myself around him, adjusting so it hurt the least. Once my cheek was against his shoulder and his arm was tucked around my waist, I grabbed the hem of his shirt and shoved it up so the arm draped over his midsection could rest against his exposed skin.

"I remember," I whispered, letting his presence sink into me. He was a peaceful guy. Despite knowing how deeply T felt, there was an inner calmness to him that soothed everyone, especially me.

"You remember what?" he asked, gently caressing my waist with his fingertips.

"You called me baby after the accident. I heard you. You wanted me to say something. I tried."

Trent made a small sound, acknowledging the memory.

"You'd never called me that before."

His fingers paused. "You don't like it?"

I pushed closer, ignoring the protest in my middle. "I do." After a moment, I went on. "I never thought I would. We weren't really the type to say that stuff."

"There's been a subtle shift between us, Drew. You can feel it too."

Against him, I nodded. "I still feel you inside me, T. I'm hungry for you. I'm so fucking hungry."

My body wasn't the only thing left vulnerable from the accident. Everything inside me was now too. The pull to Trent was so strong it left me feeling weak. My stomach buzzed from emotion, as if it was trying to digest something impossible to break down.

No one could break down the love I had for this man, the connection I felt swimming in my veins. Not even death had been able to sever our bond.

If anything, death only made it stronger.

The backs of his fingers tipped up my chin. His lips lowered so close that mine moved like we were kissing before he even got there.

"Baby," he whispered.

My heart did a cartwheel, and then I was sinking into his kiss. His lips were gentle and giving but also predatory and claiming. I opened up wider and groaned when his tongue swept in, completely dominating my mouth. With his tongue curling around mine, our lips met again and again. My hand fisted in his shirt while his hand came up to grasp my jaw, holding my face exactly the way he wanted it so he could control the kiss.

A breath hissed between us.

I was the possessive one, but now I knew what it was to be possessed. I knew what it was to surrender completely.

It was strangely liberating, leaving me drunk.

Or maybe that was his lips.

Detaching, Trent pushed my face up so he could kiss down my jawline and neck before pulling away.

"Enough." His voice was rough. Dragging a thumb over my lower lip, he sighed. "You seriously test my patience."

I went in to kiss him again. He let me, then pulled back once more.

"Lay down." He urged, gently pushing me into his body.

I settled against him with a sigh, intoxicated by his presence.

"No more bad dreams tonight, Forrester," he commanded. "Sleep peacefully."

I did exactly that until nurse Katie came into the room with needles she wanted to stick into my arm.

"When can I go home?" I grumped, eyeing the kit like it was a bad movie.

"You'll have to talk to your doctor about that." She hedged, setting it aside. "I'm about to go off shift. Patrick is here already if you want me to get him instead."

"No," I said quickly. "Just get it over with."

"He's not a morning person," Trent told her, amusement obvious in his tone. I slid him a sour glance, and he winked.

She tied some rubber band around my arm and told me to make a fist. She filled up one tube. Then another one snapped into place.

"I'm gonna need more blood, frat boy. She's taking it all," I muttered, avoiding the needle and looking at him instead.

Chuckling under his breath, he wrapped his hand around mine. "Anytime."

"Finished," Katie announced brightly, taping a lump of gauze over the hole she'd just put in my arm.

"Any chance I can get this out?" I asked, holding up my hand with the IV.

"I can probably arrange that."

"Coffee," I said next. Looking at T, I requested, "Coffee."

"I'm not sure if you can—"

I made a sound, cutting him off. "Frat boy."

Trent looked at Katie. "I'll ask about that too. I would think he can start having some of what he loves. In *moderation*."

My thoughts turned back to the kisses in the middle of the night. How I wanted more of Trent… but not in moderation.

"You're blushing." His voice was deep and secretive against my ear.

The hair on my arms stood up from the feel and sound of him so close.

I tried not to smile but failed.

"How about I change the dressing on your hand before I go?" Katie asked Trent. "Let me see how it looks this morning."

He started to shake his head, but I gave him the eye. He sighed and got out of the bed. "That would be great, thanks."

It was infected, just as I suspected, and now he was on antibiotics prescribed by my doctor. He had been so focused on me that he gave himself an infection.

It was awful…

But also kinda wonderful.

He loved me that much. As much as I hated his wounds, I loved his love more.

"Looks pretty good," Katie announced, quickly changing the dressing. "Keep it covered. Keep it dry." She glanced at the bandages she'd put on his burns too. "Same with those. I'll change those when I come in tonight."

He was going to have scars. The care he'd refused and the fact he went around with active burn wounds uncovered and ignored for so many days made the healing process more difficult. When they did eventually heal, he would be permanently marked because he'd reached through flames for me.

Trent didn't complain, though. Not once. He ignored the injuries as if they weren't even there. Only once had I seen him favor the injury, and that was when he'd gotten out of the shower last night.

After promising to ask about my IV, Katie left for the day, leaving me in the care of Patrick and a few others.

"How come I have the same nurses every day?" I asked Trent.

"Because I hired them to stay with you."

I wasn't really expecting that. "You did?"

He nodded. "They were with you in the ICU. They knew your condition from the minute you were brought in. They saw the family who sat in the waiting room for you. And even though you were in a coma, I thought maybe they would be familiar to you. I didn't want a bunch of unknowns in and out of your room daily."

The spit stuck in my suddenly dry throat. *He did that for me?* "And the security?" I asked, motioning toward the door.

He nodded. "The press snuck into your room. Got some pics of you…" He cleared his throat and glanced away. "You were in bad shape. It, ah, pissed me off."

"You punched him," I surmised, thinking back to Braeden's words.

He shook his head. "No. But I slammed him up against the wall and broke his camera. You don't need to worry about the pics being leaked online. They're gone."

"I need the bathroom," I said, starting to push up from the bed.

Appearing beside me instantly, he wrapped his arms around my upper body and practically pulled me into a sitting position. Then, using one arm, he maneuvered my legs off the side of the mattress.

"You think you want to try and stand?" he asked, still holding me steady.

I nodded.

Making sure the IV pole was out of the way, he practically lifted me onto my feet. Blood rushed to my lower half and a wave of dizziness came over me, tilting everything on its side. I gripped Trent harder, leaning into him a little more.

"You okay?" he asked, accepting the weight with ease.

I nodded. "It's weird."

"Just take it slow," he murmured, adjusting my stupid gown.

"I want some sweats." I complained.

There was a smile in his voice when he replied, "You're demanding this morning."

My eyes met his. "You gonna give me what I want?"

Golden flecks shimmered back at me. He looked a lot less exhausted this morning. He looked more like the man I loved. "I'll give you anything you want, and you know it."

Desire rose from the bottom of my feet. Against his side, my fingers curled into his shirt.

The craving in his eyes rivaled mine. A small smile played on his lips. "How about we worry about getting you to the bathroom first?"

"Cock tease," I muttered.

"Just lean on me," he instructed as he went toward the bathroom.

The weight of the cast was more than I expected. The weakness in my legs pissed me off, and the way my body trembled with the effort of just going to the bathroom was frankly embarrassing.

"Fuck," I muttered when we were almost there.

Trent stopped walking, giving me a few seconds to catch my breath. The kiss he pressed to my hairline gave me a much-needed boost of energy.

After I took care of business, Trent basically used his body to support mine at the sink as he washed my hands for me (taking care not to get the IV dressing wet).

I stared in the mirror, shocked by the man who stared back.

My silence unnerved him, and our eyes met in the glass.

I swallowed. "I don't look so good."

"You look better than you did," T informed.

It was hard to assess myself… but it was completely unavoidable. I must have dropped at least ten pounds. My cheekbones were much more prominent. The dark circles under my eyes were fierce, and various yellow bruises dotted my face. There was a cut on my forehead, which appeared to be healing, and one on my cheek.

My complexion was pale, lips dry. I seemed so much smaller than usual, especially with Trent standing behind me.

"I need a shower," I rasped, blinking at the hair that was so long it flipped out against my neck. Trent was right about my beard. It wasn't the scruff he loved so much. It was full-on grown in.

"Later," Trent said, allowing me to take in the damage.

"What about the stitches?" I asked, turning my head.

"They're back here," he answered, clearing his throat and then motioning to the area. "They, ah, actually shaved a small patch of hair. There was debris from your helmet in your head. They had to pull it out."

I winced.

Gently Trent turned my head, lifting some of the long strands to show me the shaved patch. I couldn't see all of it, but it was enough. "Guess I'll leave the hair long until that grows back."

He kissed the side of my neck, momentarily making me forget about myself. "Whatever you want."

"What's wrong with my ribs?" I asked, trying to turn to face him.

Another wave of dizziness caught me, making me stumble. I didn't fall, though, because he was there, supporting me with ease.

"They're broken," he explained as I lifted my hand to the bandage over my side.

Untying the gown at my neck, he pulled the thin fabric down so I could see the large binding.

"This?" I pointed, gazing down. I was practically a watercolor painting of ugly color. Purple, red, yellow… even some green. Fuck. No wonder it hurt so much to move.

"Your lung collapsed," Trent explained patiently, gently brushing his knuckles over the bandage. "That's where the chest tube was inserted."

My stomach dropped.

"Do you want to see?" he offered, ready to pull the bandage away.

"Have you seen it?" My voice was hoarse.

My legs were shaking. Trent felt them and shifted closer.

He nodded. "I was in the room when they took it out."

My eyes widened. "You were?"

"I think your mom was feeling guilty. She didn't have the heart to tell me to get out when I barged in."

I took his face in my hands. "Thank you. For everything you did while I couldn't do anything."

"I wish I could've done more," he whispered, tying my gown back into place.

I shook my head, making his eyes come back to mine. "It was enough. More than enough."

"C'mon." His voice was gruff.

Halfway to the bed, my legs buckled, but I didn't fall. Trent lifted me like I weighed nothing at all.

"How much fucking weight did I lose?" I bitched, glancing down at the floor.

He carried me back to the bed, held the IV pole, and managed to not jostle me at all. "I'm not sure I wanna put you down," he mused, standing at the edge of the bed, still cradling me in his arms.

I wasn't sure I wanted him to either.

Hungry. I was still hungry for him.

The door opened, and Patrick came in. He was wearing hot-pink scrubs and a pair of matching Crocs.

"Morning!" He stopped, noting our position. "Is everything okay?"

Trent gracefully put me in the bed. "Yeah, I was just helping him to the bathroom."

"Short walks are good for you. I'll get some crutches and a walker in here for you," he noted.

I started to refuse. I didn't want that shit, but Trent caught my eye and shook his head.

I fell silent.

Since when did I get so obedient?

"Did you ask about this IV?" I asked.

Patrick nodded. "It can come out. Just make sure you drink lots of liquids."

I started peeling up the tape on the back of my hand.

"Woah," Trent cautioned, grabbing my fingers. "Wait a minute."

"I want it out," I demanded.

"Well, let Patrick do it."

Patrick came over and swiftly removed it. It hurt, and I cussed at him. Trent laughed like he thought it was cute.

I glowered at him while rubbing the bandage on the back of my hand. "I want some coffee."

"Coffee dehydrates you," Patrick rebutted.

"It's made from water," I argued.

"It's a diuretic."

"How about a small coffee and a large bottle of water?" Trent compromised as though he were placating two arguing toddlers.

"One small coffee," Patrick allowed. "Your breakfast will be here shortly."

"It better not be Jell-O."

"Applesauce and eggs."

I made a face.

"The doctor will be in later to check on you and look at your head wound. By then, he should have some test results from yesterday and the labs from this morning."

"Thank you," Trent said, but I didn't.

Applesauce and eggs.

When he was gone, Trent picked up my IV-free hand and kissed the back of it. I'd be damned if it didn't put me in a better mood.

"French fries?" I asked, hopeful.

He laughed under his breath. "Let's see how the coffee sits first."

"You need to eat something," I told him.

He nodded. "I'll get something when I grab your coffee."

"Is the coffee decent here?" I asked, grimacing.

"There's a coffee cart downstairs. It's decent. As soon as someone gets here, I'll run down and get it."

"You can go now."

Before the words were even out of my mouth completely, he was shaking his head. "I'm not leaving you alone."

I didn't argue. Resolve and anxiety mixed in his eyes when he spoke, and I knew better than to push. I was the one in the hospital bed, but T and I both had scars and shit to work through from this accident.

What pissed me off most was that his scars had been avoidable.

Not too much later, the door opened again, and Camden walked in. I'd barely seen my brother since moving to Maryland, so seeing him now was also a reminder of just how bad things had gotten.

"Cam," I called, smiling. "I heard you were rattling around."

Smiling wide, he came toward the bed and offered his hand. "I was here yesterday, but I figured you already had enough to deal with so I wanted to give you a few to adjust." His eyes slid to Trent. "How ya doing, Trent?"

"Cam." Trent inclined his head. "All good. Thanks for coming."

T was cautious with my brother. It put my hackles up instantly. Had Cam said something to him?

"Why don't you go get that coffee now?" I said.

Trent glanced between me and my brother, then slowly nodded. "You'll be okay?"

"Of course. My little bro couldn't kick my ass even with me like this."

Cam guffawed. "I might be younger, but I'm bigger than you!"

"Not for long." I rebuked. "I'll gain it all back."

Trent leaned over the bed, cupped the back of my head, and kissed the top of it. "Security is right outside. Just yell if you need them."

He spoke loud enough for my brother to overhear, but Cam didn't act offended.

"Hurry back," I said because I did want him to hurry back but also because I wanted him to know I would miss him.

He kissed my head again.

"You want a coffee, Cam?" T asked on his way out.

"Nah, I had one before I came."

Outside the door, Trent said a few things to security that made the men peek around the doorframe and look in the room.

Overprotective bastard.

I loved him.

When he was gone, Cam sat down in the chair beside the bed.

"We should talk," I said.

He nodded.

More than 4% of adopted children in the United States are rasied by LGBT parents.

THIRTY-FOUR

Trent

I trusted Camden Forrester. To an extent.

It was true Ivy called him here to try and talk some sense into their parents. I also knew Cam said he supported mine and Drew's relationship. I knew he tried to reason with their father, but I also knew he wasn't successful.

Truth was it was easy to accept something from afar when it didn't affect you.

It got a lot harder to do when it stared you in the face. Especially when it was the kind of thing that literally ripped families apart.

I didn't think Cam would hurt Drew. If I thought that, I never would have given them the room.

But I wasn't stupid.

I had enough experience with people to know Camden might not be as cut and dry about his brother's relationship as Ivy.

I would buffer Drew from as much as I could, but this? His brother? We couldn't stay in that bubble I'd built around us. At the very least, we had to know who we could trust. If Camden changed his mind about supporting his openly gay brother, then Drew needed to know.

Boy also needed his coffee.

He was growly and needy all at the same time.

It fucking turned me on, pumping me full of adrenaline unlike anything else. Drew had never been one to shy away from contact, from affection, but he was almost clingy now. It might worry me if I didn't know.

If I didn't feel the shift in our relationship, if I wasn't coming to understand the way things had been realigned.

I think I liked it. No. I didn't think. I *did* like it. I liked it so much that twinges of guilt pierced me as I thought about it. About him.

I never wanted this accident to happen. If I could go back and stop it from happening, I would in a heartbeat. I would surrender my safety for his. I would do anything to keep him sheltered.

But the accident happened.

And now we were subtly different.

I was still feeling out exactly how, but Drew was more yielding. More dependent.

Of course he is, asshole. I scolded myself. *He's a busted mess, and he needs you more than he ever has before.*

But it was different. This wasn't just because he was injured.

He wants you to call him baby.

My stomach flipped, giving me a slightly shaky feeling. Without thinking, my feet hurried a little faster to get his coffee, because the faster I got it, the faster I could be with him.

Of course, the press was out.

Damn vultures. I sincerely was awed these people still hung around this hospital, hoping for a glimpse of me, the family, or even of Drew. Didn't they have anything better to do? Fuck. Go take a picture of a puppy.

If these people put half as much effort into making the world a better place as they did trying to get gossip shots, this world might not be so fucked up.

"Trent!" someone hollered as I approached the coffee stand.

My shoulder blades snapped together.

"Trent!"

I ignored them. A few clicks of the camera made my jaw tick, but I let them take the pics. They were boring shots.

At the head of the line, I ordered two coffees and grabbed a breakfast sandwich from the small heated display.

Setting it in front of me, the cashier recited the cost, barely looking up.

Shit.

I had no wallet. No cash. No phone to call someone to bring me some.

For the last week, my entire life revolved around a hospital bed. I didn't think about money or phones or food.

"Ahh…" I faltered. "I, ah, left my wallet upstairs in the room," I said, feeling like a dumbass. So nice the vultures could get my stupidity on camera for later.

"I'll have to, ah, leave this and come back."

The cashier glanced up for the first time.

"Sorry," I said, glancing at the two coffees on the counter. I picked up the one that was Drew's. "Can I take this one? I promise I'll run the money right back down." I couldn't leave his coffee here. He asked me for it. I was going to make sure he got it.

"Here, I got it," Romeo said, stepping up beside me and handing over a wad of cash. "Keep the change."

"R-Romeo Anderson," the cashier stuttered.

More camera clicks went off.

"How ya doing?" He gave the girl a smile.

I picked up the rest of my stuff, and we stepped out of the line.

"Can you pose for a couple pictures?" a few photogs yelled. "Please!"

Romeo and I stopped for two seconds, glanced at one camera, then started walking again. Questions were shouted at us until we got into the elevator and the doors firmly closed.

"Thanks," I said when the elevator started moving.

"Anytime," he said. "Glad to see you eating."

I made a sound. Why did I suddenly feel awkward? Why did my tongue feel thick against the roof of my mouth?

I stared at him a few seconds longer, wondering what the fuck was wrong with me, but then he spoke. "Everyone else already headed upstairs."

Nodding, I said, "Cam stopped in to see Drew."

"What do we think of him?" Rome asked.

"We?"

He nodded. "Your opinion is the family's opinion."

Blind loyalty. Don't ever let anyone tell you it doesn't exist. It does. And it's exactly why these people were my family even if they weren't my blood.

The elevator doors slid open. Any awkwardness I'd felt was gone. "I haven't made up my mind. I'll see how Drew is when I step back in the room.

Romeo nodded. "Good call."

"You know I really wanted to deck you for telling Drew about his father," I said outright.

Romeo smiled and rubbed his jaw. "Surprised you didn't."

"I promised Drew."

"Ah," he mused.

"At first, I was hella pissed. But then I realized that's what family does. They say the hard shit even when it's really hard."

Nodding, Romeo lowered his voice. "He needed to know. We've been just as worried about you as we have Drew."

"I really appreciate you guys being here. I'm not sure I would have been able to handle everything if you weren't."

He slapped me on the back. "Like you said, it's what family does."

As we approached Drew's room, a familiar cry echoed down the hall. My footsteps paused, but the urge to follow the sound was remarkably strong.

I am getting attached. Attached to a child that wasn't mine. *I want her.*

"Trent?" Romeo's concern interrupted the startling thoughts assaulting me.

My head snapped up. "Yeah?"

"What's wrong?" he asked, backtracking so he was at my side.

"Ah, nothing," I said, trying to shake off the feeling. I couldn't. I couldn't do it while that little peanut was crying her heart out.

Patrick appeared a few feet away at the nurses' station.

"I'll be right there," I told Romeo. "I need to ask the nurse about something."

He nodded and went ahead into Drew's room.

"Patrick," I called, going to the desk. "Why is that baby still crying?"

"That's what baby's do."

I felt my lips thin.

"I can go check on her if you want?" Patrick offered.

"You'd do that?"

"Considering you're paying me very well to basically be at your and Drew's beck and call, yeah, I can do that."

"Aren't there enough nurses around here for someone to hold her?" I griped, the sound of her cries making my heart ache.

"They do hold her. But she cries anyway. It's the NAS."

"What do you know about NAS?" I asked.

He shook his head. "Not much. I'm not a neonatal nurse."

I gazed off in the direction of the nursery. "Will you let me know when Travis gets here? I'll come by and spend some time with them."

Patrick turned thoughtful, then rummaged through a few drawers at the station. "Ah," he said, pulling out a piece of paper. "Why don't you fill this out? It's a form to be a volunteer. Nursery could always use volunteers to help out."

"Then I could see her more?" I asked, setting down the coffee to tuck the form under my arm.

"Well, no one on this floor would really stop you from seeing her now," Patrick quipped. "You're pretty popular among the nurses."

I rolled my eyes.

"But it would keep us all out of trouble."

Nodding once, I picked up the coffee. "I'll fill it out and give it to you in a few."

"I'll go see if she's okay."

"I really appreciate it."

Patrick giggled, tugged on the ear with the diamond stud, and smiled shyly. I mean, I knew the guy thought I was good-looking, but suddenly, I realized he had a full-blown crush.

Clearing my throat, I backed down the hall a little. I was kinda embarrassed.

"Trent," intoned a voice that was definitely not someone who had a crush on me.

My heart lurched, and a shaky feeling swarmed over me. Pivoting, I saw Drew's father striding down the hall toward me.

His face was dark and sour, the lines around his mouth were deep. He looked tired.

I'd be tired, too, if I had so much animosity and hate inside me.

This man made me nervous. Uncomfortable. Judged. He was someone who made me feel less than. Less than human. Less than worthy. Just less.

I hated it. I hated he had that power. No matter how much I told myself none of it was true and that he was wrong, I couldn't shake it. Maybe because he'd attacked me at my weakest moment.

Maybe because, deep down, I was terrified he was right.

Despite it all, even the tremor in my hands, I raised an eyebrow to regard him coolly. "You actually know my name?"

"I want to see my son."

A bitter flavor coated my mouth. "Sucks to have to ask for something like that, doesn't it?"

"I know you think you've won here," he said, stopping in front of me. I was taller than him, and I enjoyed looking down and hoped it made him feel small. "But I still have power of attorney. I'm still his father. And you? You're just a phase."

I bit the inside of my cheek while his words hit their mark. *Don't let him get to you.*

"This isn't a competition," I said, suddenly very weary. "I'm not trying to beat you. All I'm trying to do is be with the man I love."

He drew back as if I'd slapped him. "You dare say that to my face?"

I blinked, confused for a second as to what I'd said that was so heinous.

How stupid.

How fucking ridiculous was it that this man was offended someone *loved* his child?

Shouldn't he be thankful? I think I would be if someone ever loved a child of mine just half as much as I loved Drew.

I guess to him, my love was unworthy. It always would be.

"That I love your son?" I questioned, disgust ill-disguised in my tone. "I do. I love him more than you could even comprehend, and it's because of that that I haven't said one disparaging word to him about you."

He snorted. "I'm sure you've done nothing but fill his head with garbage since he opened his eyes."

The definition of insanity was doing the same thing over and over and expecting different results. That's what it was like talking to this man. Insanity. And now I was done.

Funny how I was so scared to set this man off before. So scared he would take Drew away. Now that Drew was awake, the fear was gone. I could say whatever I wanted to him right now and not be worried it would come back and bite me.

I didn't want to say anything. It wasn't worth it.

"If you want to see Drew, you can ask him. I don't make those kinds of decisions for him." I turned to walk away. This conversation was pointless.

"No," he called, sarcastic. "You're responsible for him being in that bed to begin with. If you hadn't dragged him down into a life of depravity, he wouldn't be being punished right now."

I sucked in a breath. My hand tightened around the coffee as so many emotions pummeled me at once. This man was good. Good at making me feel like a villain.

My vision was slightly blurry as I stared down at my feet, willing myself not to engage. Not to turn back around. It's what he wanted.

"Are you fucking kidding me right now?" The low, deadly voice cut through the hallway, commanding attention in an iconic way.

My body snapped to attention. "Drew."

He was standing in the doorway of his room, Camden under his arm as support.

"Son," his father said from behind. Just the sound of his voice made my teeth gnash together. I heard him step forward.

"Don't call me that," Drew intoned in the same quiet, deadly voice as before.

"You shouldn't be out of bed." I worried, wondering how much he heard. "I have your coffee," I added in a pathetic attempt to distract him.

"Is this the kind of shit he's been filling your head with?" Drew asked. "Is this the kind of abuse you've been subjected to while I was literally fighting for my life?"

"It's the truth," *he* said.

Drew's blue eyes whipped to his father, silencing him with a single stare. Then they came back to me, softening. "What else has he said to you?"

"Nothing worth repeating," I answered. "Let's go back to bed." I moved forward, intending to take Cam's place under Drew's arm.

Drew made a harsh sound, shaking his head once. "What else did he say?"

"He asked if he could see you."

Drew's mom stepped out of the waiting room, seeing us all there, and hurried the rest of the way down the hall.

"Drew," she said. "We came for a visit."

Anger shimmered in the air around him. "You want to visit?" he echoed, that deadly calm back in his voice. The hairs on the back of my neck rose. "All right." He agreed, settling the full weight of his stare on his parents. "Let's *visit.*"

THIRTY-FIVE

Drew

I knew. Despite having a room full of people and several conversations going on all at once, I just knew.

From day one, Trent and I always had a connection. A link I'd never shared with anyone else. After five years, I didn't think it could get deeper.

Then death came for me.

The link turned into a bond. A bond not even the reaper himself could sever.

"Cam." I beckoned my little bro, who was still sitting beside the bed. The second he glanced over, I motioned with my hand. "Help me up."

His brow furrowed, but he pushed out of the chair to help me.

Romeo and Braeden moved closer. Ivy and Rim fluttered around, making a bunch of noise about getting me whatever I needed.

Some things a man had to get for himself. Sometimes a man had to follow his instincts even when he didn't know why they were screaming.

Romeo held out a hand, ready to assist if Cam didn't support my weight, but he did and I motioned toward the door. Everyone was quiet, watching me like I was somehow possessed.

I guess I was.

"T's in the hall you said?" I asked Romeo.

He nodded. "Talking to that nurse. He said he was coming right in."

"I can get him," Rimmel offered, starting forward.

"No," I said. "I'll go."

We moved kinda slow, but thankfully, it was a short walk to the door. Cam wasn't as big as Trent. His body wasn't as solid for me to lean on. Or maybe the only person I felt comfortable enough to give my weight to was T.

Before we were even around the corner, I heard familiar voices. I also heard ugly, cruel words I wouldn't even have spoken to my worst enemy. Only, those words were not aimed at my enemy, but the person I loved most in the world.

A man who was the least deserving of cruelty.

He was standing in the center of the hallway, harsh lights overhead, an overly polished white floor underfoot. His eyes were downcast, shoulders heavy. I didn't have to see the look in his eyes to know he was hurt by what my father said.

No. Not father. By what *that man* said.

Anyone who could speak like that to the person his son loved so much wasn't really a father.

I'd been told more than once since waking up that Trent endured a lot of harshness. I knew it. Knowing something and experiencing it were two different things.

What made it even worse was that my parents saw nothing wrong with the way they behaved. My father somehow, someway thought he was justified.

And my mother?

She hurt me worse than Dad because her silence, her willingness to go along blindly with the hate he spewed, felt like ugly betrayal. Like she'd chosen a side… and the side was not that of the son she claimed to love so much. She chose her husband. She chose his ugly actions.

My parents moved past us into the room as I gazed at Trent, suddenly introspective. Wouldn't I always choose Trent over everything? Over everyone? Wasn't that the duty of a husband?

Or a wife?

Fuck me… Was I the wife or the husband in this scenario?

"Drew?" Trent called my name softly, stepping close.

Even though I was preoccupied with random and weird thoughts, I reached for him, leaving my brother's support for the one I truly wanted.

Trent took my weight without even sagging. The arm around my waist was so strong I barely had to put forth effort to stay upright.

"Am I the wife or the husband?" I asked him.

He blinked. Blinked again. "What?"

"Nothing," I muttered, dipping my head into his shoulder, mildly embarrassed.

Cam cleared his throat, and I peeked over at him.

"You two fit," he remarked, eyeing the way I basically clung to T.

"You weren't sure," Trent said, his voice not surprised.

Cam shrugged one shoulder. "I'd support what Drew wanted regardless. But it's nice to see that I actually agree with his choices."

That basically summed up our entire talk. He came because Ivy begged and because he didn't think our parents had any right to dictate my life. He'd been unsure about his personal opinion, one of the reasons he always stayed away. But being here the last week, watching my entire family… watching Trent basically fall apart without me. You could say we convinced him.

Our family had that effect on everyone. Well, everyone but our parents.

Smiling at my brother, I said, "You should come around more often, Cam."

He nodded. "I might do that. I stayed away for too long."

"You're welcome at our house anytime. The door is always open," Trent said.

I relaxed into him even more. I knew he'd been wary of Camden, but my brother changed his mind.

Cam nodded and gestured toward me. "You got him?"

"Always," T confirmed.

When he was gone, Trent dipped his head to where mine rested on his shoulder. "You sure you want to do this now? I'll have security—"

"No." I lifted my head, letting him see the anger in my eyes. "I'm not going to let what I just heard go, not for another minute."

"Maybe you should cool off first."

"If you heard someone talk like that to me, would you ever cool off?"

His eyes narrowed. "Not even if I lived in the Ice Age."

I chuckled, which hurt my midsection. I went right to him, and he tucked my body a little closer. Somehow with confidence but utterly gentle, he kissed my hairline.

I knew he was likely going to try and put this off another day, so I spoke up before he could.

"I don't have to worry about that."

His nose wrinkled. "About what?"

"About you taking advantage of my blind loyalty. Of you ever putting me in the position of choosing between you and something I didn't agree with."

Trent glanced into the room. Without looking, I knew his eyes sought my mother.

"Don't ever compromise yourself, Forrester. Not ever. Not even for me," he whispered. "I'd never do that to my daughter. To any child of mine."

I looked up from his shoulder. "Daughter?"

His eyes flew to mine, shock making them wide.

Rubbing my palm over his stubbled jawline, I smiled. "We'll go see her once we deal with this."

More shock and a twinge of panic shone brighter on his face.

I half smiled. "I feel it too."

The surprise and panic melted into softness. Melted into something that made my heart squeeze. "Are you serious?" he whispered.

"My body might be a little fucked up right now, frat boy, but my heart is working better than ever."

"C'mon." His voice was gruff as he half carried me into the room.

"Let me do it." I half whined, half complained. "My body needs to do this."

He backed off a little, allowing me to walk, but his arm stayed anchored around me. The room was packed with family, all of them watching us as we made our way inside.

"Tony. Gamble," Trent said, surprised to see them.

"Well, you look better than the last time I saw you," Gamble remarked. "But that's not saying much."

"I made him take a shower," Rimmel whispered loudly.

Everyone snickered. Gamble turned his usually shrewd, businesslike stare toward her. Humor and true affection softened his eyes now. It was the same kind of look he gave Joey and his grandkids, Sophie and Jagger.

"It's not a surprise at all that you, the littlest one in the room, got the biggest one to shower. Well done, honey. Well done."

Rimmel smiled, and Romeo pulled her into his side.

"I didn't realize you were here." T glanced around. "Where's Valerie?"

"She's with the grandkids," Anthony said of Romeo's mom. "Drew asked to see us."

Gamble nodded.

"When—" T questioned, looking at me. His mouth thinned. "A guy falls asleep one time." Twisting around, he pinned Romeo with a look.

He shrugged. "Drew asked."

"I don't know what any of this is about." Burke began, looking around the room. "But my wife and I are here to see my son. So if everyone wouldn't mind—"

"You have no right." I cut him off, my voice firm. "No right at all to ask anyone in this room to leave, to make any kind of decisions for me."

"Son."

I snapped upright, out of Trent's hold. Yes, I wobbled a little on my feet, but my balance recovered. When T reached for me, I shook my head. "I already told you not to call me that."

"This is ridiculous." Burke tossed his hands up. "You are the one who signed that will. You are the one who granted me next of kin. I was only doing what you—"

"Maybe we should wait outside," Rimmel offered, her voice slightly strained.

"No. I want everyone to stay. I want everyone to be a witness to what I'm about to do and say. That way, there will never be any doubt among anyone ever again."

"The only people in this room that doubt you are the 'rents," Braeden muttered.

"Yeah, well. Humor me," I said. "This is a family matter. Everyone in this room knows exactly what's been going on."

Getting right to it, I glanced at Tony. "Can I have the papers?"

I felt Trent straighten just behind me. My parents glanced at Anthony Anderson as he pulled a packet of papers out of a large yellow envelope.

"Drew, what—" Trent asked quietly as I took the stack Romeo's father held out.

"I'm fixing my mistake," I said, pinning my father with a stare. Holding up the documents, I went on. "This is a new will. A new next of kin is being appointed. A new power of attorney." Dividing my stare between my parents, I forged on. "Everything I have, everything I will ever have in the future, is now untouchable to you. If I collapse tomorrow, if I get into another car crash, if I get hit by a bus when I'm on the sidewalk…" I shook my head. "It no longer has anything to do with you. The only person with the right to any authority over anything of mine, including my own body, is Trent."

Behind me, Trent sucked in a breath, and I felt the faint brush of his fingertips against my side. "Drew," he whispered.

My father practically exploded. "Are you out of your mind? What the hell are you thinking?"

I pointed to myself, incredulous. *Me?* "I'm thinking that I can't stand the sight of you."

He drew back.

"I'm thinking that it was a gross error in judgement on my part when I made that original will. But I was eighteen then. I still thought you hung moon. I thought Mom loved her kids more than anything."

Her face fell when I said that, but I no longer felt bad.

These people had caused too much damage for me to care anymore.

"If you were the people I thought you were then, you wouldn't have rushed in here and kicked Trent out of the room. You wouldn't have inflicted wounds on the person I love most with words that he will never be able to unhear."

"Drew." Trent tried again. I knew he didn't want this. He didn't want me to fight my family for him.

But I would.

I had to.

For years and years, this man had been fighting for me. Thinking about it, I turned toward him. "How many times?"

His brow furrowed. "What?"

"How many times did you shield me from this kind of shit without me knowing? In the press? At work? How many times did you bear the weight of our relationship all by yourself?"

"I've never been by myself," he whispered, tender eyes roaming over my face.

I spun back to my parents, ignoring the wave of dizziness that made my world tilt. "See that?" I thumbed my hand over my shoulder at T. "That is who I thought you were when I made that will. I thought you loved me enough to always put what I wanted first."

"What you want and what is best for you are two different things." Burke maintained.

I laughed. "Says who? Says the man with a vocabulary far filthier than my way of life could ever be."

"Andrew." Mom rebuked, stepping forward.

I looked at her. "What's wrong, Mom? Don't like it when I point out the truth? You disappoint me even more than him." I pointed at Burke. "I thought you l-loved me."

I had to stop for a minute. The last part choked me up in a way I wasn't expecting. As mad as I was, I guess I was equally hurt. I guess the betrayal I felt wounded me still.

"Oh, I do!" She rushed forward.

Not wanting her to touch me, I skittered back, tumbling right into Trent.

His arms went around my waist instantly, offering steadiness. Offering a touch I would never refuse.

"I flatlined on the operating table," I announced.

Everyone in the room shifted uncomfortably. My near death was obviously upsetting for my entire family.

Shock registered across my parents' faces.

Mom lifted a hand to her throat. "W-what?"

"You didn't know that, huh? Guess you were too busy trying to control Trent and isolate me that you didn't bother to ask the doctors about my condition."

"That's not true," Burke ground out.

I felt my eyebrows rise. "Yeah?" I challenged. "Then what saved my life?"

He blinked. A clueless expression bloomed in his eyes.

I snorted. Glancing down, I saw Trent's hands clasped lightly around my waist. I covered them with one of mine.

"Trent did." I informed. "The man that you forced away from my bedside is the reason I'm even still here today. He literally opened a vein and donated the type of blood I needed, the type this hospital was out of. Without it, I would have died."

"Andrew," Mom whispered.

"I'm sure you watched the news. You know he's the one that pulled me out of the wreckage. He found a way in even when the emergency crews didn't." Gently slipping a hand under his forearm, I lifted it, showing them the bandaged burns.

"Did you even notice these? These injuries he walked around with, uncared for, while you were lashing out with ugly lies? Burns." I stared my father right in the eye. "Burns from a fire he literally put his hand through to keep me out of."

"Yes, well…"

Releasing Trent's arm, I stepped away from him, closer to my parents.

"If you really wanted to do what was best for me, you wouldn't have separated me from the man whose blood literally runs through my veins now."

His face screwed up in disgust.

I went on. "That entire time I lay in that bed"—I pointed roughly across the room—"I was partly aware of the people around me. I still remember how confused I was. How I couldn't make sense of any of the sounds or any of the people. I was scared." My voice went hoarse, and I paused, sucking in a breath and trying to get control of my emotions.

Behind me, I felt Trent move closer. I held up a hand, stopping him.

"The only voice I recognized was his. His voice was the only thing that made me a little less scared. I heard him tell me he loved me. I never heard you say that. Not once."

"*Drew.*" Trent's voice was low and rough. I knew he was probably reeling. I hadn't told him any of that. I'd held it close and kept it confidential.

His arms came around me from behind, bringing his full body against my back. His wide shoulders hunched around me, and I couldn't help but feel like he was indeed a shield, a giant human shield made just for me.

Settling his chin on my shoulder, he hugged me close without an ounce of hesitation despite our large audience.

My father stared at us, his upper lip curling.

Holding his stare, I lifted my hand, bringing it around to cup the back of Trent's head.

"You disowned me over five years ago. I tiptoed around. My sister tiptoed around. My brother never even came around. We all held our breath, thinking maybe someday… someday you might realize you were wrong. I hoped you might come to understand."

"I will never accept the choices you've made. Choices that have severed your family bonds and landed you here in the hospital."

"My family bonds are just fine," I quipped. "But you and Mom… I'd say your family is a lot smaller than it used to be."

"Andrew." Mom came forward.

My hand tightened on Trent, making him stiffen as if he were prepared to protect me.

"I won't ever forget what you've done. What you tried to rob from me. I might have been able to forgive you for the pain you caused me, but what you did to Trent? To the man I love? I'll never forgive you. I'll never forget."

Gently, I pulled out of his arms. "Can I have a pen?" I asked the room.

Gamble pulled one out of his suit jacket and handed it over.

"I need your back," I told T.

His eyes held mine for long moments, silently telling me I didn't have to do this.

"I know I don't," I whispered. "This is my choice."

Nodding, he turned, offering his back. I flipped to the appropriate pages and scrawled my name in every place required.

When I was done, I regarded my parents. "I'm a full-grown man. I didn't think it needed saying, but here I am, saying it anyway. You have no control over my life. My future. Who I love."

I found a loose piece of paper that came after all the other documents and held it up. "In addition to all the other legal shit I just signed, I asked my lawyer to draw this up as well." I glanced at Romeo's dad. "It's a document that states you, Burke and Adrienne Forrester, have *no* rights to me. You have no claim on anything having to do with me. It also states that if I ever fall into a coma or any incapacitated state ever again, you are not allowed to see me."

My mother started crying, and my father actually rocked back on his feet.

Pointing to the signature line, I showed where I'd signed. "I don't ever want to see you again. I've come to realize that your 'disowning' of me was halfhearted. A vile attempt at controlling me. I've had enough. I'm disowning you. Don't call. Don't write. Don't show up in front of me or Trent ever again. If you come to the compound, we will not open the gate."

"Andrew, no!" my mother wailed, coming forward.

I stepped back. "Stay back, Adrienne."

My use of her first name shocked her silent.

Ivy cleared her throat and silently came to my side. "Can I see that paper?"

I handed it to her.

"The pen?"

Puzzled, I handed that over too.

"Braeden," she beckoned.

B appeared, offering his back without pause. I watched my sister scrawl her name beneath mine.

"I feel the same as Drew," she announced, handing the paper and pen to Anthony.

Camden cleared his throat. "I'll sign it too."

"You don't have to," I told him and my sister. "I wouldn't ask you to do that. I would never ask you to choose."

"Yeah?" Cam scoffed. "Well, he asked me to." He pointed to our father. "Sorry, Dad, but I can't be on your side."

Mom nearly passed out. The only one who moved to catch her was my father.

"Get out," I said, suddenly exhausted.

"I'm sorry," Adrienne said.

"If apologies worked, we wouldn't need the police," Braeden intoned.

Romeo snickered.

"Trent." My father stepped forward.

I snapped upright and lunged forward. "Don't even say his name." I snarled.

The world tipped out from under me, and I swayed on my feet. A few muffled curses and hustling feet closed around me. I didn't fall, though. Trent was there scooping me up in his arms.

"You shouldn't be doing this," he scolded. "You just got out of a coma, for fuck's sake."

"I'm done now," I said, letting my head drop to his shoulder.

My parents called out to me again, but I ignored them. Braeden and Romeo acted like bouncers and bounced them right out into the hall where actual security escorted them away.

I lay back in bed while Trent pulled the French fry blanket over me. "I miss the dog," I whined.

Trent half smiled. "You can FaceTime him later." Then he paused. "Well, when I get us new phones."

"French Fry is fine." Rimmel informed him, pulling out her phone and finding a few photos. "He's with my dogs and having fun."

Turning the screen around, she showed Drew multiple pictures of all the mutts running around our compound.

"Here." Trent held a cup of water under my lips. Dutifully, I swallowed, wondering when my raw throat would feel better.

"Coffee," I croaked.

The coffee he'd gotten me appeared, and I took it with a sigh.

"If it's not hot anymore, I'll get you a new one."

When I lifted it to my lips, the cup visibly shook with the effort.

Without a word, Trent withdrew it gently, sat on the edge of the bed, and held it to my lips for me to take a sip. As I drank, I stared at him.

Pulling the cup back, I felt a bead of liquid on my lip. Trent swiped it away with the pad of his thumb, then stuck it into his mouth to suck it clean.

"Drew?" Ivy's quiet voice captured my attention.

The second I looked into her shimmering blue eyes, I sighed. "Ives." My chest tightened. Lifting an arm, I invited her close.

She climbed onto the bed, fitting herself against me. Trent tensed, no doubt worrying about my side, but I shook my head and he backed off.

Closing my arm around my sister, I hugged her close and palmed the back of her blond head.

"You really didn't have to do that, sis," I whispered.

"I already did while you were in the coma. This just proved to them I was serious."

"I'm sorry," was all I could say. "Sorry that they let you down."

I couldn't be sorry that she made this choice, though. As hard as it was, it was better this way. Ivy didn't need this kind of toxic presence in her life. She deserved better. What if she someday made a choice those people didn't like? Sometimes you had to let people go, even people you were taught from day one were always supposed to be there.

"I'm so sorry I couldn't stop them." She wailed against me. I felt her tears saturate my thin gown. "I tried. I really did."

"I know. None of this is your fault. Don't cry. I don't like it when you cry."

She started to cry harder.

"Dude. You have no skills with women," Braeden said, totally offended.

I grimaced.

"Blondie, come here," Braeden said, nearly picking her up out of the bed. "Come on. I got what you need." He sat down with her in his lap and stroked her hair.

Within moments, she quieted. He glanced at me and smirked. "Amateur."

I rolled my eyes and looked at Anthony. "Do you need me to sign anything else?"

"No, that's everything."

"Thank you for drawing up all those papers. I really appreciate it."

Tony smiled. "I've had them ready for several days. I knew what you wanted as soon as Romeo said you asked to see me."

"You're a good father," I told him. "Romeo is lucky."

"Me too!" Braeden added, as if he were insulted I hadn't said his name too.

Anthony laughed. "I consider all of you my kids."

"Especially me, though," B quipped.

The door pushed open, and I stiffened, half expecting to see my angry father scowling, but it wasn't him.

It was Patrick, and he wasn't alone. He'd brought a very loud guest.

The baby's cries filled the room as he wheeled the bassinet inside, glancing around. "Wow, full house," he said, his eyes finally finding Trent.

"A baby!" Rimmel gasped, stepping forward.

In Braeden's lap, Ivy perked right up.

"She's still crying," Trent stated, clearly unhappy.

"I checked on her as requested. She's due to eat but isn't taking the bottle. According to the nurses, she's had a rough day."

Without hesitation, Trent reached into the bassinet and pulled the baby into his chest. It still shocked me how small she looked in his arms and how I instantly worried he might break her.

"Be careful." I cautioned him as he wrapped his arms around her.

He caught my eye and smiled. "Are you worried?"

"Maybe," I echoed.

Patrick reached into the bassinet and pulled out a bottle, offering it to Trent. He took it but didn't offer it to her right away, despite her cries.

"It's okay now, peanut." He began, swaying back and forth. "I got you."

Everyone in the room was stunned silent. The last thing anyone expected was for a baby to be wheeled in and for Trent to clearly be wrapped around her finger.

"Calm down now," he told her, and remarkably, she listened. Her cries dropped a few notches, turning into fusses. Pulling her in a little closer, Trent smiled. "You're hungry again, right? Didn't want to eat for those nurses? Probably still mad they put you in the corner."

My heart swelled as I lay back against the pillow, watching him with her. The same feeling I felt seeing him with her before flooded me. The same rightness. The same possessiveness.

After a few tries, the baby latched onto the bottle and started to eat.

Patrick made a sound. "She's good with you for a while?"

Trent didn't even look up from the baby. I don't think he even heard Patrick speak.

"Just go," I told him.

"Wait," Trent called, his voice soft. "Rim."

Rimmel rushed over, peeking at the baby. "Oh, she's gorgeous."

"Yeah." Trent readily agreed.

Butterflies fluttered beneath my ribcage at the sound of his voice.

"Can you fill out that paper for me?" he asked Rimmel, motioning toward a sheet I hadn't even noticed. "Patrick needs it."

"I'll do it," I offered, snatching it off the bedside table while Rimmel handed over the pen.

"Hospital volunteer?" Rimmel read from beside me.

"I'll bring it out to you when he's done," Trent told Patrick, keeping his voice quiet. The baby fussed, and he soothed her.

The second Patrick left, Braeden spoke. "Pretty sure you can't just be holding other people's kids and wheeling them into your room."

"She's not other people's kids," I practically growled.

Everyone in the room exchanged a look.

"Whose baby is that?" Ivy blurted out.

I felt the eyes of everyone in the room. Everyone but Trent. He was staring at the baby girl in his arms.

"Drew!" Ivy was impatient.

Without withdrawing my eyes from Trent, I answered, the words tumbling out without me even thinking.

"She's ours."

THIRTY-SIX

Trent

She's ours.

I felt it in my bones. I felt it with every fiber of my being.

When I heard her cry, I experienced a physical reaction. The only other person who ever made me physically react to overwhelming emotion was Drew.

He wants her too.

Could he really? He hadn't even held her. He didn't know where she came from.

I didn't care either.

I hadn't cared from the moment I heard her crying. From the moment I picked her up without asking a soul.

Was this how parents felt when their baby was placed in their arms after birth? Instant, overwhelming love? Instant devotion?

It was new. So new to me. Yes, I loved Drew. More than anything.

But this was different.

This was somehow more.

Drew and I had been cautious at first. We danced around our feelings. Our love. We debated, and we were afraid.

It wasn't like that now, with her or with her big brother, who bravely stayed at her side despite his young age.

There was no war inside me. No debate. No worry. Just love.

I loved her. I wanted her. I wanted her brother.

I glanced at Drew. His eyes were soft, the blue like a bright summer sky on a cloudless day. I wanted him.

Our family.

His and mine.

"Really?" I whispered, speaking to him and only him.

"Let me see her." He beckoned.

She was still fussing and trembling and needed to finish her bottle. But Drew was like a siren, calling me to him, promising something infinitely beautiful.

"You have to hold her tight," I cautioned.

"I know."

I put her in his arms. She squirmed and kicked, which made me fear for his ribs. He acted like he didn't notice, chuckling instead.

"You're the smallest baby I've ever seen," he told her, his voice tender and low.

My heart did a cartwheel. My stomach dropped to my feet.

She fussed again, and he pulled her closer, making a soothing sound. The baby quieted and looked up. Her very dark eyes focused on his face.

"Hi," he whispered.

I pressed my lips together and stumbled back a bit. My vision was blurry. My lungs didn't work right.

I wasn't a man who ever cried. Until Drew almost died. Until I was shoved out of his life.

Until I put his daughter in his arms.

Ripping his gaze from the baby, Drew's found mine. "You still need to ask me if I'm sure?" he whispered.

A choked sound caught in my throat, and I rubbed at the tender spot in the center of my chest.

I shook my head. I didn't have to ask. The sight they made together was everything.

Absolutely everything.

"Is that how…?" My voice faded away. I couldn't even finish the sentence.

"Yes," he answered, returning his attention to the baby. "That's exactly how it was when I saw her with you."

"I'm sorry." Braeden interrupted the life-altering moment. "This is beautiful and all, but what the fuck is happening?"

"Think our family just got bigger," Romeo answered quietly.

"Again, I ask. What. The. Fuck?" I glanced over at B, who was glancing around the room at everyone as if silently enquiring if he was the only one with questions. He saw me looking and levelled his stare on mine. "Drew's been in a coma. You've been falling apart. How the hell did you have time to make a family of two into a family of three?"

"Four." I corrected.

His eyes widened. "There's another kid?"

Gamble stepped forward. "He does raise some interesting questions," he said. "I'm assuming this baby is suffering from NAS?"

I glanced at him, surprised. "How did you know?"

"I own part of this hospital. One of our programs is for babies born to opioid-addicted mothers. Considering her small size and the fact that there is no one to object to her being wheeled right in here…" He opened his hands as if to say, *I rest my case.*

"T." Drew beckoned. His eyes were filled with questions. And worry.

Leaning over them both, I guided the bottle back into her mouth, waiting for her to latch on. When she finally did, I motioned for Drew to hold it, then lowered on the mattress beside him.

"She's still shaking." He worried.

Nodding, I tugged the fry blanket up and tucked it around them both.

"Neonatal abstinence syndrome," I told him but was loud enough for everyone in the room to hear. "Gamble's right. She was born to a woman who was a drug addict. She's basically going through withdrawal."

Ivy made a sound and came over to the bed, leaning over Drew to look at the baby. "Poor little thing."

"I don't understand how anyone could do that to an innocent baby," Rimmel said, coming to stand beside Ivy.

"That's why she cries so much. That's why she shakes. That's why she's small. I'm, ah…" I continued. "Not really sure what other medical issues she has yet. I haven't gotten that far."

"You got far enough to fall in love," Rimmel said, catching my eye to smile.

I returned the smile. "Yeah. Well."

"It doesn't matter," Romeo declared. "A father loves his kids no matter what's wrong with them. This is no different."

My stomach vaulted, and my heartbeat doubled. *Father.*

Was that what I was?

The baby gave a yell, and Drew made a sound, trying to quiet her.

Oh God. I want to be her father.

Fear slammed into me fast and hard. Was I even capable of being a father? What did I know about raising kids? About raising kids with a traumatic background?

"Frat boy," Drew whispered. I lifted my eyes to see him gazing at me. "Don't do that."

How could I not? Braeden already pointed out that our lives were kinda in the shithole right now… How could we bring two kids into it?

What's more… Would we even be allowed to adopt them?

Holy shit. What if I was getting attached to two tiny people only to be told I was too gay to raise them?

If people could stop me from seeing the man I loved while he was in critical condition, they could definitely block me from trying to make a good life for two kids who needed it.

Standing from the bed, I paced away.

"Trent." Drew called me back.

Seeing the volunteer form Drew filled out for me, I snatched it, saying, "I'll go give this to Patrick. Be right back."

Drew called my name again, but I left anyway.

Outside in the hallway, I leaned against the wall and let out a shuddering breath. Everything beneath my skin was trembling. All my organs, nerves… my emotions.

I thought about the baby in the room, held in Drew's arms.

I wanted her. I wanted her brother.

But was I really good enough for them? I wasn't so sure.

Actress Ellen DeGeneres came out as a lesbian in 1997, shortly after the character she played on TV also came out. This made her the first openly lesbian actress to ever play one on TV.

THIRTY-SEVEN

Drew

I looked down at the tiny bundle in my arms.

Love swelled inside me like a tidal wave. It didn't matter I'd just met her. It didn't matter she would need extra care.

I wanted her. I wanted her brother. I wanted to make this family with Trent.

It felt exactly right.

I'd never thought kids were in our future. For so long, it was him and me against the world.

The baby cried out, and I lifted her to lie against my chest. She curled against me, her small fist shaking.

I glanced up at Romeo.

He nodded and went to find Trent.

Patting her back, I made a request of Gamble. "I want all the info on her and her brother you can get. I want to know what we have to do to adopt them."

Tugging his tie, he stepped forward, glancing at the tiny girl. "You know children taken from drug-addicted homes often have emotional and physical problems."

"We'll take the responsibility."

"The amount of paperwork, the amount of scrutiny and red tape you will have to go through to adopt them is astronomical."

I glanced at him. "How bad?"

"Child services will crawl up in your ass and pitch a tent there until they're satisfied," he deadpanned.

That sounded uncomfortable.

Gamble glanced around the room. "They'll be all over this entire family. Especially since you all live on the same property."

"We can take it," Ivy said.

"I'll be your legal counsel. I can call in someone who specializes in this kind of thing to assist," Tony put in.

"No matter how hard you think it will be," Gamble cautioned, "multiply that by three."

I met his eyes, keeping my stare even. "Have you ever seen me back down? I know I'm in rough shape right now, but I know what I want. Standing on the precipice of death has a unique ability of making things very clear."

Gamble nodded. "All right, then."

"You'll help us?" I pressed.

"Let me make sure Trent wants it too."

Oh, he wanted this. I felt it in my bones. In my veins. Maybe on some level, I could read his thoughts, because I knew right now, he was freaking out because he wanted this so bad. He was probably doubting himself this very second. Doubting he was enough.

He was enough. Trent was more than enough.

"Ivy," I said quietly. "Can you hold her?"

Ivy and Rimmel both nearly tripped rushing to the bed. Once I handed her over, the girls all but forgot I was there and took her off to their side of the room, cooing and fawning all over her.

Braeden and Tony moved closer to peek down at her.

"Let's go find Trent," I said, motioning toward the crutches Patrick left before.

Gamble's warnings didn't fall onto deaf ears. I knew this wasn't going to be easy. I also knew I probably had no clue just how much it would take.

The baby let out a cry, and I turned, already automatically wired to respond.

"Aww," Ivy cooed, waving me away without even looking. "She's fine." She promised.

I watched her another moment, hesitating.

Ivy finally lifted her eyes, a smile tugging her lips. "Your daughter is fine, Drew. You can go."

My daughter.

Damn, I liked the way that sounded.

THIRTY-EIGHT

Trent

I didn't stay alone for long. A large body leaned up against the wall beside me, nearly mirroring my position.

We stood there for long quiet moments, not saying a thing, until suddenly, my voice filled the silence.

"I was like a ghost in these halls. Rattling around, aching, unable to go where I wanted most."

The body beside me said nothing. He didn't even move. He just waited for me to continue.

"Just like a ghost, I saw everyone, but it felt like no one saw me. Like I was disappearing from reality, trapped in a fog filled with nothing but self-doubt and fear."

"We all saw you. We just didn't know how to reach you."

"That's why you told Drew."

"Yeah." Romeo confirmed. "That's why I told Drew. He was the only one capable of pulling you back."

"Someone else got through, though. Something else cut through the misty state I was in, offering a timeout.

No." I shook my head. "Offering a few fleeting moments when I didn't feel like I wasn't falling apart."

I glanced down at the paper clutched at my side.

"I heard her crying all the way out here in the hall. The sound bothered me. It annoyed me so much that I went off to find it. But when I found it, when I found her, I realized I hadn't been annoyed. I recognized the sound of pain. Of loneliness."

I glanced up at Romeo, and he nodded, silently telling me to continue.

"She was just laying there trembling so badly even I could feel it in my bones. She was small and in a corner, and it reminded me…"

"Of you?"

I made a sound. "Born without a choice. Fending for herself in a world where her parents clearly weren't around. My dad took off when he found out about me, and my mom only stayed out of obligation," I explained. "Then when I told her I was gay, not even obligation kept her around."

Romeo nodded.

"I was alone a lot." My voice quieted. "I didn't have a family until I met all of you."

"You aren't alone anymore, man."

"I know." I agreed and went back to what I originally meant to say. "I picked her up. I walked right in the nursery without permission. No one was even in there with her anyway. I picked her up…"

"And she became yours."

"I don't know how it happened," I echoed. "And her brother?" I added, smiling. "He rolled right up in there like he was ready to fight me for her." I glanced up, pride swelling in my chest. "Little dude was carrying a Mustang. A freaking Mustang."

"It's okay to want them. It's okay to love them."

"It happened really fast."

"Well, you didn't get nine months to get used to the idea of having a kid, but I can promise you that's how it is when you're a father. Instant love the second you lay eyes on them."

"I'm not sure I'm father material," I confessed.

"You already proved you are because you're out here thinking of them first. Because you love them."

"But they aren't mine. They aren't ours."

"You can change that."

"Who's going to give custody of two kids to two gay men?" I scoffed.

"I could probably help with that," someone said from Romeo's other side.

Straightening off the wall, I spun to see Gamble standing there, and right beside him was Drew.

My eyes flared with surprise. "Drew?" I whispered. "What are you doing out of bed?" Seeing his hands wrapped around a pair of crutches, I hurried to add, "Where is she?"

"Ivy and Rimmel are fawning all over her," Drew replied, amusement in his eyes.

A new worry overcame me. "How much of that did you hear?"

"All of it," he said, his stare darkening. "Don't you think that's a conversation for us and not you and Romeo?"

"I heard too." Gamble butted in. "I'm glad I did. Makes this easy."

My face wrinkled. "Makes what easy?"

"Using my influence to get those kids placed with you."

I faltered. Hope, but also apprehension, consumed me. "You can do that?"

His eyes sparked with a bit of challenge, then flashed with the confidence he embodied, which made him into the most powerful, rich man in the state. "Of course I can."

"You think we'd be good dads?" I questioned, the last part sticking in my throat.

"After seeing you with the baby and hearing your words? I do." Gamble agreed. "Plus, with Drew being out the entire season, you two will have plenty of time to be home to focus on those kids."

I sucked in a breath and glanced at Drew. We hadn't even talked about his recovery, about how this accident would affect his career. He had a lot to work through, physically and mentally.

Now probably was not the best time to be bringing in two kids who were going to need a lot of attention and care.

And what about next season? Gamble seemed to think Drew would be right back into racing.

I wasn't sure how I felt about that. How he felt.

"Maybe we should talk," I said to him. "You have enough on your plate right now. This could be too much."

Drew started to say something, but loud yelling distracted us all.

"Come back here!" a woman yelled. "Don't you run away from me!"

"Ow!" a smaller but fierce voice wailed.

I stiffened instantly, spinning away from everyone to look in the direction of the arguing. They were out of sight, around the corner… but I knew that voice.

"Let go of me!" Travis demanded. "I hate you!"

The woman made a startled sound. "You little brat!"

Pounding footsteps slapping against the floor grew closer, and a small body darted around the corner. His face was a mix of anger and distress, his thin arms pumping at his sides as he ran but stared behind him for whoever was giving him chase.

"Whoa, easy there," I said, taking a few steps toward him. His dark eyes turned to me, but he didn't slow.

His foster mother shot around the corner, her long skirt tangling around her legs as she rushed after him. "You're going to be punished for that!" she yelled.

Travis kept running, veering in my direction. Thin arms wrapped around my thigh and squeezed as he rotated, hiding behind me.

I felt his heart pounding against the back of my leg, and when his foster mother was within arm's distance, he cowered against me, hiding his face.

"Get over here," she snapped, flinging out her hand toward him.

I caught her wrist and shifted a little so I was between her and Travis. "What seems to be the problem here?"

"That… that *ingrate* just bit me!" She held up her hand, showing off the teeth marks that were indeed imbedded in the fleshy part between her finger and thumb. "Now step aside. He needs to be punished."

His arms squeezed tighter. I could feel the way they shook. He was scared.

Reaching down, I covered his arms with one hand. "Why did he bite you?"

The woman looked up, mildly surprised. "What?"

"Why did he bite you?" I repeated.

"Because he's completely uncivilized, has no sense of right and wrong, and doesn't listen at all."

"That wasn't the question." Drew spoke up. "I'll rephrase. What did you do that made him lash out like that?"

The woman sputtered. "You've got to be kidding me. I've got teeth marks in my hand! I'm his current foster parent. You have no right to question me!"

Moving my hand around to Travis's back, I glanced down. "Why'd you bite her, Trav?"

"She's mean!" He erupted, then pressed his face into my leg and sniffled. My heart clenched. "She said she was taking away my baby!"

All of our eyes turned to the woman. For the first time, she realized there were four very large men standing there staring at her.

She cleared her throat, tucking her hair behind her ears. "That's not what I said." She reasoned. "I—" She faltered. "He overheard me talking with someone else."

"What did he hear exactly?" I asked, feeling my eyes narrow.

Frustrated, she tossed up her hands. "He's too much of a handful, okay? He doesn't play well with others. He's aggressive. He doesn't listen. He can't even *read*!" she hissed. "He can't stay with me any longer. He will have to go somewhere else, without his sister."

Against the back of my leg, Travis started to cry.

So many things…

Oh, so many things flashed through me in that moment.

But most of all? Fierceness.

Bending down, I lifted the boy into my arms. He wrapped around my upper body like a koala on a tree. His small arms wrapped around my neck, his face buried close.

I glanced at Drew. The many emotions I was feeling were echoed in his stare.

"You're his sister's foster parent?" I asked, starting with that.

"Of course." She sniffed. "Why do you think I'm here every day?"

"I thought you just brought Travis," I replied, frank.

"Today is the last day for that."

Travis let out a yell against my neck. I rubbed a hand up his back.

"You mean to tell me you're the foster parent assigned to that baby girl and I haven't once seen you hold her or ask about her condition?"

"I'm her foster parent. Not her mother."

I drew back as though she slapped me.

Drew made a rough sound.

The woman gazed at him, then back at me. "What? I have four kids at home. When she is discharged, there will be five. I only have so much time."

"They're kids," Drew snapped. "Not paychecks."

"Who are you people?" she asked, finally seeming to understand that we were not on her side. "Give me that child." She reached for Travis. "I'm taking him to social services. I'm done with him."

I jerked out of her reach. "I'd stay back if I were you," I said, quiet. Deadly.

Romeo inserted himself between me and the woman like a brick wall.

"You're planning on surrendering this child to social services?" Gamble asked the woman, all business and no emotion.

I didn't know how he did it. I wanted to rage.

"Don't make me go," Travis whispered in my ear. "Please let me stay."

Palming the back of his head, I sought out Drew. He was watching us, a frown pulling at his features. Using the crutches, he came to my side. "Hey, Travis, remember me?" he asked, leaning close to him.

I felt him nod against me.

"Want to go with me to see your sister?"

Travis pulled back, blinking damp eyelashes at Drew. His eyes were impossibly dark, just like the baby's.

Drew's face darkened. "Where'd you get that bruise?"

I jerked back, looking down to where Drew stared. There was a red ring around Travis's upper arm and the beginnings of a bruise.

He pointed to the woman.

"You do this?" I growled, leaning around Romeo to show her the mark.

"He kept running away." She defended.

"You put a bruise on my kid," I growled.

"*Your* kid?" Her eyes went wide.

Gamble smoothly stepped into the situation. "Why don't you take the boy to see his sister? I'll speak with this lady."

Lady my ass.

More like queen of the dragons.

"Go," Romeo intoned, backing up Gamble's suggestion.

I matched Drew's pace while carrying Travis to the room. When we stepped through the door, everyone looked up.

The baby was in Rimmel's arms, and Travis immediately wanted down to go to her.

I let him go but watched closely, worried he would be upset someone he didn't know was holding her.

"Hi," Rimmel said to him immediately. "Are you Travis?"

The boy looked around at me. I nodded.

He nodded at Rimmel.

"Your sister told me all about you. She's been waiting for you to come see her."

Travis shuffled a little closer to Rim and the baby.

"Remember when I told you I had a little sister?" Drew said to Travis, who nodded. Drew pointed to Ivy. "That's her."

"She's not that little," Travis announced.

Braeden snickered, drawing Travis's attention.

"Definitely not as small as this little peanut." I agreed, leaning over Rimmel to look at the baby, who was finally sleeping. "She likes you," I said softly.

Rimmel smiled. "I like her too." She turned her smile to Travis. "Come sit with me."

Ivy vacated the chair right next to Rimmel, and Travis climbed up.

"I'm going out in the hall for a minute, okay? Stay here with Rimmel and your sister."

A look of fear crossed his features. I glanced around at Drew.

"Drew will stay with you, okay? I'll be right back."

Travis glanced at Drew, back to me, then back at Drew. When he nodded, I felt like I'd won some kind of award.

Before leaving the room, I went to Drew. "Back to bed," I ordered, slipping a hand around his upper bicep.

"Just go," he said quietly. "I can sit on my own."

Drawing back enough so I could look into his eyes, I gauged his reaction. "We haven't really talked yet."

"No." He agreed, knowing exactly what I meant.

"It's really fast."

"Yeah."

"I can't let that woman take those kids."

"Of course you can't. They're ours."

I shifted closer, my fingers tightening around his upper arm. "You really mean that?"

"Sincerely."

"We're getting married," I blurted out, our secret conversation suddenly loud enough for the entire room to hear.

Ivy gasped.

Braeden made a sound. "About fucking time."

"There's children present!" Rimmel reminded him.

Braeden glanced at Travis. "Hey, kid. I'm your Uncle Braeden. I say all kinds of stuff I'm not supposed to."

Travis ducked his face into Rimmel's shoulder.

"Don't scare him," I hissed in his direction.

"Trent." Drew called my attention back, his eyes bouncing between mine. I noted the surprise, the awe, the enquiry.

One side of my mouth lifted in a small smile. "We're getting married, Forrester. You aren't allowed to say no."

"Yes."

I blinked. "Come again?"

"Yes."

Wait. What? "You aren't going to argue?"

"You said I wasn't allowed to."

Holy shit. I cleared my throat and nodded once. "You aren't. You're taking my name too. I don't want *his* name on you anymore."

"Okay."

I pressed the back of my hand to Drew's forehead, checking for a fever. "You feeling okay?"

He smiled. "You're going to have to call me Mask now instead of Forrester."

I died. I literally died a little right there.

The second I came back to life, I lunged, wrapping an arm around his waist and pulling him into my body. He grimaced a little because I was too rough, but I didn't stop. I kissed him in the center of the room. In front of half the family… in front of our kids.

With a growl, I pulled back and ran a tongue over my lips, tasting him again. "I'm getting you a ring."

"Get one bigger than Rimmel's. Rome will be pissed," cracked Braeden.

Drew's eyes didn't leave mine. "Okay."

Oh, I liked when he submitted to me, when he yielded to every demand I made. If it weren't for his ribs and the people standing around, I would be all over him. I would be in him.

Easing back, I motioned to B. "Help him into bed."

"I have to go talk to them," I said of everyone in the hall.

Drew nodded.

I was getting married. To this guy. To my everything. I hadn't wanted to get married before.

But now I did.

Sweet Jesus, now I definitely did.

"I'll be right back," I said, still staring at his face, backing out of the room so I could look longer. My heart thumped erratically, my hands shook, and my stomach… My stomach felt as though I'd just been on an upside-down rollercoaster.

I reveled in all of it.

A week ago, I thought I'd lost everything. I feared my life would never be the same.

I'd been partially right. It wouldn't be the same again.

It was going to be better.

And Tango Makes Three, is the book written about the "gay" penguins and their chick. It is among the top ten most banned books in public libraries for 5 years in a row.

THIRTY-NINE

Drew

Travis's foster mother left him at the hospital. Basically, she told Gamble she couldn't handle him anymore and walked out.

The hospital got involved. Ron Gamble got involved.

The mayor showed up.

Yes. The mayor of Maryland.

Ron Gamble didn't play around. When you asked a man like him to do you a favor, you didn't get a signed letter of recommendation or twenty bucks. You got a visit from the mayor himself.

The head of the county court showed up too, along with the head of child services.

All of them had briefcases and sensible shoes.

I was lucky my ass wasn't hanging out of the back of my hospital gown.

You know who else showed up? Joey, Lorhaven, Hopper, and Arrow. The only two people who did not crowd my hospital room were Valerie and Caroline because they were with all the kids.

Child services accused us of trying to intimidate with large numbers to get our way.

But this wasn't intimidation. This was family. Our family. And it was their way of showing the powers that be exactly who was showing up for these kids.

Kids they accepted as their family within minutes of being told about them. Kids they didn't even have to know. All we said was, "They're ours," and that was it. Total acceptance. Total support.

My parents could have learned something. But you know, I wasn't sure this kind of loyalty could be learned. This went deeper than that. Deeper than blood.

After ten minutes with us, the director of child services, Colleen Blackstone, understood. We were asked question after question. I filled out papers until my hand literally cramped up and Trent took the pen from me.

We learned that Travis and baby girl's mother died of an overdose not long after giving birth. If Travis hadn't taken care of the baby, then carried her to a neighbor's house for help, it was uncertain where they might be today.

There were no fathers on record. No one to surrender parental rights. No other family. Travis had been abandoned at the hospital by the person chosen by the state to care for him. A person who had also left a visible handprint around his arm.

I'm glad he bit her. Bitch deserved it.

They were calling it an emergency placement.

When it was even slightly suggested Trent and I might have too much going on to be accepted as foster parents, every single couple in the room offered to apply.

Four couples. Four couples offered to take these kids on until we were deemed worthy.

It didn't really help much because none of them were already registered to be foster parents… but it meant everything.

And it moved all the powers that be in the room. These kids might be getting two dads, but they were also getting one hell of a support system. Many of which were well-liked, well-known celebrities.

The mayor signed off on it, and when the mayor greenlights something, that's all it takes.

Travis and the baby were placed in our temporary custody until more permanent arrangements could be made.

Permanent arrangements = finalized adoption.

It would take awhile. We had more paperwork, more interviews, classes to take, and God knew what else until we were granted permanent adoption.

I was confident it would go through. We were committed and would do whatever we needed to do to see this done. We were lucky because Ron Gamble was behind us, and he was an expert at cutting through red tape (without breaking the law). Most people wouldn't be able to foster or adopt this easily, but again, we weren't most people.

I used to not like that so much. Now? I thanked God for it.

Sometimes things had to go really dark for you to see the stars. And sometimes, when the stars came out, they aligned.

We still had a long way to go to make these kids officially ours. We had a lot of doctor visits, a lot of health checkups… and, ah, some aggression issues to work through with Travis, but that was okay.

The biggest, most important part was that they were with us. Everything else we could take on as it came.

"I need to get out of here," I said, tired of being held hostage by this bed.

"The doctor said your test results looked good, so it won't be long," Trent said, his voice a low murmur.

I liked it when he talked like that. It was like thunder rumbling overhead in the distant sky. It was somehow soothing, somehow demanding, and overall sexy.

He wasn't wearing a shirt again. He'd shed the layer and was sitting close to the bed, his feet on the mattress, with the baby nestled against his chest. She was dressed in nothing but a diaper, looking like a tiny, dark-headed angel. Skin to skin contact was the best thing at calming her down, so I guessed I was going to have to get used to seeing Trent strutting around this room without a shirt.

I didn't mind, but neither did anyone else, which was something I did mind.

"That's the only girl I will ever be okay with you holding without a shirt on," I told him.

He chuckled, and that low, rumbly voice made my skin prickle with goose bumps. "Your voice like that…" I said, sliding a casual glance at Travis, who was currently drawing all over my cast with a marker. "I like it as much as you like my scruff."

Trent lifted an eyebrow, interest clearly piqued. "Is that so?" He countered in the exact same tone.

I knew it was so he didn't disturb the baby, but fuck… that voice was disturbing me. Grabbing the blanket, I bunched it around my hips, hoping to cover the stiffening rod between my legs.

Trent smiled a cocky, knowing smile.

"Look." Travis patted on my knee. His small hand filled me with tenderness.

"What's up?" I asked, glancing down and trying not to grimace at the shit ton of black drawing all over the white cast.

"I made a road," he announced, placing the Mustang he always carried on his drawing to drive it around.

"Look at that," I said appreciatively. "Looks like that cast is useful after all."

Trent chuckled.

"Look, 'Rent," Travis called. Even though he was five, when he said T's name, it sounded more like "rent" than Trent.

We'd been given a lot of info on the kids, but not everything. I had an entire file beside the bed to read, but I hadn't gotten through it all yet. I would. It was important. But to me, it was more important that I actually paid attention to these kids. That I actually saw them and got a feel for who they were instead of letting a piece of paper tell me.

We were told that even though he was five, he had yet to go to school. When he'd been with his mother, he'd basically fended for himself and then for his sister when she was born. He didn't have any education, so he would need time and effort to catch up.

"I've seen a lot of car tracks, but that's the best one I've ever seen," Trent told him.

The baby started to fuss, and as Trent soothed her, Travis climbed off the bed, picked up her pacifier, and carried it over to her. Without any hesitation, he stuck it in her mouth and patted her back. "It's okay, baby."

Amazingly, she stopped fussing and sucked on the pacifier as he patted her back.

Trent and I looked at each other, a new kind of electricity buzzing between us. It was the layered kind. The base was familiar and exciting, but now it was coated with something a little heavier, something binding all that zinging chemistry together.

We were best friends first.

Then we were secretly in love.

Finally, we'd become lovers, which turned us into partners.

And now?

Now we were parents. Family.

"Husband," Trent whispered in that sexy-as-fuck voice.

My teeth sank into my lower lip. "Sometimes I think maybe we can read each other's thoughts."

"Not thoughts. Heart. I can read your heart." After a second's pause, he added, "Baby."

One thing about having kids? I couldn't jump him whenever I wanted to.

He smiled lazily because he knew I was thinking that too.

The door to the room swung open, and two girls who looked like our sisters but were partially hidden by bags came into the room.

"We're back!" Ivy said.

"Shh." T and I both admonished.

Ivy lowered a giant bag in her arms and grimaced. "Sorry," she mouthed.

Braeden and Romeo came in behind them, Romeo carrying a giant box and B pushing a stroller.

"Did you buy the entire town?" I asked.

"This is just the essentials." Ivy informed us. "We'll get the rest later."

"The essentials?" T replied dubiously.

"Babies need a lot." Rimmel confirmed.

"Is there pink?"

I laughed because Trent had been pretty adamant about wanting pink shit for our daughter. Something about wanting everyone to know she was a girl. The "pick a gender" hat, as he called it, was quite offensive to him, and it was also scratchy just like the lame blankets in this place.

Rimmel and Ivy started fishing through the bags, pulling out item after item, declaring how cute it all was, and making Romeo groan.

"They've been like this for hours," Braeden told us.

Rimmel brought a fuzzy pink blanket over to Trent, along with a pink hat with what looked like a giant furry ball on the top and an entire pink outfit that looked like a long dress.

"She needs pants," I declared. "She can't be wearing a skirt."

Ivy groaned. "Here we go."

Rimmel held out the garment. "It's a long gown. It will cover her feet, and look. It has little mittens on the sleeves so she can't scratch her face."

"I like it," Trent declared.

I pursed my lips. "Fine."

Trent lifted the blanket off the baby, dropping it on the floor, and Rimmel gently covered her with the furry one.

"We got a car seat, a stroller, diapers, clothes, hats, socks," Ivy listed. "Bottles and blankets."

"Basically the entire store."

Ivy stopped talking and shrugged.

Travis had quieted since they all came in and had squeezed closer to Trent, pushing right up against the side of his chair.

"We didn't just buy baby stuff, though," Rimmel said, smiling at him. "Want to see what we got you?" She held out her hand, but Travis shrank more into Trent.

Rimmel just smiled, knowing it would take some time.

Ivy carried over a bag, setting it beside Rimmel, and reached in. "We heard you like cars."

Travis nodded, glancing at the bag.

Ivy pulled out a few Matchbox cars, still in their packaging.

"We got you another Mustang. This one is blue. Like Drew's," she told him, motioning to her brother. "And we got you this bright-green car—"

"That's a Hellcat." Romeo spoke up from across the room. "That's my favorite. Gotta have one of those."

"This yellow one looks like your Aunt Joey's," Ivy explained.

"And this black one looks just like Uncle Arrow's." Rimmel pointed.

Travis stood there watching, absorbing it all like a sponge but not saying a word.

Trent put his hand on his back. "You like them?"

Travis nodded.

"They're for you. You can have them."

Travis glanced at Trent, and I swear every time he did that, my heart skipped a beat. The way that boy looked at him, like Trent was his rock and he trusted him totally, undid me.

Rimmel held out one of the cars, but Travis took a tentative step forward and reached for the blue Mustang in Ivy's hand.

See? He was my son. Clearly.

"Bring that over here. I want to see it," I told him.

He brought it over and climbed on the bed, holding it out for me to open. Rimmel laid a few others nearby so I could open those too.

"We got him some clothes and a pair of shoes too," Ivy said.

"Thanks," Trent told her.

The clothes he had on were too small, and I was pretty sure they were the same ones he'd had on the day I met him. It turned my stomach, and my gut reaction was to rush out and buy everything. To give him everything I knew he'd never had.

I had to rein it in, though. He would have everything he needed. And then some. But overwhelming him with stuff was not what we wanted to do.

First, we wanted to love him.

"Try that one out on the track," I said, handing him the new car. Still clutching the old Mustang in his other hand, he crawled down the bed to try out the new one.

"I smell fries," I announced, suddenly getting a whiff of my most favorite food.

Trent chuckled.

Braeden reached into the stroller and pulled out a white paper bag and waved it around.

I groaned. Oh my God, something that actually tasted good.

Braeden handed them over, and I stuck my face into the top, inhaling.

Like alcohol to an alcoholic.

"Oh, I missed you," I whispered to the still-hot, salty fried goodness.

"You need a moment alone with those?" B teased.

I pulled one out, groaning again when I wrapped my fingers around it and slid it in my mouth. I chewed appreciatively, practically melting against the bed. "I need ketchup."

"It's in the bag," Romeo mused.

Reaching into the bag once more, I noticed little man watching me.

"You like fries? They're my favorite."

He nodded.

Instead of grabbing a packet of ketchup, I pulled out the container of fries and held them out to him.

"Am I hallucinating?" Braeden declared, rubbing over his eyes like a damn drama queen. "Is that fry monster actually offering to share?"

Travis glanced at Braeden, then between me and the fries.

"Here," I said again, holding them closer. "I'll always share with you."

Travis tugged the fries into his lap.

"We actually got food for all of you," Ivy said, hurrying to grab the rest.

"Do you like chicken nuggets? Or a hamburger?"

Travis shoved a fry into his mouth and nodded.

Trent laughed. "Guess he likes both."

Ivy opened a box of nuggets while Rimmel unwrapped a burger. The girls fussed around, spreading the food out in front of him like a feast. This time, he wasn't so shy. He started eating like no one had fed him in days.

I exchanged a look with Trent, both of us clearly filled with sadness, anger, and regret.

"Can't have all that without a milkshake," Braeden announced, handing him a cup with a fat straw sticking out. "You like ice cream?"

Travis nodded, his eyes wide.

My heart turned over again when his hands wrapped around the cup and he smiled at B.

"Good man," B said, pleased, and ruffled his already messy hair.

Rimmel produced another bag of fries, setting it in my lap.

"Bless you," I said but didn't dig in. The way Trav was plowing through the food, I was afraid to eat them. He might want them too.

"Want me to hold her so you can eat?" Rimmel offered to Trent.

He gazed down at the baby asleep against his chest. Whenever he looked at her, his entire face softened. "Nah."

"Did you give her a name yet?"

I made a sound. I hadn't even thought of that yet.

To Travis, I said, "Did you give your sister a name?"

"Baby," he said around the straw between his lips.

That really wasn't much help.

"I have one." Trent informed the room.

Everyone looked at him. Except for Travis. He kept eating.

"You have a name?" I asked.

He nodded, a small smile playing on his lips.

"Well, let's hear it." Braeden pressed.

Trent's eyes stayed on my face, the small smile still lifting his lips when he spoke. "Andy."

It took a second to realize. When I did, emotion clogged my throat.

"You mean like Andy after Andrew?" Rimmel asked, then sighed.

"After Drew." He confirmed. "After her father."

I swallowed down the lump in my throat. "Isn't that a boy name?"

"It can be a girl name," Ivy announced. "It's trendy. Spell it with an 'I' at the end, and I think it's perfect."

"Andi Mask," I echoed, feeling emotion swell inside me again. Unable to keep my eyes away, I put them on Trent. He wanted to name our daughter after me.

My first name. His last name. "Part of you and part of me," I whispered.

"Part of us," he whispered back.

Across the room, Rimmel sniffled and climbed in Romeo's lap to hide her face.

All I could do was nod. Nod and fight back the tears rushing into my eyes.

"What do you think, Trav?" Trent asked. "How about we call your sister Andi?"

"Okay," he said, taking the blue Mustang and driving it across my leg.

And just like that, our daughter had a name.

FORTY

Trent

In a split second. That's how fast life can change.

One minute, Drew and I were happy and in love, and I wouldn't have changed a thing. The next, I stood helplessly on the sidelines and watched his car soar through the air and smash into a concrete wall.

There is no warning. There are no rules.

Life gives. Death takes.

We get no say in the time we're allowed. But we do get a say in how we spend it.

I protected us too much. Something I never would have admitted or even realized before all of this happened. The last thing I ever wanted was to rock the boat as we sailed along. I didn't dare ask for more, because what we had was already better than I thought I'd ever have.

Did I want to get married? Deep down, hell yes. But fear held me back. Marriage was change. Marriage might burst the bubble we lived in.

It burst anyway.

Thank God.

Yes. Thank fucking God. I didn't mess with perfection, but perfection? It came for me. It challenged literally everything. My life, my beliefs, my heart.

Turned out the perfection I thought we had was only preventing us from everything we deserved.

I was done. Done hiding in plain sight. That's exactly what we'd been doing. Announcing to the world our relationship, then asking everyone to respect it. Being careful not to hold hands or show too much affection in public. Trying to shield Drew from the media coverage when they caught our moments anyway.

I'd been open but closed off. Not in the closet… Maybe just standing in front of it.

I never apologized for being gay, for loving Drew. But looking back, sometimes it sort of felt like I was asking permission.

Fuck that. My heart didn't need permission to love someone. It just did it without trying. Why should I put restraints on something so pure? On love that blossomed in the middle of a fire? I hated it when people tried to limit love, tried to label family.

But I was guilty of it too. I was terrified our love was fragile and, if pressured too much, we might shatter.

We wouldn't. Not ever.

Feeling a strange tugging sensation on my sock, I glanced down. Travis had the marker back in his hand, but instead of drawing on Drew's cast, he had moved to my foot where it was propped up on Drew's bed.

"What're you doing there, little man?"

"I ran out of road," he said, glancing up. He had a smudge of black marker on his cheek and ketchup on his lip.

I shrugged. "All right. Draw away."

"That's a permanent marker." Ivy warned.

I shrugged.

Andi made a small sound, and I glanced down. My heart swelled every time I looked at her, and this time was no different. She was sleeping more peacefully than I'd seen, and the color in her cheeks seemed much better.

Or maybe it was because she had on a pink hat and was covered with a pink blanket.

Either way, she looked cute as hell.

At my feet, there was a bit of commotion, and Drew made a startled sound. My stare flew to the bed where he'd knocked over the milkshake and the lid popped off. What was left in the cup was now all over the bed.

"Oh no," Ivy said lightly, standing up from where she sat.

Travis scurried over the side of the mattress and ducked under the bed.

"It's okay," Drew told him. "It was just an accident."

Travis wrapped his arms over his head like a shield and scooted farther away. Ivy grabbed some napkins to clean up the mess, and Drew frowned when Travis stayed hidden.

Rising carefully, I passed Andi to Drew, pausing long enough to make sure she was covered before ducking to peer under the bed.

"You hiding 'cause you think you're in trouble?"

Under the protection of his arms, his head bobbed.

My stomach twisted, thinking about what his life had been like up until this point. How he managed to survive and adapt. How he managed to have the heart I knew he did. Had he been punished for spilling things before? Yelled at? Physically hurt?

Swallowing past the lump in my throat, I sat on the floor.

"We aren't mad," I said softly. "You aren't in trouble."

He didn't move or acknowledge what I said.

"It's all cleaned up!" Ivy announced from up top.

"See? No harm, no foul," I remarked. "Drew needed to take a shower anyway. Dude smells."

I thought I heard a little giggle, but I wasn't sure.

"I can't even argue," Drew muttered, and I grinned.

"Why don't you come out from under there?" I coaxed.

Travis shook his head.

"All right." I allowed. "I'll sit down here with you, then." Reaching up, I grabbed the blue Mustang lying on the mattress and pushed it under the bed. "Just come out when you're ready."

A few minutes later, I saw his hand close around the car and pull it into his lap.

Drew gave me a worried look, but I shook my head slightly and smiled.

Romeo and Braeden started talking about football. Rimmel and Ivy made more shopping lists, and I just waited.

A little while later, Travis crawled from under the bed into my lap.

"Are you taking me back to that mean lady?" The innocent, resigned question was like a sucker punch right to my gut.

Stricken, it took me a minute to pull my shit together before I could answer. Tugging him a little closer into my lap, tucking my arms around him, I said, "Never. You don't have to see her again."

"Are you taking my sister away?"

A low sound ripped from my throat. I felt Drew's stare, and we exchanged a look.

"I was thinking that you and your sister might like to come live with me and Drew."

"At the hospital?"

A few low laughs bounced around the room.

"No way. This place sucks." I blanched. "I mean, it's not too fun here." Rubbing a hand up his back, I continued. "We have a big house where you can have your own room. Andi too. We have a big yard and a dog named French Fry. Do you like dogs?"

He shrugged.

"He drools a lot," I explained.

"And right across the yard, Aunt Rimmel, Uncle Romeo, Aunt Ivy, and Uncle Braeden live. They have a bunch of kids around your age, so you'll have people to play with."

"Do they have a dog too?" he asked.

Braeden groaned, and Rimmel laughed. "Oh, I have lots of dogs! And a cat too. They'll love you."

Travis didn't say anything, and I kinda felt like I was failing at life. I had no idea what I was doing. What to say. Words seemed trivial right now. This kid had been let down by everyone in his life. He had no reason to trust us. Of course, he was afraid we'd abandon him too.

Rotating so I could lean against the bed, I dipped my head back and sighed.

"I know you've had a rough life. You've seen stuff no one should ever see. But I'm proud of you. Even though things were hard and the grown-ups around you were mean, you're still a good boy, and you take real good care of your sister. You're the best big brother I've ever met. I know we just met and I know Drew looks like Bigfoot with that beard on his face, but we love you. All of us. You don't have to love us back. We'll love you anyway. And we don't care if you spill milkshakes or make messes. That's what love is, okay? It's loving someone all the time, even when it's hard. Just how you love your sister."

Someone sniffled somewhere in the room, but I didn't look up. I stayed focused on the boy in my lap and hoped he understood even some of what I was trying to say.

"When I was little like you, my dad left, and when I told my mom I loved Drew, she left too."

He looked up. "Why?"

"'Cause she wanted me to love a girl and not a boy. I didn't like being alone," I told him.

"T," Drew rasped, and I felt his hand in my hair as my head leaned against the bed.

"I don't want you and Andi to be alone either. So maybe if you let me… maybe I can be your… dad. Andi's too."

Travis stared at the car in his hand, and my heart felt like it was going to implode inside my chest. Drew's fingers knotted in my hair, and then suddenly, he was leaning over the side of the bed, staring down at both of us.

"I want to be your and Andi's dad too."

"Two dads?" Travis asked, glancing up.

"Well, I'm not answering to mom," Drew muttered. "Even if I am the wife."

A strangled laugh ripped from my throat. What the fuck was he talking about?

"It's kinda unconventional," I told Travis. "Having two dads. But it's better than having one, right?" Unable to resist, I ruffled his hair. After a minute, I said, "We're the kind of dads who don't leave."

"You don't have to call us dad," Drew said, glancing at me. "You can call us whatever you want."

"Maybe just think about it," I said after a few minutes of me praying to God I didn't just say a bunch of too much too soon. "Want to play cars?" I asked, starting to shift so I could stand, but I was pushed back.

Suddenly, Travis wrapped his thin arms around me for a hug. Hesitating only for a second, I wrapped mine around him, hugging him close. My head dropped against the mattress again, chin tilting up to find Drew.

He was still close, staring down with soft eyes.

I love you, he told me without words.

I love you, I told him back.

Clearing my throat, I looked down at Trav. "You have me and Drew now, okay? We love you."

"The rest of us too," Rimmel called out.

"The rest of them too." I agreed.

Travis nodded, and something inside me eased. I knew it would take time, but this was a really good start.

FORTY-ONE

Drew

I couldn't remember the last time I showered. Like for real. It had been awhile. But with the stitches out of my head and my need to get back to feeling some kind of normal, I was pretty desperate.

Trent slid through the door, shutting it firmly behind him and leaning against the wood, and looked at me. "Hi."

My stomach did a little flip. Nerves and excitement danced along my extremities, making me feel unsteady on my already wobbly limbs. It felt like years since we'd been alone. Years since he touched me without anyone else looking.

God, I wanted him.

Everything about him.

I'd always loved Trent, but I swear, after all of this, I loved him even more. It was the most powerful thing I'd ever experienced. He was my purpose and my reason all rolled into one. He was my strength and my weakness, the only person in this world I couldn't live without.

"Don't look at me like that." He warned, his voice dropping into that sexy, low tone.

My tongue ran over my front teeth. "Like what?"

"Like you are more than willing to let me do bad things to you."

"I am."

As he prowled away from the door, the short distance between us closed. Maybe it was the size of the bathroom. Maybe it was because I'd lost so much weight, but suddenly, he seemed much bigger to me, like a wolf with total ability to swallow me whole.

"You're kinda different." The words fell out like the filter on my tongue had snapped. Like I was suddenly thirteen and couldn't remember my self-control.

"So are you," he rumbled, reaching around to tug at the tie holding the gown around my neck.

Reaching up, I caught his hand, stilling his action. "Is that okay?"

Sliding his arm around my waist, he backed us into the wall, taking all of my weight on his one arm. His other hand flattened on the wall beside my face, and he leaned in, owning his space.

Hell, owning mine too.

He moved, predatory and slow, giving me ample time to know he was coming, but sweet Lord, I wasn't prepared. I was pretty sure he could feel the pounding of my heart against his chest when my eyes fluttered closed and I surrendered to him as if I hadn't already done so the second he stepped into this room.

Before his lips claimed mine, he stopped, held still, and spoke. "You hear me complaining?" Then he abolished the slim space remaining between us.

The tightening fingertips at the small of my back torched my skin. His lips took command, and I swear my eyes rolled back in my head. His tongue was persistent, stroking across mine like a massage, twisting into every place as though he were taking inventory that I was still all here.

My head fell against the wall, chin tilting up to offer complete access as Trent ravaged me from the inside out. His body buffered mine, making sure I was completely consumed by nothing but him, and consume me he did.

Shaking hands came up to grip his shoulders, and I kissed him back until my head was woozy and all I could do was hum with desire.

Unlatching our lips, I let my chin drop as my chest heaved. Trent, still steady as a rock, pressed a tender kiss to my forehead.

Practically melting into his body, I pushed closer so he could wrap himself around me.

"I'm not hurting you, am I?" he whispered.

Fisting my hand in his shirt so he couldn't go anywhere, I replied, "No."

He held me for long moments, my body quivering against his, my cock twitching between us. One of his hands trailed a path down my back, slipping between the edges of the gown, cupping my ass.

Then he gave it a pat and pulled back.

Completely taken off guard, I blinked and nearly fell onto the ass he was still supposed to be touching.

"Whoa." Trent chuckled, anchoring an arm around me for support while reaching into the shower to turn on the spray. "Let's get you cleaned up."

I delivered a squinty-eyed glare, hoping to convey my unhappiness at this turn of events.

"You want me to help you, don't you?" he asked, untying the gown.

I made a sound. Of course I did.

Once I was naked, my cast was covered by some handy thing Patrick gave T, and the bandages covering my healing wounds were all removed, Trent reached for his own clothes, peeling them off in record time.

The shower had one of those handheld showerheads, and the water was warm as Trent directed it over my body. A low sound vibrated my throat in appreciation of the warmth of the water.

"Watch your leg," he cautioned, making sure to angle the spray away from the covered cast.

With almost all of my weight on one leg, I had to use him as support. My muscles were still weak, my body still trying to recover from the coma it had been trapped in for five days.

"You doing okay?" His voice was low because he was so close.

"I missed you." There I went again, blurting out the first thing that came to mind, not even thinking at all.

"Ah, fuck, baby," he swore. "I missed you too."

The spray went down the side of my hip, rushing down my leg and over my toes when he swooped in to kiss me again. The sensation of his body rippling against mine, of his muscles moving beneath his skin, was my aphrodisiac, and I found myself trying to climb up his body like he was a tree and my leg wasn't broken.

A low, pleased laugh filled the small shower when he pulled back, reaching to steady me.

But it wasn't funny, and I didn't care if only one of my legs was working. "I'm hungry, T. I'm so fucking hungry."

All the amusement on his face washed right down the drain in the center of the floor, and he reached around to slide the faucet into the mount on the wall.

Barely a heartbeat later, I was off my feet, my weight no longer my own to bear. Wrapping my thighs around his waist, I groaned low when my hard cock was pinned between our bodies. The muscles in his shoulders bulged and flexed as he held me, and I rubbed my fingers over the ridges, marveling at how strong he was.

"I'm sorry," I said suddenly, the words ripping out of some buried place inside me.

Trent glanced up, some of the passion in his eyes making way for concern. "For what?"

"I've always been yours… but I've never quite given in."

The alpha inside him came alive, heat and fierceness lighting his eyes, making them glitter with gold.

"You've always been enough for me, Drew." The tenderness in his voice was a direct contrast to the ownership in his eyes.

How a single man could embody so many compelling qualities was something I might wonder about forever.

"I can be more," I whispered, gripping the back of his head. "I want to be more."

His teeth sank into my lower lip, nibbling almost to the point of pain before he sucked the swollen flesh between his lips to soothe what he'd just done with his tongue. Saying I had butterflies in my stomach would be a gross understatement. My body felt like an exposed electric wire, like I was close to shorting out because my circuits were being overloaded.

He kept kissing. He kept biting, then licking.

My hips rocked against his middle, pushing my swollen head against him. Every time he breathed deep, his stomach would brush over the most sensitive spot just below my tip and I would shudder.

If he kept it up, I would fucking come without him even having to touch me. Without a single stroke to my dick.

"I should have surrendered to you years ago." I panted, leaning back to stare into his glittering eyes. "I'm submitting now, Trent. Take everything. *Please* just fucking take it."

"You do this *here*? *Now*?" he growled, diving into the side of my neck. When his teeth slid over my collarbone, my body arched into him. "Don't tempt me, Mask. Don't fucking tempt me to do something I shouldn't."

Mask.

Not Forrester. But Mask.

His.

He eased me against the wall, using his body to pin mine. The leg with the cast fell to the side, able to rest on top of a seat inside the stall.

Running my hands up his biceps and over his shoulders, I summoned him with my eyes, not giving a shit where we were or what condition my body was in, and dared him to let go of his self-control.

"I don't want to hurt you," was all he said.

"You won't."

"You have to be quiet."

Excitement skittered along my spine. "Whatever you say."

His hand slid between our bodies. The centers of his eyes expanded twice their size. The second his hand wrapped around my throbbing dick, I opened my mouth to groan, and he pinned me with a warning stare.

"If you make noise, I'll stop."

My teeth sank into my lip, forcing any groans of pleasure silent.

His hand started stroking, making my ab muscles tremble. The second his lips came back to mine, his fingers slid along my crack and rubbed over my ass.

Thickly, I swallowed and melted against the wall.

Lifting his face, Trent glanced down to make sure my cast leg was out of the way and then slid a glance to the healing wounds on my chest.

Grabbing his chin, I forced his face back up, back to my eyes where his locked and held.

His finger penetrated me while his stare devoured me alive. I wasn't sure which infiltrated me more, his stare or his fingers.

"Look at me," he whispered. "Only at me."

I nodded, obedient even as my eyes started to drift closed.

"Mask." He summoned, making my eyelids lift. "Right here," he said, sinking deeper into my body.

Pleasure and pain melded together, creating a hot-and-cold sensation all over my body. The moment I felt a twinge of pain, pleasure was right behind to soothe it.

Trent stared at me, drilling a hole right through my soul, using it to siphon out any remaining part of me he didn't yet own.

"You sure?" he asked, his voice barely audible over the spray of the water.

I nodded, wiggling a little against his fingers.

Easing out of me, he reached around, wetting his hand under the spray and then caressing my ass one more time. Shuddering, I wiggled impatiently, wanting to feel the hardest part of him claiming its rightful place.

"I don't have any lube." He reminded me again.

I pushed my still-rock-hard erection against his middle and rubbed, having to bite down on my lip to keep from making sound.

His hands grasped my hips. The strength and sureness in his grip turned me on all over again. Without another pause, he thrust up.

My body gave way. The first thrust was uncomfortable, but the tremble I suddenly felt in his body turned that little prick of pain into unsurmountable pleasure.

His hips thrust again, pushing a little deeper as my body stretched around him.

I know I was supposed to look at him, but I couldn't hold myself up anymore. I folded over, collapsing against his body, my chin resting on his shoulder. Clinging to him in a way I never had before, my lips latched onto the top of his shoulder and started to suck.

Grasping my hips, he lifted my body, sliding me up and down along his dick, making me suck harder so I wouldn't break his demand of silence.

Ripples of pleasure stole over everything else, making me feel like I was floating as I rose higher and higher on a narrow edge. Between us, my dick throbbed, making my hips rotate as though suddenly I wanted to drive.

Trent wrapped his hand around my cock and pumped, at the very same moment tilting his hips and pushing deep.

I fell back against the wall, his hand there to soften the hit.

"Baby," he murmured, sex dripping from his vocal cords.

Peeling my eyes opened, I smiled.

"You're supposed to be looking at me."

He jacked my rod and picked up the pace in fucking me. Higher and higher I went. The pressure he delivered was unrelenting until finally, blissfully, I came undone. Desire pulsed out of me, coating both our stomachs.

My eyes tried to slip closed, but he made a sound, snapping them back up. He watched me while I came. He watched me fall apart while he felt me explode across his skin.

Vulnerability curled my toes and made my stomach ache, but I let him see. I let him see just how much he owned me.

Once I was milked dry, his still-blazing stare dropped to my lips.

I leaned forward and kissed him, sweeping my tongue over his, wiggling down on his rod. I felt his nostrils flare. Inside me, his dick pulsed.

Pulling back, I anchored both hands against his shoulders and leaned my weight into the wall.

Trent started moving, pulling out and plunging in with a satisfied, voracious glint in his stare. I felt him start to come before it even burned in his eyes. I felt the bolt of energy surge through his body and into mine.

He went stiff, both hands slamming against the wall on either side of my head. His breathing was heavy, and the aftershocks of his orgasm lasted for a while.

When he finally looked up, it was with an almost drunk air, a lazy smile tugging at the lower half of his face.

"You were hungry too," I murmured.

"Starved, baby. I was fucking starving."

Taking his face, I leaned forward and kissed him sweetly. "I'll do a better job of keeping you fed from now on."

He chuckled, then slowly slid out of me. "Did I hurt you?"

"Good thing I have crutches. Might not be able to walk after that."

He blanched.

I pressed my lips together to keep from laughing. He told me to be quiet… I was obedient.

"I'm kidding, frat boy," I finally said, putting him out of his misery. "I mean, I know this is shitty timing and a less-than-desirable locale, but that was fucking hot."

He made a gruff sound. "It sure as hell was."

Picking me up, Trent sat me on the edge of the seat my foot had been resting on. "The water is going to go cold," he said, grabbing the faucet and the soap Ivy bought.

He washed me with a tenderness someone might not realize he had if they'd seen the way he'd gone at me just moments ago. Once I was clean and completely rinsed, he quickly showered himself off and shut off the water.

"You doing okay?" he asked, grabbing a towel. It wasn't a crappy hospital towel either. He'd had Ivy buy a big soft one. "How are you feeling?"

The towel was so big he was able to wrap it around me and tuck the ends together around my neck.

"I'm okay."

"I want the truth, Mask," he demanded, hard. "I want to know even if your pinky hurts."

"I like when you call me that."

Trent smiled. "I like saying it."

He dried me off in silence. The feel of his hands and the towel on my body was better than any pain pill could ever be. Once I was dry, with a pair of boxers and sweat shorts pulled on, he reached for my left hand.

Lifting it, he stared down, gently kissing the empty ring finger. "I want to see my ring on your finger."

"What changed your mind?"

He looked up.

"What changed your mind about wanting to get married? The kids?"

A dark look crossed his features, and my back hit the wall. Invading my personal space once again, his hands caged me in. "Now see here," he intoned forcefully but utterly quiet. I couldn't help it. A little thrill shot up my spine. "I'm marrying you for you and you alone. Yes, it will make it easier for us to adopt our kids, and yes, it will legally bind you to me."

"Who's the possessive one now?" I teased.

"I am." He confirmed. "No more being polite about it. No more hiding inside a bubble I build around us."

"T," I said, my brow furrowing. Is that what he thought we'd been doing? Hiding?

"I'll still shield you." He went on. "I'll shield you and my kids with everything I got... You said I was different. That's the difference."

I furrowed my brow, trying to understand.

"I'm not going to shield you quietly anymore. I won't contain everything we have to keep the blowback to a minimum. The rest of the world can take a nice long look if they're so inclined. They don't have to like it. Or even respect it. But they'll damn well keep their opinions away from us."

"Trent." I cupped the side of his face.

He pushed farther into my palm. "I spent a week... a week that felt like half my lifetime, wondering if I'd ever see those blue eyes again. I spent a week pacing the hall, being kept away from you because I'd always been too polite. Maybe a little too understanding. Fuck that. People can understand this: I don't answer to them. I regretted so much while you were out, Drew. All the times I wanted to hold your hand when we were out but didn't. All the times we ran back home to kiss and touch, for me to say out loud how much I love you. I'm not doing it anymore. I won't. I'll touch you. I'll kiss you. Fuck, I'll grab your ass and put my tongue in your mouth in the middle of Target if I feel like it."

"You never go to Target, T."

"Maybe I will now," he said, gruff. "I got kids that need stuff."

I suppressed a laugh. Oh my God. I lived this. Not loved (though, that too). I *lived* it. This was why I ran from death. This was why I rushed back into my mostly lifeless body and made my way back to him.

This is why the blood that was his and mine sang in my veins.

"I won't back down. I'm taking what I want. All of it. And most of all, what I want is you."

"I think death was good for us," I said, feeling so much pride swell my chest. Pride for him. For us.

"Shut your dirty mouth," he growled and kissed me until my eyes crossed. "Don't ever think about doing this shit to me again, Drew. I mean it. I won't survive."

"Yes, you will," I said gently. "We have two kids who look at you like you're the sun and moon."

His eyes turned emotional. "I can't raise them without you."

"Hey," I crooned, pulling him close. "I know. I'm not going anywhere." Kissing the side of his neck, I pulled back so I could look into his eyes.

"I won't back down either, okay? I won't let you bear it all anymore. I'm sorry it took all this for me to stand up to my parents. I'm sorry I didn't surrender completely…" I thought a moment, realizing. "I think holding back even just a little was my way of trying to protect you."

He nodded, understanding in his eyes. Of course Trent understood. He always did. "I know, baby. I know."

"I want to get married," I confessed.

"We will. Soon. I want to be bound to you in every way possible."

After T was dressed, he kneeled in front of me to re-cover the wound on my side. Gently leaning forward, he kissed the large white bandage, eyes looking up my body. "Does it still hurt?"

"A little," I admitted.

Standing up, he snagged my shirt off the counter.

I shook my head. "I want your shirt."

When it was in place, I watched him pull on mine and nearly got a stiffy just seeing it cling to his chest.

"Don't look at me like that." He warned.

"It's going to be a lot harder to get time alone now that we have kids," I said, partially forlorn.

He came back, covering my body with his. "Don't you worry about that, Mask. I'll always have time for you."

Out in the room, our very loud, very demanding daughter started to cry.

Both of us smiled. "How about you feed her this time, and I'll try and convince Trav to take a shower and put on the new clothes Ivy got him?"

I nodded, and he turned to leave.

I reached out, grabbing the back of his shirt and stopping him from going. Suddenly, I wasn't ready to let him go yet. I wanted just another minute. No, just another second alone with my everything.

He came back around, gaze searching mine.

"Thank you for naming our daughter after me."

"You know what?" Trent said, shuffling close again.

I loved it when he crowded me. I loved it when his arms hooked around my waist and his palms settled on my ass.

"What?" I practically crooned.

"If you hadn't gotten into that accident, if you hadn't landed in this hospital, we might never have met our kids. As shitty as this all has been, we got those kids out of it."

I nodded. "You're right."

"What's meant to be will always find a way," Trent murmured, brushing a kiss over my ear. "We weren't meant to stay in that holding pattern, baby. We were meant for this. For marriage, for kids, for *life*."

There was a small knock on the door. "'Rent!" Travis called. "Andi won't stop crying!"

"Dad's coming!" I called out, giving T a little pat on the ass to go.

Trent slid his arm around me to help me walk and opened the door. "Mom too," he told Travis, who was standing there waiting.

"Who you calling mom?" I guffawed, horrified.

"What do you think, Trav?" Trent reached down to tickle his middle. "You think Drew would make a good mom?"

Travis laughed, but I sure as hell didn't. "That's not even funny," I muttered.

"It's kinda funny," Braeden cracked.

Andi's cries turned a little more insistent, and all the joking stopped. Settling back on the bed, I pulled my shirt off so I could hold her against my chest, and Travis brought me a bottle he'd already gotten out for her.

Romeo appeared at my side, and I glanced up, doing a doubletake. He was the one cradling her in his arms. His shirt was missing too.

"Four nurses came in here to see Rome without a shirt." Braeden snickered. "Five if you count Patrick."

I raised an eyebrow, and Romeo rolled his eyes. But then amusement sparked in their blue depths. "Rim chased them all out."

She made a rude sound. "This place is ridiculous."

"The nurses here are horny as hell." I agreed, feeling her irritation.

Gently, Romeo handed over Andi. Before pulling back, he adjusted the hat on her tiny head. "I like her," he announced.

"The alpha has spoken," Braeden declared.

I looked at Trent. The only alpha I saw in this room was him.

I mean, seriously, not to be giving TMI and all, but my ass still trembled from his assault.

As if he knew, Trent looked up from Travis and winked.

FORTY-TWO

Trent

Two months later...

Steady rain pounded everything under the gray, cloud-heavy sky, turning what was previously a sunny summer day into the kind that made you want to hole up with a blanket and a beer and Netflix and chill.

"Ivy is probably freaking out," I murmured as I upped the speed on the windshield wipers.

Drew moaned. "Seriously, this shit better stop."

The sound of raindrops pelting the roof of the Infiniti QX80 I was driving abruptly halted when I drove under a thick canopy of trees leading across the property to the compound.

We'd been on the other side of the state for so long after Drew's accident that I'd grown homesick for this place. For the privacy, the trees, and our space. We'd been home a few weeks now, but I was still so grateful to be back.

Drew sighed, reclining a little farther into the passenger seat.

Reaching across, I put a hand on his upper thigh, gently squeezing. "PT wear you out today?"

He grunted. "It's getting easier."

He started physical therapy right before he was discharged from the hospital and had been going three times a week since. For the first month, he'd done it down there and we'd stayed at the apartment. But as soon as Andi was cleared for travel and she and Drew both were strong enough, we practically hightailed it back home.

Now he did his PT here and still had a little ways to go.

"I want this damn cast off."

"I know." I pacified, patting his thigh.

Technically, his cast was off. But I wasn't going to point that out. The boot he had to wear in place of the original cast was just as annoying. But at least this could come off when he showered.

And for other activities… *Know what I mean?* *wink*

"I'm not wearing it tomorrow." He grumped some more, folding his arms over his chest like a petulant child.

"Guess you'll just have to lean on me."

I felt his blue eyes, and I glanced away from the road to meet his gaze for long seconds. The air around us instantly electrified. "Guess so."

Having kids underfoot nearly twenty-four-seven didn't put a damper on our sex life. If anything, seeing him with our kids made me want him even more.

Rain started pelting the roof again, and the main house on the property came into view. There were several cars and vans parked out front, and I wanted to turn the car back around and drive away from the chaos.

"Remind me why we didn't just elope," I muttered.

"Because Ivy would have killed us," Drew replied.

"Right."

Instead of driving on by toward our house, I maneuvered around the vans to park as close to the front door as I could.

"Think Trav is okay?" Drew asked, gazing at the front door.

Andi and Travis were settling into the family better than I expected. Well, not better. I knew from the minute I saw them they were part of this family. What I meant was faster. They were settling in faster than I'd hoped.

We were a big family that didn't give each other a lot of space, and we worried at first it would be too much, especially for Travis, who was wary of all people.

There were obviously some tough moments, and the kid was stubborn as hell. If he didn't want to do something, it could easily turn into WW3 up in the house. I'd learned very quickly to pick my battles with him. It was actually a tip we'd gotten from the counselor who met with him every week.

We'd also learned a lot of stuff from some of the classes we had to take as part of the fostering-to-adopt program.

Overall, though, that boy did me proud. He warmed up to the family, and now he ran around with the other kids as though he'd been with them since he was born.

I give our brothers and sisters a lot of credit for that too. They were very hands on with our kids, and they were understanding that sometimes Travis needed a little extra attention.

"I think they would have called if he wasn't," I replied, gazing at the house.

With the wedding set for tomorrow, there were people Ivy had hired everywhere. I'd almost had someone else take Drew to PT, but Rimmel swore she'd keep an eye on Travis and call right away if he was having a problem with the strangers.

"Stay there," I told Drew, preparing to step into the rain. "I'll come around."

"It's just water," he said, reaching for the handle.

"Mask," I intoned, commanding his attention.

There'd been no transition, no learning curve to him answering when I called him Mask. It was instant, as if that had always been his name.

When he turned back, I was leaning over the center console, crowding his space. "Stay put until I come around."

He gave a slight nod, letting his hand fall back into his lap.

My stare dropped to his lips, which parted almost instantly, the perfect invitation. Holding his stare, I leaned in closer, kissing him fully on the mouth, making sure our lips were good and melted together but not closing my eyes.

"Blue is my favorite color," I rasped when I finally pulled back.

His tongue ran over his lower lip, licking what was left of me into his mouth.

Later. I promised myself.

I didn't flinch when the rain splattered my shoulders and weighed down my hair. Jogging around the matte gray SUV, I pulled open the passenger door, leaning in to where my almost husband waited.

He'd left his seatbelt clasped.

Smiling faintly, I leaned around, making sure my hand brushed fully over his crotch on my way to undo it for him. The belt retracted automatically, but me?

I stayed where I was.

Rain pelted the part of me still outside the car, but inside, we were dry. The pattering sound, along with the cloudy lightning, set an intimate atmosphere.

When I turned my face just a fraction, our noses nearly bumped.

"Tomorrow's been a long time coming," he murmured, rubbing a hand across my freshly shaven jaw.

"I would have waited longer." The time I'd wait for him was infinite.

Pushing off the seat, he kissed me this time.

Muffled sounds from somewhere nearby were just that… muffled. All my senses were consumed by the man whose lips were on mine.

"Trent," Drew said, pulling back from the kiss.

"Hm?" I said, blinking open my eyes.

"Dad!" someone yelled. "Dad!"

"That's not one of ours," I said, leaning back for more of his lips.

Drew's hand covered my shoulder, stopping me from continuing forward. "Yes, T. Yes. It is."

"Dad!"

Recognition slammed into me, and I jerked back, hitting my head on the doorframe as I spun around.

Travis was standing on the front porch. He was jumping up and down, a phone in his hand. But it wasn't the way he looked or even the happy smile on his face.

It was what he was yelling.

"Travis," I called out, my heart hammering heavily against my ribs.

The smile on his face got bigger, and then he was running down the steps, rushing through the rain, eyes focused solely on me.

"Dad! You're home!"

A strangled sound nearly choked me.

His feet splashed over the driveway, and I barely had time to brace myself for the way he launched himself at me.

Catching him, I lifted, and his legs went around my waist. "I've been waiting for you to get here."

"Is something wrong?" I asked, pushing through the veil of emotion pulling me deep as concern took over.

"I caught this shiny Pokémon!" He held up the cell, showing me the screen with some Pokémon character that apparently was really important in the center.

Did I mention this kid loved Pokémon?

He was obsessed.

I stared between him and the phone, trying to catch up to what he was saying. The entire time, rain fell splashing us both.

I was glad for the rain. Glad because it disguised my tears.

"Did you call me dad?" I whispered.

He nodded, a shy glimmer coming into his eyes. "But you didn't answer."

My heart stumbled. "I'm sorry, bud. I didn't know it was you. You've never called—" I paused, trying not to make this a thing.

But holy fucking shit, this was a thing.

A *big* fucking thing.

"You've never called me dad before."

"You said I could," Travis said, lowering his eyes.

"Hey, hey," I hurried to say, taking his little chin in my hand. When he looked at me, I smiled. "It makes me so happy when you call me that."

"Really?"

Rain slid between my lips as I nodded. "I'll always answer from now on, okay?"

Travis nodded. Then he held up the phone again. "Look!"

I blinked, trying so hard to focus on that fucking creature he was so proud of, but oh my God, I couldn't. All I could do was stand there and hold my son.

My son who'd just called me dad.

Abruptly, I rotated, wanting to share this moment with Drew. He was right there. He'd stood from the car and was right behind us, rain slicking his hair and clinging to the beard he'd yet to shave.

"Did you hear?" I whispered.

He nodded, eyes filled with emotion, and I wondered if some of the rain on his face was actually tears too.

"Dad!" Travis yelled again.

"What?" I said, my voice a little raspy.

"Not you," Travis said, pointing right at Drew. "My other dad."

Drew tossed out a hand, grabbing the top of the door to steady himself. A whole host of emotions played across his face, and I reveled in it.

It was the best movie I ever watched. This moment, I knew, would become one of my greatest memories.

Drew's throat worked, and he nodded. "Yeah?"

"Look! I caught this!"

His eyes glanced at the screen but then back to our son's face. "That thing lives in my phone now?" he asked, making a face.

Travis nodded. "Your phone's cool!"

"What about my phone?" I asked, making a face.

"Your phone is cool too, Dad, but not as good as my other dad's."

I hugged him. I couldn't hold back. I crushed him against my chest, holding him tight as I stared at Drew.

"What in the world are you doing out in the rain?" Ivy called across the driveway. "Get in here!"

Pulling back, Travis smiled at me. "I got a haircut!"

I noticed his hair for the first time. It was shorter than it had been before, and it wasn't uneven anymore. "Aunt Ivy said it was a surprise for the wedding!"

"You're going to be the best-looking man there," Drew told him.

"The hair lady is still in there. Aunt Ivy says you have to get a haircut too!"

Drew grimaced, and I laughed.

Ivy yelled for us again, and I set Travis down. "You go first. I have to help your dad."

He raced back off across the driveway and up the steps to the house. I was about to turn toward Drew when Ivy gave a low shriek, making us both look up.

Both of us started laughing. Travis, who was definitely wet from the rain, was shaking his head like a dog in front of her, splattering his aunt with water.

"Kid's a savage," Drew said proudly.

"Takes after his dad," I said.

Drew's eyes softened. "Which one?"

"Who cares?"

Noting his booted foot was still inside the SUV, out of the rain, I offered him my back. "Let's go."

"What?" Drew said, suspicious.

I slapped my shoulder. "Jump on."

He hesitated, but his laugh floated over my shoulder. "You asked for it."

"Ye—" My reply was cut off when he literally leapt onto my back. "Argh," I said, nearly toppling over. Recovering, I stood, hooking my hands under his knees and lifting him a little higher. "How much weight did you put on?" I teased.

"Not enough." His voice rumbled right beside my ear.

"Give it time, baby," I said, no longer teasing. "You've been through a lot. So has your body. You'll get back to where you used to be."

He made a soft sound and shoved the car door closed. Seconds later, his chin rested on my shoulder. "You gained back everything you lost. I swear you got bigger," he muttered.

I laughed. "I had to. I gotta haul you around now."

"Fuck you," he said, but it was practically a term of endearment.

"You know, I wouldn't mind if you stayed this size," I confessed. "I like carrying you around."

"I live with a bunch of giant football players and my own personal giant," he quipped. "I look tiny next to you guys."

Turning my head, I told him, "You take up the most room in my heart."

"Don't sweet talk me." He grouched, but he wasn't really grouchy. He was charmed.

"Now, baby," I teased, heading toward the house. "You can't be grouchy the day before our wedding."

"Ivy's making me get a haircut."

"I miss the scruff," I said.

I felt his small jolt of surprise. "You said you liked the beard."

"I like you any way I can get you. But the scruff has always been my kryptonite."

"Noted," he murmured, and it brought me back to the first time we'd ever kissed. When I'd been so twisted up inside from his proximity that I'd blurted out just how much I liked his unshaven jaw. That was exactly what he'd said back then too.

Ivy and Travis disappeared somewhere in the house. The voices of the pack of kids we all created echoed somewhere close by.

"Hey," I said, pausing before the pre-wedding family craziness took over everything. "You're mine later."

"Aren't I always?"

I smirked. Well, yes. He was. "I mean we have a date."

He drew back. "A date?"

Nodding, I hefted him a little higher onto my back.

"We're inside. You can put me down now." He reminded.

"I don't want to."

When he settled against my back once more, I reveled in the way his arms looped around me from behind. How every part of him was touching me.

"We have a date?" He went on. "The night before our wedding? Isn't that kinda… unconventional?"

"Who the fuck cares?"

He considered that for all of two seconds. "Okay."

"I'll pick you up in a few hours." Gently, I put him down on his feet and handed him the crutches.

"Where are you going?"

"To see my daughter," I said. It had been a couple hours. I missed that sweet face.

"I want to come too."

"Drew!" Ivy appeared. She sounded like Bridezilla, and she wasn't even the bride.

Drew was.

Ha. I made a joke.

Funny, right?

Somehow, he got it into his head that he was the "girl" in the relationship. I tried to tell him there was no girl in our relationship, but I knew he still pondered this. He must have been talking to Braeden.

"Andrew!" Ivy scolded. "Look how wet you are. Come on. The stylist has been waiting. You're getting a haircut."

"Ives—" He started to protest.

"Don't you Ives me. You look like a caveman. That is not a good wedding look. I want to see your face in the wedding photos."

"Fine." He relented.

I gave him a wave as Ivy hauled him away. "I'll see you tonight."

"Where we going?" he called out.

"It's a surprise!" Ivy declared.

He glanced at me for answers, but I shook my head. She was right. It was a surprise.

FORTY-THREE

Drew

After my trip to the salon, aka Ivy's stylist who made a house call in the center of our kitchen, I tried to go home.

She wouldn't let me. She gave me a pouty lip and started crying because I was finally getting married and she was "so happy."

Why did girls always cry when they were happy?

So I caved like the big brother I was and let her shove me into the shower, a fresh stack of clothes I didn't even know I owned piled on the bathroom counter. I swear my sister had a closet full of clothes—not just for herself but for everyone.

Good thing the house was so big.

When I was done, I went to find Trent and my kids. I was starting to have withdrawals from them. When Travis rushed out of the house, calling for his dad, my heart damn near burst out of my chest. Hearing him say it to Trent was just as good as when he turned his dark little eyes and said it to me.

I loved them. More than I seriously ever thought possible.

Rimmel was sitting in the center of the living room floor, which was strangely quiet, with a pink bundle in her arms. London, who had been the baby of this family up until Andi came, was sitting in front of her, stacking some jumbo blocks together.

She wasn't quite two yet, but she was a tiny version of her mother. Dark hair, small build, and an innocence shining in her blue eyes. The eyes were the only thing she'd gotten from Romeo.

"Look at all these pretty girls," I said, trying to maneuver around the furniture.

The twenty-five dogs that were Rimmel's harem all jumped up and practically formed an army in front of them like I was some kind of enemy intruder.

Fine. Twenty-five was a bit of an exaggeration. There were probably like six in here right now. But there were more around here somewhere.

All the ruckus they were creating made the one-eyed cat, Murphy, stand up indignantly from the arm of the sofa so he could saunter away.

As if sensing I was grossly outnumbered, Fry rushed in from the kitchen, shoving up against my side to join in the barking.

I patted his head because he was a good boy.

"Down, boys," Rimmel said, amusement in her tone. "It's just Drew."

The dogs obeyed her as if they didn't know almost all of them were bigger and could take her down.

Although, these dogs were smart. They knew if they tried, the alpha of their pack would charge in here and make them all suffer.

"I don't think they like the crutches," Rim said apologetically.

"Yeah, well, me either."

Fry jumped up on a nearby chair and flopped down. No one batted an eye at the animals jumping on the furniture in this place. It was a common occurrence.

The only person who kinda minded was Braeden, but he put up with it because he was forever Rimmel's BBFL.

BBFL = big brother for life.

London grabbed Ralph's tail on her way to me, and the dog didn't even bat an eye. When she was farther up his body, she tugged his ear, using it for balance.

"Lo." I smiled, forgetting the crutches to pick up my niece and kiss her cheek.

She planted a wet, messy kiss on my cheek, then wiggled to get down and go back to her blocks.

Did I mention this girl had a glowing golden halo to Romeo? He loved all his kids, but his baby daughter who looked just like his wife? Good luck and Godspeed to any man who ever came around here for her, because he'd never live.

Add the fact that she had four older brothers?

May the odds be ever in her favor.

They weren't. The odds were not in London's favor. I wasn't sorry, though. I had a daughter now too. I fully understood Rome's position.

"Where's my girl?" I crooned, reaching down to lift her out of Rimmel's arms. When she saw me, she smiled.

Her smiling at me gave me the exact same feeling as when Travis called me dad.

"Guess I don't have to ask if you recognize me," I said, and she smiled again.

Pressing a kiss to her dark hair, I snuggled her close as she kicked her feet. She was still small but no longer frighteningly so. She'd gained some weight. Her cheeks were chubby, and the doctors were pleased with her overall health.

"Where's Travis?" I asked.

"With Trent," Rim answered, clapping for the tower London made.

"All the wedding people leave?"

"Most of them. The rest are down on the property. Ivy is making them put up a tent in case it rains tomorrow."

"Poor people," I muttered.

Rimmel laughed.

"So what do you know about this date I'm going on tonight?" I asked.

She smiled. "Everything of course."

I turned, showing her my ear.

"Oh!" She feigned surprise. "I think I hear Uncle Trent outside!" Rimmel stood, reaching down to pick up her daughter. "Let's go see."

"Brat!" I called as Rimmel ran off.

"You calling my wife a brat?" Romeo said, coming in from the next room.

"Drew!" she called from the front entry. "Your fiancé is here!"

I rolled my eyes but smiled.

"Give me my niece," Romeo said, reaching for Andi.

I pulled her back, making a face. Her stare was already focused on me, and it made me want to be a better man. It made me want to make sure she had the best life possible.

"You be good for your Uncle Romeo and Aunt Rimmel," I told her. "We'll be back later, okay?"

She made a couple sounds, and I kissed her cheeks. "Love you, peanut."

Once she was in Romeo's arms, I went to the front door, where a very familiar and satisfying sound made the air purr.

The fastback, which was as awesome as ever, sat near the door, engine rumbling, body shining. Trent was behind the wheel, and Travis was sitting on his lap.

"Dad!" Travis yelled, running around the front end. "Dad! Look! I got to drive. Dad let me drive the fastback!"

Rimmel's intake of breath made me glance at her.

"Best wedding gift ever, right?"

Tears shimmered in her eyes, and she nodded. "Best ever."

"You drove that all the way up here?" I asked, ruffling his dark hair.

"You look different," he announced, scrutinizing my face.

"I got a haircut and shaved."

He nodded. "Guess what? We're going to the movies too."

At the bottom of the stairs, Trent groaned.

I grinned. Guess the secret was out of the bag. "You are?"

"The home theater," Romeo said from behind.

Dropping onto my knee in front of Travis, I smiled. "Have fun, okay. Be good for your aunts and uncles. We'll be back in a little while."

"Okay." He nodded.

"You're okay with me going out with Dad for a while?" We tried not to spend too much time away from the kids. The most I was away was when I was at physical therapy or some other medical appointment. I'd had a couple meetings with Gamble, but he'd come here for them.

I worried that maybe us being gone for PT earlier and then leaving again tonight might be too much for him.

Travis nodded. "Blue and Jax are going to help me catch more Pokémon!"

"Ah," I mused and pulled my phone out of my back pocket. "Guess you'll need this."

I was seriously considering getting the kid his own phone. Yeah, yeah, he was only five. But he pretty much commandeered mine… I needed a phone too.

He took it, putting his finger on the sensor and unlocking the screen. He was struggling a bit learning how to read, but little man knew how to work a phone better than me.

In a burst of movement, Travis flung himself forward, wrapping his arms around my neck. Momentarily shocked, my eyes lifted to Rim, who smiled. Closing my arms around him, I cleared my throat. "Call your dad if you need anything."

"Okay." He pulled back and ran up the stairs, yelling for Blue, Jax, and Nova.

"He'll be fine." Rimmel assured me.

"Yeah," I said, looking after him. "I know."

I felt a hand slide under my arm, and then I was being lifted back to my feet. I didn't have to look to know it was Trent.

"Thanks, guys," he said.

Romeo and Rim waved us off, practically throwing us out and shutting the door behind us.

"The movies, huh?" I ribbed Trent, giving him a lopsided smile.

He groaned. "Last time I tell him a secret."

I laughed, but it quickly turned into a gasp of surprise when my back hit the front door.

Trent's body pressed all along mine, one hand on my hip, the other caging me in. His eyes were lit with fire, narrowed and gazing around my face as if he hadn't seen me in years.

I recognized his hunger. It was the same kind he always made me feel.

Smiling faintly, I lifted my chin, turning so he could get a good look at my jawline.

A ferocious sound rumbled in his chest, and the hand at my hip suddenly wrapped (gently) around my neck.

"You shaved." He grunted, the pad of his thumb rubbing over the stubble.

"Technically, I trimmed it." I corrected. "Gotta give my man back the scruff he loves so much."

Trent dove into my neck, lips latching on and making my eyelids drop closed. The hand on my neck slid up a little so he could hold my face exactly where he wanted while he kissed and sucked along my jaw. Making a sound of approval, he drew back to rub his nose along the prickly hair, his fingers tightening on my jaw.

"So fucking good," he mumbled, kissing toward my mouth and claiming my lips.

Both his hands wound around my neck, pushing up into my newly cut hair. He massaged my scalp and totally messed up the style.

When he pulled back, he tugged my lower lip with him, and my hand slid into the back pocket of his jeans, squeezing his ass.

"I like it," he said, sweeping his stare over me again. "The scruff and the hair."

The hair was still fairly long on the top, but the back and sides were all cut close.

"Gotta look good for my groom tomorrow," I said, pleased he liked what he was seeing.

Surprising me again, Trent scooped me up, carrying me down the stairs to deposit me into the passenger side of the fastback.

I'd driven our "parent car" a few times since we'd gotten home, but not the fastback. Since it was a clutch, I needed two feet, and the broken leg I was sporting cramped my style.

We'd barely been out in the Mustangs at all (his or mine) because we always had the kids. I wanted something big and protective around them, something they would feel safe in. A sports car wasn't exactly that.

The accident was still too fresh in my mind. It still haunted my dreams sometimes.

Reading me, Trent picked up my hand across the center. "Thought you might want to take a spin in your car tonight, but I can go get the SUV."

"No," I said, giving him a smile. "This is perfect. I miss this thing."

"I know." He agreed gently. "She'll be here when you're ready for her."

His understanding and automatic acceptance of everything and anything I felt never ceased to inspire me with awe. I honestly believed Trent was one of the most empathetic people I'd ever met.

I was goddamn lucky he was the father of my children.

"What movie are we seeing?" I asked, eyes twinkling.

As we drove away from the house, he made a rude sound. "I'm not telling you anything else."

"Maybe I should call Travis."

Another sound ripped from Trent's throat. "He called me dad." His voice was stricken. "*Dad, where are you taking Dad?*" he quoted. "Fuck, I'd have told him anything."

My hand covered his on the stick shift. "I understand."

After a moment, T smiled. "I'll drive, you shift?"

Some nerves skittered along my back, but I shoved them down and nodded. We hadn't done this in a long time.

It didn't matter. We still drove perfectly in sync.

FORTY-FOUR

Trent

A date the night before the wedding?

Why the hell not?

Besides, there was something I needed to do, and it definitely couldn't wait until after the wedding.

The only time alone we'd had since before his accident were stolen moments, middle-of-the-night rendezvous, and trips to physical therapy.

With Andi and Travis settling in more and more every day, I thought it would be okay if we just took a few hours for us.

"Hey, frat boy?" Drew called as I pulled the fastback into the parking lot.

"Yeah?"

"If you wanted to watch a movie, why didn't we just do it at home, in the private theater."

Turning off the car, I pocketed the keys and twisted to face him. The lot was dark, only a few lamps overhead providing shadowy light in the interior. "Because I wanted to come out with you. Because we don't need to hide at home. Because if I put a movie in our theater, we'd have six kids piled on top of us and a bunch of drooling dogs."

"You mean we don't have to watch a cartoon tonight?" Drew gasped, shock and awe all over his face.

I laughed. "Most of all, I wanted to be alone with you." Not bothering waiting for his reply, I jogged around the car to open his door.

"Stop treating me like a girl," he bitched.

"Your leg is broken." I reminded him. Leaning down in the doorway, I said, "And I'm treating you like I love you. Like maybe I want to marry you."

"Maybe?" He scoffed.

I nodded, making a sound of agreement. "Maybe."

"Help me out," he said, holding out his hand for me to take.

Ignoring his hand, I swooped in, grabbed his waist, and tugged. When he was on his feet, I glanced in the back at the crutches, and he made a face.

"Want another ride?" I asked, turning.

He jumped on my back, and I couldn't help but smile. "Who would have thought you would be the kind of guy to love a piggyback ride so much."

"Put me down, frat boy."

"No."

"You know," he said, "if you wanted us to be alone, coming to a public movie theater kinda defeats the purpose…"

"Look around the parking lot, Mask."

He was quiet a second as he swiveled around, making a noise near my ear. "Why is the lot empty? Are they closed or something?"

"Or something," I said.

"Trent, what—"

"Stop talking. Let me surprise you at least a little bit," I muttered. Geez, the guy was nosy tonight.

The inside of the theater was just like the parking lot outside. Empty. But it was lit up and definitely open.

A teenager with a red hat with the theater logo on the front smiled at us from behind the concession stand. "How are you doing tonight, Mr. Mask?" Then his eyes went over my shoulder. "Mr. Forrester?"

"It's Mask." Drew corrected automatically.

He never used his old name now. He didn't answer to it anymore either.

The kid nodded. "What can I get for you?"

"Fries, extra ketchup," I told him. "Popcorn, two sodas, and…" I glanced over my shoulder. "What candy do you want?"

"Fries."

I rolled my eyes. "Skittles," I told the kid.

He nodded. "We'll bring it in for you if you want to go ahead to your seats."

"Thanks." I headed off in the direction of the theater, and Drew tapped me on the shoulder. "Yes?" I asked, amused.

"You didn't buy tickets. And since when does this place deliver your order?"

Lowering, I put him on the floor and then turned to face him. "Since I rented the entire place out for the night."

Drew's eyes widened. "You did what?"

"I said I wanted to be alone with you."

"So you rented out an entire theater?"

I shrugged.

He blinked.

I held my hand out between us. "Hold my hand."

He did, leaning heavily on me as I led him down the hall.

"What movie are we watching?"

"You'll see," I said, guiding him into one of the smaller theaters. I could have chosen the biggest one, but it wasn't necessary. I wanted the smaller space. I wanted the room at the end of the hallway.

Plus, it was less to decorate.

The second the door closed behind us, Drew stopped, turning to look at me.

I smiled.

He pointed to the candles lining the dark, narrow hallway leading into the theater. "You did this?"

Taking his hand again, I nudged him forward. "Come on."

Candles flickered and shimmered, creating a soft glow through the short hallway, and under his feet, yellow rose petals covered the space between them.

When we made it around the corner to the seating, Drew halted again, eyes roaming everywhere before settling on me. "Frat boy."

"I know you told me once you weren't the type to need romance, but I kinda wanted to give it to you anyway," I said, nerves making me incredibly nervous.

This was the first time I'd ever done something like this. At least for Drew. For us. I'd strung lights, lit candles, and cut out a hundred paper stars for other people's romances. I don't know why it took so much to do it for my own.

Maybe, like Drew, I thought it wasn't necessary.

Maybe I thought a guy like me didn't think I deserved it.

Fuck all that.

I was taking it. The romance. The love. Everything.

"I can't believe you did this," he said, awed.

His head hit my shoulder, and our hands entwined as we stood there gazing around the space that was lit dimly by hundreds of candles. And I literally mean hundreds.

But they were the flameless kind. Theater rules.

There were also a few battery-operated paper lanterns strung around the room and sitting on the stairs leading up the rows of seats. Large bunches of white balloons were tied to the row behind the one where we were sitting, and there were a few big bouquets of yellow roses sitting close to our seats.

He glanced at the screen, which was just white, and back to me. "When did you have time to do this?"

"I always have time for you."

Leaning in, he kissed me, a simple kiss turning into something deeper, something longer lasting. When at last he pulled back, his eyes were glassy and held a dreamlike quality.

"You like it?"

He nodded, his smile shy.

"Follow the petals," I said, then decided against having him walk. Picking him up, I carried him the short distance up the stairs to maneuver toward our seats, which were dead center and in the perfect place.

The armrest between the two red leather chairs was already up, and there were blankets and pillows stacked on the seats beside ours.

Depositing Drew in one chair, I grabbed a giant pillow/ottoman thing and slid it under his booted foot, making sure he was comfortable.

While I worked, I felt his stare the entire time, and frankly, it was giving me a hard-on.

"Why yellow?" he asked when I shook out a blanket to drape over his lap.

Looking at the yellow rose petal stuck to his foot, I smiled. Reaching down to pluck it off the toe of his boot, I laid it in the palm of my hand, offering it to him.

"Because…" I began, sliding into the seat right beside him. I sat so close our bodies brushed together. "In roses, yellow is the color of friendship, and this is how we began, isn't it? With friendship."

"You're my best friend." He agreed. "You'll always be my best friend."

"Mine too." I agreed, feeling a lump of emotion forming at the base of my throat.

"You know," Drew said, squinting at me. "This is kinda like that first weekend together… our first go at being more than friends."

I smiled. It made me happy that he totally understood what I was going for here.

"The couch. The blankets…" His eyes drifted to the screen. "You gonna have them play *Terminator*, T?"

Chuckling, I nodded. "You remember."

"Like I would ever forget. Our first kiss blew apart my entire world." He reminisced. "I was so fucking nervous."

"You were shaking." I agreed.

"I didn't feel ready... but seeing you in that bar that night, with other men throwing themselves at you..."

"They weren't."

His stare silenced my lips. "The fuck they weren't. I almost had to blow the whole place up."

What a drama queen. I liked it.

He grunted as if he was still pissed off about the gay bar. "I was so scared I'd lose you. The thought of losing you to anyone else... a woman, another man," he listed. "It eclipsed everything else."

"You and me," I mused. "We're very motivated by the idea of losing each other."

"I can't live without you, frat boy."

"Ditto."

"That kiss changed my life. Then you blew apart my world again with a blowjob..." He grinned.

I rolled my eyes. Dude loved his blowjobs.

"Thank you for taking a chance with me," I whispered, rubbing my palm over his jaw. "Thank you for loving me."

Our lips were just about ready to touch when I heard the concession workers enter the theater. I didn't pull away. I continued kissing Drew in spite of them.

The teenagers were at the end of our row when I looked up.

"Thanks, guys."

They carried over all the food and slid it onto some tables that pulled up in front of the seats.

"Can we grab anything else for you?" the boy in the red hat asked.

"Nah. We're good," I told him. "You can start the movie now."

Before they were even gone, Drew was eating the fries. "I need ketchup."

I opened a few packets and slid it in front of him so he could dunk them in. I watched him eat, totally amused by his never-ending love for fries.

A few minutes later, he glanced at me, shoved the rest of the fry in his mouth, and grabbed a big soda to take a long drink. When he was done, he held it out to me, nudging my lips with the straw. Technically, I had my own soda. But as always, his tasted better.

After I took a drink, he fed me some popcorn and ripped open the giant bag of Skittles lying front of us.

"Taste the rainbow, T." He invited.

"I'd rather taste you."

Forgetting all about the food, he leaned in, and we made out until the screen at the front of the room went dark.

"It's starting," he whispered against my mouth.

Piling the blankets over us and pulling him as close to my side as I could get him, we watched the classic movie that would probably always have special meaning to us.

I made it through the opening credits before my hand began wandering. At first, his eyes stayed focused on the screen even while my hand fondled the back of his neck, his newly cut hair, and played along the jawline of his rugged face.

I was transported back five years to that first night with Drew. To the first time I got to touch him. To the butterflies that turned my insides to a mass of quivering mush. I'd been scared to touch him but desperately wanted to do so anyway.

Every inch he'd move closer, every lingering stare… hell, even breathing the same air in that moment had been overwhelming and thrilling.

Maybe it wasn't quite like that now, but it was just as good. Familiarity had its advantages too.

Like how I knew the space just below his ear made his arms break out in goose bumps when I sucked it. How the space behind his right knee was sensitive to the touch and how I knew exactly when he stopped seeing the movie and only felt my hands.

As he stared ahead, my fingers dragged down his chest, covering one pec before sliding over to do the same with the other. He blinked, but it was more like a drag of his eyelids. Like he was suddenly very sleepy and had to fight to keep his eyes open.

My hand kept going, and his eyes grew heavier.

Under the blanket, my hand brushed over his cock, which was rigid beneath the jeans he wore. I only stroked it once before pulling away and making him turn his head to finally look at me.

I smiled, knowing he wanted me to keep touching that particular area, but my hands had other ideas. The ripped jeans he was wearing were like a playground, offering glimpses and teases of different patches of his skin.

Something on the screen in front of us exploded, but neither of us reacted.

His body trembled when my fingers dove beneath one of the rips, caressing his skin. The light from the screen cast ever-changing shadows over his features as he stared. "Frat boy."

I looked up.

He shoved me back into my seat and climbed into my lap, straddling my stiff cock and rocking against it.

"You were hard that night too," he murmured.

I stayed relaxed against the seat, staring up at him with passion-drunk eyes and reveling in the weight of him in my lap.

Our chests bumped together when he kissed me, and the thin string of restraint we'd sort of been holding on to snapped.

Tugging the shirt off his body, I sucked one of his nipples into my mouth, bunching the warm skin stretched across his back in my palms.

His moan of pleasure spurred me on, spiking the adrenaline already pulsing through my system.

Moving to the second nipple, I reached between us and unbuttoned his jeans. His hands were doing the same, and soon, both of our straining dicks were out.

Drew's hand wrapped around both of us. The feel of his silky skin rubbing against me as he jacked us both made my head fall back against the seat.

He rocked against me, and the sight he made on top of me, nothing but a dark shadow with the screen at his back, made my hips thrust upward in reply.

"Drew." I moaned, trying to lift him off of me, wanting to slide down his body and take him between my lips.

"You sure we're alone right now?" He panted, pushing me back into the chair.

I nodded, reaching between our bodies.

Lunging forward, he slid his tongue into my mouth, and they battled it out in a sweet, sweet war.

When my dick was slick with pre-cum and I was nearly suffocated with the need for more, I pushed him back so I could pin him to the chair and suck him dry.

"No," he said, reaching around into the back pocket of his jeans and tossing a packet of lube against my chest.

By the time I glanced at it and then back up, he'd already shoved his jeans down and was reaching for mine.

"We don't have to," I said, even though I fucking wanted to so bad.

His teeth flashed. "You fucking want me bad right now."

I caught his hip as he was climbing back into my lap. "Drew."

The seriousness in my tone made him pause. Our eyes met. "Is this why you think you're the wife?"

Even though he was shadowed by the bright movie behind him, I could see his big smile. "What?"

"Ever since the accident, you've been the one, ah, on the receiving end." This was awkward. And hella hard to talk about when my hormones were raging to be inside him.

But I'd deny myself. I'd deny myself all the pleasure in the world if it meant making sure Drew had what he needed.

"You mean I've somehow become your bottom," he said boldly.

He was a lot better at saying things bluntly. Even more so since he almost died.

"Well, yeah." I agreed.

His throaty laugh made my cock jerk. His hand wrapped around it and stroked, making me forget about this conversation.

Focus.

"I'm serious." I forged on. If he could be blunt, so could I. "I know I've been kinda… demanding lately."

"Savagely bossy is more accurate," he said but then finished his words with another jerk of my shaft.

I moaned.

"It doesn't always have to be me." I panted. "I'll be—"

"I like being your bottom," he announced, releasing my dick to grab the lube still lying on my chest. "I like when you're demanding. I like when you're inside me. I like knowing that I please you."

My hips thrust at his words. "You trying to make me come with just your words?" I ground out.

"Just telling you like it is. Just telling you all the stuff I've held back."

"I fucking love you."

He used his teeth to rip open the packet. The slippery stuff was warm from being in his pocket, and my body jerked when he first coated me with it.

"I'm not saying I don't ever want to top you again."

"You can have me whenever you want me." I promised, wanting his hands back on me.

He added more lube, and breath hissed between my teeth.

Grabbing the blanket he'd been covered with, he draped it around his shoulders and adjusted his body.

I held my fingers out between us, and he squeezed out what was left in the packet on the ends of my fingers.

The second I rubbed against him, his body sagged closer to mine. I was impatient and needy, but I took my time making sure he was moisturized, then dragged my hand up to wrap around his cock.

He moved with confidence, as if he definitely mastered being my "bottom" even though technically he was totally on top right now.

The first push of our bodies merging made me bite into my lower lip. And when he sank down over me completely, I jolted up, grabbing both his arms, and bit down lightly on his chest.

We were alone, but me screaming with pleasure might not keep us that way.

At least the movie was loud and would cover up most of the sounds we made.

Grabbing my head in his hands, Drew pulled my mouth off him and stared down, riding my dick like the true professional he was.

I pulled his head down so we could kiss, both of us falling back against the chair while he fucked me until I couldn't see straight.

When he started to whisper my name over and over against my ear, I knew he was at his peak, so I reached between us and brought him over the edge.

He buried his face in my neck, muffling the sound of his moans, his hips still riding me even through the orgasm ripping through his body.

Before he was even done, I lost control, surging up into him, pouring out every last drop of desire into his body.

I was sweating when I collapsed back with him against my chest. Both of us breathing heavily, our legs trembling.

Before I was even recovered, I started to shift so I could pull out, but he made a sound of protest, curling closer against my body.

"Stay," he murmured.

"I don't want to hurt you."

"You don't hurt me, T. My body loves you."

I stayed nestled inside him, because really, there was nowhere else I wanted to be.

I rubbed his back for a long time, enjoyed the tickling sensation of his scruff against my chest, and inhaled his familiar scent while the movie played.

Eventually he shifted, so I gently lifted him up to slide out of his body.

"I love you," he whispered.

Even though the movie was louder, his words were all I heard.

Snatching his shirt from nearby, I tugged it over his head. When it appeared through the center of the fabric, I leaned up to kiss him. "No, baby, I love you."

He smiled, and it was the cutest fucking thing I'd ever seen.

No, seriously. I'd seen a lot of cute shit. I had a baby daughter. But this? *Goddamn.*

"We should get cleaned up," I said. "The movie is almost over." I helped him first, making sure he didn't put too much weight on his booted foot, making sure he was cleaned up and covered before I even worried about myself.

Once he was back in his seat with a blanket on his lap, I took care of myself.

Not too much longer, the credits for the movie started to roll.

"Thank you for this," he said, turning to me. "For tonight."

Cheekily, I lifted an eyebrow. "Who said it's over?"

"Is another movie playing after this one?"

I nodded. "Watch." I gestured to the screen.

Drew turned back, and I smiled at his profile.

Terminator went off.

Another movie came on.

Ours.

It is reported that Andrew Buchanan was the first gay U.S. President. President Andrew Jackson referred to him as "Aunt Nancy" and "Aunt Fancy".

FORTY-FIVE

Drew

This wasn't at all what I was expecting.

When the first photo filled the giant screen, I looked over at Trent.

He smiled and gestured for me to keep watching. But how could I watch the screen when he was right there in front of me?

How could I tear my eyes away from his strong profile, his handsome face that was suddenly filled with nerves and shyness?

Trent reached out, palming the top of my head and turning it so I had to look at the movie playing before me.

Our movie.

Trent made a "movie" about us.

Photo after photo of us played, showing us at the track, inside the Mustangs, eating fries at some shithole diner off the interstate.

There were selfies. There were candid moments the family had caught without us realizing. There was even a badly recorded video of us surfing at the beach.

Tears blurred my eyes as I looked back over the last five years I'd spent with this man. With my best friend. My soulmate.

There was no one else. There never could be.

I lived and died for Trent. He was my blood. My oxygen and everything in between. All the hate we'd experienced since "coming out" seemed trivial now. Losing my parents suddenly felt like a worthy sacrifice. Hell, death itself even seemed unimportant.

I'd relive that car slamming into the concrete and listen to my father's hateful words a thousand more times as long as we ended up here.

The song playing in the background nudged a tear out of the corner of my eye. It was by Calum Scott, and it seemed completely written for us.

(It wasn't, but it sure felt like it in this moment).

Finally, the picture changed, and a photo of our family filled the screen. Me, Trent, Andi, and Travis. Four people. My entire world.

The song stopped playing, but I continued to stare.

"Drew." Trent beckoned, his voice like velvet on a cold autumn day.

I looked over, and my heart started to quake.

He was down on one knee, the look on his face completely sincere, with an open ring box poised in the palm of his hand.

"I never really asked." He began, giving me a shy smile. A smile that undid all the laces holding me together. "I pretty much demanded, and then Ivy took over the plans."

"I don't care." I gasped, trying not to cry.

"I know," he said gently. "But I do. I thought about it, and every single couple in our family had some type of epic proposal. Hell, we helped set up a lot of them. But what did I give you? An order. A demand."

"You gave me everything."

He smiled. The box in his hand seemed a little unsteady.

"I can do better than that," he whispered. "I know the wedding is tomorrow, but I'm still asking now. Will you marry me?" He looked me right in the eyes, casting a spell that could never be undone. "Will you let me take care of you for the rest of your life?"

"Yes."

He started to go on but then realized I already answered. "Yeah?"

Oh my God, his crooked tooth appeared in that lopsided smile. I nodded. "Yeah."

Blowing out a breath like he hadn't dared to breathe, he ripped the ring out of the box and threw it somewhere I'd probably never see again.

The lights in the room gently lifted, offering just enough brightness for me to see what he slid onto my hand.

"Shouldn't we do this part tomorrow?"

"Screw everyone else. I want this moment for us."

I laughed.

"Besides, you know how hard it's been calling you Mask but not seeing a ring on your finger?"

"Ring or not, I'm always yours."

"I want the ring," he declared.

Bossy bastard.

I glanced down, taking in the thick black band with a row of round sparkling diamonds through the center.

"Diamonds." I scoffed, smiling. "Really?"

"Fuck yes. My baby gets diamonds."

I laughed, and my stomach floated from all the butterfly wings.

"I love it," I admitted, watching the way the light caught on said diamonds.

Trent took my hand and kissed the band.

"Since we're doing this now," I said, leaning my hip up to reach into my pocket to pull out a band of my own. "I have one for you too."

"That's been in your pocket this whole time?"

"I've been carrying it around on the daily since I bought it. So many times, I wanted to slip it on your finger."

Grinning, he offered his hand.

I slid the band home, and he looked down and laughed. "Diamonds?"

"Fuck yes." I copied his words. "My baby gets diamonds."

His was the color of gunmetal, dark gray.

Clearing my throat, I said, "And technically, it's not diamonds."

"They're blue," he said, still staring at the ring. Lifting his stare, he said, "Like your eyes."

I knew he'd understand. "Sapphires."

"It's perfect."

"I'm not taking this off just to put it back on tomorrow during the ceremony." I warned.

"No one would dare suggest it."

I knew that technically, he wasn't my husband until tomorrow, but my heart didn't give a crap about technicalities. To me, Trent was already officially mine.

Jimi Hendrix pretended to be gay to get out of the army in 1962.

FORTY-SIX

Trent

Romeo was my best man. Braeden was Drew's.

We stood under some elaborate yellow rose archway erected in the backyard, and it didn't rain a single drop. I swear the clouds were scared of Ivy.

All our friends and family were in attendance, and though we tried to keep it pretty small, we knew a lot of awesome people.

The press was kept out, and Ivy tied bunches of white balloons to literally everything, which blocked the view of the drones that would occasionally fly overhead.

Sure, the press probably got some air shots, but they'd be shitty and that made me kinda gleeful inside.

Not because I wanted to hide, though.

Not because I was ashamed.

Not because I worried Drew's parents would see the images online.

Mainly, it was because *GearShark* had the feature story and would release "official" wedding photos with our cover story.

Yep. Another cover story. This time, I wasn't holding back. Why should I?

And shit, this cover story alone would pay for both my kids' college education.

Andi made the prettiest flower girl I'd ever seen. She outshined even her fellow flower squad of Nova, London, and Sophia.

Who could resist an angel baby being pulled down the aisle in a basket of roses?

Fake roses. Not real ones. I wasn't having my baby girl poked by thorns.

Travis, Blue, Jax, Asher, and Jagger were the ring bearers, but the boys had no rings to carry. Instead, they all drove down the aisle in mini cars. Travis drove a Mustang. Of course.

Then he stopped his car halfway down the aisle so he could get out and catch another Pokémon that magically appeared in the middle of the wedding.

We, of course, stopped everything. Kid had to catch the Pikachu.

Once all the kids were wrangled and their cars were parked behind the flowers, we said some heartfelt vows, which sounded something like this:

"I, Drew, take you, frat boy, to be my bossy husband. I won't share my fries with you, but I'll eat the tomatoes off your burgers and I'll wear all your shirts even when mine are clean. I swear to love you in this life, the next one, and even in death. Thank you for being patient and kind, for always protecting me, even when that meant you were hurt. I'll never be as good a man as you are, but you picked me anyway. And I'll do everything in my power to make you happy. You gave me the family I never knew I was missing, and if that wasn't enough, you gave me the blood flowing through

your own veins. I'm not just me anymore, Trent. I'm us. I literally don't exist without you."

Yep. He said all that.

I had to get a tissue from Braeden.

Don't worry, though. He had to get a tissue from Romeo.

"I, Trent, take you, Drew, to be my wife. Oh! Wait. I mean husband."

Everyone laughed. Except Drew.

"I'll always put ketchup on my plate for your mountain of fries, make your coffee just the way you like it, and tie a knot in the straw paper that you always toss my way. You can wear my shirts and I'll wear your boxers, and I'll always be your number one fan. My whole life, I was lonely, missing a lot of shit I was too scared to reach for, but you literally sped into my life and made me even more afraid not to try. Without you, I'd be alive, but not living. I'd be a man, but only half. I would have loved but never known the meaning. You're my reason, you're my truth, and you have a really nice ass. If my life is a book, you are the story. A story that only begins and ends with you. Thank you for being a father to our kids. Thank you for letting me love you, and thank you for being brave enough to hold my hand. I never thought we needed to get married, but now I can't imagine you as anything but my husband."

When we were finally official, I picked him up in front of everyone and kissed him until my arms couldn't hold him up anymore.

And there we were. Husband and husband. One life with two hands. Surrounded by people who loved us unconditionally and allowed us to love them the same in return.

Maybe I'd have to concede to Ivy on this one. Maybe this was better than just doing things at the justice of the peace.

Travis and all the kids were off, likely draining the battery on Drew's cell. Andi was being hoarded by Romeo's mom, and everyone else was probably off drinking pear-infused champagne.

Speaking of, I reached over and plucked the crystal glass out of my husband's hand before it could make it to his lips.

"Hey," he protested, spinning around. When he saw it was me, he gave a wry smile.

"No drinking during recovery, Mask."

"It's our wedding," he whined.

I lifted an eyebrow that I knew was perfectly sculpted. Ivy made me get them threaded.

"You need alcohol to get married to me?"

A sly glint came into his sexy blue eyes. Snagging the tie hanging around my neck, he tugged, bringing me close enough to kiss. His tongue swept past my lips, into my mouth, and over the roof. The back of my neck heated with desire, and I pressed my lips a little harder against his.

The silk he was still clutching slipped through his fingers the farther I straightened.

"If you won't let me drink it from the glass, I'll just have to drink it from your lips."

"I'll allow it," I declared.

He smirked, and it made me want to eat him.

Grabbing the lapels of the custom black leather jacket he was wearing, I tugged him close, taking into consideration his leg was still healing.

"I like you in leather," I told him, dropping my voice to the octave he loved. "It looks good with your scruff."

"Yeah?"

I nodded. "I like even more that it has my name across the back."

Instead of making Drew wear a classic tuxedo jacket, Ivy got him a custom-made black motorcycle jacket with "Mask" painted in white on the back. He wore it with a pair of black tuxedo pants, a white dress shirt, and no tie. Drew hated ties.

But apparently, he liked mine, because he pulled it again.

"You should keep this tie," he whispered.

"Noted."

He smiled slyly. "You look good in a tux."

Drew got to wear a cool "race car driver" outfit to our wedding, while I got to be classic with a black tux, black vest, and black silk tie.

I even wore black dress shoes. Drew got sneakers with silver studs on them.

I would have complained to Ivy, but like the clouds, I was scared of her too.

"I look better *out* of one."

His tongue darted out to wet his lips. "Can't argue with that."

"I love man love," Braeden said, sidling up to join us.

"You drunk?" Drew asked as I tucked my tie back into the vest.

"Drunk on love."

"Rome," I yelled. "Get your boy."

Romeo appeared instantly, and Braeden slung his arm around his shoulder. "If I was to ever have man love, it would be with Rome."

Romeo made a choked sound.

We all laughed.

"Right, Romeo. I'm totally your man type."

"I don't have a man type."

"Rome. You gonna do me like that?"

"I ain't gonna do you at all."

B dropped his arm from around his best friends' shoulders and started away. Sighing, Romeo grabbed the back of his neck, hauling him back. "You're totally my man type, B."

Braeden hugged Romeo. "I know."

"How about we get you some food?" Romeo suggested, taking away his champagne glass and handing it to me.

"I hope they got sprinkles," Braeden quipped.

"Rome," I said, stopping him before they could walk off.

He turned, meeting my eyes, knowing the serious note in my voice.

Setting the empty champagne flute on a passing tray, I turned completely toward him.

"Thank you. For everything."

"You don't have to thank me. We're family."

"Yeah. I know. But that's especially why I'm thanking you. You didn't have to be my family. But you are. You're better than any family I could have been born into. We've known each other a long time… since freshman year. You always treated me good, considered me a friend even when I hung back and kept to myself."

Romeo nodded.

"You even accepted me when I told you I was gay."

"We love man love!" Braeden exclaimed.

"No more talking." Romeo hushed him.

Braeden wrapped his arms around Rome from behind, giving him a back hug. Romeo rolled his eyes but reached up and patted B's hands where they clasped across his chest.

"I'll always be here for you," Romeo answered.

I nodded. "I know. I also wanted to apologize."

He drew back, surprised. "For what?"

"For being rough on you in the hospital. I took out a lot of anger and frustration on you when Drew was in the coma. You never said a word. You just took it and let it slide. You used your celebrity status to smooth over the people I pissed off. You told *him* that it was you who got the security and hired the nurses so he'd let them stay. I snubbed the charm you used more than once, and I more than once considered punching you in the face."

Romeo laughed, his blue eyes shining. As he did, a lock of blond hair fell over his forehead and his wide shoulders shook with amusement. "Bro, you don't have to apologize. It's all forgotten. You've always been there for us too. You take care of Rim when I'm on the road. You make sure she doesn't lock up the shelter alone at night. You had my back all through college, even when you got shit at the frat for it. When Rim…" He cleared his throat. "When we lost Evie and the press tortured us, you and Drew would distract the press in ways I knew you weren't comfortable with just so we could breathe."

"We love you, man," Braeden blabbered, still hugging Romeo.

I held out my hand, and Romeo shook it.

"Now, if you don't mind, I have to sober him up before the princess sees the state her husband is in."

When they were gone, Drew circled around behind me, slipping his arms around my waist.

"What are you doing?" I asked.

"Braeden made me want to cuddle you."

I laughed.

"Trent," called a voice I hadn't heard in a while, making me smile.

I looked up as Liam Mattison and his wife Bellamy approached.

"Liam," I said, offering my fist to pound it out. Letting go of me, Drew did the same. "Thank you so much for coming all the way from Colorado for the wedding."

"Perfect timing," he said. "The ski resort's off season is now."

"Bellamy," I said, leaning in to hug the blonde at Liam's side. "You look beautiful as ever."

"And as pregnant as ever," she said, cradling the small bump at her middle.

"Dude, give the poor girl a break." Drew ribbed Liam.

Liam laughed. "Hard to do when my girl looks like she does."

Bellamy blushed.

"This is number… four, right?" I said, trying to remember how many kids they had now.

I'd only met the first two, Shaw and Noah, when our family went to BearPaw Resort for vacation after we met Liam at a Hall of Fame Event. (Dude is an Olympic medalist for snowboarding!) Bellamy had been pregnant with number three, which had been a little girl named Everly. And now she was pregnant with this one.

Bells nodded. "Yes. Number four. And after this one, I'm *done.*"

"We'll see," Liam murmured.

"Don't you let him talk you into any more kids," Alex exclaimed, joining the conversation, his wife, Sabrina, in tow.

Alex was basically Liam's brother and helped run BearPaw resort. He used to be military… and when I say military, I mean he was a badass.

"You gonna end up with twins like us."

"Sabrina," I said, reaching out to hug his wife. "How are Daniel and Donovan?"

"Rotten as ever!" She laughed.

"Bellamy!" Rimmel exclaimed, rushing up to the group from behind.

I stepped aside so she could slip between me and Drew. London, who had a giant gold bow around her head, smiled up at me, and I plucked her out of Rim's arms.

"Lo," I said, holding her above my head and making her laugh.

Bellamy, Rimmel, and Sabrina started going on about everything as though they didn't talk regularly on the phone.

"Dad!" Travis yelled, making both me and Trent turn and reply, "What?"

He appeared out of nowhere, his hair messy and the jacket to his suit long gone. Half of his shirt was untucked, but he was smiling.

Seeing what was coming, I casually stepped behind Drew, offering some extra support for the moment Trav flung himself at him.

"Oomph." Drew groaned when he caught him, his body slightly rocking back into mine. Once he was steady, I stepped back around him to look at our son.

It wasn't that Drew wasn't strong enough to catch Travis. It was just that Drew was still healing from the accident, but he refused to tell Travis he couldn't launch himself at him.

"What are you doing?" Drew asked.

"Can I have cake?"

Drew glanced at me. "What do you think, Dad? Can this little savage have some cake?"

"Only if I can have some too."

"Is this Travis?" Liam asked, stepping forward.

Trav tucked his arms around Drew's neck.

"Yep, this is our son, Travis," I said. "Trav, this is Liam. He gets medals for riding a snowboard."

Travis's eyes widened.

"And he has a really big dog named Charlie," Rimmel added.

"Cool!"

"We're going to get cake," I told everyone, handing London back over to her mother and shaking Liam's and Alex's hands. "Thanks for being here. We're going to have to bring the kids back to the resort when Andi is a little older."

"Anytime." Liam agreed.

One the way to get cake, I plucked Trav out of Drew's arms because I still worried about his ribs and leg.

"Since you're married, does that mean we're a family now?" Travis asked.

Drew and I both stopped walking.

"We've always been a family," I told him. "Since the first day I saw you."

"But now you can adopt me, right?"

We exchanged a look. I hadn't realized how much Travis understood. How much he heard without actually being told.

"Yeah, buddy," I said, truthful. "Now we can adopt you. We already signed all the paperwork. We're just waiting for them to, ah, mail it back."

It was hard to explain all the legal shit involved in adopting a child to a five-year-old.

"Does that mean I can stay with you forever and ever?"

Drew stepped forward, ruffling the back of Travis's hair. "Forever and ever, okay? We'll always, always be here for you."

"Andi too?"

"Of course!" I scoffed. "Can't leave out my little peanut."

"I love you, Dad."

I choked.

"I love you too, son," I said without hesitation, even though it was hard to speak. "No matter what, okay? I'll love you no matter what."

"Forever and ever," Drew added.

Travis hugged me, and Drew quickly swiped the tear off my cheek over his little shoulder. Oh my God, a child's love was so pure. It was the purest thing I'd ever experienced.

"What about me?" Drew asked when Travis pulled back.

He held out his arms, and Drew pulled him close. "I love you too, Dad."

Damn. This was the best day of my life.

"Cake now?" Travis asked, completely oblivious to the giant gift he'd just handed over.

"You can have the entire thing," I said.

When we made it to the cake table, I handed him a fork and pointed at it. He started eating.

There was a good-size hole in the side when Ivy came running over.

"Oh my God!" She gasped. "You haven't even cut that yet!"

"He wanted cake," Drew told her.

She tossed her hands up in the air. "Then why didn't you just cut him a piece?"

"He told us he loved us," I said.

Ivy's eyes filled instantly with tears. "Eat the whole thing, honey. Whatever you want."

"Thanks, Aunt Ivy," he said and shoved more in his face. There was icing all over his shirt and cheeks.

"He's adorable," Ivy declared and hugged both me and Drew at the same time.

"Thank you for planning this wedding, sis," Drew said, pulling back. "It's seriously better than anything we could have done ourselves."

"You two deserve it. After all this time, after everything…" She sniffled and waved at her eyes like she was afraid to cry more. "I just love you both so much."

"We love you too," I told her.

Jax, Blue, and Asher came running over, all of them in the same savage state Travis was in. "Cake!" they all declared and reached for it with their hands.

Ivy nearly fainted.

"There's a cupcake table," she announced, pointing. "Cupcakes!"

The boys went racing off toward it.

"You can stop worrying now." I assured her. "Even if they did eat the cake before we could cut it, this is still the best day ever."

Romeo and Braeden joined us, Braeden looking a lot more alert than before. "Hey, no one told me we were having cake," he announced and put his hand in the hole Travis made.

"Braeden James Walker!" Ivy bellowed.

Well, maybe he wasn't as sober as he looked.

"It needs sprinkles, blondie."

Everyone burst out laughing. Even Ivy.

"I give up," she said. "You're all a bunch of ill-mannered cavemen."

"But we love you, baby," Braeden drawled.

"Kiss me," she demanded.

Braeden kissed her, and she squealed because he had cake all over his face. And his hands.

The DJ started playing a new song, the same one I used in the movie I'd made for Drew.

"Come on," I said, grabbing his hand.

When we stepped onto the dance floor, everyone started to clap. And chant, *"Kiss, kiss, kiss…"*

I kissed him.

"Dancing really isn't my thing, T," Drew said when I pulled back, leaving my arms around his waist.

"Just stand really close to me," I whispered. "That's all I care about."

He laughed under his breath and mirrored my position. Sliding my hands up his back a little, I pulled him closer and started swaying. "Foot okay?" I asked.

He grunted.

"I love you," I whispered.

He echoed, "Love you back."

I kissed him again.

The first openly gay doll, Gay Bob, was released in 1977. He had a pierced ear and his box was shaped like a closet.

FORTY-SEVEN

Drew

I was sitting in Trent's lap, and my hair was messed up from his hands constantly running through it.

Sweet Lord, I was turning into Rimmel. Thank God I didn't wear glasses.

I glanced around the full table for an empty chair. There wasn't one. It was the reason I was sitting in his lap to begin with.

Actually, no, it wasn't. I was in his lap because I liked it here. But there really weren't any chairs.

His broad hand slid underneath the back of my leather jacket to rub over my back. "You're hot." He frowned. "Take this off," he murmured, reaching for the jacket.

"No." I refused. "I want to wear it."

"Its July. You're wearing leather." He scowled.

"But it has your name on it."

He pursed his lips. He couldn't argue with that.

"You feeling okay?" he asked, changing tactics. Still, there was no less concern in his tone.

"I'm fine, frat boy. I promise."

"It's been a long couple days." He worried more. "This has been a lot."

True, this had been a lot more than we'd been used to as of late, but it was good. It was nice to feel like we were really getting back to normal.

Pressing my forehead to his, I repeated, "I promise I'm okay."

"We have business to discuss," Gamble declared, stepping up to the table like he was the head of it.

I guess he kinda was.

"Dad." Joey groaned. "We're at a wedding, not a business meeting."

"You know how hard it is to get all my kids in one place these days?" Gamble announced.

Jagger, Joey and Lorhaven's youngest, was sitting on Joey's lap and clapped and laughed at his grandpa's declaration.

"At least someone in this family appreciates me." He grumped, giving the boy a grin. Jagger laughed again, his green eyes and wild, curly dark hair making him look like the perfect accomplice.

"Traitor." Arrow grumped.

Lorhaven gave him the evil eye. "What'd you say to my son?"

"Where's Sophia?" Gamble asked, looking around for his granddaughter.

"Playing with Nova," Joey replied. She looked beautiful as ever in a curve-hugging gold glitter dress and her wild mane of hair pulled up into a high ponytail.

Lorhaven was wearing leather too—but he didn't look as good in it as me—and his arm was draped over the back of her chair, his body swiveled toward his wife and son.

Across the table, Arrow sat so close to Hopper he was practically in his lap, and there were three empty plates in front of him.

"You've been driving really well this season," I told him. "More cautious than usual, though."

"I'm still at a good ranking," he said, sliding a glance in Hopper's direction.

Ahh.

"A damn good ranking." Hopper agreed.

I nodded. "Proud of you, kid."

"I'm not a kid," he muttered but then smiled. "Thanks, Drew."

"And you," I said, turning my attention to Lorhaven. "Now that I'm not in front of you, you're number one."

He scoffed. "It's not like I haven't beat you before."

I inclined my head. "You've beat me before."

"Not often," Trent added, always at my back.

"Down, boy." Lorhaven hushed Trent, but it was without the usual heat in which he usually snapped at him.

"You definitely have this season in the bag." I went on. "You look good out there."

Lorhaven sat forward, leaning his forearms on the table. "You've been watching?"

"When I can."

Lorhaven glanced at Trent. I think they shared a look.

"Whoa, whoa," I intoned. "What is this?"

"What?" Lorhaven asked.

I turned to T. "Did you two just have a conversation without words?" I made a face. "Are you two actually getting along?"

"He was there when you got hurt." Trent shrugged. "He sat beside me in the hospital and worried beside me. He supported us even when other people wouldn't."

Pursing my lips I nodded. "And now you're like linked telepathically?"

Lorhaven burst out laughing. "Are you jealous, For—" Halting, he corrected himself. "Mask?"

"No!" I said.

Everyone laughed. Even Gamble. Guess I'd spoken a little too fast.

"I'm just used to practically prying you two apart while you snarl at each other." I defended.

"You almost died." Trent said simply, his palm settling on the back of my neck. "And I don't really know why I don't like him anyway."

Joey laughed, which made Jagger laugh too.

"Okay, so what's with all the eye speak, then? What'd you say?"

Lorhaven grinned, grabbed his beer off the table, and took a long pull of it. Trent delved his fingers into the hair at the base of my neck.

Leaning up, his lips brushed my ear when he whispered, "The only person I'm linked to in any way is you."

I smiled.

Sitting back, Trent finally answered. "He was asking how you're doing."

I looked at Lorhaven. "Why don't you just ask me?"

"'Cause I wanted the truth."

I gave him the finger. Joey covered Jagger's eyes.

"No one would blame you if you have some, ah, stress about driving again," Arrow said, understanding deep in his voice.

"You having some trouble since I crashed?" I asked him point blank.

Arrow shifted uncomfortably. "Uh, yeah."

Hopper made a sound. "Not him. Me."

"Hopp," Arrow said, reaching for his hand.

"It's okay, A. Everyone here knows I got a history with accidents too."

And so Arrow was driving more cautiously because he was concerned that Hopper was worrying about him too much.

"If your head's not in it, that's dangerous too." I cautioned Arrow. Just thinking about him going through what I did turned my stomach.

Hopper stiffened and then knocked back the rest of the beer in front of him.

"I know. That's why this is my last season."

Lorhaven stood up so fast his chair fell over. Hopper spit out the beer he was still swallowing, and Gamble looked gobsmacked.

"I'm guessing from the reaction around the table you haven't told anyone about this," Trent said.

"No. But this isn't a split decision. I've been thinking about it awhile."

"A," Hopper said, wiping his mouth with the back of his hand. "You should have talked to me about this."

"I've always said I'd just drive for a couple years. It's been more than a couple. I've had a good run. I've been successful. I'm ready to retire."

"Arrow." Hopper leaned toward him.

"I like driving, but I love you. Seeing that fear in your eyes every time I get in the car—" He stopped and shook his head. "I've had enough. We both have."

I felt kind of responsible for this, for the kid hanging up his keys.

Trent's arms wrapped around me from behind, tugging me back, and I gave him my weight almost readily. "Your demons don't have anything to do with theirs," he whispered. "Let them work it out on their own."

I turned my cheek toward him, and he kissed it lightly, somehow soothing all the turmoil inside me.

"We're not done talking about this," Hopper declared.

"We can hash it out over family dinner next week." Gamble decided.

They had family dinners like we had pancake Sundays.

Arrow just nodded like he already expected the fight. But he was calm. He was secure in his decision. It was done in his mind, and so it was done in mine as well.

He glanced at me, and I nodded, telling him silently I understood. I guess we had some stuff in common. We both loved another man. We both faced ridicule from people who were supposed to love us. We both drove fast, and now both of us sat here pondering our future and what speed could do to the people around us that we loved most.

"I don't think I'll be calling you kid anymore," I said.

He smiled.

"Arrow." Hopper tried again, but A silenced him with a single action. A kiss.

"Drew," Gamble barked, making me glance away from the couple.

"What?"

"You have an interview in two days."

"I know."

"*GearShark* is paying damn good money for this."

"We know," Trent said this time.

"You sure you're up for this?" he asked.

We'd stayed pretty quiet to the press. The NRR issued a statement after I woke up from the coma, updating the public about my condition and confirming I would (obviously) be out the rest of the season. They also confirmed the cause of the crash was a faulty tire that blew at the perfect wrong moment, and when that happens under such perfect conditions, the track turns into a shit storm.

The family never commented on the rumors about my parents, the "fight" at my bedside, or any of the other epically dramatic shit the press was conjuring up. We also kept quiet about Andi and Travis because the last thing we wanted was the press breathing down our kids' necks. There was speculation about the kids too, of course. I mean, we'd been seen with strollers and car seats… and, well, the kids.

"We're up for it." I nodded.

"They're going to ask some hard shit."

"And we're going to answer it," Trent deadpanned.

"What about next season?"

And there it was.

The question everyone tiptoed around. The question I knew everyone speculated about, but no one asked. Would I return to driving? Or was this the end of my career?

Feeling the obvious tension vibrating my body, Trent sat forward, wrapping himself around me from behind. I liked it. He felt good. Secure. He helped banish the panicky, confused feelings that sometimes resurfaced from when I'd been in a coma.

We hadn't even talked about this yet. We'd been too busy grabbing hold of each other and our kids to think about anything else.

"I don't know," I finally said.

"Dad," Joey said, handing Jagger to Lorhaven and pinning her father with a hard look. "It's their wedding day. You can't bring this up later?"

"The interview is in two days," he muttered.

"And I'll tell them exactly what I'm telling you. I don't know yet. I don't—"

Trent gave me a light squeeze and spoke over my voice. "When Drew makes a decision, we'll let you know. Until then, back off."

Everyone went silent, all sort of surprised that Trent would dare talk to Gamble that way. I wasn't surprised. It wasn't the first time Trent shielded me. Hell, it wasn't even the millionth. And it definitely wouldn't be the last.

"Fine." Gamble allowed, not offended in the least. "But I need to know by the end of summer."

Trent stiffened, but I patted his hand, trying to calm him down. Business was business, after all.

I nodded. "Okay."

Everyone sat there broodily for a few moments, as if Arrow's announcement and my indecision brought down the mood.

Gamble cleared his throat. "And, uh, either way…" He began, making me look up at him. "Either way, there's a place for you in the NRR, on the track or the sidelines."

Relief I didn't even know I needed filled me. The absence of its insurmountable weight overwhelmed me. "That really means a lot to me."

Gamble grunted. "Well if I don't keep you around, you won't stay out of trouble. Besides, you gotta work off all the money I had to pay out to keep that husband of yours out of a cell."

Trent groaned. "I issued apologies to everyone."

"'Cause human resources made you." Lorhaven snickered.

"More than you would do," I snapped.

"Damn right. Those assholes deserved every beating Trent gave them."

Trent grunted in appreciation.

Was this the twilight zone?

"No more business talk." Gamble was brusque and signaled a server with a tray of champagne. In seconds, we all had a flute in our hands. "A toast," he said, raising his glass.

All six of us lifted the glasses.

"To Drew and Trent, for beating the odds more than once. May you have a long and happy life together."

"Here, here," everyone rang out, and then we all drank.

I only got one sip before Trent confiscated the glass from my hand.

How ridiculous but also incredibly endearing.

FORTY-EIGHT

Trent

The house was dark and still when Andi started fussing. Even though I'd been dead asleep, my eyes sprang open immediately. I always had the same reaction to my daughter when she was upset: I didn't like it. It was almost like I was hardwired to instantly want to soothe her, to make whatever the problem was go away.

Pushing up, I leaned over the bassinet pushed close to our bed to reach in and lift her out. Her arms and legs were flailing as she gave me her best hangry cry.

"All right now, peanut." I soothed, laying her against my chest. "Let's eat."

"What's wrong?" Drew's sleepy head lifted off the pillow. Even with only the glimmer of the nightlight, I could see his wild blond hair sticking up everywhere.

Dude was such a mess.

I really liked messes.

"I'm getting Andi a bottle. You can go back to sleep."

"I can help," he slurred, making a sleepy groaning sound. Drew was not a morning person… He wasn't a middle of the night person either. God love him, though, he tried.

The little boy sleeping between us rolled, smacking him in the face.

"Ah!" he grunted, falling back into the pillow.

I chuckled. "You better stay put. Don't wake him up."

"He hit me in the face, and you're worried about me waking him?" Drew grumbled. "Is this what happens when you get married? I'm the bottom of the totem pole." He accented his whining with a yawn.

Andi was a little calmer since I was holding her, so I went around the bed, stepping on a squeaky dog toy and then stumbling over a metal race car lying on the floor.

"Fuck," I muttered.

From the bed, Drew laughed. "Karma."

"I was coming over there to kiss you, but I think I changed my mind," I quipped, taking my daughter and heading for the door.

For a guy who was a grouchy grump when having to wake up, he sure did move stealthily when he wanted to. His warm hand curled around my bare bicep, not pulling me around but his touch enough to make me stop.

When I pivoted, one of his hands gently cupped the back of Andi's head, and the other cupped my jaw. Leaning over, he kissed me softly, slipping me a little tongue.

I liked tongue.

"Come on," he drawled, taking my hand and leading me downstairs into the dimly lit kitchen.

We used to sleep with not a single light on in this house. But now we had nightlights everywhere and kept the light above the stove on for when we had to get up with Andi.

Shuffling to the fridge, Drew pulled out a bottle and popped it into this thing that heated it up for us, which was a gift from Rimmel.

Andi fussed while it heated, so I gently rocked her while we waited.

The second it beeped, Drew snapped it up, wiped off the outside, and then tested the temperature on the inside of his wrist. "All good," he said, handing it over.

Andi didn't have much trouble latching onto a bottle anymore, so the second I offered it to her, all the fussing filling the room stopped and she started to eat.

She ate a lot and had already put on a few pounds since we brought her home, but she was still my little peanut and probably always would be.

"You look sexy standing there half naked, feeding my daughter," Drew said, padding across the floor toward us.

"Dad." Travis's voice floated around the corner, and then he stepped into the kitchen, dragging a stuffed Pikachu with him. His hair was sticking up everywhere, and his feet were bare.

"Yeah?" we both said at the same time. It didn't matter which one of us Travis wanted, we both always answered.

"Where'd you go?" he asked, walking up to Drew.

French Fry's toenails clipped across the solid floor as he followed along behind his boy. Ever since Travis got here, Fry had become his shadow.

Drew picked up Travis, and my heart tumbled when he immediately relaxed against Drew's body, the stuffed toy dangling over his shoulder and down his back. "Andi wanted a bottle."

"She eats a lot."

Drew chuckled and carried Travis back upstairs with me happily trailing behind.

Both my husband and son sprawled out on the bed before I even got there, with Fry taking up the entire foot of the mattress. Drew lay on his back, one arm flung up over his head and the other around Travis who pressed into his side, hugging his toy.

I stood beside the bed, staring down at them for a few moments before getting in myself and leaning against the headboard to finish feeding Andi.

Her dark eyes stared up, making me feel like I was her entire universe. "I love you," I whispered. "You're my favorite girl."

Her lips let go of the bottle, and she made a small coughing sound. But then she went right back to eating.

Travis fell back asleep almost instantly, and when he shifted, it was to fling his animal across Drew's face.

From underneath the yellow blob, Drew made a sound. Chuckling, I reached over and peeled it away.

"We need a bigger mattress," he declared.

"Doesn't matter how big of a bed we get. We'll all still roll over to be as close to you as we can."

His head turned toward me, and when he smiled, his dimple appeared. "This isn't exactly the way I pictured our honeymoon."

"It's better," I confessed.

His head bobbed. "Way better."

Once Andi finished her bottle, had on a dry diaper, and was swaddled up in the pink blanket she loved, I settled back into the sheets.

"Are you asleep?" I whispered.

Drew made a sound.

"You nervous for tomorrow's interview?" I whispered, again.

He was quiet a moment, but then he replied, "No, not nervous."

"Do you know what you're going to say?"

He shifted beneath the blankets and son, turning so we were facing each other in the dark.

"How come you've never asked me?"

I knew he meant about racing. About if he would return to the track.

"Because whatever you want to do is fine with me."

He rubbed his cheek against the pillow, eyes focused on me. "Even if I say I still want to drive? Even if you will worry every time I get behind the wheel?"

"Even then."

"Really?" he asked, partially surprised.

I nodded, no longer able to resist the urge to rub my palm over his rough jaw. "I know how much you love racing, Drew. What a big part of you it is. I would never ask you to deny that part of yourself. I would never ask you to choose between racing and your family. You can have both. You can have whatever you want. All I want is for you to be happy."

Drew's hand covered mine where it rested against his jaw, gently tugging it down so he could kiss the center of my palm. "I seriously don't know what I did to deserve you."

"I wonder the same thing every day."

"I think I want to race again," he confessed, nerves and excitement playing over his face at once.

I nodded, my own nerves and excitement whirling inside me. "Then that's what you'll do."

"But I'm afraid."

"I think that's probably natural," I said gently. "You've been through a lot."

He shook my head, scooting closer toward me. "Not of wrecking again."

His brows drew together. "Of what, then?"

"Of hurting you. Of making you feel like I'm willing to risk everything we have for a race."

My heart squeezed. "Is that what you'll be doing?"

"No," he said, rough and a little too loud. Travis shifted against him, and we both looked down, worried he would awaken.

He didn't, though. Little man stayed fast asleep.

"No." he said again, this time quiet and gentle. "Nothing is more important to me than you and the kids. I swear it."

"I believe you."

Leaning forward, his lips latched onto mine. The kiss felt like a hug. A warm, strong hug for the lips. Everything inside me warmed and tingled. Everything inside me felt loved.

"I can't go out like this, T. I can't let one bad crash sideline me forever. I was at the top of my career. I loved what I did."

"And then everything changed."

I heard him swallow in the silence that followed. "Yeah." His voice was raw. "Everything changed, and it put you through hell."

"You too."

He made a sound. "I don't care about me. But you. Travis and Andi…"

"You want to finish your racing career on your terms. You want to go out at the top, not in a mass of crumpled metal."

"I should have known you'd understand." His tone was warm, his lips softly curved in a smile.

"I do, and it's okay. We can't not do the things we love because it's scary. If that were the case, you and I probably wouldn't even be together."

His face darkened. "That's not even an option."

I smiled. I liked when he was growly.

"Return to racing when you're ready. When you are physically *and* mentally ready. Give them hell, and take your title back."

"Yeah?" His teeth flashed.

"I'll be right there cheering you on."

"I won't race forever. I'll take a job at the NRR, something less risky." He promised.

"Okay."

"Thank you," he whispered fiercely. "Thank you for always being exactly what I need."

"Get some sleep. The crew will be here early," I told him.

"Kiss me first," he demanded.

Leaning over our sleeping son, I kissed him languidly until he sighed in satisfaction.

I'd be lying if I said him getting back on the track didn't make me apprehensive, but I'd meant every word I said. And after everything we'd been through, I knew that doing anything less than exactly what we wanted was not the way we were meant to live.

I had faith that fate would take care of us. Just the way it had up until now.

No one said life would be easy, but it didn't have to be in order to be happy.

GEAR*SHARK* PRESENTS
TRENT & DREW MASK

An exclusive tell-all feature by Emily Metcalf

I'm coming to you today from behind the walls of a notorious compound on the western side of Maryland. Acres of land surrounded by a stone wall and attainable only via a large wrought iron gate are quite imposing when first approached.

I wasn't sure what to expect when the gates swung open, allowing me and our team at GearShark *behind the coveted walls. But I can say what I found was somewhat surprising. Though the property is very large and it is no secret that the people who live here are blessed with fat bank accounts, nothing is pretentious.*

Nothing screams of money and privilege, except, of course, the two large houses positioned deep into the acreage. But even those, which are enormous and beautifully built, do not invoke an air of celebrity. Instead they just make me feel like I'm being welcomed by family.

As I drive under the canopy of mature trees, dogs race across the open grass and children run about with them. I know which house belongs to our featured couple immediately because right beside it is a massive garage and Drew's famous blue fastback parked out front.

A large, hairy dog, of which breed I cannot determine, is lying by the front door, and a boy with incredibly dark hair and eyes sits beside him with about a dozen race cars scattered around.

There are chalk roads drawn everywhere—down the concrete steps, over the walkway, and even around the driveway. A larger toy Mustang, the kind that small children can drive, is parked beside Drew's fastback, and I have to say I find it incredibly charming.

Now here I am, sitting in the middle of the home our feature cover models share, a place that is simply done in mainly black, white, and gray but is livened up by the pops of colors from all the toys and baby items scattered about.

This is the first interview given by either man after the tragic and quite dramatic accident that cut short Drew's racing career with New Revolution Racing. Since his accident a few months ago, rumors have swirled and headlines have highlighted the turmoil this race star has faced.

Trent nor Drew have spoken to the press… until now.

We at GearShark are honored and thrilled to welcome back these beloved boys for a raw and eye-opening interview where the notoriously private men have promised to come clean and tell all.

And once these boys have spilled the tea and your thirst is quenched, you can flip through a few exclusive photos we've been given permission to share from their recent wedding (yes, they're married!).

Ladies and gentlemen, fasten your seatbelts and let's get this interview started.

Interview key:
GS = GearShark (that's me, Emily!)
DM = Drew Mask (not Forrester anymore!)
TM = Trent Mask

GS: *First things first. Thank you for allowing* GearShark *the privilege of coming into your home.*
DM: *Thank you for coming all the way here for this interview.*

GS: *It's truly my pleasure. It's wonderful to see you again. It's been quite awhile.*

TM: *You're looking beautiful as ever, Emily.*

GS: <Yep, Trent is as charming as ever. And honestly, I think he's gotten even better looking!> *Thank you so much.*

GS: *Drew, you are looking well. Better than I honestly expected. How are you doing after the crash?*

DM: *I'm alive, and alive is a pretty good thing.*

<At this point, Trent reaches over and takes Drew's hand, linking theirs together. It was casual and natural and done without any kind of hesitation. I'd also like to note these boys usually shy away from any kind of public affection.>

GS: *So you did almost die, correct?*

DM: *Yes. I flatlined on the operating table.*

TM: *I don't like to think about that.*

GS: *I'm going to ask some hard questions. Are you ready?*

DM: *Ask.*

GS: *What is it like to almost die? Do you remember any of it?*

DM: *Yes. Some people might call it a near-death experience. I saw myself in surgery, I saw the doctors operating on me, and I saw the monitors flatline.*

GS: *Were you scared?*

DM: <pauses to consider the question> *I was confused more than anything, and then I was scared. I remember looking for Trent.*

GS to TM: *How does it feel to hear that as he was dying, he looked for you?*

TM: <His face is visibly pale, and I can't help but remember the photos the press took of his haggard state during that crucial time.> *I don't think I can put it into words.*

GS: *Can you try?*

<Drew stiffens. I note the way his hand tightens around Trent's. I have a feeling he's about to tell me not to pressure his husband, but Trent speaks up first.>

TM to DM: *It's okay, I know the end of the story.*

<My heart totally flutters when Trent kisses the back of Drew's hand.>

TM: *I feel helpless and small. It's quite literally my worst nightmare for Drew to need me and me not be there.*

GS: *Let's talk about that for a minute. About some of the rumors that still circle, even months after the accident.*

<Both guys nod.>

GS: *There have been many reports as well as a very heartbreaking image circling the internet that say you were thrown out of Drew's hospital room and banned from his bedside. Is that true?*

TM: *It's true.*

GS: *Why?*

TM: <Glances at Drew, who nods.> *Drew's parents showed up at the hospital with a will Drew had crafted when he was very young. It named his parents next of kin and basically control over his medical care.*

GS: *Drew, you didn't have control over yourself at the time?*

DM: *I was in a coma.*

GS: *What were the extent of your injuries exactly?*

DM: *Uh…* <He seems to not quite know>

TM: *He had broken ribs, a collapsed lung, a traumatic brain injury with stitches and debris in his skull. He also has a broken leg and various other minor contusions and lacerations. He also had swelling of his brain, was on a ventilator for several days, and had a chest tube.*

GS: *How was it seeing him like that?*

TM: *It was the worst thing I've ever experienced in my entire life. If I could have traded places with him, I would have.*

GS: *You caused quite a ruckus at the crash site. There are also several reports that Ron Gamble, ah, paid off several of the emergency workers that you attacked while trying to get to the car Drew was inside.*

TM: *Ron Gamble is an upstanding man who would never do anything that wasn't lawful.*
GS: *That's quite a political answer.*
TM: *It's the truth.*
GS: *Do you deny that you were aggressive at the crash site?*
TM: *Why would I deny it? There are videos floating all over the internet showing it.*
DM: <grins>
GS: *What was going through your head at that time?*
TM: *Nothing. All I could think about was getting to Drew and getting him out of that car. He was pinned, and the rescue workers were having a hard time getting to him safely.*
GS: *But you didn't care about your safety.*
TM: *My safety depends on Drew's.*
GS: *Those scars on your wrist, what are those from?*
DM: *That's from when he reached through the fire inside my car to get me.*
GS: *You put your hand through fire?*
TM: *Yeah.*
GS: *Would you do it again?*
TM: *A million times over.*
GS: *Back to the hospital. So Drew's parents had you removed from the room. Why? Were you still acting aggressively like at the crash site?*
DM: *Trent isn't aggressive. He's extremely protective. There's a difference. And he didn't do anything wrong.*
GS: <I think perhaps Trent isn't the only protective one>
DM: *My parents kicked him out of the room because he's gay. Because we are in a relationship.*
GS: *And your parents don't approve?*
DM: *No. My father is dead set against it. He disowned me five years ago.*
GS: *That must have been very painful.*
DM: *It was. I spent a long time doubting myself. Fighting against who I really was to be who they wanted me to be.*

GS: *But you don't do that anymore?*

DM: *No. I learned that real love doesn't have limits. Real love doesn't have boundaries or rules.*

GS to TM: *There's a photo.* <I pull out the copy of the infamous photo of Trent clearly grieving alone in a hallway.> *This was leaked to the press. Is this you?*

TM: *Yes.*

GS: *Did you know this photo was being taken?*

TM: *No. I thought I was alone.*

GS: *Was this after his parents made you leave his bedside?*

TM: <His voice loses some of its strength.> *Yes.*

DM: *I hate that photo. Put it away.*

<I put it aside>

DM to TM: *Seriously, T. Where the hell are your shoes? What's with those thin clothes?*

TM: *I was wearing scrubs because my clothes were bloody and dirty, and they wouldn't let me in to see you that way.* <He frowns.> *I'm not really sure why I wasn't wearing shoes. I don't remember many details from those first couple days.*

<For a moment, I feel like a third wheel because Drew wraps an arm around Trent's neck and pulls him into his shoulder. I'm fascinated by the two large men hugging each other and the tenderness that Drew shows as he strokes Trent's hair.>

DM to TM: *I'm sorry.*

TM: *Don't be sorry.*

GS: *So Drew's parents kicked you out of the hospital room because you're in a gay relationship?*

TM: *Yes. I think he was hoping Drew would have some type of amnesia and he could erase me from Drew's life without any resistance from him.*

DM: *Shows how little my father knows me. I won't ever forget Trent. Ever.*

GS: *What happened when you woke up?*

DM: *I asked for Trent.*
GS: *He was the first person you asked for?*
DM: *Duh.*
GS: *How did you feel when you realized what your parents had done?*
DM: *Ashamed. Angry. Responsible.*
<Trent looks at Drew, a frown pulling his face.>
TM: *Responsible?*
DM: *I should never have allowed things to get that bad. If I'd had the courage to cut them out of my life completely, they never would have been able to hurt Trent that way.*
TM: *They're your parents.*
DM: *No. They're just people with bad hearts.*
GS: *Is this why you got married? Maryland recognizes same-sex marriage, so you now have all the legal rights a spouse has.*
DM: *I married Trent because I love him.*
GS: *I don't think you've ever said that in an interview before.*
DM: *Surely, I said it when we came out.*
GS: *But probably not since then. And you've touched him more in the last ten minutes than I have ever seen in the last five years combined.*
TM: *We aren't being lowkey anymore. We aren't going to refrain from showing how we feel or even saying how we feel for the benefit of others. Doing things for the benefit of other people only hurts us. I care more about Trent than anyone else.*
GS: *So you have a lot of skinship?*
DM: *What the fuck is skinship?*
GS: *<giggles> You touch each other a lot. You're intimate with each other.*
DM: *Are you asking me if we have sex?*
TM to DM: *Easy, Mask.*
TM to GS: *Yes, we touch all the time. It's been very difficult to hold back when we are out in public. <Trent glances at Drew and smirks.> And of course we have sex. Do people really think we don't?*
GS: *Just asking the questions the people want to know.*

DM: <Snorts> *You're a dirty woman, Emily.*

GS: *If I was dirty, I would ask you to kiss.*

<Trent grasps the back of Drew's neck and pulls him in. Their lips collide, and I'm telling you I see some tongue.>

TM: *Next.*

GS: <Is it hot in here or is it just me?> *Okay, so you got married because you love each other.*

TM: *For a long time, I was afraid to get married. I was afraid it might ruin the perfection I thought we had.*

GS: *You didn't have perfection?*

TM: *No.*

GS: *Do you now?*

DM: *We're pretty fucking close.*

TM: *Stop saying fuck. This is a professional interview.*

DM: *You just said it.*

GS: *Who's the top and who's the bottom?*

<Both men stare at me, stunned.>

DM: *Emily. This is a family magazine.*

TM: *Who said we have to be one or the other?*

DM: <chokes>

GS: *Do you have any kind of relationship at all with your parents now, Drew?*

DM: *None. And I never will.*

GS: *There is no room for forgiveness? Even if they see that they were wrong?*

DM: <Slowly, he shakes his head> *Some wounds are just too deep to come back from. I might be able to forgive what they did to me. But to Trent? I'll never forgive.*

GS: *How is your recovery coming from the wreck?*

DM: *Slow but good. I'm just waiting on this leg to catch up to the rest of me.*

GS: *Have you been behind the wheel since?*

DM: *We bought an SUV. I've driven that a couple times.*

GS: *Not your Mustang?*
DM: *It's a clutch, and I need two feet to drive.*
GS: *Okay, what kind of SUV did you buy?*
TM: *It's an Infiniti QX80.*
DM: *I'd rather have a Ford.*
TM: *He'd rather have a Ford.*
GS: *So why not a Ford SUV?*
DM: *'Cause I thought this was better for my kids.*
GS: *You bring me to my next talking point.*
TM: *Bring it.*
<There's something slightly different about Trent when I see him this time. He's a little less reserved, a little more in your face. No less charming. In fact, this could be the reason he seems even better looking than before. He'd always been confident, but now he is… *more*.>
DM: *Emily, are you checking out my husband?*
GS: <Busted!> *Me?*
DM: *Stop it. Stop it now.*
GS: *You are currently in the process of adopting two children, correct?*
TM: *Yes.*
GS: *Names, ages, gender?*
TM: *Travis is five, and Andi is a few months.*
GS: *Andi is…*
TM: *She's a girl. Her name has an "I" at the end.*
DM: *But she's named after me.*
GS: *Andrew. Andi. Whose idea was that?*
TM: *Mine.*
GS: *Did you always have plans to adopt?*
DM & TM: *No.*
GS: *So how did this come about?*
TM: *My brother told me this once—*
GS: *Which brother?*
TM: *Does it matter?*
GS: *You have very famous brothers.*

TM: *It was Romeo.*

GS: *Please continue.*

TM: *That's how fatherhood is. The first time you lay eyes on your kids, you love them. You know they're yours. That's how it was when we met Travis and Andi.*

GS: *The timing of this coincides with Drew's hospitalization. Reports are stating that you met the children at the hospital.*

DM: *I know this is a tell-all, and we'll tell you as much as we can, but details about our kids are off-limits. The adoption is still going through, and frankly, the press is scary. We won't do or say anything that might jeopardize them.*

GS: *Your foster daughter and foster son are Asian, is that correct?*

TM: *Our daughter and our son. Period. Never refer to them as anything but that ever again. And yes, they're part Korean.*

GS: *You love them.*

DM & TM: *Duh.*

GS: *What's it like being new fathers?*

TM: *Overwhelming, scary, but the best.*

DM: *What he said.*

GS: *What's one thing you didn't expect about being parents?*

DM: *How small our king-size bed really is.*

TM: *That love could be so infinite.*

DM to TM: *You're making me look bad, frat boy.*

TM: *I love you.*

<Drew doesn't seem surprised by the abrupt declaration of love. He just smiles.>

DM: *I love you, too.*

GS: *How long until the adoption is final?*

TM: *Hopefully, not too much longer.*

GS: *How do the kids fit in with the rest of the family?*

DM: *Like it was meant to be.*

GS: *Drew, you said you almost died. How did death change you? Are you now more scared of death than before?*

DM: *Death made me grow up. All the way up. It made me realize that life can change in an instant. One minute, you're happy, and the next, everything crumbles around you. I realized I'd been holding back without really meaning to. I don't want to live like that.*

GS: *And the fear?*

DM: *I think death always conjures up some kind of fear. Not necessarily the dying part, but the being separated from the ones you love the most. Even in death, I looked for Trent. Even in a coma, he was the one voice I always heard. I'm not really afraid anymore because I've seen death, because I learned that not even death can keep me away from Trent.*

GS: *I didn't think I'd need a tissue for today's interview.*

<Trent leans forward and pats me on the shoulder.>

GS to TM: *What about you? What did death teach you?*

TM: *That life is never perfect. It can't be. So reaching for more is okay. When life pushes, it's okay to push back.*

GS to TM: *Have you ever thought of writing a book about your experiences as a gay man?*

TM: <laughs> *A book about me would be boring as hell.*

DM: *I'd read it.*

TM: *That's because the entire thing would be about you.*

GS: *Drew, all of us at GearShark are wondering about your racing career. Are you planning to return to the NRR, or are you retiring?*

DM: <reaches for Trent's hand> *I'm coming back.*

GS: *Really! This is exciting news! Your fans are going to be so thrilled.*

DM: *I'd like to personally thank all my supporters for their well wishes and love during my accident and recovery. I know I've been quiet across social media and so has Trent, but we are grateful and we have read all of the love sent our way.*

GS: *Was making the decision to return to racing difficult?*

DM: *Of course. I have a husband and kids now. Being a race car driver, especially for the NRR where there are no rules, is dangerous. But we talked about it—*

GS: *By we, you mean you and Trent?*

DM: *Of course. I'd never make this kind of decision without him. And we've decided that I'll make a comeback when I'm ready.*

GS: *Any idea when?*

DM: *I'm not sure.*

GS to TM: *Do you really want Drew back in the driver's seat? Aren't you scared?*

TM: *If I shied away from everything that scared me, I'd never leave my house.*

GS: *A big, confident guy like you is scared of that much?*

TM: *You'd be surprised.*

DM to TM: *You're the strongest guy I know.*

<Trent smiles.>

TM: *I know it's risky. But cars are in Drew's blood. And we want to be examples to our kids that you don't quit when things get really hard. You rise above.*

DM: *I don't know how many more seasons I have left in me on the track. I've been doing this awhile now. But I know I want at least one more.* <grins slyly> *I gotta come back and reclaim my title from Lorhaven.*

GS: *So you think Lorhaven will be this season's champion?*

DM: *Of course.*

GS to TM: *What about you, will you continue on working for the NRR?*

TM: *Yes, and as Drew's manager. But right now, we're both on extended leave of absence. We want to be with our kids. And with each other.*

GS: *Thank you for being so forthcoming in today's interview. I feel like we got see a whole other side to the both of you.*

DM: *Thanks for sitting down with us.*

GS: <I'm about to get cheeky.> *Can you kiss again?*

<Trent laughs, but Drew leans in, taking Trent's face in both his hands, and kisses him deeply.>

DM: *Good?* <He totally swipes his thumb along his lower lip. These guys are hot, you guys!>

GS: *Very.*

GS: *One final thing. Could you offer any kind of advice or words of wisdom to any out there who might be struggling with life, death, or acceptance?*

<Drew looks at Trent.>

TM to DM: *Why are you looking at me?*

DM: *You're the deep one.*

GS: *No pressure.*

TM: <laughs under his breath> *I don't think I'm qualified to give anyone advice about life. But what I can say is that you shouldn't be afraid to follow your heart. Even if your heart leads you on a path less traveled. Even if the path is full of potholes and sticks. Denying your heart is sort of like denying life, because if you aren't doing what you truly want, then are you even living? Also, change doesn't have to be bad. Even if the catalyst for that change is. Change is uncomfortable, but so is being stuck somewhere you don't belong.*

DM: *That's my husband. I like him better than French fries.*

GS: *Thank you for sitting down with us and for the exclusive look at your wedding. Nice rings, by the way.*

<Drew sports a black wedding band with round diamonds around the circumference, while Trent's band is dark grey with blue sapphires in the center.>

TM: *Thank you for all the support you and the entire staff at GearShark has shown us.*

And that, loyal GearShark readers, is the sit-down, in detail, that I had with Trent and Drew Mask.

By the way, isn't it adorable that Drew took Trent's last name? I think it's so easy to see why these boys have captured everyone's hearts and continue to be some of the most talked about racers in this country. We here at GearShark will be on hand when Drew Mask makes his comeback at the NRR, whenever that may be, and of course will have full coverage of it all. Until then, we wish Trent and Drew nothing but the very best as they embark on marriage and fatherhood, something I think we can all agree these guys will excel at.

And hey, do this journalist a favor. The next time you see Drew and Trent in public—or any couple who looks just like them—smile brightly or offer a kind word. The world knows enough hate, so let's show it some kindness, especially to those who love without limits.

At the age of 24, Leonardo Da Vinci was arrested for gay sex. Twice. He was acquitted both times. If he had been killed, the world wouldn't have the Mona Lisa or The Last Supper.

FORTY-NINE

Drew

I lived.

I died.

I was given a second chance at life.

Turned out what I wanted in my first life was exactly the same thing I wanted in my second.

Love. Happiness. To be nothing but myself.

I didn't get it exactly right my first time around… but still, things were pretty damn good. So now I totally surrendered to everything I ever wanted but maybe was too scared to have.

I'd always loved Trent.

Now I loved him more. Now we had a son and a daughter we could love the way we weren't when we were small.

This was what life was. The good and the bad. The high and the low.

It's sleeping with a Pikachu on your face and dog drool on your feet. It's waking up to a fussing baby and a son who calls you dad, not because it's your title by birthright, but because you earned it in his eyes.

Most of all, it's drinking coffee made by the man you love and knowing he owns you—that you were brave enough to give yourself over completely, body and soul.

I honestly had no idea what life might throw at me and Trent next.

But it didn't matter, because whatever it was, we would be together.

> Sometimes the best revenge is no revenge at all, but rather leaving it all in your rearview as you drive away.
> - Trent

EPILOGUE

Trent

The second I knocked on the door, my nerves spiked.

I'd been calm the entire way here. Calm and collected despite how hard the decision was. It had taken a lot to get on that plane a few hours ago.

Not because of the destination, but because this was the first time since his accident that I was away from Drew for longer than a few hours. This was the first time I'd ever been away from my kids.

My kids.

Two words I never thought I'd ever say. Two people I never thought I'd have. Hell, having Drew as my other half was quite honestly more than I deserved. I considered it pushing my luck to ask for or even want more.

I'd been content being an uncle.

Until those kids came into my life. And now I couldn't even fathom ever not having them.

Which is why I was here today. A place I never thought I'd be.

Life was like that, right? Filled with *nevers*. Layered with people and situations that didn't seem possible.

Fate knew no boundaries. Fate did what it had to do to find a way… and that included putting you through hell. 'Course, how would a man be able to fully appreciate heaven if he hadn't danced with the devil?

Footsteps on the other side made me straighten. The door swung open, and our eyes met instantly. His, which had been curious and even, I daresay, friendly, turned to shock.

"What the hell are you doing here?"

It was a voice I never wanted to hear again.

See what I mean about fate? Never say never.

"Mr. Forrester," I said, dipping my chin. "I have something I'd like to say to you."

His upper lip curled. "I don't want to hear it."

The door slammed in my face.

I knocked again and braced myself for a blast of anger when it opened again.

This time, though, it was Drew's mother. When she saw me there, her eyes widened. "Trent?"

"Ma'am."

The door opened much wider, and she came partway out onto the porch. "Is Drew with you?" she asked hopefully, searching for her son.

"I came alone."

A hand flew up to her throat. "I-is he okay?"

"Drew's fine." *No thanks to you.* Shaking my head, I discarded the thought. "I have something I'd like to say. I won't take up much of your time." Glancing at the watch on my wrist, I added, "I have to catch a flight back home in an hour."

"You flew here because you wanted to talk?"

I shook my head. "Not talk. I just have something to say. Then I'm going home to my family."

A flash of hurt could be seen deep in her eyes. I didn't feel bad for her. I never would. Drew's parents made their choices, and they would have to live with them.

I actually felt kinda sorry for these people because someday they would probably look around and realize all the shit they gave up. Someday they might look in the mirror and wonder who the hell was looking back.

Or maybe they might never know. Maybe their ignorance and intolerance would never change despite everything it cost them.

I couldn't and wouldn't concern myself with however it ended up for them. I was here right now for me. For me and me alone.

"Camden told me about the kids," she whispered.

"*Our* kids." I corrected. "Mine and Drew's."

She hesitated a moment, then said, "Do you have a picture?"

"Can I come in?"

"Of course," she said, swinging the door wide and motioning me inside.

Burke was standing in the middle of the family room, staring at the door. "I told you to go."

"Yeah," I replied. "I know. I'll go as soon as I say what I came to say."

"I told you I don't want to hear it."

"I think after everything, the least you could do is give me five minutes."

"Burke!" Adrienne scolded, coming into the room. "He flew all this way. At least hear him out."

Burke slid a look at his very obedient wife, then back to me. "Hurry up."

"Can I get you some coffee—"

"No." Burke cut her off.

"Thanks for the offer," I told her anyway.

This house looked exactly the same as when Drew and I came here to tell his parents about us. The day he was disowned. It felt different, though.

Emptier. Colder. Not at all like our family compound with the kids and dogs and people everywhere. Our walls nearly burst with love. I could feel it all the way here in North Carolina.

I drew strength from that and stepped forward.

Burke flinched.

I held out a hand, showing I meant no harm, then held it out, wanting to shake his hand. Incredulous, he stared between me and my outstretched arm.

After a few minutes of silence and no attempt to offer his hand, I pulled mine back.

"Thank you," I said.

Both his parents stared in stupor.

I half smiled. "Surprising, right?"

"What kind of game are you playing?" Burke intoned.

"No game." I shook my head. "I came because I wanted to thank you."

"For what?" Adrienne asked.

"For making me stronger."

They both stood there, not sure what to say. They didn't have to say anything at all.

"If it wasn't for you, I might never have expanded my world. Drew and I might have just lived together as we had been and never reached for more. I'd been scared all this time without realizing it. Scared to put us out there, to risk what we had. Scared someone would hurt him the way you have hurt me. I wanted nothing more than to shelter him. To love him."

Listening, Drew's mother sank down on the sofa, gripping the arm.

"Fate intervened. Fate showed me what life might be like without him. If you hadn't come and forced us apart, if you hadn't threatened to keep him from me, I might never have known."

"Known what?" Adrienne asked.

I didn't look at her, though. I watched Burke, who, though he tried to hide it, wanted to know what else I would say.

"Known that we were stronger than that. Stronger than your hate. I realized I couldn't protect Drew from people like you. But we don't have to bury ourselves to avoid your wrath. We can rise above it."

I felt lighter already. Less burdened. Carrying around hate weighed so much. I was tired of bearing it. I didn't have room anymore. I had a husband and two kids who would get all of me and nothing less.

"So thank you for giving me the courage to get married to someone I love more than myself. Thank you for showing me what kind of father I want to be. A father who loves his kids no matter what. A father who would do anything to make sure they are happy and safe. A father who will put aside his own prejudices for the sake of love."

"Why, you little shit…" Burke swore, rushing me.

I didn't flinch. I didn't stare at the fist he had squeezed tight.

Adrienne jumped up, gasping. "Burke!"

"He's taunting us," he insisted.

I shook my head. "No. I'm not. I'm letting you know that I acknowledge the role you played in our lives. I'm putting it to bed. When I walk out of here today, it will be with no more hard feelings or ill will. You might have taught me how to hate, but your son…" I smiled, twisting the diamond band around on my finger. "Your son taught me how to love. And his love is so bright your hate is insignificant."

His arm fell at his side. His fist unclenched. Unmistakable remorse flashed in his stare.

"That's all I came to say. I have to go now. I have a plane to catch."

I didn't look back when I walked out the door. I didn't have to. There was nothing behind me anymore.

Outside, the sun was bright, the air was warm. Halfway to the car, someone ran outside behind me, their rushed footsteps echoing across wood.

"Trent!" Adrienne called.

I stopped and turned, standing there in the sun while she remained in the shadows of the porch.

She swallowed thickly, tears dripping down her cheeks. She couldn't speak, but I saw a lot on her face. I heard a lot in her expression.

I smiled. "You don't have to worry about Drew. I'll take care of him."

Her lips rolled inward; her chest heaved. Then slowly, she nodded.

The house grew smaller and smaller in my rearview as I drove away. By the time it was gone, so was the rest of the weight I'd been carrying for years.

It felt good.

It felt right.

It felt like fate had most definitely found its way.

And fate? It was better than anything I could have ever imagined.

THE *END*

#Trewlove Forever

Author's Note

This book was a long time coming. And when I say a long time, I mean years. Yes, years. I had the idea for this book probably about two years ago. I had the cover done a little over a year ago. This started document sat in my computer for months and months and months.

I kept everything about this book a secret. The plot. The fact that I was even considering another one. It was SO hard to keep this a secret because I was asked nearly every day when Trent and Drew would get another book. When would I write more for these guys?

At first, I said never. I'm done. But this idea kept on in the back of my head. They whispered that maybe I wasn't done. And I wanted to write this book. Badly.

I've said it very often that Trent is my most favorite character. Trent & Drew are my favorite couple. Yes. Even over Romeo and Rimmel. *Gasp.* I will also say that in my own opinion and from my own standpoint, I think #Junkie and #Rev are my best books. I'm very proud of them, maybe because I never thought I could write a male/male romance story. Why? Well, for one thing, I'm not a gay man. How could I write in that perspective?

But guys… The passion I feel for this genre, for these guys, it is currently unmatched. The love this series and this couple specifically has gotten is incredible, and it means so much to me. Even if you can't relate to them, it doesn't matter because we all *feel.*

So because of my intense love, I sat on this book. I sat on this idea. I debated in my mind over and over and over again. Could I write this book? Could I do these boys justice? Could *#Fate* live up to *#Junkie* and *#Rev* (in my own eyes). What if I messed with "perfection?" What if I ruined the entire series with one bad book?

I was plagued with these questions. I almost didn't write this. It took so much courage to finally just do it. I said, well, if it turns out bad, I won't publish it. I won't tell anyone I wrote it. I was inspired for the blurb by my own struggles with this story. "Why mess with perfection," right?

On top of that, I knew this would be an emotional book for me. I didn't want to put Trent through all this. I didn't want him to hurt. I didn't want people to be mean to him. I didn't want to see Drew fighting for his life. And honestly, I didn't want to piss off readers.

But I pushed on. I'm glad I did.

These boys deserve a beautiful ending. Even more beautiful than the one they had before. Yes, their life was amazing. Yes, they were happy. But there was so much left unsaid. Unfelt.

And now there isn't.

They found their pot of gold at the end of their rainbow. I'm proud of these boys. Proud as if they were as real as you and me. They changed me. It's kind of odd to say that, to *know* that two men who basically live in my head changed me. But they did. They opened my eyes so much, and because of that, I will carry them in my heart for the rest of my life.

I don't know if this book is up to par with their other books, but I *feel* it. I feel them and I know they're happy, and honestly, that's good enough.

I tried to pack as much as I could into this book. Glimpses of everyone and moments of laughter. How far we've all come since 2014 when #Nerd released.

I'd like to give special thanks to Colleen Blackstone for offering some insight to adoption and children born with NAS. I tried to write that particular plot point with truth and accuracy. I did take some creative license to move things a little faster, so I hope no one takes offense in anything I wrote.

Also, special thanks for Adrienne Ambrose and Kaydence Hebert for the brainstorming sessions and encouragement to get this book out there and complete. Books like this take a team effort, and I definitely couldn't have done it alone. As always, thanks to my editor, Cassie McCown, for her hard work at editing, even when I send chapters late.

And to all of you who asked—*for years*—for this book. I hope this is everything you wanted it to be. I hope you are happy with the life these boys chose, and I hope this book gave you all the feels. Thank you for loving Trent and Drew and for keeping them in your hearts for as long as you have. I appreciate you.

See you next book!

XOXO,
Cambria

About Cambria

Cambria Hebert is a bestselling novelist of more than fifty titles. She went to college for a bachelor's degree, couldn't pick a major, and ended up with a degree in cosmetology. So rest assured her characters will always have good hair.

Besides writing, Cambria loves a pumpkin spice latte, staying up late, sleeping in, and watching K drama until her eyes won't stay open. She considers math human torture and has an irrational fear of chickens (yes, chickens). You can often find her running on the treadmill (she'd rather be eating a donut), painting her toenails (because she bites her fingernails), or walking her chihuahuas (the real bosses of the house).

Cambria has written in many genres, including new adult, sports romance, male/male romance, sci-fi, thriller, suspense, contemporary romance, and young adult. Many of her titles have been translated into foreign languages and have been the recipients of multiple awards.

Awards Cambria has received include:

Author of the Year 2016 (UtopiaCon2016)
The Hashtag Series: Best Contemporary Series of 2015
(UtopiaCon 2015)
#Nerd: Best Contemporary Book Cover of 2015
(UtopiaCon 2015)
Romeo from the Hashtag Series: Best Contemporary Lead
(UtopiaCon 2015)
#Nerd: Top 50 Summer Reads (Buzzfeed.com 2015)
The Hashtag Series: Best Contemporary Series of 2016
(UtopiaCon 2016)

#NERD Book Trailer: Best Book Trailer of 2016
(UtopiaCon 2016)
#Nerd Book Trailer: Top 50 Most Cinematic Book Trailers
of All Time (film-14.com)
#Nerd: Book Most Wanted to be Adapted to Screen: (2018)
Amnesia: Mystery Book of the Year (2018)

Cambria Hebert owns and operates Cambria Hebert Books,
LLC.

You can find out more about Cambria and her titles by
visiting her website:
http://www.cambriahebert.com